W9-CCL-634

The
Rebellion
of
Miss Lucy Ann
Lobdell

William Klaber

GREENLEAF
BOOK GROUP PRESS

Published by Greenleaf Book Group Press
Austin, Texas
www.gbgpress.com

Distributed by Greenleaf Book Group LLC

For ordering information or special discounts for bulk purchases, please contact Greenleaf Book Group LLC at PO Box 91869, Austin, TX 78709, 512.891.6100.

Design and composition by Greenleaf Book Group LLC
Cover design by Greenleaf Book Group LLC
Cover photo ©iStockphoto.com/Ann_Mei

Publisher's Cataloging-In-Publication Data
(Prepared by The Donohue Group, Inc.)

Klaber, William.
    The rebellion of Miss Lucy Ann Lobdell / William Klaber.—1st ed.

    p. ; cm.

    Issued also as an ebook.
    ISBN: 978-1-60832-562-7

    1. Lobdell, Lucy Ann, b. 1829—Fiction. 2. Transvestism—United States—History—19th century—Fiction. 3. Lesbians—United States—History—19th century—Fiction. 4. Historical fiction. I. Title.

PS3611.L23 R43 2013
813/.6   2012951080

Part of the Tree Neutral® program, which offsets the number of trees consumed in the production and printing of this book by taking proactive steps, such as planting trees in direct proportion to the number of trees used: www.treeneutral.com

TreeNeutral®

Printed in the United States of America on acid-free paper

13 14 15 16   10 9 8 7 6 5 4 3 2 1

First Edition

*I intend to write a book in which I shall
give a full account of my adventures
whilst I adopted male attire.*

Lucy Ann Lobdell, writing in 1855

PART I

Bethany

Assuming the name of Joseph Lobdell, Lucy went about the country as a music teacher. While teaching at a school in Bethany, Penn., she won the love of a young lady scholar, a member of one of the leading families of the village.

—New York Times, October 7, 1879.

1

THE TRAIN WAS late the day I ran away. Those waiting stood quietly—the women tightening their shawls, the men taking turns looking up the tracks. When it finally came in, the southbound number seven snorted and hissed, its damp breath spilling over the travelers as they said last good-byes and dragged their belongings up the metal stairs. I stayed by the stationhouse, my reasons for leaving growing smaller by the moment. Perhaps it was all a mistake. I should turn while I could and go home.

But my heart knew what my head could only suppose—that I had to leave or surely die. So when the steel wheels began to grind, I strode toward the train, and as the last car rolled by, I took three quick steps and leapt upon its stair. With my bag in one hand and a rail of cold iron in the other, I looked back as Callicoon and everything I knew slid off into the distance.

Had it been warmer I might have stayed out on the landing, but soon enough I went inside. The car smelled of cigars and was painted green, but more than that I couldn't say, as I took the first empty bench and lifted my newspaper. After a minute or two, I lowered it enough to let my eyes steal about. I saw pieces of faces and all sorts of hats but nothing that belonged to anyone I knew. Safe for the moment, I set the paper aside and looked out toward the river. There were no leaves yet on the trees, and as the sun flickered through the gray branches, I could see on the glass a faint reflection of myself, appearing and disappearing like a spirit trying to enter the world. The image was stranger still, for my curls were now gone. My neck felt oddly cool, and I knew the skin there was too white, even for the early spring. As for the rest of me, I was dressed in a canvas shirt and britches. My breasts were bound by a length of muslin.

I had thought in the morning that I'd fashioned a good imitation of a man, but later, at the train station, I wasn't sure. I found myself looking away from strangers, as though my eyes were windows through which they could see in just as I saw out. A woman, of course, is expected to avert her eyes, to draw a curtain as is proper, but for a man, looking away invites suspicion.

The conductor was my nearest worry. Could I meet his gaze and not reveal myself, or would he see the eyes of a wayward woman? In his blue coat he resembled a constable, and I imagined his damp hands on the back of my neck, tossing me off the train at the next stop. For a time he seemed content to trade stories with those up front, but then he turned and began to work his way up the aisle. I went back to my newspaper and pretended to read, but I could hear his wheeze as he approached.

"Ticket, sir."

I held out the stub and looked straight at him. His eyes were red and runny, and to my surprise, they darted away. He had something to hide, or more likely hidden, a bottle perhaps. Without a word he punched my ticket and moved on.

The train continued its parade down the valley, announcing itself at every chicken coop and hay barn, while my thoughts, with less noise, went the other way—back to Basket Creek. At this hour, Father would be in his chair before the fire, pipe in hand—my flight yet unnoticed, for they all thought I'd gone hunting. Brother John would be out in the barn, and Sarah would be in the kitchen with Mother, making some unkind comment about me, no doubt. Mary, bless her heart, would be upstairs playing with Helen. Sarah and Mary are my sisters.

And Helen?

I cannot hide her, so you might as well know. Helen is my daughter, left behind.

* * *

She came into this world seven months after my husband George ran off. By then I was back at Father's house, and the neighbor women helped at the birth. Mother was there, of course, neither gentle nor kind. Even afterward, I was merely tolerated by her, as though my daughter had been born out of wedlock.

Helen was a beautiful, spirited child, but I didn't feel the joy a mother should. First, there was George Slater's betrayal and then Mother's ongoing disdain. Yes, my husband had left me, but was that my sin or his? It wasn't even what Mother said so much as how she went about—nose in the air. A couple of months of that, and I started hunting again, in good part just to get away from her. While I was in the woods, Helen was with my sisters. In truth, I didn't give my daughter half of what I'd given my brother when he was little. Still, we had our playful times, especially once she was up and about. After dinner I would get on my knees, and Helen would ride my back, shrieking with delight as I neighed and pawed at the floor. And when I put her to bed, I would calm her by singing the lullaby that Mother had sung to me—the one about the fairies in the meadow.

As far as paying work, there wasn't any. Not for a woman. I earned my keep at my father's house by chopping wood and bringing home deer meat. I liked to hunt, though for most, a woman carrying a rifle was like a two-headed calf—something to look at and turn away from. Father wasn't bothered—he'd given me the gun and taught me to shoot out behind the barn. But brother John didn't like it and neither did my mother. I didn't care. They couldn't keep me from it, and in tramping the ridgelines, I gained a taste for what it might be like to be a man. Once while in my buckskins, I met a peddler on the river road. We walked near a mile, talking the whole way, my rifle on my shoulder and my hair in my hat. He never guessed and I didn't tell him. Nor did I tell anyone at home, but I went to bed that night feeling the excitement of it.

The autumn Helen turned three, the schoolmaster at Long Eddy, Mr. Pritchard, fell ill. I was offered his position, as there was no one else. I was good at the teaching, not just because I knew my numbers and letters but because I hadn't forgotten what it was like to be young. I didn't spend all my time taking the fun out of everything, which, by reputation, Mr. Pritchard did at every opportunity. I liked the work and was grateful for the appointment—grateful until I opened the school's book and saw that my pay was only one-half that of Mr. Pritchard. I didn't say anything, but after a few days of weighing it, I decided to stand up for myself. I wrote a careful letter demanding my due, but it never got sent. The schoolmaster became well, and that was the end of my teaching.

In the spring I became housekeeper for Raspy Winthrop, a widower with three children who lived along the river. Mother said his real name was Jasper, but I never heard anyone call him that. I went to work for him because I wanted to do my part and bring money home, but all I got was one dollar a week when men working the same hours made ten. Worse, Winthrop looked at me like I was a calf bound for market.

One afternoon while I was baking, he came up behind me—I could smell him. He put his stubby hands on my hips, but I knocked them away and told him I'd skin him like a coon if he did it again. He just laughed through his greasy whiskers, and I didn't tell anyone. Why give the hens of Long Eddy something to cluck about? Instead, the very next evening, I had to endure Mother saying how the prospects looked good for Mr. Winthrop's freight business, meaning him, his wagon, and two scabby mules. Ten wagons and twenty mules, it would have made no difference. How could anyone even think it? But they did. A week later, without a word of warning, Raspy Winthrop announced that he and I would be getting married, as though his saying it would make it so.

"You jus' gotta learn," he said, chewing the words, "which side the bread the butter is on."

And that's the way he, my mother, and most people saw it. If I did more work than I was already doing, got no pay for it at all, and in the bargain allowed him to take his pleasure with me, I would have, in everyone's eyes, risen in station. For my part, I would have thrown myself off the Callicoon Bridge before sharing a bed with that man. And his proposal was an insult. Even my no-good George said that I was dear when he proposed. Believing him was my mistake, but at least he said it.

Did I protest? Tell Winthrop what a hog he was? No—not in those words. I just knew, deep within, that as a woman I could do nothing for myself or my daughter. We would learn the thin charity of others, like the widows and orphans in the Bible, allowed to pick up the stray grains of wheat. Of course, I could have heeded my father, but I didn't. Now I was damaged, and it would be Winthrop or someone like him. I could be either housekeeper or wife, indentured servant or slave. I wanted no part of it. I took off my apron and told Winthrop that from then on he could bake his own bread and butter whatever side of it he liked.

I returned home and secretly set about my preparations. I oiled my rifle, wrapped it in burlap, and hid it in the woodshed. I walked to Long Eddy and checked the times for trains. I went down to the root cellar and retrieved the small box with the money given me on my marriage day.

Three days later I rose while it was still dark and put on a shirt and britches, clothes my brother had outgrown. I cut my hair by candlelight and wrote a note saying that I'd gone hunting. Then I went to the small bed where Helen lay asleep. She was three but still had that milk-fed smell. I kissed her gently so as not to wake her. I told her I was leaving to find work so I could provide for her—that I loved her and would return. These words were spoken true, and as I walked the Callicoon road that morning, the thought of Helen in her bed did not weaken my knees but rather gave me strength for the journey to come.

* * *

It was dark when the train pulled into Port Jervis. The station was filled with people waiting to get on the train or to meet those getting off. No one made way for me, and I had to use my elbows. When I reached the street, I found it lit by gas lamps, something I had never seen. The light danced off the cobblestones and floated in the fog that drifted up from the river. I stopped to watch it, but others pushed past me as though it were nothing. Laughter and loud conversation led me to the Canal House Inn. I followed two men in long coats into a hall filled with men drinking mugs of beer. After a quick look about, I cut a path through the room to where the inn-keeper sat adding numbers. He was a small, wiry man, but on his stool behind the counter he seemed imposing.

"Have you rooms to let?" I asked, my voice cracking on the last word. The innkeeper looked up, and I coughed as though clearing my throat.

"Two bits for jus' yerself," he said looking back down at the ledger. I nodded and with a shaky hand signed his book *Joseph Israel Lobdell*, taking the name of my grandfather, gone years now but still missed by me. Granddad had never made me feel less than my boy cousins, and once I heard him brag about how well I could shoot. And when he died, he left me money as he did the boys—money given me on my marriage day and not a nickel of it spent until now. Would my taking his name insult him? I didn't think so. More likely, he'd be up in heaven having a good laugh.

The room at the inn was no larger than a horse stall, but I sat on the bed, happy to be alone. I undid my shirt and then the wrap, suddenly able to breathe again. It would take some getting used to, although, in truth, I never had much of a chest, even after nursing my Helen. I lay back and looked at the ceiling, wishing to rest and think about nothing. But the candle let off a flickering light, and I began to see strange faces in the cobwebs above. I would have gone at them with a broom had there been one.

A little later I was downstairs, bowl of soup in hand. I made my way through the crowded room till I found a table with an empty place. Already there, bent over their bowls, were three men in oil-stained overalls. I was ready to meet them in the eye, but no one looked up as I sat down. They just slurped the broth and belched in turn.

I sat before my soup and looked at my spoon. Should I too slurp? But then what if I did it wrong? Safer to be quiet. I found the broth a little briny, but the mutton was good, and tasted all the better because I hadn't spent the day cooking it. With food in my belly, the clamor in the room turned melodious. I sat and watched as men gestured, guffawed, and slapped each other on the back. I liked it. I liked being there. And why couldn't there be a hall where women could go and do the same? A regular slap on the back might do us all some good.

After a while, I got up from the table, not wishing to remain the only one without beer in hand. I found a hallway that led to a room where men sat in large chairs and smoked cigars. I would have been more out of place in that room, so I stayed in the hall and looked at the notices posted there. I had the faint hope that someone might be looking for a schoolteacher or a music teacher, but there was nothing like that. A carriage was for hire; a wheelwright sought; a teamster needed. But then a notice in bold letters caught my eye: TO ADVENTURERS! OPPORTUNITIES IN HONESDALE!

The bill was faded and worn, but I read it top to bottom. Then, when no one was looking, I took it down and put it in my pocket.

* * *

That night in my room I wrote a letter home. Using a careful hand, I said only what I had to, not wishing to pile one lie upon another:

> Dear Mother and Father,
>
> I have left Basket Creek in search of work. Please forgive me. I will return for Helen when I have a proper place to live. I am sorry I did not heed your warning about Mr. Slater, but I hope I can redeem my mistake. John, Mary and Sarah have been so dear with Helen, and I am truly grateful for all the love you have given me.
>
> Your devoted daughter,
> Lucy Ann

I folded the page so I could post it in the morning, but there was a tight feeling in my throat as though more words wanted to come. I took another sheet and began a wild scrawl: *Dear Ma and Pa. I have cut off all my hair and I'm wearing John's clothes, the skunk. If Reverend Hale could see me now, he'd have me tied up and burned, for sure. Please tell him that I'm staying upstairs at a den of sin with many drunken men below. No, George isn't with them, but you were right—he was a drunk and a lout. But that didn't make me a harlot. Tell John that his dumb old knife is under the bucket in the barn, not far from where he left it. And kindly suggest to Sarah that she should, once a month, as hard as it might be, give a thought to someone other than herself. I don't know where I'll sleep tomorrow. Your footloose first-born, Lucy Magdalene.*

When my scribbling was done, I felt better. I took the second note to the lamp and gave it to the angels to deliver, watching it burn as I held one corner. Then I shed my brother's clothes and got into my grandfather's flannel shirt, the one that I had slept in for years. I reached for my hairbrush and then realized I wouldn't need it. Brushing out tangles was a chore I didn't like, but now I felt deprived. I wanted to be home in front of the fire, sewing or darning—I didn't care. I wanted to talk to Mary. I wanted to lie down with Helen and kiss her good-night.

This would not do. This would not do at all. A woman crying upstairs at the inn would be the end to everything. Thinking then to summon other spirits, I went into my bag and pulled out my violin. The lacquer glowed orange in the dim light. I plucked the D string for good luck.

I was eight when Father taught me to play. He told me the strings were magic, and I had seen it for myself. Father could wave that bow and make a tear roll down my face. Or he could lift me out of my chair and make me dance like a fool. Not anymore—his hands had become swollen and stiff. The violin was mine. I had even thought to offer instruction on it or in dance, as I had received training in both while at school in Coxsackie. But in Long Eddy it was hard enough to get children into the classroom to learn their letters. There was no one who would sit still for music lessons, much less pay for them. I looked at the violin and imagined the songs I might play. My tiny room could have used a little magic, but, not wishing to draw attention, I put the instrument away.

2

I WOKE IN the morning to the smell of spilled beer. I was in a lumpy bed, looking again at the cobwebs—no faces there now, only spiders. I dressed, all the while aware of the letter on the table that I'd written the night before. I felt an urge to tear it up, but I put the letter in my pocket and went downstairs. After porridge at the tavern, I walked to the mail depot and posted it to Long Eddy.

Coming out of the depot, I noticed a shop across the street—a shop that sold clothes for men. I went over and peered through the glass in the door but couldn't get myself to turn the knob. I had bought clothes in a store only twice, each time in Albany with my mother and never as a man. How was it done? I stood in place like a statue, till I thought people might be looking. If they were, they saw me leave with a purposeful step as though remembering some errand. A minute down the street I stopped to scold myself—if I were to live as a man, there would be things more difficult than this.

I returned to the shop, stepped inside, and was greeted by the smell of brushed wool. It took a moment for my eyes to adjust, and as they did a young man appeared as though birthed by the clothes hanging nearby. His starched shirt was gathered gracefully above the elbow and his head was held high, as though he too were performing for some unseen audience. Might he be of service, he asked, making a sweeping gesture with his arm. I didn't curtsy in return—just said I wanted to buy a few things. The man's eyes traveled my body, while his face did its best to hide a grimace. Was I deserving of the clothes in his store?

The shopkeeper led me to some shelves off to the side, all the while speaking in an overly mannered way. "Would the gentleman like this? Would the gentleman prefer that?" I didn't know what to say. I wanted to slap him.

My host sighed and gathered his patience. "Can you describe the occasion?"

Suddenly, a new truth came to me—I mustn't hesitate when it comes to deceit. "Yes," I said. "I'm going to visit my aunt in New York."

With mere mention of the grand city, the man looked at me with new eyes. He took down a pair of smoke-gray britches and, from another shelf, a white shirt with a stiff collar. He handed them to me, and I went behind the curtain. When I came out, I stood before the mirror and looked at myself as I thought a man might.

As I continued to admire my new clothes, the shopkeeper fluttered about. His fingers brushed imagined dust off my shoulders. Then they went to my waist and began to wander, as though, perhaps, to assure a proper fit. I felt myself stiffen. Then his hand moved over my bottom! I nearly jumped. For a woman, this was a brash liberty; for a man, I didn't know. In no position to make a fuss, I let the moment pass.

In less than an hour I came to own the britches, several shirts, and a pair of leather shoes. I had spent a good part of Granddad's money and might have given more thought to my shrinking purse, but I didn't. Feeling cheerful—victorious even—I bade my nosey-hands friend good-bye and returned to the inn to collect my belongings. A short while later, dressed in my old clothes, the new ones in my bag, I set out for Honesdale, Pennsylvania, some fifty miles up what everybody was calling *the ditch*.

The barge canal ran along the east bank of the Delaware. The river was rushing with the spring rains, but the canal was calm and the towpath firm—good walking, the only dangers those left behind by the mules. I did my best to stride like a man, and it wasn't hard, for I had done it often while hunting. The boats going in my direction were lightly loaded, but those coming the other way were filled to the brim with stone coal. As the canal had only one towpath, I was curious as to how they could pass without becoming tangled. But the etiquette was as formal as the moulinet, a dance figure we had learned at school. The boat heading for the Hudson, being burdened, moved to the far side, dropped its lines and let the lighter boat pass over, the maneuver so graceful that little time was lost by the ceding vessel and none at all by the favored one.

Midday, at a place called Monroe's Lock, I bought some bread and cheese and found a sunny place to sit. After my meal, I reread the notice taken from the tavern:

TO ADVENTURERS!
OPPORTUNITIES IN HONESDALE!

The DELAWARE & HUDSON CANAL has opened a field for enterprise. The Subscriber offers for sale, on moderate terms, a number of lots in Honesdale. The titles are indisputable. In HONESDALE the Merchant meets his goods from New York; and there the Farmer finds a ready market for his Husbandry. The social amenities are good, and the churches are Presbyterian, Methodist, and Baptist. In each is a Sabbath School. Inquiries may be made at the office of the Subscriber, which is to be found at the Tavern in Honesdale bearing his name: Daniel Blandin

I had chosen the bill with no more thought than a page of the Bible selected by chance, yet I was obeying it with the same devotion. I was in need of a place to go, and I took this for my sign. Honesdale sounded like a town with promise, and I felt as though I knew someone there—Mr. Daniel Blandin. I folded the notice and put it away, my letter of introduction. Then, to keep myself company, I took out my violin and scraped some melodies, mostly sad ones. After several songs, a whiskered boatman appeared, bringing his mules to water. With him was a boy wearing overalls and a slouch hat.

"That's a fine piece of fiddle playing," said the man. "The name's McAdams, Captain Jake McAdams. This here's my driver, Little Nick."

"Joseph Lobdell," I said, rising to shake hands, as I had seen men do. I had chopped many a log on Basket Creek, so my hand was strong, but it was small. McAdams swallowed it in his sweaty paw but didn't crush it. Our eyes met, and the captain appeared satisfied.

"Are you headed in or out?" I asked.

"Runnin' light to Honesdale," he said. "Be lucky to pay the feed."

I nodded my sympathies, trying to speak no more than I had to. What words I did say, I roughed up in the back of my throat. When the captain learned I was going his way, he invited me to ride with him. A little later we stood on the deck of the *Mary Ellen* and watched the mules returned to the traces, the driver slipping the harnesses over their heads and tightening the buckles under their bellies. I was more or less doing the same with the unfamiliar belt around my waist, not quite able to find the place where it was comfortable yet would still keep my brother's britches on my narrow hips.

Seated on a barrel nearby was a woman whose hips were anything but narrow—the captain's wife, I thought. "That's Martha, our cook," said McAdams, speaking as if she were at a distance. I waited to greet her with a nod, but she didn't turn or lift her face.

McAdams next motioned to a hatch and a steep ladder. Something told me not to go, but I didn't know how to refuse without appearing strange. I took the ladder and watched as the sky became a small square, wondering with each step down if I were to be locked away and sold into bondage. My feet hit bottom in a dark room that smelled like vinegar. Nearby, I could see a table and a coal stove. Further on were two smaller rooms with bunks. A window high up provided a meager ration of light and air—a perfect prison.

The captain's legs appeared on the ladder. When he got down, he turned and gave a satisfied nod. "This here's where we all live. It can be cold and blowin' a gale up top, but down here you'll be snug and dry."

I had to laugh at myself. I had read too many pirate stories as a girl. Still, I felt uneasy, and when we returned to the deck, I looked for a sheltered corner, vowing to sleep topside in any weather short of a blizzard.

As we got under way, the captain asked if I would play some tunes. I was happy to do most anything that wouldn't require talking, so I unwrapped the violin and bowed the most cheerful melodies I knew: "Horse and the Moon," "The Rusty Shuffle," and "Lazy Ole Daisy." The notes floated out into the afternoon, and for a while it seemed as though the land and the people on it were the ones in motion. The music brought smiles to those walking the towpath, and several waved or called out as we went by.

The captain liked the playing well enough, but once it was done, he was ready to talk. "You been on the ditch before?" he asked. I shook my head. "Well, she's a hunert miles from Kingston to Honesdale. The *Mary Ellen* carries ninety tons and needs only five foot of water." The captain then mentioned some recent trouble—the canal company had tried to lower the hauling fee. "Most the free owners like myself refused to carry," he said, spitting overboard. "A bunch of us dressed like Indians jumped a company boat near Wurtsboro. Lit her on fire. You should've seen it when the flames reached the coal dust—blew like she was carrying gunpowder."

I paid my fare that afternoon by giving the captain half an ear, making the occasional nod as he told his stories, all the while imagining conversations taking place at home. I had never been hunting for more than two days running. They would worry as it got dark—my letter wouldn't arrive for another day. In the meantime, with his bad legs, Father couldn't go looking for me, and I doubted my brother John would even bother.

A sudden silence from Captain McAdams interrupted my drift. His attention was forward, and I turned to see three piers of stone rising out of the river. It was a bridge of some kind, but not like one I'd ever seen. It had curved shapes and high walls, as though it were the guarded gateway to a lord's castle. But there was no castle, only the bridge, lit up by a sun now low in the sky—forest and mountain on one side, forest and field on the other. And the two figures at the end, who might have been footmen with pikes, were, instead, old men with fishing poles. I looked back at the captain. "What is it?"

"Mr. Roebling's Bridge," he said proudly, "and we're goin' over it."

I wasn't sure I had heard him right, for I had never seen a bridge that carried one river of water over another. But when we got closer, I saw it was true, though I didn't know how it was done. McAdams was bragging on how the bridge had to carry not only the barge and its tons of cargo but the weight of all the water needed to float that boat some thirty feet above the river. According to him, the whole thing was hanging by wire rope. I knew that couldn't be true, but before I could think more on it, the towpath changed from dirt to oak plank, and the hooves echoed loudly as the mules pulled the boat out over the Delaware. By then I didn't care if angels were holding it up, as I was seeing the bridge in a whole new way—one life of mine on the near shore, an entirely new one on the far.

3

HONESDALE WAS NOT the polite place I had imagined—certainly the canal basin wasn't. Dead rats floated in the black water. It stank. On the wharf men were shouting and cursing as they hauled carts and stacked crates. I jumped off the *Mary Ellen* and had taken but ten steps when I was shoved aside by a man carrying a large sack. "Watch your arse!"

Compared to Port Jervis, Honesdale seemed the more roughly hewn, though, as I would discover, it was better in two respects—the number of drinking halls and their signs. Over every tavern door were brightly painted boards with seafaring expressions and short poetical works. *The seaworn sailor here will find / the porter good, the treatment kind.* One portrayed a canal boat next to a flagon of beer. *This is the ship that never sailed / this is the mug that never failed.*

The notice that I'd taken in Port Jervis directed me to Blandin's Tavern on Main Street, a block east of the basin and a more respectable avenue. The tavern stood proud on the corner of Fourth, and, like the others, its motto hung by the door.

> 'Twas thus the Royal mandate ran,
> When first the human race began;
> The friendly social, honest man,
> What're he be,
> 'Tis he fulfills great Nature's plan,
> and none but he.

I blinked and read it again, never having seen the problem so briefly put. None but *he*, indeed!

I stepped through the swinging door and was greeted by a sour smell that I remembered from the tavern in Port Jervis. At several tables men were drinking and talking in afternoon voices, but I went unnoticed except for the man rinsing glasses behind the bar. He looked at me without expression and went back to his work as though I were a fish not worth the bother. I took a breath, approached, and at the last moment the barkeep looked up with a questioning eye, as though he'd been watching me the whole time.

"I'm looking for Mr. Daniel Blandin," I said, herding the words like sheep.

The man took his time wiping a glass and then threw his chin toward a table in the back. "He'd be over there."

The master of the house was a large man with thick eyebrows and thinning reddish hair. With him were two others, talking and laughing. Not knowing what to do, I stayed where I was and asked for a beer. When it came, I held the mug tightly and tried to look as though I had done this many times. But simply holding the beer wouldn't do, so after what I judged a proper moment, I raised the glass. My first few swallows disappointed. I had imagined that the enthusiasm surrounding the drink would somehow be reflected in its taste.

When the two men rose to leave, I took my beer and walked up to the table. "Mr. Blandin?"

The man looked up, pleasant enough. "And who might you be, lad?"

"Joseph Lobdell, sir." My hand wanted to reach for the paper in my pocket, but I spoke of it instead. "I saw a bill bearing your name in Port Jervis."

Mr. Blandin smiled. "I'm afraid you're a little late if you're looking to purchase a property on Main."

"I'm not. I'm not here to purchase land."

A twist of surprise showed on the man's face. "What then? You're not here to load coal, that's for sure." He let go a laugh, and I felt funny in the knees. My life as a man was near its end—that seemed clear. I wondered if I might turn and run out of the place, but what good would that have done? I'd just have to keep running. There wasn't much to do except spit it out.

"Well, sir," I said in a tin voice, "your notice spoke of social amenities, and I am a music teacher. I seek to open a school to instruct young people in the art of dancing. I thought you might offer me some direction."

Mr. Blandin put his mug hard to the table and coughed as though the beer hadn't gone down right. "Dancing?" he finally said. "Does this look like a ladies' shop?"

"I've made a mistake," I said, glancing about for a path to the door. "I'll go."

"Not so fast," said the tavern keeper. "I like to get to know my guests."

I didn't like the sound of this, and as my host looked me up and down, I felt like a mouse cornered by a cat—a cat more eager for entertainment than for a meal. The man's eye then came upon my bag and the neck of the violin sticking out. "Can you play that?"

A hesitant nod was all I could manage. Mr. Blandin folded his arms and gave the order. "Do it."

I took the violin from my bag and brought it to my chin with the small hope it would buy my freedom. Had I been asked to sing, I couldn't have hit one true note in five. But the strings felt no fear, and my fingers knew their way in the dark. I played "Brennan on the Moor," and when I stopped, every head was turned.

Mr. Blandin rose. "Well done!" he said, giving me a hearty clap on the back. I felt the binding wrap loosen. "Have you eaten?"

"No, sir," I said, holding myself so as to not come undone. "Not since morning."

The tavern keeper motioned for me to take a chair. The noise of conversation returned to the room as I looked about in disbelief. My father had spoken true—the strings really could cast a spell. Moments before, I'd been laughed at. Now I was a guest. Dizzy from the reversal of fortune, I grasped the chair's edge as I sat.

My host called over his shoulder for two bowls of stew. Then he asked where I was from. I pulled myself straight and said that I was from a town near Albany, where I had studied music. Two steaming bowls were set before us, and Mr. Blandin dipped his bread into the gravy.

"A dancing school," he said, nodding slowly. "Might work. People seem to need all kinds of things these days."

Had I heard him right? My face must have asked its own question, for Blandin bent forward and lowered his voice. "I'll let you in on a little something. A few years back, Bethany was county-town here in Wayne, but then Honesdale took it from Bethany, and I confess I had a little somethin' to do with it."

The man swallowed some more beer, while I pursed my lips and nodded as though I knew what he was talking about. Then he spoke in a near whisper.

"But living among us, there are some who believe that Honesdale will continue to its destiny, overtake Harrisburg, and govern all of Pennsylvania. They imagine grand occasions with guests arriving in fancy carriages. So you'll have a clientele, son, as long as people have high ideas, which I think we can depend upon."

Mr. Blandin speared a small potato and brought it to his mouth, where it vanished in a single swallow. "Now, what won't be so easy," he said, "is finding a proper hall. But there must be something. I'll ask around."

"That's very kind," I said, still not entirely sure if he were serious or making fun of me.

A wave of Blandin's hand said the favor was of no consequence. He pulled his chair closer. "Now let's you and I discuss a little business of our own."

I imitated his gesture and leaned toward him. What could our business be?

"Not long ago, we sadly lost our piano player," he said, looking over to a dusty piano in the corner. "So you might like to come by in the evening and play a few songs on the fiddle. I'd give you dinner. It wouldn't be first-pickin's, but you'd be fed."

Surprised and pleased, I accepted the offer. I then asked if there were a simple place to stay nearby.

"You could stay here," he said, motioning toward a stair. "A dollar a week, two with breakfast. The room ain't large, but it's yours alone. Sheets every three weeks."

"I would like to stay here," I said. An approving nod was followed by a handshake. An older man named Damon took me upstairs.

As promised, the room was small—bed, table, and window. I pulled aside the curtain. Over the building behind, I could see the barges lined up on the far side of the basin. Beyond them were mountainous piles of stone coal. I couldn't see where the coal was being loaded, but I could hear the rattle as it ran down the chutes.

Damon left, and as the door closed behind him, it revealed a mirror that seemed to have a history. Its frame was scorched, and a crack ran up the glass. The left side offered a true image; the right produced a reflection you might see in broken water. I stood before the good half and ran my fingers through my hair, missing my brown curls as though someone had stolen them. My face looked undressed. While growing up, I had waited for it to become round and full, like the faces of the pretty girls I knew. It didn't. It stayed angular. This was now helpful, perhaps, in my deception, though my smooth skin made me look more like a boy than a man. I considered not washing my face for a while and then thought of rubbing in a little coal dust, a ready supply on the windowsill.

4

I WAS TIRED and the bed beckoned, but rather than rest, I decided to take what was left of the day and explore the world beyond Mr. Blandin's Tavern. I redid my wrap and put on the shirt and britches I had purchased in Port Jervis. The new clothes added a month or two to my twenty-five years. I felt respectable.

I left my room, walked down the stairs and out the door to discover the Honesdale that might imagine itself an important town. There were stores of every kind on lower Main Street. They all had painted signs as one might expect, but most didn't need them because they had large windows that showed what there was inside to buy. Farther up, I came upon a hotel, several churches, and a red brick courthouse on the town square with its walkways and benches. I sat on one and watched people pass by, trying to guess at their troubles or schemes. No one gave me any notice, a good measure of my disguise, but after a time, I began to think about home. My letter had arrived by now, and I could almost see the looks and hear the words as though I were in the room—John, Sarah, and Mother voicing their outrage, each of them secretly glad I was gone; Father shaking his head but saying nothing unkind; Helen and Mary looking lost and betrayed. I vowed to make it right to them when I could.

In the failing light a man approached, his hat pulled low. I near fell off the bench when I recognized my scoundrel husband, George. Had he run away to this very town? It wasn't him, of course, only my busy mind, which wasn't a bit embarrassed to be proved wrong but went ahead and imagined George passing by anyway. In this drama, I would follow him and witness his dissolutions in some saloon. It wouldn't be all that enter-taining, not that part of it, but after things had gone on a while, I would go up to him and start a conversation, watching with great interest his drunken confusion as the man he was talking to turned into his former beloved. That might cure him.

* * *

George Slater was not my first boyfriend. That honor belonged to Wil-liam Smith, who would walk with me after school when we lived in Westerlo. Not for long. Father put a stop to it, saying I was too young for *romances*. I hadn't even considered it a romance, but Father's meddling made it one. For a while, William and I left little notes to each other under a particular rock.

After Mr. Smith, there was Henry St. John. I was fifteen then, and this I did consider a romance, but it bloomed for only a few months. He fell ill. After he had taken to his bed, I wasn't allowed to see him for fear I'd get the cough, so we smuggled short letters by way of his sister. Then one cold afternoon she brought a note written in a bad hand. "You are my treasured memory," it read; "Pray for my soul." A week later I watched them lower his box into the ground. I was shattered, certain he was my one true love, his being taken from me somehow proof of that. But spring came and then summer. No one spoke of Henry, and his memory slowly became more a sadness than a sorrow. By then, there was George Slater.

He was a pretty boy with dark hair that fell over a troubled brow. He thought this or that about everything, not shy during our walks after school. I found his brash opinions entertaining, not seeing that most of his stories had to do with some clever trick he had played or some injustice done him. I was young, and to me, he seemed like a poet set upon by cruel fate—his mother was dead and his father a drunk.

I liked having a handsome young man pay me attention. But as George's attentions increased, I liked it less. One day he declared his love and said he wanted to marry me. It wasn't a real proposal, more an expression of regard, but even so, I told him I wasn't ready, and that was true. And I wasn't sure if I really loved George—loved him enough to marry him. You shouldn't wonder about a thing like that.

Father had no good opinion of George, but he didn't forbid my seeing him. He just said that it might be best if I went to live with my aunt and attend the academy in Coxsackie. Anxious to escape, I agreed. And in truth, while at school, I didn't think about George all that much. I had other friends there, mostly young women, for the young men at the academy were, with few exceptions, kept in their own classes and let out a half-hour after we were sent home.

In my final year at school, Father wrote that he was selling our farm. He had purchased a cabin and two hundred acres near the Delaware River, *a beautiful wilderness* he called it. When I arrived some months later, I found our new land as Father had said. We built a sawmill that first year and lived the life of pioneers. It was hard work, and I didn't mind the privations.

The next year, the railroad came up the river, and suddenly we could sell at a good price any amount of lumber that we could mill or any amount of bluestone that we could chisel out of the hill behind our house. Most of what was grown in the valley stayed in the valley to feed us or the livestock, but just about everything else—honey, maple syrup, hemlock bark, milled wood, and stone—was well worth the effort if you could get it down to the station at Long Eddy. And we weren't pioneers anymore; nobody in the valley was, because now anything you'd ever want could arrive by train. It even brought George Washington Slater, who one day knocked on our door wearing a store-bought shirt and a bow tie. We went for a walk along the creek, and he proposed for real. He said he had always known that I was meant for him. He said that he had heard me call in the night—heard me call so many times that he had to come find me.

This was all like out of a story, and I couldn't remember the hesitations I had felt before. My family was beginning a new life, and I thought that God probably meant for me to begin one too. And I didn't just have God on my mind. I would see Clarence and Katie Sykes walking arm in arm, laughing and leaning against each other, and a warmth would spread over me. I imagined them going home together and what would happen there. I imagined this so often I thought I might be sinful. But sinful or not, I wanted what Katie had. I wanted a man who would kiss me and touch me and lie with me and talk to me in the dark of night. And then suddenly there was, right in front of me, a handsome man—I will not lie—a man who had come all this way just to do those very things with me. I said yes.

I told Father the news when we were in the barn. He was limping by then from the pain in his swollen legs. That pain seemed to spread to his face as he set aside the bag of feed. "Lucy, dearest," he said still breathing hard, "the man you marry is your choice. But if you want my blessing, you will wait." Father then offered to hire George for six months so I might better learn his character.

I didn't see the generosity of Father's offer. My head was filled with things that I wanted, and I didn't want to wait. I resented him for opposing us. And when I told George, he acted as though Father had offered him not a job but an insult. This anger echoed my own feelings and made me more certain of George's love. We told Father we would marry, with or without his consent, and so forced him to give it.

The wedding took place at the church in Long Eddy. George wore the shirt and bow tie he had proposed in. I was in my pretty yellow Sunday dress. Reverend Hale presided, though I wished it were someone else.

To me, Reverend Hale was just a crabby old man, and that would have been fine if that was all there was to it. But I think to Reverend Hale I was something wicked, or at least that's how he acted. I never knew why. Was it because I didn't go around frowning like he did? Was I somehow bathed in sin by my God-given nature? Was every young woman? I didn't know what he thought, but as I walked down the aisle on Father's arm, I saw a look in Reverend Hale's eye that made me shiver. And, surely, it can't be a good thing to be led in your sacred vows by someone who thinks you're evil. I wonder now if he didn't insert some secret curse—that would explain a lot. But living where we did, there really wasn't a choice. If you wanted to marry, it would be Reverend Hale.

My minister was not the only chilly wind blowing that afternoon. What I didn't know in those headstrong moments when I forced my marriage on my father and my family was that when the day came, I would have to be happy for all of them, for they were not going to be any more than polite. And so, with the crinoline holding out my dress, I went like a hummingbird, flower to flower, hoping to receive love, warmth and approval. But I didn't find that precious nectar, except, of course, from Mary, without whom I mightn't have finished the day. And George Slater was no help. For all his ardor and impatience, he now acted put upon, as though getting married was just my idea. So while I was trying to cheer those around me, I also had to keep him merry—no small feat with George, even on the best of days, as I would find out.

After the wedding, we had a celebration with food and dancing in the hall behind the church. Many friends and neighbors were there, and they, at least, seemed perfectly happy to have me wed. Later, without the crinoline, I played the fiddle at my own wedding, and those moments were the happiest I remember of that night. The next day I went into Long Eddy expecting people to treat me special, as they had the night before. No one did. I was now just plain married folk.

George and I rented a cabin about a mile from my father's house, and George went to work at Mr. LaValley's mill. I was glad to have a house of our own, small as it was. I expected to be happy, but once we moved in, all of George's tenderness fell away. I will not bother with a full list of his mean doings, much of it served with foul words. Briefly put, his complaints might have to do with the meal I had made. Or that I was not sufficiently pleased to see him when he got home after work, stinking of drink, whatever hour that might be. He wanted me to be loving no matter what growl he gave as he came through the door or what insults followed, as though a loving mood were like feed for hens to be put out whatever the weather and not something that two people made with each other. Soon enough, I came to understand that none of it had to do with whatever he said it was about. When a person is drunk and mean, he will find something wrong. I stopped worrying about the meal or about being loving. Things were just the same, no matter what I did.

One evening, when he had come home drunk and I had complained about it, he struck me across the face and threw me out of the house, my mouth bleeding. I waited till he fell asleep and then crept back inside. I vowed to leave him, but the next day he cried like a baby and told me that God should strike him dead if he ever did it again. I stayed, thinking that he was truly sorry and would keep away from the drink.

He did—for five or six days. Then he came home from the mill with another man and ordered me to set a place for him at our table; he would be staying with us until his own cabin was finished. I didn't want someone else sharing our tiny house, but I got out another knife and fork. A week later, George came home drunk and accused me of things I could scarce believe, suggesting I had spent time with our boarder in a personal way, giving our guest the love I was withholding from him. And by that time I *was* withholding the love from George, the drunken imposter, staying true to the man I had once loved, waiting for him to return.

George didn't actually come out and say it. He just kept asking with a leer if I had *enjoyed* my time with our boarder the night before. I said that if he had come home when he should have, he wouldn't have to make up stupid stories. I don't think George believed that I had been unfaithful, but the idea seemed to excite him in some way. "Deny it?" he shouted. "Well then show me that you love me." I knew what he wanted, but it made no sense. Had I been unfaithful, would an act of love between us undo the wrong? I wouldn't let him near me.

When our boarder came in that night, I told him he had to go. I didn't say why, and George was perfectly pleasant to the man, which I thought strange considering all that had been said. And when George came down with a fever the following day, I was glad—it made sense of things.

My George stayed in bed for three days. I brought him tea and soup. At first he seemed like a sick little boy. But then he told me he was going to die and wanted me to promise that I'd never remarry. I told him he wasn't going to die, and I wouldn't make so selfish a promise. I thought it was the fever talking, but a couple of days later, when he was better, George started ranting and calling me a whore for wanting to lie with another when he was in his grave. That night I dreamed that he stabbed me with a knife.

The next morning he again abused me with foul words. As soon as he was gone to work, I put some things in a bag and walked down the creek to my father's house. I spoke of an argument, ashamed to give an account of George's behavior. It didn't matter. A few days after that, George Slater sold our cow and just up and disappeared.

5

I CROSSED THE bridge to the upper village and took the road north. Nearly a week had passed since my arrival in Honesdale, and I had yet to find a room for my school. Now I was following Mr. Blandin's directions to a glass factory in a stone building that was to be found on the flats below the village of Bethany. It all seemed rather unlikely, but I walked on till I came to the described building, covered with the veins of creeper vine. A man in a leather apron was waiting by the door.

"John Stevenson," he said, offering a scarred hand.

I took the hand and looked into his weathered face. "Joseph Lobdell."

Mr. Stevenson had talked to Daniel Blandin and knew I was there to see his upstairs hall. Without another word, we passed through the door and into a large room that looked like Satan's kitchen. Teams of sweating, shirtless men were working a row of furnaces. We stopped before one and watched as the headman dipped a pipe into a cauldron and gathered a molten ball. This he shaped by turning and blowing while his assistant fed the fire. The two exchanged only looks as they passed each other with red-hot irons and glowing glass, the ball slowly taking the shape of a heavy mug, like those used every night at Blandin's. I had always seen men as clumsy to the bone, but standing there I marveled at how graceful they can be when there's a purpose to it.

At the end of the room, a hall held a set of stairs. I asked Mr. Stevenson if there was another route in—the way we had come wouldn't be suitable for young students. Mr. Stevenson laughed and pointed to the clutter at the hall's end behind which I could now see a door. "Somewhere in my office there's a key."

I had been told that the second floor had once been a meeting room, so its condition surprised me. There was debris everywhere—broken crates, an odd assortment of chairs, and some sort of workbench. Dirt and sawdust covered the floor, and the windows were so grimy that one would have to guess at the weather. I knelt down and pushed aside the dust. The planks were smooth and tightly fit.

"Maple," said Mr. Stevenson proudly.

I gave a nod. "So I see."

I asked about the rent, and Mr. Stevenson replied with a modest sum. I tried not to act like I thought it low, but he saw my face. "I'm glad to do what I can," he said, "for any friend of Daniel Blandin." We shook hands again, and I left quite pleased. I had, it seemed, stumbled upon a great secret society—a world in which everything is accomplished by a wink and a nod.

I walked back to town and went to the offices of the *Honesdale Democrat,* where I placed a small advertisement that would appear the following Tuesday.

> Joseph I. Lobdell, Professor of Dance, announces the formation of classes in dance, voice, and violin for Students of all ages. Those interested should come at four in the afternoon on Thursday to the meeting room at the Dyberry Glass Factory.

I was back at the glass factory the next day. I had given myself only a week, so I had no time to burn. Instead, I burned rubbish. After that, I swept the floor and cleaned the windows. On Monday, I borrowed a mop from the tavern and washed the floor three times. The next two days I spent on my hands and knees, putting wax on the maple. The wood glowed yellow, and the wax put a civilized smell into the room. It also put dirt under my fingernails. I thought about leaving some to roughen my appearance as it would aid in my deception at the tavern, but I didn't, because it wouldn't help me as a music teacher. I was looking over one shoulder, then the other.

I had, of course, started my journey with a greater fear of men—that

I would do or say the wrong thing. So far that hadn't happened, but men are not known for noticing things. Women, on the other hand, notice near everything. My fear began to grow that one of them might catch some detail that a man would never see—a book held to the breast, a button unfastened with two fingers, an eyebrow lifted in doubt. But in spite of that fear, I stopped along Dyberry Creek on the advertised day and picked a bouquet of purple phlox that ended up on the table by the door.

At the appointed hour, eight or nine mothers arrived, coming in twos and threes. There were children of various ages. I was formal with the mothers but did my best to make them feel at ease, speaking with humor and not condescension. I think I charmed a few.

Some older girls arrived. They put their names on the list but did not engage me in conversation. Instead, they stood off in a corner, whispering and casting glances in my direction. I wondered if they thought me handsome.

* * *

My room upstairs at Blandin's was adequate but not more than that—just a place to sleep. I might on occasion sit there and read the *Democrat*, but usually I would do that downstairs. And there was little to see out the window except for the piles of coal and the privies in the alley. From my bed I could hear their doors creak at all hours. I didn't feel any danger when I went there. Aside from the drunks who piss into the canal, men and women do their business in private, and visitors don't come calling. And it's not a comfortable seat whoever you are, what with the cold drafts and smells that ain't lilacs.

As far as washing, I would do that in my room with a bucket of water made warm in the kitchen below. I would use the same water to wash things that could not go to the woman down the street, picking a day when the sun was coming through the window and the cotton would dry on the back of the chair.

All of that was easy enough. The evenings downstairs were less so. Mr. Blandin made it known that I was there at his request, but I still felt out of place, as one might expect. I was unpracticed at the banter, and I often found myself forcing awkward laughs a short moment after those around me. I sat at a table off to the side and soon had a chair that was considered mine. I was shy at first about playing the violin, but the men seemed to like it and began making requests. I knew many tunes, but not the canal songs with their refrains about low bridges and unruly mules. These I had to learn. One evening a scruffy coal loader named Jimmy Lawson called out for me to play "Never Take the Hindshoe."

"Don't know it," I said over the din.

Jimmy rose to his feet, unsteady. "I'll sing it fer ya." Blandin's became quiet.

Jimmy had been drinking and wasn't any choirboy to start with, yet he managed to stumble his way through a song that warned against getting near a mule's private parts, for, as it said, "the business end of a mule is mighty ticklish." With these words, the room burst into hoots and howls—the mere mention of private parts, even those of a mule, the cause for great laughter.

But not every canal song was of low humor. The boat men also entertained a variety of romantic notions—songs about the perils of the canal and verses about tearful ladies left behind, sung plaintively as if they had set sail for China. As silly as those songs seemed to me, the men enjoyed them. Soon, I came to share their good spirits, more so after I discovered that a glass of beer made it all go a little easier. In time, stubborn mules and private parts became funny to me too.

What didn't become funny were the cruel comments about the boatmen's cooks or wenches, as they called them. These were unmarried women who, for pitiful wages, did the cooking and cleaning. Even after the meals were served, their duties were usually not complete until the master of the boat was fast asleep. I would feel myself flush when they were mocked, but, of course, I said nothing. Worse, I had to display some merriment, so I got good at acting amused when I wasn't. And if I didn't laugh heartily enough at a crude joke, it could be forgiven along with my other faults—I was slighter than most and didn't drink whiskey or chew tobacco. But because of these shortcomings and, most surely, because I was there at the invitation of Daniel Blandin, I became, soon enough, everybody's little brother.

* * *

I stood with my arms folded until my students realized that nothing would happen unless they were still. When all was quiet, I recited the very words that had been said to me just a few years before: "Dance is not a series of learned figures. It is a formal gesture between a man and a woman. You will learn the manners."

And thus it began with the etiquette: the proper way to approach a lady, when to bow and when to curtsy, how to escort a partner to her seat, when to withdraw. I told my students how I had been taught at the academy by Miss Burchett, a matron who always looked like she had just eaten a lemon and who recited rules till we were saying them in our sleep. To lighten the load, I scrunched my face and imitated her nasal declarations. "A gentleman is *always* introduced to a lady. A lady is *never* introduced to a gentleman."

My students laughed at the mimicry, but in Miss Burchett's class we hadn't even smiled for fear we would be made to sit in the corner. Miss Burchett acted like Moses come off the mountain—commandments for everything, and all of them designed to keep the sexes apart. "All intimacy ends with the dance!" she would proclaim at least once a week. And that, without fail, would lead to her golden rule: "It is better to be deemed prudish than indiscreet." These rules had no good effect that I could see. For my part, I would have welcomed anything that might have even passed for indiscretion, a recollection I did not share with my students.

In the lessons that followed, I started in on the quadrille: how the couples were numbered, their positions, where the head of the hall would be. Then came a walking tour of the basic figures: right and left, ladies chain, forward two, and chassez. By the second week it was time to play the violin and call out the figures. Soon my students could perform a simple version of the quadrille. Ahead of us still were the so-called promiscuous figures, more complicated maneuvers in which partners switched for a portion of the dance.

On Monday and Wednesday I had nine students, four boys and five girls, ages twelve to fifteen. On Tuesday and Thursday I had seven young ladies. Four of them—Sarah Clemson, Jane Brower, and the Blackstone twins—were age sixteen and from the upper village of Honesdale. Dorothy Millen, Evelyn Sanders, and Lydia Watson were a year or two older and from the village of Bethany. The girls in my older class constantly exchanged looks and whispered to each other. I ignored it, though at times I felt excluded, as though I were back at school. And did they really believe I was a man? That thought continued to astonish me. It seemed that they did, but how long would they? After all, they looked and smelled like girls to me. How did I look and smell to them?

I had expected my younger students to be the more difficult to teach. They weren't. They listened and did what they were told. My older girls were the ones who bridled. They sighed and put on bored expressions, making it clear that they were oppressed by the dreariness of the province. I had little patience for it.

"Are you too good for this?" I asked one afternoon. The silence said I was close to the truth. "Would you prefer the society of Baltimore?"

Miss Millen glanced about nervously. "I just don't want to dance like my grandmother."

"We would like to learn the waltz," said Miss Watson.

"And the mazurka," said Miss Sanders.

I held back a smile. I had planned all along to teach the waltz, but now I thought to use it as a carrot. "Very well," I said, as though a bargain were being struck. "I will teach you the waltz. And the mazurka too, perhaps. But only after you show me that you have mastered the quadrille."

The girls brightened, and the next few lessons went quite well. Even so, during our recesses, the Bethany girls would go off by themselves, and in observing them, I noticed a curiosity. In years past, I had sometimes heard young women variously compared to dolls, angels, or fillies. I had thought the imagery insipid, if not insulting. Why couldn't they just be young women? But now, oddly, I began to do the very same thing, at least in my thoughts. Plain and round, Evelyn Sanders was a stuffed doll that one would hug at night till the seams gave out. With skin you could see through and hair the color of wheat, Dorothy Millen was a porcelain figure with folded wings, something you would set upon a shelf. And Lydia Watson, with her sturdy frame, dark skin, and long brown hair? She was a horse running loose in a field.

* * *

While reading the *Democrat* one morning at Blandin's, I came across a notice placed by the Young Men's Literary Society. It was for a lecture titled "Bleeding Kansas" to be given at the Cornell Hall that evening. I decided to go, wishing to hear a man of the world speak on a public issue, an experience that had not been mine before.

I arrived late so I could stand out of view at the back. It was a warm night for May, and the hall was dense with smoke and the strong odor of men's bodies. I couldn't see the speaker, but his voice was clear. "Now we have all heard it referred to as *popular sovereignty*. Sounds most upright, does it not? But what do we call it when men from Missouri cross over to murder and pillage those who have settled the Kansas land with the idea of freedom? *Popular sovereignty?* No! Call it by its real name. *Popular thuggery!*"

The room exploded with cheers. When the speech was done, men went this way and that, as those wishing to exchange greetings with the speaker had to push past those trying to leave. As I waited for things to sort out, a gentleman in a tailored waistcoat came up to me. "I am Kenneth Burton," he said with a slight bow, "former chairman of this august organization, now demoted to the reception of new members. My friends and polite enemies call me Burton."

I gave a nod. "Joseph Lobdell."

"The dancing teacher."

"Yes," I said, surprised.

"Well, Mr. Lobdell, I'm heading to the Hotel Wayne for some light supper with a couple of friends. Would you join us?"

I was unsure of what to do, but the man appeared well-intended, and saying yes seemed the easiest thing. We left the hall and set off down Main, he asking polite questions about the music school while I wondered when it would come clear that I knew nothing about political matters.

We entered the hotel and were led to a table that seemed to have been held for Mr. Burton—or Burton as I soon came to call him. The dining room was full, and there was the hum of people speaking in low voices, nothing at all like the usual noise at the tavern. Moments later we were joined by Mr. John Marbury, treasurer of the Literary Society, and Mr. Howard Chase, a banker who had a seat on the Board of Merchants.

"Well, what did you think of our little meeting?" Marbury asked, once he was seated.

"Quite lively," I said, thinking this would be a good thing to say.

Burton snorted. "Of course you found it lively. You thought you were attending a literary convocation but found yourself in a nest of barnburners. I tried to resist, but I was deposed."

"Burton," said Mr. Chase, "you were not *deposed*. Your term had expired, and someone else was elected. You were not chairman for life."

"Well, no thanks to you." Burton then turned to me with mischief in his eye. "You know, there are some who believe that I am opposed to the political transformation of the *literary* society because I have sympathies for the South—which, of course, I do. There are even whispers that I am a spy—"

"Oh, Burton, please!" groaned Chase.

"Of course, for that to be true," continued Burton, "you'd first have to imagine someone in Richmond actually caring to know what is happening in Honesdale, Pennsylvania."

"As you can see," said Marbury, "our Mr. Burton has a flair for the dramatic."

"And what's wrong with that?" asked Burton. "I thought I'd founded a book club, but it turns out I've started an ill-mannered political party. This is bitter fruit."

Mr. Marbury rolled his eyes, and I had the sudden warm thought that I was not about to be exposed as a bumpkin, but was, instead, being fought over.

"What our good friend Mr. Burton refuses to concede," said Chase, "is that attendance has grown tenfold since the society began political discussion."

"Yes," said Burton, "and if we were to start singing bawdy songs in church, I'm sure the numbers there would increase as well."

I laughed. I couldn't help it. I liked this Burton. And Honesdale, I decided, was something more than I had imagined. The town, it seemed, was being run about by ideas—first, a serious and impassioned speech; then, amusing and irreverent conversation. The mixture was intoxicating, and I returned to Blandin's tavern feeling giddy—not angry that this world was generally denied to women but excited that it was now open to me.

6

THE SCENT OF apple blossoms drifted in and made everyone light-headed. The girls chattered like squirrels, and I let it go on, remembering my days at school. Finally, I raised my hand. The hall became quiet, and I gave the news: we would begin the waltz. A cheer rose up, but I cut it short. "Don't be fooled," I said. "The steps are not difficult, but the grace is found only with patience and practice."

I put out my arms as though holding a partner and performed the dance. Then I took the violin and played a song I knew only as "Laura's Waltz." I bowed the melody three times, telling the young ladies to remember it, for we would dance while the violin was silent. "We will hum the melody, at first," I said, "then just hear it on our own." Doubtful looks came back at me, but I had seen it taught this way in Coxsackie. According to Miss Burchett, it would break the habit of *following* the music. I didn't have much of an opinion on that, but it did solve the problem of seven dancers.

The girls from the upper village formed pairs. Evelyn and Dorothy made the third. Lydia and I, the fourth. I had danced with my girlfriends at school, so taking the man's part was not new to me. "The gentleman," I said, "places his right hand on his partner's back, the lady her left on his shoulder. Dance as though you have a fat pillow between you."

As I spoke, Lydia and I assumed the posture. The others followed. When all were ready, I gave a nod. We stumbled with the melody right away, the girls unable to hold their laughter. We tried again to the same result. After that, we did better.

When the lesson was done, the girls put on their cloaks and began to leave, except for Lydia, who walked to the open window. Once the others had left, I went over to her.

"What's out there?"

"Horses and hay wagons," she said, looking at the fields.

"And a couple of dogs, it would seem."

"Yes. Down by the creek. They've got something up a tree."

"You danced very well today," I said.

Lydia kept looking out and didn't reply. I thought I should say something more, but before I could she turned and set her green eyes on me. "Professor Lobdell, would you take me as a student on the violin?"

I held back a small laugh. Such drama. "I am a music teacher, Miss Watson. Of course, I will take you. You will need to speak to your mother."

A wisp of a smile crossed Lydia's face. "Mother has already agreed."

* * *

I sat in my room, lamp lit, pen in hand. My letter home was weeks overdue, but one fear or another had kept me from it. I didn't want to tell more lies, and what could I say about my new life that wouldn't be one? Worse, Basket Creek now seemed like a story someone had told to me.

I had lived on this earth for twenty-five years. Those years held my girlhood, the barn out back, my first horse, my sisters, and the daughter I had birthed—all that had ever been real to me. But now, here were these few weeks in costume where no one knew me and nothing looked familiar. If one of these worlds was to be the real and the other the dream, you might think that two decades of life with family would be the waking state and the brief costume drama the dream. And that's the way it was—at first.

But in just a handful of weeks, that changed. The costume drama was now my waking state, and what I had thought was my real life had become the dream. All my anchors had come loose—even my Helen, I'm ashamed to say. I had set out with her in mind, to find freedom for us both, but now I didn't know how the pieces fit. There was no script for me to read, not that there is for anyone. My plan was simply to get through each day without being discovered, everything else to be revealed, including how to present myself in a letter.

I thought I might write things in a general way, simply telling Helen and the others that I was alive and they were still in my heart. I hadn't finished the first sentence when it occurred to me the letter couldn't be sent. It would bear the mark of Honesdale. Given half a chance, brother John would travel some distance to find me or spy on me or spoil whatever good thing I had found. I thought about handing the letter to one of the barge captains at Blandin's and asking him to mail it in Kingston. But what man would not be curious as to why? He would open the letter, and I'd be tarred and feathered for sure.

So there it was. I could not write the truth, nor could I send a lie. I was alone—like Jonah, swallowed whole and spat up on a foreign shore. And by having started and stopped a letter, I had opened the gate to memories that ran in my mind as though through a lantern. I saw a little girl playing with a spotted dog by a creek in Westerlo. Then that creek became the Basket and the little girl turned into Helen.

At the start, I thought she was part of me, so firmly attached in taking my milk. But once Helen began to talk, there was never again a doubt about that. She was who she was and had something of her own to say about everything, often talking to herself or to imagined friends. Once I heard her scold a toy horse that Father had carved, telling it not to be naughty. She was mimicking me from the day before when I had lost my temper, and I, no doubt, had been imitating my mother.

Helen slept in a crib beside me, and if she woke from a bad dream I would wake also. Once, when she was two, I heard her crying and brought her to my bed. "Mommy," she said as I lay down beside her, "what made Aunt Elsa die? Was she bad?"

"No, dearest," I said. "She was old. She got sick and died."

"Am I going to die?"

I wanted to reassure her, but I knew that I mustn't lie—about this, of all things. "Yes, my dearest girl. We all die."

"But I don't want to," she cried.

I gathered her to me and told her that she didn't have to worry about that for a long, long time. I didn't try to explain heaven to her young mind. Indeed, how to explain it to anyone? Helen might imagine a heaven with all of us brought together before the hearth at our home on Basket Creek. But I might imagine us before the hearth in Westerlo when I was young and all seemed safe. And so when we all do meet again in heaven, whose fire do we sit before? And who would be the grown-ups and who the children?

* * *

Miss Watson's violin lessons began the next week in the hour after dance class. I expected her to be an eager learner. She wasn't. She showed nothing of the intent she displayed when she proposed the instruction, acting almost put upon as I tried to teach her the strings. I began to wonder if she really cared about the violin, or then again, perhaps I was pushing too hard.

At the start of the third lesson, I thought to try a little conversation, asking Miss Watson if she had always lived in Bethany. She said she had and asked where I was from. I told her I grew up on a farm in New York, and that much was true. But I knew the smaller past I had, the safer I would be, so I invented one without siblings and told an awful lie. "My parents died when I was at the academy in Coxsackie," I said sadly, "in the year of the fever."

I held my breath and waited for lightning to strike me dead, the vigil broken by Lydia's voice. "I'm sorry for your loss," she said, her eyes filling with sympathy. I felt the urge to invent more tragedy but instead asked about her family.

"They're on all sides of me," she said, lifting her eyes to the heavens. "If you counted aunts and cousins, we'd almost be a beehive. My uncle Karl has a farm north of town where he raises horses. In the summers I used to ride with my cousin Jason, but then he left to find his own land in Minnesota."

"And your father—his business is trees?"

"Trees, yes, trees," said Lydia, her arms extending as though they were branches. "The bigger and more beautiful, the sooner it shall be killed."

I felt myself smile. "I think, Miss Watson, most people would describe what your father does as harvesting."

Lydia sat back in the chair. "I know. There should be no complaint. We want for nothing."

"But you seem to have one."

An awkward silence followed. I had gone where I should not have. "Don't pay me any mind," I said trying to go back. "We all have—"

"No, you're right," said Lydia, interrupting. "But it's not the trees. It's not. It's just . . . " Her eyes went to the floor, and her voice went there also. "I don't think I've ever seen my father make my mother laugh. I've often wondered how it was that they married."

"Oh, I'm certain they have attachments," I said, trying now to fluff the pillow. "The simplest of reasons are sometimes the hardest to see." I had just mimicked my Aunt Bertha who used to say vacant things like that when I was a girl. Lydia didn't like it any more than I had.

"Then tell me, Professor," she asked, "what are *your* simple reasons— the ones that brought you to Honesdale?"

My thoughts ran about like ants while I did my best to look composed. "Well, if you must know, Miss Watson, I came here, because I was told that Honesdale was a place of unrealized social aspiration."

"Oh, my," said Lydia, her hands meeting in a gleeful clap. "Are you here to fulfill that aspiration or frustrate it?"

I held back a smile. "At the moment, Miss Watson, I'm more concerned with what might be said if no music is heard from here." And with that, I began to play the violin, so that someone passing might hear music, as though a lesson were being taught. First I played my part, then hers, that of a student who is learning and none too well. I played so badly that Lydia brought her hand to her mouth to keep from laughing.

"This is the best lesson so far," she declared as I put the violin down.

"Yes," I agreed. "You've played not a note, and if it goes on like this, I won't accept payment."

"Well, I can't bring the quarter back and keep coming. What would you have me do with it?"

I thought for a moment, playing her game. "You go to church on Sunday?"

"Yes, of course. It's boring. I hate it."

"I'm sorry to hear that. But since you'll be there anyway, just slip it in the plate."

Lydia smiled as she considered the plan. Then she shook her head. "No, Professor Lobdell. I think it would be best if I gave you the quarter and learned to play my own bad notes."

7

THE PIANO ANNOUNCED the hymn, and the congregation stood to sing all four verses of "Awake My Soul." When it was over, we could hear the annoying groan of a Presbyterian pipe organ a block away. I smiled inwardly, thinking of my outspoken Miss Watson suffering in her pew up in Bethany. As for me, I had no great fondness for sermons, but I had liked singing hymns when we lived in Westerlo, particularly in the summertime when the windows were open and God could hear better. And sometimes I felt God's presence—not just in church but when I was alone at night or off in the woods hunting. He would speak to me—not with words but with thoughts and feelings. But when I tried to tell about this at the Methodist meeting in Long Eddy, Reverend Hale told me to sit down and not talk nonsense. "The word of God is from the Bible," he said, pounding his fist, "not from clouds or stars!" I vowed not to go to another meeting.

But I hadn't kept that vow. Once again, I was in a Methodist church, this one a block above the town square in Honesdale. I was lonely and felt the call. And, of course, Reverend Hale wasn't there. Instead, there was a younger man, Reverend Albright, whom I had gotten to know after prayer meeting the week before. I listened with hopeful interest as the young reverend spoke from the pulpit on the parable of the talents. He made no more sense out of it than I'd been able to do on my own.

After the service, as we exchanged greetings by the door, Reverend Albright asked if I would wait and walk with him. A short time later, he and I were advancing clockwise around the town square. My minister walked with a measured step, his hands firmly clasped behind him. I secured my hands in like fashion and right away felt more highly born.

The day was warm, and many people were out. Reverend Albright nodded the occasional greeting, but the good pastor was not the picture of ease. His lack of social graces matched his frayed appearance, but I was not put off by any of this—his unruly shock of hair and rumpled clothes I saw as emblems of humility. I think he found comfort in my company, because I, like him, was from somewhere other than Honesdale. I knew from our previous meeting that he didn't feel welcome in his parish. He had been sent from seminary to assist the much-beloved Reverend Webster who had died just four months after the young pastor's arrival.

"They have not forgiven me," he said in a low voice. "They think Webster would still be here if I hadn't come."

"Things should improve with time," I said, as though I had seen this circumstance before. The advice brought me a moment of satisfaction, but no comfort to my minister.

"No, Joseph," he said, not breaking step, "it gets worse. Quite daunting, really—a wall of faces staring back as I speak. And I'm certain that this one is totaling the receipts for the week, and that one is scheming to punish some matron across the aisle for a slight she has imagined."

"You'd see the same anywhere," I said. "I wouldn't bother myself."

"I can't not," said my pastor. "As I stand by the door, I want to say, *What an ugly bonnet, Mrs. Johnson. Did you eat too much cabbage last night, Mr. Barstle?*"

I laughed. "Reverend, you must not fret so."

"Malcolm," he replied. "Please call me Malcolm."

* * *

Lydia and I came to terms over the violin. She could keep coming for lessons if she would give her full attention to the instruction, which would occupy the better part of the hour. The rest we could chat or fritter away as we liked. With this as our agreement, she applied herself and made acceptable progress. We decided that she would bring the violin to her house on

Tuesday nights so that her mother and sisters could hear her practice and not harbor grand expectations.

After just a handful of lessons, Lydia became informal, calling me Joseph when the others were not there. I could have corrected her but didn't. I liked her company and saw in her a bit of myself. And in return, I began using her given name, calling her Miss Watson only when I wanted to feign a scolding. Soon, she was staying beyond the hour, content to read the newspaper while I swept the room. One day in early June, I walked over to the window where she sat holding the *Herald*. She cleared her throat and began to read aloud:

> The Steamship Atlantic arrived yesterday, bearing news that the Russian Embassy has again left Constantinople. The Czar was said to be furious at the rejection of his demands by the Sultan, declaring he would have vengeance. In London the price of funds has declined.

"Joseph," she said, not looking up, "would you rather have dinner with the Sultan or the Czar?"

"I don't know. Are they coming to town?"

She turned the page and began to read something else:

> Last Sunday we observed that all the saloons in Honesdale were closed. Let the town continue to enforce the ordinance, and let it include the barbershops and ice cream parlors. It may sadden some dandified idlers to be denied the privilege of getting shaved and oiled upon the Sabbath or of cooling their palates with ice cream, but plain and industrious citizens will cheerfully sustain the authorities.

Lydia set the paper aside, got up, and walked down a narrow board in the floor as though it were four feet off the ground. "Joseph," she said, moving her hands to keep balance, "why would God be offended by ice cream? Is it awfully wicked to cool one's palate? Or is it the slurping? I rather think it's the slurping, don't you?"

I laughed.

Lydia stopped her balancing act and turned to me. "Beardslee's a prig," she said, referring to the editor of the *Herald* and using a word that might merit a mouthful of soap were she at home. "If he really wanted to improve the Sunday promenade, he could protest the fashion of the barge owners to parade around the park as though they command ships at sea." She lifted her shoulders and walked stiffly as though navigating the corners of the town square. "Have you seen the blue coats and brass buttons?"

"I have," I said. "I saw one last week with epaulettes."

"Yes! And where is our Mr. Beardslee when we need his protection against such a thing? Out filling his belly with bratwurst, I'm sure." Lydia picked up her shawl. "Such a sour man; it's hard to imagine how he has children."

* * *

I returned to the tavern that afternoon to hear angry voices coming from the back room. I couldn't make out what was being said, but I heard the word *poser*. A sick feeling went to my stomach. I looked over to where Damon was sitting and saw the *Honesdale Herald* spread on the table before him. Then from the back room I heard the name Beardslee coupled with other words I should not repeat.

Howkin Beardslee had no friends at Blandin's. The editor of the *Herald* had appointed himself the conscience of the town, and something or someone was always leading it to ruin. Beardslee's worst bile was saved for Francis Penniman, editor of the rival *Democrat*. Almost weekly, Beardslee would accuse Penniman of doing the Devil's work—catering to special circles like the "godless Literary Society," which was now, somehow, according to Beardslee, in league with the saloon owners.

The door to the back room swung open, and Blandin and four men came out—saloon owners every one. A broad-shouldered fellow was in a rolling boil. "Daniel," he said, grabbing Blandin's sleeve, "if we let that bastard push us around now, there'll be no end to it."

Blandin shook his head. "Heath, sometimes you just got to let the fire burn out."

The others nodded, and the man let go of Blandin's shirt. "I'll fight him by myself if I have to."

"So would I," said Blandin. "Let's just see if we have to."

The men left, and Blandin drew a beer and came over to where I was now sitting with Damon. My curiosity gnawed. "So you're going to stay closed on Sundays?"

Blandin looked at me like I was a child in short pants. "No, we're just going to do things when it's time. Now where do you think all those fellows—I'm talking about the wharf rats—where do you think they'll go on Sunday if they can't go to the saloons?"

I gave a shrug.

"They'll go up to the square! They'll stand around and stare like lost dogs at all the fine people out for their parade. We'll give it another Sunday and then start opening earlier in the day. Won't nobody say nothin'."

8

THE SPEAKER WALKED to the head of Cornell Hall. He gave no greeting. He didn't smile. Instead, he took out a newspaper and held it up: *The Charleston Mercury*. He opened it and began to calmly read notices for lost property.

> Run away, a Negro woman and her child. A few days before she left, I burned her face to make the letter T.

> One hundred dollars reward for my man Achilles. He has both ears notched at the top and is well scarred from the whip.

Lost property seemed to be a common problem in Charleston as the notices went on and on. When the list of horrors had been recited, the speaker put down the newspaper and broke into a spirited denunciation of something called the Slave Act. It had to do with runaways. I had never seen a slave, yoked or runaway, and had never heard of this law. But those around me seemed to have heard of it, and by the time the speaker was done, Cornell Hall was a sea of indignation. Everyone had something to say to the person next to him, except me who was there alone and thinking about a warm bowl of stew. I was looking for an open path to the door when I felt a tap on my shoulder.

Mr. Burton and I took the same table at the Hotel Wayne, this time just the two of us. I was expecting to see the mischievous eyes of our first meeting, but those eyes seemed troubled now. "They are preparing themselves for war," he said, referring to the evening's meeting.

I was surprised and my words came out on their own. "I don't think that speaking of injustice is the same as making for war." It was an unintended challenge—what did I know of these affairs? Burton looked down, and I braced for his certain withering response.

"You are right, of course," he said, looking up and meeting my eye. "If I might rephrase, I suppose what I find repugnant is the comfort taken in moral outrage."

"But you believe it's leading to war?"

Burton refolded his napkin. "Of course it is. Why, just last Saturday they staged a battle on the meadow at Indian Orchard."

"Who did?"

"The militias of Honesdale and Hawley—in parade uniform, complete with hats and feathers."

Burton's review of the battle dress was delivered in a light Virginia accent that to my ear gave it a courtly charm. And beyond that, despite the clothes I was wearing or who I was supposed to be, I found him to be a handsome man. His brown hair lay loosely on his head, and his eyes, the same color, didn't dart about, but moved slowly and settled upon one thing. And when they settled on me, I could feel it. There were moments when I thought I might blush as though he could know that I liked the way he looked.

Beef was the featured fare that night at the Wayne. After we ordered, I thought to ask about the start of the Literary Society. What authors had been the subject of meetings?

"We began with Irving," Burton answered, as though I should join him in some frustration. "He's the patron saint of Honesdale, you know."

"I didn't know," I said. "I thought he was from New York."

"Yes," said Burton, trying to be patient, "but he visited here some years ago—they won't let you forget it. He stood in the park and declared Honesdale to be the epitome of American industry and beauty. Everyone was there." Burton raised his eyes as if some sympathy might come from above. When it didn't he leaned forward as though to tell a secret. "But in close company, I am told, our Mr. Irving referred to the town as *commonplace*. His work then grew in my esteem."

I smiled but didn't dare laugh, glancing about to see if anyone had overheard. Then, thinking it best to move on, I asked about the more recent authors.

"Dickens and Poe," he said. "But it's Thackeray now. Everything's Thackeray, at least in New York City it is. If I can find enough people to forgo political debate long enough to read a book, then we shall have a meeting on him in a month or so. Would you care to borrow *Vanity Fair?*"

I was delighted by the offer and agreed to walk to his house after dinner.

In the last light of evening, Burton and I crossed the bridge to the upper village and walked up North Main, the boulevard that boasted the grand houses of Honesdale. We turned onto Dyberry Place, where the homes were more modest, Burton's cottage among them. Once inside, Burton ushered me into a sitting room that held a fireplace and two large chairs. One was clearly where my host spent his solitary hours; the other held a stack of newspapers. Burton moved them to a small table and invited me to sit. He seemed unaccustomed to visitors.

"You subscribe to the *Tribune*," I said, looking at the newspapers. It was a well-known New York City journal, one I had come to know when I lived in Coxsackie.

"I don't," said Burton. "Greeley came last year and spoke to the society. Now they just come."

"But you read them."

"Yes," he said, taking his chair, "for Bayard Taylor if for no other reason. After his last journey, he came here and lectured on the mysteries of the Arab world. Of course, after Beardslee got done with his slander, several windows at Cornell Hall were smashed. Still, were I given another life, I would come back as Mr. Taylor himself."

Burton stared at the dark window across the room as though it looked out on some foreign land. He seemed to know something about everything, and I liked that about him. But why, I wondered as I eyed his profile, did he favor me? I had been nowhere and knew no one, including Mr. Taylor. And what had brought him to Honesdale? It seemed an odd pairing. Then suddenly Burton turned, and our eyes met. What did he want?

"So is Mr. Taylor your only interest in the *Tribune?*" I asked, my voice unsteady.

Burton acted like he didn't hear the tremor. "No. After Mr. Taylor—that is, if I am not paralyzed with envy—I move on to Mr. Ripley's reviews of books."

"They please you as well?"

"Sometimes," he said, tapping a finger on the arm of his chair. "But often our Mr. Ripley will praise good intention and overlook defects in craft—an idealist of some repute. You know that he founded Brook Farm."

I shook my head, unable to hide my ignorance.

"A noble experiment," Burton said in mock reverence. "Men of learning were to plow the fields, and men of labor to go to lectures. The sexes would partner freely—the more base emotions, such as jealousy, to wither away in the sunlight of reason. It failed, of course."

Burton said these words like he drew comfort from them. Then he gave his head a little shake. "But I brought you here to get a book."

* * *

The sun streamed past Lydia and sparkled in the dust I had set adrift with my broom. She had her face buried in the *Herald*, and when I joined her, she began to read a notice:

> A Beautiful Head of Hair is the grandest ornament belonging to the human frame. How strangely the loss of it changes the manly countenance, causing many to hear jests and sneers. To avert such unpleasantness, OLDRIDGE'S BALM OF COLUMBIA stops the hair from falling off and a few bottles restores it again. It likewise makes the hair curl beautifully and frees it from scurf.

Lydia looked up. "Joseph, do you live in terror of losing your hair?"

"I don't," I said, swallowing a smile. "This is not one of my fears."

"Then what is one of your fears?"

I held my face steady while I reviewed the choices. To be found out? Pilloried? Tarred and feathered? I had a lot to choose from, but I needed an answer that would die where it was.

"I have a great dread," I said, "that more of my students will seek lessons on the violin. What about you?"

Lydia rolled her eyes but let it go. "I fear," she said, "that I shall be trapped, stuffed, and placed in a museum. I fear I shall spend my life in this place and never have an adventure. Never find love."

"But have you not already found love? I heard one of the girls say something about you and a young man named Horton—that you would be betrothed."

Lydia raised an eyebrow. "Really? I find it interesting, Joseph, that people have news about me of which I am ignorant. Would you say it was relevant that David Horton has never had a conversation on this subject with me? I would. And what's more, if he were to have one, he might be surprised to learn a few of my thoughts." Lydia seemed more annoyed than angry, as though she had never held expectations of this young man.

"Have you known him long?"

"Most of my life. We grew up in the same church. He was older but still chased me about after service. Now he's started his own timber business, and I'm the envy of every girl in Honesdale."

"Except yourself, it seems."

Lydia let out a small laugh. "Dorothy thinks I've gone mad. If there was a simple way to do it, I'd give him to her. I would. Evelyn understands, though—plain, old nutcake Evelyn. She is the least comely of all my friends, yet she has her Walter. Did you know they promised themselves to each other on Evelyn's seventh birthday?"

"So you want something like Evelyn has?"

She shook her head. "No, I want what my cousin Jason has. Land and horses. I want the life of no woman I know."

I chased any true feelings from my face. "Why is that?"

"Because there's nothing for us," she said, a piece of her accusation aimed at me. "Do you think that if paid work existed for women, we would abandon men altogether? Is that what you all fear? How would you like it, Joseph, if your only choice was between a distasteful marriage and the hell of spinsterhood?"

Lydia's fierce green eyes searched the room, while I wondered what

Joseph, the dance teacher, would say about all this. Perhaps something encouraging. "I believe," I said, "a day will come when this will not be so."

Lydia wasn't comforted. "What day, Joseph? When will this come? How will this come?"

My failure to answer hung in the air. Lydia broke the silence.

"Dance with me."

I hesitated, not sure that I had heard her right.

"I want to dance the waltz with you, Joseph. We do it every week."

"Well, yes, of course," I said, oddly off balance. "Would you like me to first play the violin?"

"That would be nice."

I picked up the instrument and played "Laura's Waltz." The bow seemed to have a will of its own, and the melody took on a sweetness I had forgotten with its classroom repetition. When done, I took her hand, and we arranged ourselves. We started to dance, our movements stiff at first. Soon, however, we began to turn in ever-tighter circles, more vigorous than any we had done in class.

"You know," I said as we whirled about, "where I was taught, a woman who leaned back so in the turns was thought unseemly, the posture a demonstration of abandon."

"What a strange idea," said Lydia. "I should think abandon is why we dance. Why do *you* dance?"

I gave her my best smile. "I'm told it has a good affect upon the organs."

"Nonsense. Joseph, stop teasing and tell me something true. Why are men never accused of showing abandon? Why a crime at all?"

"Perhaps because you are the frail sex, and we don't want to see you hurt."

"Oh, really?" she said as the room continued to turn. "Well, I think it's the other way. I think most men are stuffed and sewn together none too well. And you would restrict our movements so you don't split and spill the sawdust." And with that, she closed her eyes and leaned out even more.

9

I ENJOYED THE noise and the banter at Blandin's, but an entire evening of it, every night, was a lot to do. The meetings at Cornell Hall and the dinners at the Wayne were welcome changes. On those occasions, I could come back to the tavern at a later hour and play the violin when everyone was some distance down his path and ready to be amused.

Prayer meeting on Wednesday night provided another haven. It took place in the small hall behind the Methodist Church, the dusty smell of the hymnals bringing me back to when I was a girl and sitting in the pew in Westerlo. The people at prayer meeting were dressed in everyday clothes, and all who attended were welcomed like family—the warmth of family was something I greatly missed. And beyond that, I didn't feel like the deceiver when I was there. I was dressed as a man, yes, but surely God could see under my shirt, so I wasn't fooling Him. And what difference did it make to the others? Man or woman, we were there to worship our Lord.

Reverend Albright presided over these meetings, reading the scripture and leading us in prayer. After the meeting, most of the parishioners would head back to the upper village while Albright and I would go the other way, he to the parsonage on Second Street and I to Blandin's. My minister knew where I slept, but he never asked me a thing about the tavern, as though only unspeakable things happened there. I thought it a little strange, but I didn't take this reluctance as a warning. I didn't know what evils he had attached to the place, but I didn't think they had attached themselves to me in his mind. I didn't want to explain myself and was comfortable when we instead talked about his vexations.

One night in June the good reverend appeared particularly ill at ease. He stumbled while reading Leviticus and made a mess of the benediction. Later, on the street, I asked if anything were wrong. He took a dozen steps and then said he needed to be married. I came to a stop.

"Malcolm, is this a want of yours or an expectation that you feel from others?"

The moths fluttered around a nearby streetlamp, while Reverend Albright looked at me like a martyr seeing his fate. "I don't think they will accept me until I am," he said. "It has to happen sometime."

My minister might have been buying spools of thread for all the emotion he showed. I felt like wagging my finger but instead asked further. "Is there someone in the church you are drawn to?"

"Abigail Jenkins," he said, looking down, "but she gives me no encouragement."

So this is what it was about. I took a breath. "Malcolm, if you were a young lady, what fears would you have concerning marriage to a minister?"

Reverend Albright cast a glance at his Bible, knowing the answer wasn't there. "She might fear that our life would be—," he paused for a moment, "would be . . . well . . . dreary."

I was surprised. He had found the point and spoken it plainly. I wanted to help. "Show her it doesn't have to be."

"How?"

"Make her laugh, Malcolm. Believe me on this. Tell her a funny story."

"Joseph," he said, almost pleading, "I don't know any funny stories."

"Of course you do. They're all around us. Tell her about the lady and her ugly bonnet. Have you confessed attraction to her?"

"No," he said, looking dismayed. "I assured her that my feelings were only the most proper."

I lifted my eyes to the heavens. "Malcolm, don't assure her about so many things. Let her know that you're made of flesh and blood."

My friend gave a look of warning. "The flesh, Joseph, is the province of the Devil."

That made me laugh. "Malcolm, you give food to that flesh every day, do you not? Are you doing the Devil's work each time you put a piece of bread in your mouth?"

Reverend Albright wrinkled his brow as though he wanted to quote scripture. Nothing came. "There's really not much to it," he said, finally. "When it comes to the ladies, Joseph, I'm just a bumbler."

* * *

I saw Burton at the next Society meeting, and we agreed to have dinner later that week. On the chosen night, I walked to the Wayne, *Vanity Fair* in hand. I entered the dining room, and the head waiter nodded as though I were a longtime customer. Burton saw my approach and stood. I paused and, for the briefest unthinking moment, waited for him to pull my chair. He looked at me, and I came to my senses, giving my head a quick shake. "I got a little lost in my thoughts."

"About what?"

"Mr. Thackeray's book." It was the easiest thing to say and nearly true.

"Indeed! And what did you think of our Miss Sharp?"

That was a question. Just how approving should a man be about a woman who did as she pleased? And, of course, I loved Becky Sharp. Without family or dowry, she raced through the book, living by her wits and running circles around men. I took my seat and thought to mute my opinion. "She was a most engaging character."

"*Engaging*," said Burton, tasting the word.

I didn't like this—I wanted him to chew on something else. "So who did you favor?"

A smile settled at the corner of Burton's eye. "I was rather fond of Lord Steyne," he said.

"You could not have been," I protested. "He was a monster!"

"Well, well," said my friend. "Weren't they all?"

Kenneth Burton was nothing more than a naughty child. I would have scolded him but didn't want to give him the satisfaction. He held court at the Hotel Wayne as though everything could be seen from his chair. For all I knew, his work for the bank was done there as well.

He liked to observe, that much I knew, and he saw things in unusual ways. His manner, his pleasure in watching the world pass by, suggested to me that life for him was a masquerade in which any particular costume was as good as any other, which might explain why he seemed to enjoy my company—and why I enjoyed his. But would the pleasure remain if I were in a dress? Somehow I didn't think so. I was drawn to him—found him intriguing and handsome. But he would want a genteel woman, grown up in lace and practiced manners, and not a backwoods girl who hunted weasels. Even so, sitting across from him, I tried to imagine it—tried to imagine me as Mrs. Kenneth Burton.

And along with that silliness, I began to wonder if editor Beardslee wasn't right. Perhaps the Literary Society really was a cabal, but one made up entirely of those who were pretending to be someone they were not. And Burton was there, just as he said, to bring in new members. Seen that way, *Vanity Fair*, with all its lies, was the perfect initiation.

I handed him the book with a thank-you. Burton gave me another in return: *The Scarlet Letter* by a Mr. Hawthorne.

"More secrets and deceits?"

"You can be sure," he said with a wink.

This pronouncement, of course, made me eager to read the book, but rather than inquire more about it, I asked my friend if he had always loved to read. The words were barely out when I realized the question had a feminine tone. My eyes searched Burton's face for any trace of suspicion. His brown eyes met mine.

"When I was little," he said, "my mother read to me every night. First, stories that would interest a boy. Then poems and plays. We would read whole chapters while Father was out. Later, I would hear them argue." Burton looked past me to the far corner of the room, as though the echoes of those angry words were yet to be heard there. I stayed still, surprised to hear him say something that did not have an edge or a double meaning. "She was beautiful, Joseph. Long, dark hair, dark eyes. I, unfortunately, resemble my father. I was afraid that because I looked like him she would stop loving me too, but that's not how it happened." Burton paused. "She died when I was sixteen."

"I'm sorry for your loss," I said. "But then, not everyone feels such a bond with his mother. I envy you that."

I thought Burton would continue on about his childhood, but for a reason I could not detect, the spell broke. "Joseph," he said as though waking from a nap, "we need someone to call dances at the evening jubilee on the

Fourth. Abram Stryker has done it for years, but he can hardly stand now. Would you? I'd be grateful."

Had I heard him right? Perform before the whole town? No. I wouldn't do it. I wouldn't.

Burton sat back with a contented smile, as though he could hear the shouts in my head. And, of course, there was no saying no. Not to Burton. Seeing how things were, I mustered what cheer I could and said I'd be happy to help. Burton nodded and thanked me politely on behalf of the celebration committee. Now I was the one to smile.

"Forgive me," I said by way of explanation, "it's just that I wouldn't have thought you so involved in the festivities."

"Oh, I won't set foot outside my door that day," Burton said quickly. "But I have served on the committee for seven years. I'm in charge of *arrangements*."

"Meaning what?"

"I make sure that everything ends up where it's supposed to, which means I mostly settle disputes."

"Burton, it's a picnic. What disputes?"

My friend appeared amused. "Well, let us say that a certain Bible society held a favorable position in the square last year, the northeast corner, to pick a place. Should that be reason for them to have it again? Some people think so. Others think it should be the very reason they don't get to have it."

"Why bring it to you?"

"Because I don't care."

I didn't understand and it must have shown.

"Joseph, I'm not from here. I don't know whose grandmother was mean to someone else's grandmother twenty years ago. I could probably run for judge, though the temptation for mischief might be more than I could bear. I'm safer with the celebration committee."

I didn't think about Burton's use of the word *safer* just then. But on my way back to Blandin's, it struck me as an odd choice. Safe from what? It wasn't a big question, because I was more concerned with my new plight, which definitely would not make me safer. In ten days I would stand on a stage in Honesdale's public square and call dances. As I walked down Main Street, I rehearsed calamities that might save me—a flood or a broken leg.

* * *

An hour after discussing *Vanity Fair* at the Hotel Wayne, I was seated at Blandin's Tavern playing "Arkansas Traveler." Jimmy Lawson, the large-bellied coal loader who liked to poke fun at me, came over and, in front of the others, asked me to go with him and some friends to the Rusty Buckle, a saloon on the canal. There a man could enter the back room, pay two bits, and a curtain would be drawn aside to reveal a woman, naked. I was assured that for some small additional money, she would bend and pose.

"Come with us," he said. "A little hair peeking out from a lady's arse might grow some on your face."

"And then what?" I spat back. "I could look like you?"

There were a few chuckles at this, and Jimmy gave a snort. "You ain't probably never even seen a woman."

"Oh, don't lay your money on that," I said, unable to keep the grin off my face.

"I ain't talking about yer mum or yer sis."

"Nor am I, sir," I said, as though insulted. "For I am able to pleasure my eye from time to time, and the money gets paid to me."

Jimmy blinked. "Well, how do you work that?"

"Nothing to it," I said. "Why, just last month I was playing the fiddle at a wedding not far from here. The bride got up to dance a jig, and I played 'The Devil's Britches.' Faster and faster I played and faster she danced till soon she was standing in just the clothes God gave her. I'd do the same right now, but from the look of you, I'd guess the result wouldn't be so appealing."

There was a brief silence before those around us burst into laughter. Jimmy looked confused but then laughed with the others. A short time later, he and his friends left for the Rusty Buckle and its delights. I played a few more songs before going to my room. It had been a full evening. I had talked books with Kenneth Burton at the Wayne and traded barbs with Jimmy Lawson at Blandin's—talk and nonsense I would have never known had I been in a petticoat. I felt pleased with myself.

But as I got into bed, the good feelings abandoned me. I had to wrestle with darker thoughts—those I often had when there was no one to distract me. What, I wondered, was being said about me in my house or along Basket Creek? But then how could anyone there know even the smallest part of my sins? My trespass was not that I had left my daughter to look for a better life for us both but that I had come to so enjoy my new life without her. The Music School, the Literary Society, the tavern, Malcolm, Burton, and Blandin—never had my life been so full. But alone in the dark, it all felt like some bargain made with the Devil. And trying to sort that out—the good and bad of it—was like trying to untie a knot left out for the winter.

It had always seemed to me that when you travel, the surroundings change but you remain more or less the same. But now I began to think that if you come to a fork in the road and take one turn instead of another, you not only end up in some other place, you become some other person—not very changed in many instances, but perhaps greatly changed in others. And I had taken a road that had led me to somewhere and someone entirely new. I had left home seeking a place for myself and for Helen, but in leaving her and starting a new life, I had invented a me who was, in many ways, not her mother.

I still wanted to make a home for the two of us, but that dream seemed distant. When I tried to think about it, I would imagine renting a cottage outside of town where Helen could come live with me. I'd have to invent a story. But, then again, Helen would have to be old enough to understand the deception, and at what age would that be? In truth, I didn't know how it would work. I hadn't so much as chosen a fork in the road as I had set out on a river in a tiny boat—a boat that was going wherever the water went, my best efforts doing no more than keeping it upright.

10

FROM MY CLASSROOM on the second floor of the glass factory, I could look north and see the fairgrounds. Tents and wagons appeared on its fields, more each day as July drew near. The coming celebration was much the talk at Blandin's—loggers and firemen spoke loudly of the coming events while I quietly prayed for rain. I had never performed on a stage and wondered what I would look like. How would I sound? I talked from my throat every day to sound manly, but if I tried to shout that way, I might end up squawking like a catbird. And why all the plans and fuss?

When I was a girl, Independence Day was a simple occasion, taking place in a meadow by a lake south of Westerlo. All morning wagons arrived with friends and cousins jumping out like young birds from a nest. The women presided over the food in the shade of a large elm. The men gathered some distance away, smoking cigars and throwing horseshoes.

An old sycamore stood by the lake with a thick strand of hemp hanging from its limb. The boys in just their britches would take it and swing out over the water. We girls went off by ourselves and skipped rope, pretending not to notice the boys and the fun they were having. The summer I was nine, I went into the bushes and stripped down to my shift. Then I ran to the tree, swung out, and let go, hearing laughter and cheers as I hit the water. When I got out, I got a good scolding from my mother.

Later that afternoon, as he did each year, Father took us out on the lake, the boat pushing forward with each groan of the oars. We all begged for our turn rowing, and here my brother John had no more rights than my sisters and I. Mary and Sarah, of course, did little more than splash everyone. On the far side was a cove, so thick with lilies you might think you could walk on the water. We always came upon an egret or heron, and in those moments, it seemed that there would never come a summer when we would not take that ride.

* * *

On the morning of the Fourth, as Joseph Lobdell, I joined the parade up to the Bethany fairgrounds. The near meadow held events for children— sack races and the like. In the meadow beyond the grandstand rose like an open-sided barn, decked out in flags and banners, and filling quickly, as many were there to see Winter Wheat run in the Dyberry Derby. Lydia's uncle Karl had a horse in the race, a filly named Sophie's Birthday. I was curious as to how she would do against the unbeaten Pike County stallion, but I didn't go to the track. I didn't want to be cornered and led into conversations. Or sit where lots of people could see me. They'd get their chance later.

I walked across the great meadow to where the fire companies were laying hose back to the creek. The contest was to see who could shoot a column of water the greatest distance. For weeks, the Honesdale Fire Brigade had drilled with its new artillery piece, called, affectionately, *Le Deluge*. Confidence in the town was high, judging from the bragging at Blandin's. The pumper required six strong men, three on each side, to push and pull the levers that forced the water out the hose. The firemen poked fun at one another as they readied their machines.

Then I saw him.

It wasn't the first time, for I had seen David Horton about town on several occasions. He was, as Lydia had said, something to look at. His sun-darkened face was framed by sandy curls, and his shoulders were at the chin level of the two young men he was walking with. As he made his way into the crowd, I saw several young women cast glances in his direction. I turned back to watch the firemen.

The competition did not turn out as the Honesdale firemen had hoped. The Carbondale company bested the two teams before it by throwing a stream of water almost two hundred feet. But the wind that had been blowing in their favor died before the Honesdale firemen had a chance to shoot, and when they did, they came up two feet short. The Honesdale men wanted the Carbondale men to shoot again, without the wind. They wouldn't. I heard shouts and insults.

I turned from the bad manners to see a large, red balloon rising from the field across the way. I hurried over, as I had never seen such a sight, though it wasn't a complete surprise. The week before, the balloonist, a Mr. Henri Sinclair, had advertised that for one hundred dollars each, he would provide two fortunate souls "an experience for the ages." Mr. Sinclair, however, had only one taker—a Honesdale storekeeper named Whitaker, who, from the comments I heard, was the very last person anyone expected to see ascending into the sky. But there he was, dressed for church and trying to smile even as the basket rose and his cheeks paled. Mr. Sinclair in leather cap leaned over the rail and waved.

I watched the balloon rise and then felt a sudden danger. I looked around and found a pair of eyes hard on me. They belonged to David Horton, a good thirty paces away and watching me as I had watched him a short hour before. Our eyes met, then others got between us. It was not a friendly moment, but what could he know? What was there to know? Had Lydia spoken of me in a way to make him resentful? Had someone else said something? Feeling unsteady, I looked up at the balloon, now floating south—Mr. Sinclair still hanging over the side. When I brought my gaze down, David Horton was not in sight.

Along with others, I walked back to the first meadow, where we were joined by those coming from the racetrack. Winter Wheat had won. Sophie's Birthday had taken a respectable fourth. On the far side of the field, the Honesdale Guard was standing at attention in a double line. An officer on a horse trotted down the line and shouted a command to an officer in the front. That officer gave a crisp salute and turned and repeated the command to another officer, who saluted and repeated the command. Finally, a volley of musket fire rent the air, announcing the end to the morning events—the dry, sweet smell of gunpowder drifting over us. Then the Guard, in dress uniform, complete with hats and feathers, marched down the field and formed the vanguard of a ragged parade back to Honesdale.

* * *

The town square looked like a tiny village, what with all the tables and tents lining the walkways. Charities and Bible societies sold woolens, quilts, cookies, pies, and cakes—all to benefit one deserving something or another. I strolled about and smiled at the thought of Burton hiding in his house. Then I saw Lydia up ahead with her two younger sisters, stopped before a table covered with sewn dolls. I went the other way.

Early in the afternoon, picnic lunches were auctioned to benefit the orphans' home, the highest bidder not only receiving the treats within the basket but the company of the young lady who made them. Most of the girls in my older class had prepared baskets, including Lydia. I soon observed that the winner of each auction was understood from the start, the bidding only to make the young man pay a proper price for the attentions he sought.

I watched from a distance as David Horton, with just token resistance, won Lydia's basket. They walked off together, he carrying the basket, she taking hold of his arm and laughing at some remark. I was surprised, thinking I would see at least some trace of her dissatisfaction with this young man. Nothing.

Again, I went in the opposite direction, forcing smiles as I wandered about. Had Lydia been misleading me? And if she had, why did I care? David Horton was her affair. I told myself this several times, yet I couldn't shake the feeling of being discarded. It reminded me of a time at school when a girl with whom I shared my closest thoughts suddenly took a liking to a young man. Overnight she forgot me. It took me months to get over it, and now I had similar feelings as I watched Lydia and David walk off together. But this made no sense, because Lydia hadn't put me aside. She liked me and, moreover, liked me as a man. And there it was. Standing in the town square, I realized that I had been playing my part so well that I was feeling a man's resentment. I didn't want him touching her.

* * *

The lanterns were lit as it began to get dark. Abram Stryker gamely limped onto the stage and assumed the duties of ceremony. Behind him was an assemblage of horn tooters and fiddle players, of which I was one. Stryker made some announcements and then got things started by calling several dances. After the first sweat was broken, he spoke about Honesdale's good fortune in now having a school of music. "I would like to introduce to you a young man who has made quite an impression in his short time with us—our very own Professor of Dance, Mr. Joseph Lobdell."

I tipped an imaginary hat to mild applause, stomped three times, and, as arranged, we began a very spirited rendition of "Cow Bell Crazy." Everyone clapped and yelped, except one older man who danced a jig as we went flying through the piece.

"Now, folks," I shouted. "Pick your partners; we're goin' to Virginia!"

In a minute the lines were formed, and I called that reel and a couple more. Everyone was in good spirits, and my voice didn't betray me. The rebellion, instead, came from my eyes. From the stage, even in the dim light, they found Lydia and David, still together. I could see every movement—each time she took his arm, laughed, or leaned on him in a playful way. She was having a perfectly wonderful time.

"Now that I've got some of you looking for a chair," I said, as though I was having the most fun of anyone, "we're going to go a little slower. Partner up, those of you who wish to dance the waltz."

As I had arranged, some of my students took to the floor, Lydia now with Dorothy. They were joined by several older couples I didn't know. With a nod, the band began a rehearsed but ragged version of "Laura's Waltz." The couples began to turn, stiffly at first but then more naturally, like whirlpools left by an oar, the grace of the dance seeming to point to the town's bright future. Blandin stood nearby, a glass of beer in hand and a big smile on his face. I had not forgotten the day when he mocked the town's social aspirations, but now he stood there proudly, like a dog by a box of puppies.

I thought a cheer might rise up when we finished the waltz, but as the final note faded, I heard an unhappy ripple run through the crowd. A moment later, Constable Gary rushed to the stage. Breathing hard, he informed us that a riot was taking place at the canal basin. The rail workers from Hawley had come over and drunk themselves into a mean state and were attacking people and breaking into stores and maybe even starting fires, because Gary asked for the pumper. "There are good citizens," he said, "your neighbors, who badly need your help. I want every man to step forward!"

No one stepped forward, because that would have been the wrong direction. Instead, they began to move quickly toward the canal. I handed my violin to Abram Stryker and followed with no idea of what I thought I would do when I got there. Then someone called my name. I turned and saw Blandin, a half-block away. Using his big voice he asked if I would go over to the tavern and stay with Damon. I waved and turned downtown, happy for a task. At the tavern, I found Damon, guarding the door like a piece of grizzle—plug in his jaw, a rusty musket across his lap and a big coon grin on his face that was maybe meant to scare people.

"Do you have powder and wadding for that?" I asked, looking at his unconvincing weapon.

Damon spat on the floor and kept grinning. "If it were pointed at you, would you bet that I didn't?"

From the tavern we could hear the commotion down by the canal. It was, by all accounts, a nasty event but not a long one. Once the men of the town appeared in strength, the rioters quickly got the worst of it. Some were bloodied and arrested. Others ran away. Many of the town's defenders then found their way to Blandin's, which had been closed during the festivities. With them came Jimmy Lawson, on his own feet but kept upright by a man on either side. Jimmy was bleeding from a terrible gash on his head and another on his shoulder. I cleared a table and looked at Damon. "Get me a clean cloth and a bottle of whiskey."

Jimmy was laid on the table while someone ran to get Doc Richardson. Damon returned, and I soaked the cloth with whiskey and began to clean the ragged wounds, no doubt the work of a broken bottle.

"Joseph, my boy," said Jimmy, flinching a little, "you have the touch of a woman." There was laughter, and I looked at my hands, slender and smooth against his rough skin.

"Is that so?" I said, pulling the wound apart and pouring whiskey straight into the shoulder. Jimmy let out a yell, and there was laughter again.

Doc Richardson came through the door, already bloody from the evening's work. Jimmy took a look at Doc's black bag, grabbed the whiskey, and took several heroic swallows. Doc told Jimmy to lie still, poured some more whiskey into the wounds, and then dug deep with needle and thread. When the sewing was over, Jimmy got up, belched, and, with his good arm, slapped Doc on the back as a thank-you. Then, with great energy, the oral application of whiskey having taken effect, he told his tale of the riot.

11

I MOVED THE chairs as though to sweep the floor, but the floor didn't need sweeping.

"Did you have a pleasant time on the Fourth?" I asked.

"I suppose," said Lydia, not looking up from the paper.

"You and David certainly seemed to be having good time."

"Yes." Lydia kept reading.

"What did you talk about?"

"What do you think?" she said putting the paper aside. "We talked about what people talk about."

I didn't like the manner. We didn't have to do the lesson. But before I could end the day, Lydia stood up. "Joseph," she said brightly, as though a new person had jumped into her skin, "Mother asked me to invite you to dinner this week. Will you come?"

This sudden change and the invitation that came with it caught me off balance. Dinner at Lydia's house? It wasn't a good idea. I should have pleaded my duties at Blandin's, but something else came out. "And do *you* want me to come, Miss Watson?"

"Of course," she said, as though I had imagined her evasions. "What's got into you?"

* * *

The Watsons' white house stood at the near end of Bethany village. A large porch guarded the front, and its stairs creaked as I went up, each one warning against my visit. Emily Watson answered the door, a reserved, handsome woman with her daughter's dark features. I took the hand she offered, bent at the waist, and looked up into a pair of familiar green eyes. Mrs. Watson invited me in and called upstairs to Lydia, bringing forth instead Lydia's sisters, Beth and Julia. Each sought to claim me.

"Let Professor Lobdell be," said Mrs. Watson. "Next year you can be in his class."

Lydia appeared on the stairs like a princess in gingham. She gave a playful curtsy and led me into the parlor where Mrs. Watson joined us. I was a little stiff, but Lydia and her mother did their best to make me feel at home. Helping was the aroma of roasting meat and the prospect of food cooked only once and not many times like that served at Blandin's.

We chatted about the season and the music school. "I had hoped," said Mrs. Watson, "that you would bring the violin so we might hear you play."

"Mother!" said Lydia. "Professor Lobdell is our guest."

Mrs. Watson threw a look at her daughter and turned back to me with a smile. "Forgive me. It's just that we did so enjoy your playing on the Fourth."

"For as long as that lasted," I said, hoping that the unpleasantness could now be laughed at.

Not by Mrs. Watson. "Such a disgrace," she said, no doubt speaking words that had been said many times that week in the finer homes in Bethany. Down at Blandin's, the brawl was a merry topic, as though it had been one of the planned events.

Lydia's father came into the room. His determined eyes and scarred hands pointed to the days, now gone, when he would skid the logs himself. But how does a man who subdues forests receive one who teaches girls to dance? Henry Watson didn't seem to know. He gave the smallest greeting, nodding his head but not offering his hand. The awkward moment was saved by the Watsons' housekeeper, who came in to announce the dinner.

Henry Watson took his chair at the head of the table, while Mrs. Watson sat at the other end. I was seated next to Lydia. Beth and Julia across. Henry

Watson said the blessing, and the food was passed—roast lamb, greens, and mashed turnips.

"Well, Professor Lobdell," said Mrs. Watson, "I hear you're quite the regular at Cornell Hall with its many visitors. What news do they bring?"

This was as it should be. I was the guest and the man. Mrs. Watson would ask questions of me, and I would respond in an engaging way if I could.

"I fear no one brings tidings of joy," I said. "By all accounts, there's trouble in every direction."

Mrs. Watson sighed. "Wherever can it all be going?"

This, again, as ordained. My part was now to say the thing that would put everyone at ease. But before I could, Julia jumped in. "Is there going to be a war?"

"Oh, I don't think so," I said. "This sort of thing has been going on for a long time. Most of it is posturing." I was parroting a view I had heard at the Literary Society. If pressed, I wouldn't have been able to say who was doing what to whom.

"I hope there's going to be one," said Julia with a child's innocence. "And father bought a forest, so they can make the boots!"

There was a sudden silence as Mrs. Watson gave Julia a look that would have burned the pudding. Lydia stared down as though to make sure nothing spilled off her fork. I too inspected the silverware, a little confused and not daring to cast my eyes in Henry Watson's direction. Finally, he spoke.

"There is a great difference, Julia," he said slowly, his displeasure for all to hear, "between being prudently prepared for war and hoping for it. A Christian man does not hope for war." He turned to me. "I am in the wood trade, Mr. Lobdell. I bought, not long ago, a superior stand of hemlock, the bark of which is filled with tannic acid. If war comes, there will be a need to tan leather. If war does not come, the profit will arrive a little later."

Henry Watson descended into a stillness that coiled around me. Lydia gave her head a slight shake to say I shouldn't be bothered, but I was. Henry Watson appeared put upon by my presence. And perhaps it was my imagination or the lack of a handshake, but he seemed to not even regard me as a man, to which, I must say, I took insult.

The conversation stumbled a bit from that time forward, but Mrs.

Watson did her best and that was good enough. Later at the door, she graciously offered her hand. "You must promise, Professor Lobdell, to visit our house again."

Mrs. Watson moved aside, and Lydia stepped forward. "Yes, Professor Lobdell," she said, echoing her mother, "you must come again." She then offered her hand, and when I took it, she gave my fingers the lightest squeeze.

* * *

For the next week, the town baked like an oven. Dogs found what shade they could, and well-mannered people lost their tempers over trifles. Farmers kicked at the dust and only talked about a second cutting.

On Thursday, I sent the class home early to no one's complaint. Lydia stayed on, but all we did was sit by the window in hope of a breeze. The air was thick and still. But then, as though summoned, a breeze did come. Clouds of gray and purple swooped in from the west like giant birds of prey. A rushing noise moved through the fields and tree lines. A bright spark. Then a crash that sounded like God had knocked over His wardrobe.

Sheets of water poured from the sky. A man ran along the road, trying to reach shelter. Then, realizing that not a dry bit of him was left to be saved, he stopped and let out a silly laugh. Taken by the moment's drama, I turned to Lydia. She was looking toward the creek, seeming lost in thought. But then, without turning, she spoke.

"When I was little," she said, "Mother would let us run in the rain behind our house wearing hardly a thing." That memory brought a smile to the part of her face I could see. "If we were in a meadow out of sight, Joseph, I would do it now. Would you join me?"

"You would not," I said, trying to scold, but all the while imagining her running in the rain, shift clinging to her flanks. "And no, I wouldn't join you. I'd like to keep my reputation and remain in town a little longer."

Lydia laughed. "Well, aren't you the modest one. You'd have to promise to cover your eyes and never tell a soul."

Cover my eyes? Never tell a soul? I knew what she was doing, and this time I wasn't going to play the prude. "I think, dear Lydia," I said, now meeting her eye, "the most I could promise is that I would not tell."

I saw her start to color, but she quickly danced away. "I loved those summers," she sighed, as though nothing had been said about running in the rain. "I would turn so brown. Mother used to say that she was going to give me back to the Indians."

"Did that frighten you?" I asked, happy to move on.

"No, I liked it. I liked when she played with us, my cousins and me. Sometimes she would chase us, and we would scream as though a beast were loose in the woods. But there were so few moments like that."

Lydia then asked about my mother. Did she play games with me? For an instant I was back in our old house in Westerlo, looking out at an apple tree that had come down in a storm when I was ten. As far as games, I didn't remember much of that. What I remembered was Mother being sick a lot. Headaches. Sudden noises like a door closing might be enough to send her to her room. I learned to be quiet and move carefully; we all did—a complicated story, so I put a simple lie in its place.

"She was playful," I said. "Not all the time, of course."

"When did you last see her?"

"Oh, several months ago."

Lydia seemed to lose her balance. "But, Joseph, you said she was dead!"

In the warmth of new deceptions, I had forgotten my old ones. My mind raced back to fill the breach.

"So she is," I said, as though Lydia had not heard things right. "She's buried beside my father in New York. I visited her grave before I came to Honesdale."

Lydia wrinkled her brow. Behind her eyes I saw more questions, but I was rescued by a sudden rush of hail. For several minutes it fell, the size of small, dried peas. We captured these pellets with outstretched hands, refreshing our faces and laughing.

That night I thought back over the afternoon's storm and what it had brought forth between Lydia and me. She had challenged me with a game that was beyond propriety—all that running-in-the-rain talk. I had protested, but that protest wasn't very convincing. And it was gone for good the moment I said I wouldn't tell but might look.

So Lydia had proposed a flirtatious game, and I had played. I wasn't sorry. I liked it. And I didn't really care if it was or wasn't proper. I had never cared a fig about proper. Beyond that, I didn't think it was strange to feel so drawn to her. After all, I was living as a man. Life was presenting itself to me as it presented itself to a man, so it was natural for me to find Lydia beautiful and enchanting. The better I played my role, the more beautiful she would be.

* * *

The rainstorm had broken the heat, and the following night Cornell Hall was bearable. After the lecture, I walked to the Wayne to dine with Burton, who was to follow. I was almost to the hotel when up ahead I saw David Horton and two friends. They didn't see me. They might have already been drinking, because they were pushing at each other and laughing loudly. I moved to the shadows and watched as they bellowed and hooted their way down the street.

When I got to the hotel, I took a seat at Burton's table and watched as men who had been at the meeting entered and sat at the remaining tables. A few minutes later, Burton came into the room with the evening's speaker, Mr. William Casey. With them was Mr. Francis Penniman of the *Democrat*. Mr. Penniman looked every bit the newspaper man, as he stopped and shook hands with several men seated nearby. His spectacles were framed by unruly eyebrows and his wool vest displayed a gold watch chain, all of this befitting a man of his age, which I thought to be a little north of sixty. Our out-of-town guest, Mr. Casey, was younger, with more hair on his head and more flesh about the face. He had lectured that evening on "The Danger to Our South," a lesson that continued over a plate of beef and cabbage.

"You have to understand what's at stake," he said, chewing loudly. "Depending on how thin you slice the bread, there could be four to eight new states down there. And they'd all come in slave, with just as many senators as New York or Pennsylvania."

"Could that really happen?" asked Penniman.

"My dear friend," said Casey, "as we speak, there's an expedition in New Orleans ready to sail for Nicaragua. To capture it and make it a state. Yes, it has rich soil. Minerals too. But there are ways to get at them without granting voting privileges in our sacred halls. *Presidentes* come at a rather reasonable price."

"But, sir," I said, a little surprised. "Did you not say this evening that our southern neighbors should be free from interference?"

Casey glared at me and pointed his fork. "Interference is what's being planned in New Orleans. But in the world of nations, there's a rightful place for the strong. We see it in nature as it is handed down from heaven."

I nodded as though all had been made clear. Burton winked.

Mr. Casey finished his dinner and ordered two pieces of pie. Once these were dealt with, he retired upstairs. Fewer people were in the room now, and it was easier to talk in a normal voice. Mr. Penniman turned to me. "I'm happy to finally meet you, Mr. Lobdell. Burton speaks well of you."

I glanced at Burton, but he gave a blank look as though to disavow anything to come.

"I wonder," Mr. Penniman continued, "if you might be interested in a position at the *Democrat* this autumn? I was impressed by your conduct tonight."

"But I hardly said a thing," I protested.

"Ah, but you listened! You found the weak point in our guest's fortress, and you did not press the attack when there was nothing to be gained. These are qualities not lost on an editor."

The offer was most certainly Burton's doing. Even so, I felt as though Mr. Penniman had pinned his gold watch to my chest, and I had a brief vision of myself at the head of Cornell Hall. I tried to hide these inflated feelings, saying that I knew nothing about newspapers. Penniman would have none of it.

"Everyone learns on the job," he said. "You can do it, or you can't."

"But I have the music school."

He shrugged. "We can work around that."

Once again, I was swept away. Mr. Francis Penniman, owner and editor of the *Honesdale Democrat*, thought me worth my own hours. I stopped looking at the gift horse and said I would try my best for him. We agreed to sit down in September.

I left the Wayne with a light step. My fortunes were on the rise. I would need new clothes, a better place to sleep, and a bank account. I had not opened one before, fearing that questions would be asked or references required. What money I made, I handed to Blandin to keep in his safe—two, sometimes three dollars a week. Soon, with a second income from the newspaper, I was certain to save more, money for our future, mine and Helen's. And this night, as I walked down Main, my daughter was very much on my mind. In the autumn, I would begin to send money home—I'd find a way. In a year or two, Helen might come to me, perhaps as my niece. I didn't know how it would all work, but that night it seemed it could.

The next morning, I warmed a bucket of water and brought it to my room, washing myself up and down with a rough cloth as I often did. I had just put on my britches when the door to my room swung open—the latch hadn't held. From the corner of my eye, I saw Damon in the doorway, peeking out from behind a pile of sheets and towels he was bringing around. I gave him my back and quickly put on my shirt. I didn't think he had seen the evidence, but my hurried actions must have looked peculiar. I turned back and tried to smile. He gave me an odd, searching look and then put the sheets on my bed.

* * *

I wrapped the violin while Lydia sat and read the *Herald*. She seemed strangely quiet, and I didn't have much to say. But then she began to read aloud—a story about a fire in a mine near Carbondale—a fire that could not be put out and now burned in unknown directions. Would the city fall into the newly created chasm? No one knew.

"A strange way for the world to end," she said, putting the paper aside. "To be burned up from the inside." And with that, she began to recite something that at first sounded like scripture.

In the 'ginning was the Wurts. And the Wurts was good.

And the Wurts begat Hone who did what he could.

And Hone begat Carbon, and Carbon 'gat Hawley,

and they all rode to town in a little painted trolley.

And Hawley 'gat Jervis by a mule team driver,

and the two lived together in a shack by the river.

And the Wurts stole a boro, and the Hone stole a dale,

and the Jervis stole a port, and they all went to jail.

How many years did they serve without bail?

I laughed. "What, in heaven's name, was that?"

"Oh, just something Evelyn and I made up. We used to skip rope to it."

"I was a fair skipper myself," I said, not seeing the mistake.

Lydia looked surprised. "Really? There weren't many boys I knew who could do it at all. They jumped like grasshoppers." I braced for more questions, but Lydia got up and stared out the window. "Have you ever been over there, Joseph? To Carbondale?"

"Is it nice?"

"Oh yes," she said, still looking out, "if you like grand homes with porches on the second level. But what do you see when you stand on them? Mountains of coal, piles of slag, and on every surface a black dust that surely darkens the soul."

I looked at Lydia like I was seeing my younger self, though we were only six years apart. She saw the world as black and white, good and evil, one or the other to win. I had seen it that way. Now I believed that the world was just a pudding of good and bad and would always be so. But I liked that Lydia felt the way she did, and I argued with her sometimes just to see the color run to her face.

"Oh, aren't you the serious one," I said. "I rather think the human spirit is on an upward course."

Lydia turned. "Well, you might feel differently if you'd been here last year when they hanged Harris Bell."

"Was that not for a murder?"

"Surely, but my goodness, the fascination!" Lydia picked up her shawl and draped it over her arm. "People started gathering in the early morning, Joseph, just to see the man as he was marched up the street. There was a fence to hide the gallows, but ladders were brought, and people paid money to climb them. And when it was done, our good citizens took the rope and cut it into pieces, so each could have a memento of the occasion. Imagine." Lydia's eyes burned, and had they been turned on a pile of leaves, it might have burst into flames. She was beautiful.

12

I GOT BACK to Blandin's to find the tavern oddly crowded for the late afternoon—merchants and bargemen sharing tables, of all things, many of them with soot-darkened faces. I soon found out why. There had been a fire south of town. The men had gone out to fight it, but the fire kept advancing, driven by a wind that was pushing it toward the coal yards, which, had they begun to burn, would have been the hellish end to everything that had ever called itself Honesdale. Then the wind died, and the town was saved—all of this while I was teaching girls to dance. That night I played many a merry tune.

But that Sunday, Reverend Albright saw no cause for celebration. In its place he read the story of Lot. He spoke with such passion that I started to think that he would have liked to see the town burn. But it didn't burn, and Reverend Albright knew why. God had spared Honesdale the fate of Gomorrah as He had spared the city of Zoar. We should fall to our knees and give thanks—we should be grateful for this warning to turn from our wicked ways. Our sins piled together had called forth the fire. God's mercy had stopped it. I saw heads nod in agreement.

After service, Reverend Albright and I walked to the square. I intended to challenge his sermon, for I didn't believe that God burned cities, despite those Bible stories. Maybe those cities burned because someone knocked over a lamp. And why was Lot's wife turned into a pillar of salt? What did she do?

But Reverend Albright and I didn't talk about the sermon. His troubled thoughts were elsewhere. "Have things not gone well with Miss Jenkins?" I asked.

"They have not," he said, fussing with his parson's cap. He didn't say more, so I could only imagine. Had he tried to tell a joke? Confess his desire? Why had I even suggested it?

"Malcolm," I said, wishing to change the subject. "I'd like to tell you about a story. By Mr. Hawthorne. About a village pastor. One day he comes to church wearing a veil—"

Reverend Albright waved his hand. "I've read only one work by Mr. Hawthorne. I'll not hear of another. His Reverend Dimmesdale was an insult to men of the cloth."

"Insult? Don't men of the cloth wrestle with sin like the rest of us?"

"Of course, but that's not the problem."

I took a breath. "What *is* the problem?"

My minister looked up as if to search the clouds. "Books should be morally uplifting. Unfortunately, that appears to be beyond your friend Mr. Hawthorne."

My friend Mr. Hawthorne? I was losing patience. "And just what is my new friend's great sin, if you care to tell me?"

"Mr. Hawthorne was a founder of Brook Farm," he said, folding the crooked sticks he had for arms. "You may know that their grand build-ing—they had some fancy name for it—that unholy building burned to the ground. Burned by the hand of God, of that I am certain."

Brook Farm, again. Had the place still existed, I would have gone there just to see it for myself. Burton thought it misguided. Reverend Albright saw it as outright sinful—so much so that God had burned the place down. I didn't believe it. And I was getting tired of my minister's small-minded lessons.

"Malcolm," I said, "if God weeded the wicked by fire, I think we would smell smoke every day of the week."

Albright stood there gaping like an old hen, no doubt searching for scripture in his old hen head. I walked away.

* * *

The girls stared dreamily out the window as they waited for class to begin. I had done the same in school. Back then, I might have imagined myself out with my father and the farmer's militia. In those dreams I would be on a pinto, carrying some secret message past the sheriff's patrol. But I was old-fashioned, even as a youngster. My students, I was sure, were not thinking of daring deeds on horses.

To refresh their interest, I began to teach the mazurka. At first, there was much stamping of feet and ragged jumping about, the imagined music not helping. After several attempts, I retired to play the violin, and we imagined, instead, our eighth dancer.

Lydia stayed for her lesson, but it didn't last long. Once we were done, I told her of my quarrel with Reverend Albright. She laughed.

"Joseph, he's a prune. When are you going to see this?" And then, as if to help me, she pinched her face and spoke through her nose. "*Make a mournful noise unto the Lord, all ye lands. Serve the Lord with sadness, come before his presence with frowning.*"

I took a step back.

"Oh, goodness," said Lydia, "the psalm will survive." She tried to make light of it, but my face must have said more than I wanted it to, for suddenly she turned away as though to hide. A moment passed. And another. Finally she spoke, her voice low and pleading. "Joseph, I'm not sure there even is a God. There would be some evidence, don't you think?"

"Evidence?" I said, dismayed. "Dear Lydia, the signs are all around us. God is everywhere—in the forests and the fields, the trees and the rivers."

Lydia ran her fingers along the sill. "Joseph, if you tell me that God has a seat on the Board of Merchants, then I agree He is all powerful. But the trees and the fields? We cut them down."

"Have you not *ever* felt His presence?" I asked, hoping for something we might share.

A vacant look settled on Lydia's face, as though she had opened a gift and found nothing in the box. "When I was a girl," she said, "I used to pray. I would beg God to come to me, to touch my head, to show me some sign He was there. Sometimes I would tell myself that He had touched me, but it never happened." She got up and began to gather her things.

I didn't want her to leave. I reached out to stop her. "Dance with me."

Lydia seemed surprised, perhaps imagining that I was angry. After a moment, she nodded that she would. Without a note on the violin or another word, we arranged ourselves and danced without smiles or laughter. I felt wooden and foolish. The waltz didn't bring us closer but only showed the distance between us.

When we finished, Lydia didn't move. We stood holding each other. Then, like a flower folding itself for the evening, she nestled gently against me. I put my arms full around her, and we rocked slowly, her head on my shoulder, my lips brushing her neck. I could feel her breathe.

Then she pushed away, looking out from under her lashes and speaking in a whisper. "What you must think of me."

If I had been braver, I would have told her the truth about everything. But all my instinct was to protect what had just happened. Protect it so that it might happen again. But the moment still called for truth, so I gave it, in half measure. "I love you, Lydia. That is what I think of you."

"Oh, Joseph," she sighed as she looked away. Then, as though not to wake us, she left.

* * *

That night I wrestled with large thoughts. Now that the words had been spoken, it was plain—I was in love with Lydia. Was such a thing possible? Could a woman love another woman? I had never heard of it, though when I was young, I would sometimes hear things whispered about two spinsters who lived together. People would laugh and say they were married. I thought it was just something funny to say. When I was older, I heard a preacher speak out against the sin of unnatural unions. I didn't know what these unions were, but a woman loving another woman might surely be one.

This troubled me some, but not as much as you might suppose. And before I am judged from the far off comfort of a chair, please remember that everything had changed for me. Up was down, red was blue, and some part of me had come to see myself as a man. And as such, my feelings toward Lydia were as natural as the morning mist. Of course, Lydia didn't know the truth, and there was nothing natural about that. It was all such a tangle.

But there was a place where it wasn't a tangle—a special, quiet place, beyond the reasons and the thoughts. There, in a room of its own, in an attic with sloped ceilings, a part of me just loved Lydia and didn't care about the rest. I went there that night, hugging my pillow and remembering over and over the smell of her hair and the pulse of her neck until those thoughts brought me into a generous sleep.

* * *

My retelling of Reverend Albright's street lessons brought a smile to Burton's face. "Morally uplifting?" he said, raising his eyes. "Please, I'd rather a cold bath."

"No you wouldn't," I said. "But what does he have to fear from Mr. Hawthorne?"

"Oh, he has everything to fear," said Burton. "Mr. Hawthorne has, I'd say, a sympathy for our darker nature." For Burton, of course, that was a compliment, but, even so, it turned out he didn't really like *The Scarlet Letter*. Prynne was too good, or something like that.

As for me, I liked it, but I didn't tell Burton why. I felt a kinship with Miss Prynne. She wore a damning letter across her breast, while my breasts themselves, bound under my shirt, were my transgression. I might have been a character in the story. Why not? My every day was a fabrication. And with our embrace, my conduct toward Lydia had become a moral failing. Every time I thought about it, I resolved to tell her the truth. But how? The truth would be so shocking that Lydia would have to tell another, and then I would be ruined and have to give up everything and flee. So, I'd have to replace one lie with another—a story, say, of my hand already promised in marriage. But that would be no simple tale to tell. Lydia would ask questions, and there would have to be more lies—lots of them. My head ached with it all, and I began to dread seeing her.

Thursday came and with it the dance class. When the others left, Lydia asked if we could spend our time outside. We walked to the creek and chose the path that went upstream. I thought about telling her my new story, the one about my betrothed back in Westerlo. But I hadn't worked it all out, and the day was so beautiful I couldn't bring myself to spoil it.

We walked farther and soon found ourselves in a small, overgrown meadow. We sat where the grass was soft and watched the clouds scud down the valley. A warm breeze lightly rippled the field. Then it fell away, bringing a silence that was challenged only by the occasional bee.

Lydia took a stalk of grass and traced loops in the air. "When I was young," she said, "I used to think that if one was a girl, one stayed a girl, in the same way if one were born a pony, one stayed a pony."

"Not me," I said, turning to her, "I always wanted to grow up."

Lydia kept looking at the sky. "It wasn't that. I just thought grown-ups were a different breed. But, yes, now that I'm about to become one, I don't want to."

"Does it really seem that awful to you?"

Lydia brought her eyes back to mine. "Yes, Joseph, it does. And do you know where it frightens me most? In church."

The silence spoke my confusion. Lydia seemed annoyed.

"Have you really not noticed, Joseph? Would not Sunday be the day and church the place to see joy if there were joy to be seen? But you don't see it. The women and the men—they have looks on their faces like they're so very tired of it all."

Lydia turned away, and a wood thrush began its afternoon song. I lay back and closed my eyes. A minute later I opened them and saw her above me. Her face was surrounded by blue sky and clouds, as though detached from her body—something one might see in a dream. Her fingers touched my cheek, and her eyes searched mine. She kissed me on the mouth, gently at first, then fiercely—my hands finding her soft places.

13

THE NEXT MORNING, in bed, I relived our moments by the Dyberry, remembering the pleasure of Lydia's kiss. But those warm thoughts were soon pushed aside by the question—would my touch bring her the same delight if she knew my true nature? I didn't know and couldn't bring myself to think more about it. I got up and went downstairs.

Over breakfast, I saw a notice in the *Democrat*—a Mrs. R. Parsons had a room to let in her carriage barn. I very much needed a new place to live, a room where men would not pass my door at all hours, a room where I could heat my own water and bathe. I finished my bowl of oats and set off for the upper village.

It might have been home to a large family, it was surely big enough, but no sound came from the house as I stepped onto the porch and knocked. Then I heard footsteps, and the door opened to reveal a gray-haired woman in a baking cap. I asked if the missus were home, and she laughed and said she was the only Rebecca Parsons there that day. When I told her why I had come, she took off her apron and put on a shawl.

We walked to the barn, and Mrs. Parsons asked if I were new in town. I told her about the music school. She said she had heard of it. When I told her I was staying in a room upstairs at Blandin's, she smiled and said she could see why I might be looking for another place to sleep.

Once in the barn, we went up a dark stairway that led to a long, bright room. At the near end was a bed with a feather mattress and at the far end, a small iron cook stove. In the middle, a table and chair sat before a window that looked out onto wild roses grown high on a trellis. I made no effort to hide my pleasant surprise.

The rent was modest but came with duties to the main house and to the grounds, these to begin in a month when the present boarder was to leave. I had time enough in the morning to do the work, but I did say that I would not be home a great deal later in the day if she were counting upon my presence. Mrs. Parsons frowned.

"I'm not looking for a companion," she said. "I just want someone who'll do what's needed. I'd be pleased to have you if it suits."

I walked back to the lower village, thinking about the future. I was soon to have a retreat a little like Burton's, and only a few streets from his. In the colder months, I could sit by the stove with a book in my lap and a cup of tea beside me. Perhaps this was the place where Helen could join me. If I did well for Mrs. Parsons, if I were diligent in my duties, she might allow my niece one of the bedrooms in the main house. It was more thinkable there than at Blandin's.

* * *

Lydia sat by the window in her pinafore, hair tangled loosely about her shoulders. I should have taken out the violin and begun the lesson, but I kept finding small things to do. I hadn't seen her since the day of our kiss and had no idea of what was to be said. And if she were happy to see me, it didn't show. She just sat there, almost hiding in the *Democrat*.

"Joseph," she said finally, not looking up, "do you know Arthur Crum? I mean, do you know who he is?"

"Yes," I said, grateful to be speaking any words at all. "He hasn't killed his jailer, has he?"

"No, he was hanged. Listen to this."

> After Mr. Crum was pronounced dead, a scientific examination of
> his head was conducted by Doctor Crawford, the noted phrenologist.
> According to the doctor, the head was twenty inches in circumference.

The perceptive faculties were said to be strong, the reflective weak.
Other organs of good disposition were found to be atrophied, while
the back of the head was oversized, indicating sensuality and cruelty.

Lydia rose and came to where I was sitting. Suddenly her hands were
rummaging about in my hair. "Joseph," she said, accusing me, "your soft
hair is a disguise. You're really a monster."

I tried to look amused. "And how do you know that?"

"Because the back of your head is so large!"

"It's not true."

"It is," she replied. "And I shall have to report you to Doctor Crawford.
What will he say? Your sensual nature, yes, but cruelty as well? Why must
the two go together?"

We danced that afternoon. I kissed her softly, but my hands did not
presume to their liberties along the Dyberry. Lydia seemed impatient. She
broke off the embrace but held on to my hand.

"Joseph, when we dance, do you hear music in your mind?"

"Yes," I said. "Of course."

"I mean, do you hear the actual notes?"

"It isn't remarkable, Lydia. It happens all the time."

"Not remarkable?" she said, letting go of my hand. "To hear music that
is not played? Joseph, if you wanted, could you hear that music played on
a piano instead of a violin?"

"Surely."

"But I could be hearing a violin. So if we were hearing it at the same
time, would it be a duet?"

"Well, I'm not sure you could call it a—"

"Would we have to be in the same room?"

I was now lost, and my face must have shown it.

"What I am asking," she said, "is how do we do it? How are the notes
made?"

"We use our faculties in some way," I said, no longer feeling playful.
"What's this about?"

Lydia looked to the floor. "Well, Joseph," she said with gathered courage, "if by using our faculties, as you say, we can hear music that's not in

the room, and we can hear it at the same time," her eyes came up and challenged mine, "what other melodies might we dance to?"

Before I could answer, she picked up her scarf. "Good day, Professor Lobdell," she chirped, and down the stairs she went.

I shook my head in disbelief. She was shameless. And wonderful—that is, if she had proposed what it seemed she had. Then I thought that I had imagined too much and that it was *my* mind that needed to be washed with lye soap. But a minute later, as I was preparing to leave, I heard the door slam and quick steps. Lydia ran into the room, hurried over and kissed me on the mouth. "Tonight I'll hear what notes I want, and you can do the same." She gave me a wild look and ran back down the stairs.

That night, alone in the dark, I imagined Lydia. And the thought that she was thinking about me in the same way was like dried hay to a fire. Safe by myself, I could kiss her and touch her as I pleased, and I did so without remorse and with better result than anything I had known in my marriage bed. But as soon as I ceased my imaginings, the same truth stood before me—I had to put things right between us. But how? As I had discovered, resolving to put things right with Lydia and actually doing so were not the same. Our grassy nest along the Dyberry had been the perfect place to tell her, if not the truth then at least some lie that would put an end to our romance. I couldn't do it. I was swimming in her eyes, and all I wanted was for the moment to continue.

I lay in confusion. Was there anything I knew for sure? Yes. I knew that I was in love with Lydia and that she was in love with me. Or, rather, she was in love with Joseph. So that meant that she was in love with me so long as I was Joseph. But was I? I tossed about in the dark and felt the need to talk to my God, but by what name would He know me? Then it came. If God would accept me as Joseph, then surely it would be all right for Lydia.

* * *

That Sunday, I returned to church. I wanted to be part of His flock—part of His flock as Joseph. I wanted to sing hymns. I wanted my prayers to go to Him in a chorus, so they couldn't be separated or ignored. And as I stood and raised my voice in praise, I felt a peace come over me. Reverend Albright preached on Jesus and the Mount. I had never heard him speak so beautifully on God's loving purpose. Even so, I wasn't eager to come face-to-face with my minister. But when our eyes met at the door after service, I saw what I thought was regret for what had happened. "It's good to see you, friend," he said. "I thought we'd lost you."

"You haven't lost me, Malcolm," I said, trying to assure him and the Master he served. "And I haven't read any more books by Mr. Hawthorne."

Reverend Albright gave an approving grunt that for him was almost a laugh. He asked me to wait, and a little later we started toward the square. A light rain was falling, but my declaration about Mr. Hawthorne, made in jest, seemed to have raised my minister's spirits. "Yes, Joseph," he said, continuing the conversation, "I think you and I would do better to stay with the Holy Book."

"Indeed," I replied, feeling light and generous, "and argue about only the smallest of things."

I had said this to put him at ease, but Reverend Albright gave a disapproving look. "Are there small things when we speak about the Bible?"

I took a breath. This could not be a serious point between us. "My friend, when I read in Genesis that Enos was nine hundred years old, I understand it to mean that he lived many years but not necessarily nine hundred. Does that change the message of Our Lord? Is anything lost?"

"Only your immortal soul."

It's a joke, I thought. But my minister's stone face said that it wasn't.

"Malcolm," I said, almost pleading, "can't we can find God's message in these stories without embracing every word?"

The rain came harder, and Albright lifted his chin as though I had challenged the truth of the Flood itself. "The road is clearly marked, Joseph. Don't stray from it."

I should have walked away, but I couldn't. "Malcolm," I said, "when you arrive at the mill, the miller doesn't ask what road you came by. He asks about the quality of your grain."

Albright's eyes caught fire. "You would compare our Lord to a miller?"

"Sooner a miller," I said, now wanting to spit, "than a schoolmaster who would discard a student over a misspelled word. I can remember no such teaching by Jesus of Nazareth."

Malcolm Albright held up his hand as though to stop me and the rain. "Joseph, I must defend the church—just as our Lord expelled the unworthy from the temple—"

"Those were the Pharisees!" I protested. "The moneychangers!"

"Yes," he said, with a satisfied smile. "That's exactly who they were. They brought with them the iniquity of the day. The *isms* are the iniquity of our day—Deism, Universalism, Transcendentalism."

I wanted to slap his pocked face, but this time I did walk away. His voice followed. "You carry their plague."

* * *

That night, tortured thoughts circled the room like banshees. When I fell asleep these became my dreams. In one, an intruder entered my room. I watched him in the dark, unable to cry out. Then he leapt upon me and we struggled. I choked him until he was dead. Still in the dream, I lit the candle. It was Lydia dressed in a shirt and trousers.

I woke the next morning in a strange sweat. I could hear men below and went downstairs to find Blandin and several others talking in low voices. Cornell Hall had burned a few hours before, the pumper arriving in time to save the town. I had slept through it.

I walked up the street to see for myself. It was a horrid, smoldering sight. Strange too. The roof and insides were gone, but the front of the building with its grand doorway stood almost untouched, as though one could enter as before.

I wasn't sure if my dinner with Burton was still to happen, since the lecture clearly wasn't, but that night Burton was at his table. He did his best to act calm, but his eyes darted about in a manner that was not his. "I don't know how it burned," he said, "but I know who, even if he didn't light the match." Burton's words were as hard as any I had heard him speak. Little doubt he was talking about editor Beardslee and his campaign against the Literary Society. I had someone else in mind.

Burton had spent the afternoon trying to find another hall to host meetings. None had agreed. Beardslee had referred to the Society as *godless* so often that the churches were not eager to help. He asked if I might speak with the Methodists. I told him how I'd been cast out by Reverend Albright. Burton smiled, perhaps the first of his day.

"Be happy to be done with him," he said. "The poor fellow would be better off down at Ludlow's, putting dried beans on the scale." That made me laugh, but when I looked up, Burton was not laughing with me. "Joseph," he said, "you don't need his approval. You don't need anyone's approval."

Burton had never before spoken to me in such a manner. His words signaled an odd change to our conversation, and I wondered if the fire had affected him in some way. He leaned toward me and brought his voice down.

"My friend, you are not like other men." A chill ran up my back. "If you know me, then you know that such things do not escape my notice. You do not act like other men. You do not speak like other men. You are different. I know it, and no one else need know, but you don't have to pretend with me. I believe that we could have a closer relationship. A special relationship."

I held still, not entirely certain what was happening. I think the blood ran from my face. Burton became alarmed.

"Joseph, you needn't fear anything from me."

"I know that," I said in a whisper. I pushed the spoon about with my fingers while I wondered whether it was still possible to pretend that I hadn't really understood his meaning. Then I took the napkin from my lap and put it by my plate. "Kenneth," I said, using his Christian name for the first time, "you have befriended me, and I hold you in the highest regard. But I need now to retire." I stood up. "I look forward to many more evenings with you at this table." What that meant to him, I don't know. He seemed in disarray, for once unable to control a situation with his words. I bade him good night and fled back to Blandin's, straight to my room.

I lay on my bed in the dark, my head aching. Only then did I allow myself to think of Burton's proposal, for I had feared displaying any reaction to it in his presence. Now I felt revulsion. But why? Because I believed his feelings toward me were unnatural? That he loved me as a man? I had to laugh, for if Burton had feelings of desire toward me, they would have to be more natural than what I was feeling toward Lydia Watson.

But perhaps I had it wrong. Maybe Burton had fallen in love with the woman he had discovered. I wrestled with that idea but could remember no occasion when Burton showed the smallest interest in a woman. No, I was sure that I had understood him, but even if I hadn't—even if Mr. Kenneth Burton loved me as a woman and wanted me for a wife or even a hussy—it didn't change a thing. I loved Lydia.

14

I WAS SHORT with my students. I wanted them gone. I wanted to listen to Lydia read the news. I wanted to laugh at the troubles of others. But when the class did leave, Lydia was in no mood to play jester to my frowning face. She asked if I had eaten worms for breakfast.

I owed some explanation, but I certainly couldn't tell her about Burton. "I've been cast out of the church," I said, offering what I could. "Albright thinks I'm a Deist, whatever that is."

Lydia would now say something bad about Reverend Albright, call him a sour pickle or something. She didn't. "Oh, why do you care?" she said, annoyed. "It's all just hocus-pocus. *Though I speak with the tongues of men and of angels and have not MONEY, I have become as sounding brass and—*"

"Lydia stop! Stop mocking everything." She stepped back, seeming frightened by my outburst. A moment passed. "I'm sorry," I said holding out my hand. After a hesitation Lydia took it, and we came together, rocking gently in an embrace. "Just speak your heart," I said softly, "that's all you need do."

I thought we might stay entwined, but suddenly Lydia released herself. "Well then, speak it I will." She paused and then continued in a softer, less certain voice. "Joseph, I lie in bed at night and wish that you were with me, to touch me and kiss me and talk to me when I wake up in the lonely hours. But there's something you must know." She took a breath. "I've seen the life my mother lives. I don't want anything like it."

I held my face steady. "What would you have in its place?"

Lydia tugged on her sash. "Minnesota."

"What? The territory?"

"My cousin has written of its beauty and open spaces. I don't need comforts, Joseph. I want to be free. I want to go to Minnesota and raise horses." Lydia blushed. "Well, didn't that sound just awful. What must you think?"

I thought everything, and it spilled out of me. "Lydia, I know that here I'm just the music teacher, but I have lived the plain life. I know horses. I ride well. And I can track and hunt. I'm a crack shot with a rifle."

Lydia clapped her hands and gave a little jump. "Oh, Joseph! We shall marry and go west." Then she caught herself and became still. "Will you marry me, my dear, dear Joseph? You must."

At that moment, a dropped book might have fallen to the ceiling. The earth stopped turning, and wishes became logic. I could give Lydia the freedom she wanted, and our union, born as it was out of love, would be blessed by God. And what she had yet to learn was small next to what we now knew—that we wanted to be with each other. And I had found more pleasure in her embrace than anything in my marriage bed. Why couldn't the same be true for her with me? We could make a life for ourselves in the wilds of Minnesota.

"Oh dearest Lydia," I said, with my last ounce of reason, "I think we should talk about this."

"But, Joseph, you do want to be with me?"

"I do. Yes. Very much."

"And would you go with me to Minnesota?"

"I would, but this is sudden. As a gentleman, I should allow you time to think it over."

"I've thought it over."

"And what about your father?"

"I will see to my father."

"But, Lydia, there are things you should know."

"Such as?"

I took a breath. Did I have the courage? "Such as, all I have in this world is one hundred and fifty dollars and a rifle back in New York."

"I have money," she said. "My grandfather left us each a thousand dollars. Once I am married, it's mine. Then we can decide when we want to go west. Anything else?"

"Yes. I am descended from wolves. And you have to leave within the minute, so we should talk about all this when we can do so without hurry. I think we should take another walk up the Dyberry. Can you come on Saturday?"

Lydia thought for a moment and said she'd come at noon. Then, to seal the agreement, she gave me a peck on the cheek. "I can't wait to tell Evelyn," she said as she pulled away.

"Don't!" I warned.

"Evelyn and Dorothy are my friends," she said, looking offended. "I know their secrets and they know mine." And before I could caution her further, she hopped down the stairs like it were any other day.

I set off for Honesdale, my worries dragging close behind—Reverend Albright had my soul roasting in Hell; Damon was looking at me strange; Burton was hoping for heaven-knows-what; and Lydia wanted to marry me and go west. All of it seemed beyond my control, except, perhaps, the last. Lydia and I would meet on Saturday. We would walk up the Dyberry, but this time I would set things right. I would tell her about my hand already promised, or I would tell her the truth—one or the other.

After a late breakfast the next morning, I walked to the canal and took the towpath east, wishing to think about things without the distractions of the tavern. But once I was out of town and imagining our planned walk up the Dyberry, the choices that had seemed so clear the night before made no sense. After all that had happened, I couldn't very well say that I had just remembered my betrothed back in Westerlo. That was no choice at all. And as difficult as the truth would be, if Lydia knew my true nature, there was a chance that she would still want to go with me—go to Minnesota and live a life that would be ours. I came to a stop and decided to do what I already knew I had to—I would tell Lydia everything. I would tell her about Helen and George Slater. I would take off my shirt. Then she could choose, and if we were not to be married, I would leave town by dark. I was afraid of it, but there was also a comfort in the resolve.

It was early afternoon when I got back to Honesdale. As I started down Main, I saw three men ahead. Two of them I didn't know, but one was familiar. Then I near froze in alarm. The man was not from Honesdale—it was William Patterson, a timberman from Long Eddy! He was not a friend, but he knew who Lucy Lobdell was and might recognize her, even in disguise. He would certainly know she'd gone missing.

I kept my head down as I went by, but I felt his cold stare on my back.

* * *

Saturday, and Lydia was coming to the glass factory to plan our engagement. I would tell her the truth and accept my fate. I was there for more than an hour, but Lydia didn't appear. I became increasingly fearful and hoped very much that she hadn't yet spoken to her friends or her mother about our plans. Then a knock. I went downstairs, thinking that I had carelessly latched the door behind me. But the door wasn't locked, and when I opened it, I saw a gray-haired lady, the Watson's housekeeper. "This is for you," she said, offering an envelope and nervously looking around. "It's from Miss Lydia."

I took the envelope. Perhaps Lydia had fallen ill, and I would make some reply. But the woman hurried away in a manner that frightened me. The note said all.

> Dear Joseph, Some terrible accusations are being made about you that
> I know cannot be true. An unspeakable humiliation is being planned.
> Guard yourself without delay. Lydia.

I had been found out. There could be no other meaning. And no comfort in Lydia's professed disbelief, for if she did not believe the accusations, she would have come herself and not warned me to flee. And no hint at all that she wished to come with me.

Desperate to escape, I took the road back to Honesdale at a fast walk, not sure if I were moving away from danger or closer to it. After the Bethany turnoff, I saw in the distance two men on horseback coming toward me. On any other day I would have thought nothing of it, but I went into the bushes and was well hidden by the time they passed at a canter. I only got a glimpse, but one of the men, I was almost certain, was David Horton. I counted to thirty before taking to the road again. The riders had disappeared around the bend, and I couldn't tell if they had gone toward the glass factory or up to Bethany.

I reached Honesdale and walked down Main Street fearing every passerby. Up ahead I saw Francis Penniman standing outside the office of the *Democrat*. He was having a conversation with someone whose arms were making wild gestures. I crossed the street to avoid them.

At Blandin's, I went straight upstairs to collect my things. I stuffed my bag in haste, all the while worrying about my money. It was in Blandin's safe, but I hadn't seen him when I came in. Was he in the back? Would he give it to me?

A sudden bang and the door to my room swung open. It was Damon, and his withered face was looking mean. "Daniel wants to see you, missy. He wants to see you now."

With no choice I tied my bag and followed Damon down the stairs. There were a few men at the tables, but I was afraid to look in their direction. Blandin was now behind the bar. Our eyes met, and he motioned for me to go into the back room.

Blandin followed me into his office, closed the door, and threw the bolt across. It was just me and him. I didn't know what he had in mind, but three of me would have been no match for him, if he were looking to settle things that way. He put his hands on his hips and looked at me hard. "There's gonna be trouble, son," he said, voice steady. "You need to go. You need to go now."

I didn't know why he was being calm and kind. I had made a fool out of him in front of the whole town. Any other man would have bellowed or lashed out, but Daniel Blandin didn't even need to unmask me.

"Yes," I replied in a whisper. "I've gotten my things."

Blandin nodded and went to his safe. He pulled out the envelope with my money then turned to me. "Which way will you go?"

I had no answer.

"Listen," he said, "there's no time to lose; they'll be on horseback."

"Who'll be on horseback?"

Blandin gave a disbelieving snort. "Who do you think? Horton and his friends. I'll try to slow them down, offer them some drinks when they get here, but that'll just make things worse if they catch you. And you don't want that to happen. Do as I say—take the towpath."

"Won't they know I went that way?"

"They will, so you have to be smart about it. Where the Pike branches off, there's a store. Go in and buy some tobacco and ask the distance to Hawley. Then go on down the towpath, as though you're goin'to Hawley. Half a mile or so there'll be a footpath that goes up the hill. When no one's looking, take it. It will bring you over to Narrowsburg. They'll go right on by."

Blandin then crossed the room and undid the bolts on the rear door. It groaned as it opened onto a narrow alley. He turned and offered his hand. "Take care of yourself, Joseph."

"Thank you for your kindness," I managed to say, aware that he now took my hand gently. A tear rolled down my cheek, then another. I was crying like a woman.

PART II

Manannah

The townsite of Kandiyohi was surveyed and platted in October of 1856 by a party of Minneapolis gentlemen. Upon the most commanding prominence overlooking the lake, these enterprising men had reserved four blocks as "Capitol Square" two years before the capital lands were located, indicating that some understanding existed between the townsite promoters and the parties who were to select the new capital lands.

—*History of Kandiyohi County*, The Pioneer Press, 1905, describing the apparent under-the-table dealings of the company seeking to move the Minnesota capital from St. Paul to Kandiyohi, a land scheme that Lucy Ann Lobdell became part of when she, with her rifle and posing as Joseph, was hired to guard the Kandiyohi site.

15

THE RAIN BEAT down in a single-note chorus. Above the din I could hear the creek rushing, but in the dark I couldn't see it. My feet were my eyes, and had I not been familiar with the road, I would have stayed at the station, lonely but dry.

The glow in the window said that someone was still awake. I gave a quick rap and entered as though I had been gone only a day. Indeed, once inside, I saw that everything was where it had been—the broom in the corner, the chair by the hearth, and in it Father, asleep. Beside him stood my mother in her bedclothes, eyes wide.

"Lucy?"

"Yes, Mother."

I knew she would be angry. She had every right to be. Even so, I wanted her to set it aside, if only for a minute. I wanted her to cross the room and hug me—happy to see me safe. But she stayed where she was, her face in a knot. "What's happened to your hair?"

I set my bag down and tried to stay calm. "Where I went," I said, "it was easier to work if my hair was short."

John and Sarah came running down the stairs, followed by Mary. The older ones froze when they saw me, but Mary jumped like a goat and threw her arms around me without a thought of the water dripping from my outer-shirt. This moment of sisterly love didn't wake my father or soften my mother.

"What kind of work?" she asked as I let go of Mary.

"Men's work," I said, hoping that might put an end to it. Mother's face filled with more questions, but I spoke before she did. "Is Helen upstairs?"

"Well, I see you still remember her name."

I pretended not to hear those words as I took the wet canvas from my shoulders and hung it on a peg by the door. Then I reached out and took Mary's hand. "Will you take me to her?" Mary gave a bright nod, but Mother just stood there blocking the way. Our eyes met in a cold stare. A moment passed and then another. She moved aside.

I followed Mary upstairs and into her room. Helen lay asleep in Mary's bed. She had twisted in the blanket and her pink feet stuck out the side. I could hear her breathing as I drew near. I looked at my child for a long moment, feeling everything from joy to shame. Finally I knelt down and kissed her gently. "I don't think I should wake her right now," I said softly.

I was not just thinking about Helen and the surprise it might cause to be woken this way, but about what I could manage in my own weary state. Mary didn't understand and pushed past me, less cautious. "Oh, I wake her all the time—she always goes right back to sleep." My sister gave my daughter a little shake. "Helen, look here. Mommy's come back."

Helen opened her eyes and smiled at Mary. Then she saw me and started to cry. I was scaring her, as I had feared.

"Helen, darling," I said, leaning forward and touching her shoulder, "I know I look different, but it's me. I've come home."

My daughter pulled away. Mary reached out and took her hand. "I'll get her back to sleep," she said. "We'll do this in the morning."

I bent forward and kissed Helen again and then got up to face whatever was waiting down below. I could hear conversation, but as I came down the stairs, it stopped. Father was awake now, and he, at least, was happy to see me. He stiffly rose from his chair and kissed me on the cheek. Mother, John, and Sarah looked on.

"The return of the prodigal son," said John, landing hard on the final word.

I turned to him. "Aren't you a little glad I've come back?"

"It depends on how disgraced you are."

"Disgraced?"

"Yes. You went away with a man?"

I wanted to throw something. "I did not."

John forced a small laugh. "If you didn't, then it's probably because you think you are one." I was standing there in his clothes, so there was little I could say to that.

"Men's work?" asked Mother, as though there could be no reason for it.

"Well, what would you have me do, Mother? Stay on with old Winthrop for a dollar a week? Marry him? Would that make you happy?"

My mother wasn't moved. "It was you who wanted to marry George Slater," she said. "Couldn't wait. Wouldn't listen to anyone. You made that bed."

It was unkind to throw George Slater in my face, but she was right. It was my doing and no one else's. But the meanness in the room wasn't my doing, and I had no way to meet it. Afraid I might cry, I turned and ran back up to Mary's room. She was asleep with Helen, or nearly so. I lay down on the rug beside the bed. I hadn't slept in two days, but still it was hard in coming, as bits and pieces of pointed conversation drifted up from below.

* * *

Neither Mary nor Helen was in the room when I woke. It was already light and I rose with the hope that a night's sleep might have made everyone more kind. But downstairs, Mother looked at me and didn't even give a good-morning. "Why are you wearing your brother's clothes?"

I tried to stay even. "You've seen me in these. I've worn them before."

"Yes," she answered, "when you were working in the barn."

"Well then, it's no great sin if I wear them, is it?"

Mother's face began to color. "I want you out of them right now."

"She can have the clothes," said John from across the room. "She can wear them all the time if that's what she wants. But she won't be any sister of mine. I'll not be laughed at by the whole town."

My brother was eighteen now, and I could see no trace of the little boy I had once loved, the boy I used to carry on my back and roll with in the grass. And if he fell and scraped his knee, I would run to him with a funny face to make him laugh again. Why had he turned against me? Because I was the oldest? Or was it because Father had taught me to shoot and ride and play the violin, things that other girls were not taught by their fathers?

I hadn't come back to Basket Creek with the idea of staying in men's clothes. I hadn't had time to think about it. But now everyone was telling me what to do, and I didn't like it. I looked at my mother and dug in my heels. "I'll dress myself."

From across the room, the woman who had brought me into this world met my eyes and answered with words as hard as river ice. "Then you can't stay here."

I knew that Father wouldn't let that stand. He loved me and had always told me that no matter how big I got, I would never stop being his little girl. While I was away in Honesdale, my memories of him had been from the past—when he would grab me with his strong arms and throw me into the air as I shrieked with laughter. I remembered peeking at him in the candle-light as he unwrapped his rifle to go out with the farmer's militia. Mother begged him not to go—men had been killed—but Father said it was the right thing to do. I felt proud of him and wished I could go with him.

I turned to my father and saw a man I hardly knew. I had not let him grow old in my mind, and so now, suddenly, he had aged twenty years. He was not a man on horseback with a rifle strapped to his shoulder; he was a man in a chair holding a pipe in a hand that couldn't stop its shake.

Father understood that it was for him to speak, so he set aside the pipe and sat forward. "Let's all just calm down now," he said, "and come to our senses." The room was still. He had said the sensible thing, which we all expected. Now he would proclaim the law and say that I could never be cast out of the house. But he didn't. He didn't say anything else, and what he had said was meaningless. He might as well have told the sky to stop raining.

I forgave my father—his hearing wasn't good, and I don't think he had understood much of what was being said. And even if everyone did calm down, what good would it do? Soon William Patterson would be back from Honesdale with stories about me, for surely he now knew, even if he hadn't recognized me on Main Street, which most likely he had. And what would Mother or John say once they heard that I had been betrothed, or nearly so, to a young woman in Honesdale? What would anyone say? My daughter would hear her mother taunted and mocked, the fodder for a year's worth of Reverend Hale sermons. I couldn't possibly stay. I had nowhere to sleep and no prospects for work—not teaching children, that was now sure. And I wasn't going to marry Raspy Winthrop. I'd sooner die a long, cold death, but not in Long Eddy, where everyone could watch.

My eyes dropped to the floor. "I'll go."

I went out to the woodshed and took my rifle from its hiding place in the rafters. When I returned, Helen was on the far side of the room. She had been in the kitchen with Mary and had heard everything. She knew I was leaving and that she was not. Indeed, no one thought otherwise. I had little money and nowhere to go. And who could say what would become of me? I could sleep under a bridge and not eat for days, but would it be right to do that to Helen? I was the one without a home, not her.

I called to my daughter to come say good-bye. She stayed by the kitchen door, face twisted. She had not forgiven me, and why should she?

My heart fell apart like wet bread. It may have shown, for all at once Helen crossed the room. I went to my knees and gathered her to me.

"Helen, dearest, I have to go away again."

Her arms tugged at me. "Will you come back, Mommy?"

"Of course I'll come back," I said, wanting it to be so. "But if something should happen and I don't, you must always know that I love you." I pushed back and met her dark eyes. "Helen—always know that your mother loves you."

I cried on the road to Long Eddy. I had lost everything and everyone. Helen, Mary, Father, Lydia, and yes, even Mother, Sarah, and John. Without them, what was left of me? And where could I go?

I stopped and watched the night's rain rush down the creek, following a leaf through the riffles, as though it were a boat that could take me to a new place, a place where no lumberman from Long Eddy would find me. And what would I do when I got there?

Suddenly by the creek, it came to me. I'd do what Lydia and I had planned. I'd raise horses.

16

"PULL THE DAMN captain out of the whorehouse!" shouted one man.

"Let's get on with it!" called another.

We were on the wharf in Davenport, and people were making their opinions known. The object of scorn, the steamboat *War Eagle*, sat before us, two days late in departure. I think the crew on the riverboat found the fuss amusing. They could have come out and told us we would leave that morning, but instead they started feeding the boilers. When the first smoke appeared, a ragged cheer rose up. The mate came on to the upper deck, but he wouldn't speak until all were quiet. "Listen well," he said. "We'll begin loadin' up the fore plank, but only them with cabin passage. The rest of you'll wait." A groan came from those who had pushed to the front. I was at the back, so I didn't care.

I had come to Iowa by way of Cincinnati, where I had spent the winter washing dishes and mopping floors—guarding my money, not afraid to sleep cold or miss a meal. When the weather turned in March, I traveled to Davenport. There I bought common passage on a steamer that would take me to St. Paul, a graceful side-wheeler that had an upper deck with rooms that rich people could sleep in.

Once the cabin passengers were on and safely tucked away, the rest of us were allowed to board. Up we went, and to watch the crush, you might have thought we were staking claims for gold. But it was berths we were looking for, and when I got inside, I discovered that they were stacked two high with little room between. Most of the bunks had been taken, but I did find a lower one that was empty and no worse than the others. Then a hand grabbed me from behind. "That there would be mine. I seen it first." I turned to see a heavy man with sores on his mouth. I glanced about for another place.

"No! He was here before you." The words had come from a strapping young man on the bunk above, a clean-shaven fellow with determined eyes. The heavy man shrugged and went away.

"Thank you," I said. "I'm Joseph Lobdell."

The young man gave a nod. "Owen Carter. What puts you on the river?"

"Oh, I'm running away." My foolish candor had invited the next certain question, but Mr. Carter didn't ask it. He just said something about doing the same and went back to reading what looked like a letter. I stowed my things and glanced about. No cough or snore or anything else was going to be private, and any changing of clothes would be under the covers. Still, I was aboard and would be heading north within the hour.

When the whistle blew, everyone ran outside to watch. The boat shuddered as the great wheels began to dig at the water. Out into the river we went, and soon Davenport passed out of sight, as did all of civilization. A little later, the mate called everyone on the lower deck inside. Once we were all squeezed in, he stepped up on a box so we all could see him.

"All right, you flop-eatin' wharf rats," he said, "you're now citizens of your own little country. Here the captain is God, and I'm the archangel. And so long as we're out on the river, we don't have to answer to the bloody governor of Iowa or nobody." The mate smiled and showed his bad teeth. "Now listen well, 'cause I'll say this once. If you are so much as seen on the deck above, you'll wish your mother had never bared her arse to your pa."

These words were plain enough. Everyone understood that to the Minnesota Packet Company we were no better than cargo. Worse than cargo, because we moved about and had certain needs, whereas cargo remained where it was. When the mate left, a few people said choice things. Then most of us went back outside to look at the swampy woods and the occasional shack with chickens and dirty children—grown men too, doing nothing but sitting on stumps and watching the river.

I walked to the steamer's back end where I found a dozen bales of burlap stacked against the cabin. I climbed up on one and made a nest for myself. Then I untied my bag and brought out my violin. The instrument had done well for me in Honesdale, but not since then. In Cincinnati, the saloons didn't take to the fiddle. The same was true in Davenport. And a day earlier, on the wharf, I had stopped an officer of the *War Eagle* and asked if the company might like me to entertain the passengers. The man looked at me like I had mange.

"I'm sure you'd love to get on the cabin deck," he said, curling his lip. "Love to get your hands in people's pockets too, I'd bet."

I sat on the back of the *War Eagle* and began to play the violin. I would entertain myself and the common folk. A few of those nearby leaned back and closed their eyes as though the music were bringing them to another place. It did the same for me, the place being the glass factory on Dyberry Creek.

I had not seen Lydia in eight months, yet all through the winter I had thought of her. I wanted to write. I wanted to speak my heart and make my apology. But I knew that I should not—I shouldn't appear in her life again in any form, so she could go forward with the fewest reminders of my deceit. I was a deceiver and a liar. I couldn't deny it.

But one part of that burden I no longer carried. I didn't struggle any more with what it all meant. Whether I had loved Lydia as a man loves a woman or if I was just an oddity of nature—none of it mattered. I was not looking for a husband, nor was I looking for a wife. I could not imagine loving anyone other than Lydia. Women who were not Lydia held no more interest for me than men did. For whatever reason, I had loved her. Now she was gone.

And gone also was any love-fevered notion of having become a man. I hadn't become a man and didn't want to. What I wanted were the freedoms that came with being a man. I wanted to work for pay and come and go as I pleased—those privileges and others that came to me so long as I was wearing britches and addressed as Mr. Lobdell. And in that disguise, I sat on the back of the *War Eagle* and played a dozen songs. Then a young man in ship's uniform appeared.

"Please come with me," he said. With some dread, I put my violin in my bag and followed him up the stairs to where I had been told not to go. I didn't think they were going to hang me from the yardarm, but I did think I was to be taken to task for playing music without the mate's permission. But when we got topside, the young man showed me to a chair in the forward parlor and told me that if I were to play the violin, I could eat my dinner with those on the cabin deck.

How had this come about? Perhaps some passengers above had inquired as to why those below were being entertained while they who had paid more were not. I thought it best not to ask and instead offered my hand. "Joseph Lobdell."

The young man took it grudgingly. "Mickey Harrelson."

"And what's your position?" I asked, seeking to be polite.

"Mud clerk."

I couldn't tell from his manner if this were a real position or if he was just having fun with me. "Forgive my ignorance," I said, "but what is a mud clerk?"

Mr. Harrelson shrugged as if to say it was not a position of importance. "I check everything that comes on or off the boat. Match it with the bills of lading."

"And you like working on the river?"

"Yes, I want to be a captain someday." Mr. Harrelson's eyes drifted out to the gray water. "Of course, when I was a boy, all I dreamt about was being a pilot. He is higher than the captain, you know."

"But that's not your dream now?"

The young man shook his head. "And it wouldn't be yours neither. You recall that girl in school who could spell every word, no matter how long it was?"

"I do," I said, holding back a smile.

"Well, to be a pilot you need a memory better than that, 'cause you need to know every snag and wreck for a thousand miles of river, see in the dark, and talk to God too."

Just then there was some shouting down below. Mr. Harrelson frowned. "It's like this every year. The first trip upriver is ugly. When they lower the plank in St. Paul, there'll be a crush worse than at Davenport, as though they think they're going to race to the Suland and claim the best piece for themselves. What's your business in Minnesota?"

I gave the mud clerk a big grin. "I'm racing to the Suland."

"Whatever for?" he asked, as if there could be no world beyond the river.

"I want to raise horses."

This was the first time those words had passed my lips, and I felt the thrill of it. Mr. Harrelson gave a slow nod that I took as cautious approval.

* * *

A little after the noon hour, the *War Eagle* tied up to a flatboat filled with cut wood. The mate blew a whistle, and half a dozen men appeared, among them Owen Carter, the young man who bunked above me. Their job was to carry wood onto the steamer. They did this in return for rights to the grub pile, a disgusting mound of leftovers set out for the crew.

The mate yelled and cursed at the men to work faster, though none that I could see was being lazy. Then, out of nowhere, he gave Owen a shove. Owen stumbled and almost dropped his wood. He righted himself and looked hard at the mate. The mate's smile became wide, as though inviting him to do something. Owen paused but then turned and continued on with the wood. The mate was called away, and that was the end of it.

Late in the afternoon a raw wind drove many people back into the parlor. There was not a great deal of society on the boat, the season being early, but what there was sought to gently advertise itself. Where one sat and with whom became a subtle dance. I watched from my chair and played songs, and because the words were not sung, I could play whatever I liked. I even played a certain song about a mule's private parts, sweetly, as though it were a waltz.

But all displayed gentility came apart upon the clang of the dinner bell. The women were given their own table in the back parlor, and when I saw the manners displayed by the men, the reaching and grabbing, I understood why.

Beyond providing my dinner, my duties upstairs gave me access to the cabin water closets—far superior to anything below. There I was able to wash in private with a basin of warm water. And as to the fear of being discovered, I felt in less danger on the riverboat than I had in Honesdale. On the *War Eagle,* everyone was out of place, so I wasn't an object of interest. And I had been living as a man for a year and no longer looked at people for that extra moment to see if they suspected me. I continued to speak from the back of my throat, but I had already found that it's not the pitch that makes words manly. It's the certainty, deserved or not.

I stayed late on the cabin deck that first night, and when I went down, the lower deck was dark. I found my bunk and made myself as comfortable as I could. I had barely gotten settled when I heard a low growl. "He touches me again, I'll slug him one." It was Owen Carter, speaking, it seemed, to himself.

"Don't do it," I said, knowing he was talking about the mate. "That's what he wants."

"I don't care."

"He can have you whipped," came a voice from across the aisle.

There was a brief silence. Then Owen's voice. "He just better be careful."

* * *

The next day, the small, green leaves changed into buds as we headed north and backward in season. A person had to be well wrapped to stay outside. When the wind picked up or a shower fell, those on the cabin deck retreated to the parlor, which was warmed by stoves at either end.

Around noon the boat put in at Galena. The men were called to wood-up, and once again, the mate began to berate them for no apparent reason, calling them women, among other insults. I kept my eye on Owen from the deck above, though the mate didn't seem to pay him special attention. But when Owen passed on his third run, the mate stuck out his foot and tripped him. Owen fell against the cabin wall, and the mate laughed for all to see. I had seen the whole thing and it was done with purpose. I had the sudden thought that the mate did this on each voyage, picked some strong young man to humiliate—to show that in his position he could do whatever he liked. The normal chatter on that side of the boat stopped as everyone watched to see what would happen next.

Owen once again righted himself without a protest as though nothing were out of the ordinary. Without looking at anyone he rearranged the wood he was carrying, and I hoped that this meant that he was going to continue on without any trouble. And that's the way it seemed it would go. But once the wood was secure, instead of moving away, Owen stepped toward the mate and for a long moment looked him in the eye. The mate wasn't smiling now, appearing uncertain himself as to what was in store. Then, without any change in expression to serve as warning, Owen dropped the wood. The heavy pieces fell, and the mate's sudden attempt to pull his feet back made the top half of him lurch forward. In this posture he received Owen's fist, the contact making an awful, cracking noise.

The mate screamed in pain and fell back against the rail and then down onto the deck, blood gushing from his nose. In a matter of moments it was all over the place. The mate managed to raise a bloody hand and point at Owen. "Get him."

The men nearby remained still as their arms were full and they owed the mate nothing but wood. Then several burly crewmen appeared out of the boiler room. Seeing them, Owen turned and ran to the back of the boat. Next thing, he was up on the rail, leaping across six feet of water onto the wharf where he landed hard and was grabbed by a constable.

"Bring that man on board," screamed the mate, spluttering blood. "He assaulted an officer!" The constable looked up and said nothing. "Bring him up here, I say!"

"I seen what happened," the constable said. "This man is in the State of Illinois and will stay in my custody."

The mate might have made a bigger fuss, but his nose was broke. He was brought up to the officer's quarters from where you could still hear his cries and cursing. I ran down to the main deck and then inside where I found someone stuffing Owen's bag. It was Josiah Johnson, who slept across the aisle, a man traveling with his wife and two boys. I rolled Owen's blanket and followed Josiah out the riverside door. We made our way around the back and then worked forward to where, below, Owen stood beside the constable, no longer in his grasp.

* * *

When I came on deck the third morning, I saw that everything had changed. The river no longer looked like a river. It was miles across and surrounded by turrets and bluffs. I found Mr. Harrelson by the rail.

"What is this?"

"Lake Pepin," he said. "The Dakotas call it the Lake of Tears." He stopped there, leaving it to me to ask him *why* they call it the Lake of Tears. Mr. Harrelson gave a sly smile. "They are said to have cried 'cause they didn't murder the first white men who came upon it." I laughed. Mr. Harrelson then pointed to the far shore. "That's Maiden Rock."

I looked over to a piece of high land with a cliff facing the water. "Is it a famous place?"

"Oh yes. An Indian girl is said to have thrown herself off. She was to be married but loved another."

I looked again at the precipice and the jagged rocks below it. "And the brave she loved?" I asked. "Did he follow her over the cliff?"

The mud clerk gave a shrug. "I never heard anything about that."

The boat moved forward that night with no turns or shudders, as we were still on the lake. When done with the violin, I stayed topside and watched the men play poker. The game took place at a round table near a sign that said, "Gambling on the *War Eagle* is strictly forbidden." I already knew from Mickey Harrelson that the sign was there only so a man couldn't complain to the captain if he woke in the morning with his land stake gone.

I was familiar with poker from my time at Blandin's. Nothing at all to the rules—some hands were higher than others, and the high hand won. The real game was in making people think something that wasn't true. If you had good cards, you wanted others to think that they weren't that good, and sometimes, at just the right moment, you could win with nothing at all. It was a game where a man's nerve and a woman's keen eye might work well together, but I never dared play at Blandin's—I was too busy being the little brother.

I watched for a time, gaining a sense of how each man played—whether he liked to bluff or just ride his luck. Then a man got up and said he was done for the night. I waited to see if his chair would be taken. When it wasn't, I took it and said the words I'd been itching to say all those months at Blandin's. "Deal me in."

A certain quickening of the pulse comes with sitting at a table and gambling with money—a feeling of danger and sensation. I could see the tightness in faces, feel the heat off bodies. I felt the vibration in the floor and was aware that this room of peeling elegance was floating into the wilderness. I had climbed into man's sacred cave.

Thirty dollars was what I gave myself to play with, one quarter of what I still had. My first few hands were so bad that I got out of the way in a hurry. Then I got lucky and won two hands. The pots were not large, but suddenly I was working with other people's money. Only two at the table played with caution. The others were just loudmouths. When they won, they acted like they were born clever, and when they lost, they took pains to show how put upon they were by fate. Some drank too much. The conversation became coarse.

"The first redskin I see," said a heavy man across the table, "I'm gonna shoot'im right out. Don't care if it's no squaw, neither." There was laughter, as though he had told a funny story.

"Why shoot 'em," said another man whose eyes were red, "when you can sell 'em whiskey at any price?"

"And get what?" said the heavy man. "Some stinking shells or last year's jerky?"

That was the prelude to another game of seven stud. By the fourth card up, the heavy man opposite me had two jacks and two fives showing. I had a king, two sevens, and an eight showing. Underneath I had a jack and a nine. I shouldn't have even been there, but I did have possibilities and my winnings had made me a little reckless.

The man with the two pair bet five dollars, as though he already had what he needed underneath, only four of us still in. The man to my right dropped out with a show of disgust, as though some good friend had let him down. I had already decided to fold, but then I noticed the man to my left scowl. He should have stayed still. If he was leaving, I had a chance. I called, and the man to my left tossed his cards. It was down to me and the heavy man across the table.

The two pair looked real good, sitting there like eggs in a pan. But I didn't think their owner had anything else. He was the bragging kind, and if he had the full house, he'd be getting ready to crow like a rooster. It wasn't there. That was good as far as it went, but he still had me beat. I needed a seven, a ten, a jack, or a king. Any one of those would win the hand for me—I was almost sure. I had one of his jacks, and I had seen one of his fives earlier.

When the final card came, I lifted its corner. It was a queen and no help. I held my face steady and looked at the man across the table. He wasn't eager to meet my eye, and that told me what I needed to know. Still, he had me beat. But the riddle was his to solve, and he must have been feeling a little naked. Everything he had was there for all to see. And why was I still in? I couldn't be there with just two sevens—the dimmest wit on the boat would know that.

Sensing that he was now the prey, the man tapped his finger to say that he didn't want to bet. It was for me to do it, and I didn't want to push too hard—didn't want him to think that I wanted him gone. And I knew for him it wasn't only the money. He also feared the moment when whatever I had underneath would appear and make him look the fool. I let out a sigh and then put in five dollars as though sorry it had come to this. The man folded. I nodded like he had done the smart thing and tossed my cards face down.

That night I won near forty dollars. And so taken was I by the drama that had I been a man and could have borne the scrutiny, I would have, then and there, become a riverboat gambler.

* * *

The next morning, the rail became prime property, as many wished to get an early view of St. Paul. From a distance, the town looked a little like Cincinnati, perched as it was on several large terraces above the river. At the boat landing we were greeted by every imaginable proposition—land to buy, maps to goldfields, offers of transport, the company of ladies. Everything that one might imagine as a need was offered in fact or fancy.

Lodging in St. Paul was for the rich. Those with little money lived in camps on the land north of town. I bought some bread and smoked buffalo and joined the parade to that meadow, already busy with those who had arrived before us. The end nearer St. Paul was filled with shanties in which people had stayed the winter. Several served as stores, selling just about anything that might be useful. I bought some rope and canvas to make a tent. Others did the same. We moved through the field until we found some open space.

I pitched my tent near that of Josiah and Agnes Johnson. That night we made a common fire and cooked and shared what food we had. After the meal, I took out my violin to celebrate our arrival. Agnes's face brightened when she saw me lift the bow, but every song I played ended up sounding sad. Soon, all of us were sitting quiet, thinking about loved ones left behind.

17

I CAME OUT of my tent at first light to find people standing close to their fires and speaking quietly, each word taking the form of a small cloud. Agnes Johnson offered me a tin cup with sweetened tea. I thanked her and washed down the heel of bread that I had from the day before.

Those in camp with work in St. Paul began their walk to town. Others, like me, went to a wall at the edge of the meadow where offers of work were posted. From these I learned that common labor was paid a dollar a day. Skilled men earned two. There was also work for women, washing or cleaning—this at fifty cents a day, better pay than in Long Eddy.

A notice posted by the *Daily Minnesotian* caught my eye. The newspaper was looking for an apprentice, and I decided to see about it. A short while later I was walking up the rutted road that was Washington Street. From the river St. Paul had looked a little like Cincinnati, but now I saw that it was quite different, and not in a good way. No one in St. Paul, it seemed, built a building and then cleaned up after themselves. Odd boards, shingles, crates, and broken pipes lay about as though they were supposed to melt away with the snow.

The offices of the *Minnesotian* were in a two-story building at the head of the street. I went in and right away came upon an old coot of a man leaning over a table, magnifying glass in hand. He knew I was there but wouldn't look up. I cleared my throat. "Walk to the back and speak to Mr. Owen," he said, never lifting his head.

The door to the back room had a panel of frosted glass with *J. P. Owen* painted on it. I knocked. No answer. I knocked again.

"Hold on to your britches," came a voice from inside. A minute later the door opened, and I was looking at Mr. J. P. Owen himself. I told him that I was answering his notice, and his whiskered face made no effort to be pleasant. "Ever work at a newspaper before?"

"Yes, sir," I said, crossing my fingers. "For Francis Penniman of the *Honesdale Democrat*. In Pennsylvania."

Mr. Owen frowned as though Pennsylvania was not a good state in which to have worked at a newspaper. Then he handed me a broom and told me to sweep the shop. This I did, trying to be swift and thorough. All went well until a tray of cold type hit the floor. One of the typesetters had knocked it over, but I was standing close by. Mr. Owen suddenly appeared, looked at the mess and then at me. I was on the street a minute later— couldn't even tell you what the J. P. stood for.

The following day I answered a notice for kitchen work in the Hotel American. It was at the center of town and easy to find, what with all the fancy carriages lined up in front of it. I entered by the grand door and found myself on a plush carpet in the great lobby. I had never seen the like, even in Albany. Polished brass was everywhere and crystal hung from the ceiling.

I had been there but a moment when a well-dressed gentleman appeared by my side as if by magic. "May I help you?" he said, looking down his long nose. I told the man why I was there, and by his expression he made it plain that I had entered by the wrong door. He then took my elbow and firmly guided me through the lobby, smiling for all to see, as though he were helping an old woman. Once we were out of sight, the smile fell off his face. Through another door and I was handed over to the master of the kitchen.

Alberto Curasco was a heavy man with pocked skin whose words had an odd accent that I later learned was Portuguese. The kitchen was his kingdom, and before he had said a word, I saw him bellow at some unfortunate soul. Then he looked at me and snorted. I peeled potatoes and scrubbed pots the rest of the day.

The rich people who stayed at the American dined in its grand parlor that could seat a hundred. The fare was beef, buffalo, chicken, or pork served with potatoes, cabbage, and greens. Pies and cakes were offered for dessert, and Mr. Curasco was pleased when I showed some ability with butter and flour.

At the end of the day, Mrs. Johnson always had a large kettle simmering with soup. She made enough for her family and half a dozen others, nearby men who paid for their dinners. This gave me an idea, for there was much discarded food at the American. I introduced Mrs. Johnson to Mr. Curasco, and the two made an arrangement. Twice a day, the Johnson boys would arrive at the back of the hotel and leave a little later hauling buckets filled with scraps. Soon, the Johnsons had an eatery. Dinners of thick soup and bread were fifteen cents, and in a matter of days, they had to turn people away.

During this time I purchased, among other items, a strop and folding razor. Twice a week or so, I would stand outside my tent and run the blade over my face, making the contorted expressions and careful motions of a man who had something to shave. This must have looked real enough, for no one said a thing, one way or another. And what was the worst someone could think? That I was a young man eager for the rituals of manhood? That was a common enough story, and one that would do me no harm.

* * *

I worked in St. Paul six days out of seven. At night I found companionship in camp, either helping at the Johnsons' eatery or playing the violin by the fire. The violin always brought memories of home, and these were not easy for me—more difficult still, because I had not yet written. It was well past time, but I was afraid. Not afraid as I had been in Honesdale, that my brother or someone would come find me, but rather afraid that my two lives, the one before and the one now, were so different that they could never touch, or if they did, something bad would come of it. Finally guilt overcame fear, and I sat one night at Mrs. Johnson's table and wrote a letter to my daughter.

> Dear Helen. I am in Minnesota Territory. Perhaps Mary can show you on a map where that is. There are redskin Indians out here, though I have seen only a few as I am working in a big town called St. Paul. Soon, I'll go west and claim a piece of land and raise horses. Perhaps someday you will come, and we can ride together. I miss our woods and our home on Basket Creek. Most of all, I miss you, my darling. I don't know when I will see you again, but please know that you are always in my heart. Mind Grandma and Grandpa, and give everyone a big hug for me. Your loving mother.

I put down the pen, unhappy with what I had written. But I had no idea of what else to say. And it wasn't as though I had told lies. I was in St. Paul and would go west and raise horses. And if I could tame the land, then Helen might join me on ground that would someday be hers. This was the hope. With a farm I might, in some small way, still be true to Helen, and even to Lydia. But carving a farm out of the wilderness was no small thing—witness the steady stream of men and women flowing back into St. Paul, people who had hurried west in high spirits and returned in rags. I thought it best to find a situation.

Each day I searched the notice board for work that might take me west. There were occasional calls for carpenters or blacksmiths, but most notices were for work in St. Paul. In the meantime, I went to bed each night with food in my belly and a dollar richer, money I would need later, even if the land were free. And so the summer passed, till I began to think that I would travel west the following spring.

* * *

One morning on a free day in September, I saw a notice that offered two hundred dollars for guarding a claim over the winter in a place called Kandiyohi. Curious, I followed the directions to a building with a painted sign:

WHITE BEAR LAND CO. I opened the door and came in on five hard-faced men leaning over what seemed to be a map.

A man with thick arms and curly hair took a step forward as though to block my view. "What do you want?"

I took a step back. "I saw your notice to guard a claim."

The man came toward me, put his hand on my shoulder and hurried me outside. Once on the street, he looked me over without a smile. "So you want the job?"

"I might," I said. "Where is this place? And how do you say it?"

I suppose I wasn't the first to ask that question, 'cause the man laughed and then kindly broke the word into four syllables. "It's sixty miles due west," he said, "but to get there you need to go north to St. Cloud."

"Is it good land? Good for horses?"

The man laughed again. "Sure it is, but the land you'd be sittin' is spoken for."

"And what will I live in?"

"Well it's log and not sod, if that's what you're wonderin'. It's got an iron stove, and you and the other man will be well supplied. Your partner is already out there. What can you say for yourself?"

I thought and then remembered something my father used to say. "Well, sir, I always try to finish what I start and do what I say I'm gonna do."

The man nodded his approval and told me his name was Tom Flynn. He then asked if I had a rifle. I said that I did and could hit a squirrel at forty yards. I think Mr. Flynn liked that answer, because he asked me again if I wanted the job.

Despite his gruff manners, there was something about Flynn I liked. And I believed him about the cabin and the supplies, so I put out my hand. If all went well, I'd come away with two hundred dollars and be that much closer to getting my own place. But why did it pay so much? And why did I need my rifle?

"Not meaning to pry," I said, "but just what's so valuable out there? I mean, that you'd need to guard it."

Flynn paused and looked around. "I'll tell you, but not until we're on the trail. I'll be going with you and the last wagon." We agreed to meet in two days, and I walked away wondering what it could be. A vein of gold?

I returned to our camp and found Agnes Johnson tending three pots of soup. "You're home early," she said, looking to see if I was walking steady.

"I'm leaving," I said, proudly. "Going west to guard a claim."

Mrs. Johnson gave a sad look. "We'll miss you, Joseph. But I know you'll do well out there."

I had known her only a few months, often sitting with her by the fire after the dinner was served. Sometimes I'd play checkers with her boys, and perhaps that had something to do with it, but in some small way I think Agnes Johnson had come to adopt me. In that moment, I wished she really were my mother, or rather wished my mother were more like her.

I put up a sign asking twenty dollars for the tent and the spot which in four months had become a good one, the shanty town having grown. I had it sold by dark and made ten dollars' profit on land that wasn't mine. I could have made twenty.

18

TOM FLYNN AND I traveled by coach to St. Anthony, where we boarded a steamer heading north. Two days later we were in St. Cloud, a poor cousin to St. Paul, but its streets were busy with people and wagons. We took rooms in a small hotel, all paid for by the White Bear Company. At dinner we sat at a table and ate buffalo. Flynn finished his before I was half done and ordered another plate. He dug into that one as though it were his first.

For all his appetite, Tom Flynn was only a little heavy in the belly. His face was heavy too with scars from years of scraping it with a blade. This was his third trip since spring to Kandiyohi, and he'd been there twice the year before. He said he was from Ohio and had come to St. Paul when it was still called Pig's Eye.

"Nobody back home thought Tom Flynn would amount to nothin'," he said, pointing his fork. "Someday, when this is done, I just might pay their fare so they can come out and see."

"See what?" I said, thinking I might get Flynn to tell me what I'd been hired to guard. He smiled and said nothing. Just then, something touched my leg. I looked down to see a scrawny, three-colored cat making a sad appeal for food. I slipped her a piece of buffalo, and she ate it in a single swallow. Then I heard a sharp yell, and the cat ran for the door. The hotel keeper came over. "She won't stay out of here," he said by way of apology. "I'm gonna have to shoot her."

Five minutes later the cat was at my feet again. I looked at Flynn. "Can

I take her?" He raised his eyes as though I were a soft-hearted fool. I took that for a yes and carried the cat to my room. I put her on the bed, and she lay with her paws outstretched. I named her Cleopatra.

In the morning, Flynn and I met up with two men and a heavily loaded wagon. We headed out of St. Cloud on the rough road that went south, my bag and rifle on the wagon, as was Cleo, who, already certain of my devotion, watched as Flynn and I walked behind. Until this moment, my travels in Minnesota had been on the river. Now I was walking through new land and breathing its ripe smells. It was an odd patchwork of woods and grassland, the forest and prairie, meeting and claiming what they could, the swamps taking the rest. The trees were familiar, maple and ash, oak and cherry, but there were no sudden rocky rises like there were in New York. And other than the ruts in the road, there was no sign that men, white men, had yet lived on this land—and they hadn't, because until recently it had all been Indian land. There had been a treaty—some sort of payment. But had everyone agreed? Were there savages still out there? Flynn's men had their rifles loaded and within reach.

At midday we stopped to rest. I sat on a log next to Flynn and told him it was time. What was this about?

Tom Flynn gave a boyish smile and replied with a question. "Well, are you ready to be the very first citizen of the future capital of all the Northwest?" I didn't know what he was talking about.

"Next month," he continued, "White Bear will file a plan for a new city. It's to be called Kandiyohi, after the county it's in. When Minnesota becomes a state, it'll need a new capital—something in the center, not over by Wisconsin. If the lines get drawn the way we think, Kandiyohi will be sittin' pretty."

I wasn't sure I had heard him right. "And you'll own all the land?"

Flynn shook his head. "We've given a lot of it away already, or rather promised it. But there's plenty to go around."

My employer was clearly pleased with himself, and I was not put off. I liked this scheme. It gave me confidence that we would be well supplied. *The capital of all the Northwest.* It had a ring to it, and I'd be the mayor of the place, at least for the winter. In that moment, my dream of raising horses fell away, and I imagined myself an important person in this new city. Maybe in a few years, I too would be inviting people to come out and see it. And I liked that I wasn't going to be guarding gold or something that people might want to take from me. Who would want to steal some plain, ordinary land when you couldn't take it anywhere, and there was so much of it to start with? When I asked this of Flynn, he said that his company had spent a lot of money on this city already, and he didn't want to come out in spring and find someone else on the land. It was my job, mine and my partner's, to make sure that didn't happen.

We headed south again in the afternoon. And spending every hour with Flynn and company introduced a new problem. Certainly, I could find the time and place to relieve myself in private, but I soon saw that simply peeing in private wasn't enough. Once out of town, men peed quite casually in the presence of one another, usually just turning and facing a tree or a bush. If I didn't do this, it would, after a time, appear strange.

And so that afternoon I began to pretend to pee like a man, something I never had to do in Honesdale. I would stop on the trail when Flynn was a short distance ahead, turn my back and face a tree. I would spread my legs, throw back my shoulders, and engage my hands, the left holding my trousers, the right feigning the more specific task. I was amused by the playacting and wished, not for the first time, that I had a hose for this purpose, it being opportune.

Late in the day we came upon a broad meadow where another track came in from the south. Already there, at the far end, was a great camp with a large circle of wagons. We set up on the near end, but I could hear the beat of drums and the notes of what I thought were flutes.

"What in heaven's name is that?" I asked.

Flynn laughed. "The Bois Brûlés."

"Who are the Bwaa Brulay?" I said, imitating the sound of his words.

"Go and find out. They're friendly."

Curiosity got to me, and I went over to their camp. A double circle of wagons, perhaps forty, formed the outer rim. I had never seen the like.

They were carts, really, with only one axle and wheels taller than myself. The rails and spokes were made of bent wood. Not one piece of metal anywhere.

Inside the circle, men and women danced around a large fire. The men wore coarse blue jackets with brass buttons and red sashes. Their jaunty caps had tassels, and their leggings were decorated with beads and quills. The women wore similar decoration. They were every shade of brown, and among them were some of the most handsome people I had ever laid eyes on. They talked in a strange language and laughed loudly, which is pretty much the same everywhere.

The music came from mouth harps, flutes, and drums. It wasn't so much a melody as a repetition of chords and rhythms. After nodding along for a while, I took out my violin and joined them, earning smiles all around. Later, waving, I bade them good night.

I returned to our camp and found Flynn by the fire. "So who are they?"

"The answer to that question," he said, poking the coals, "will make some men rich. I plan to be one of them." He kept me in the dark for another moment and then relented. "They come from Pembina, along the Manitoba border. They're the descendants of fur trappers, Frenchies and Scots mostly with Cree and Ojibwa women. Beautiful to look at, wouldn't you say?"

"They have their own tribe? How many are there?"

"Maybe four or five thousand."

I looked at my employer in disbelief.

"Well, those old trappers were hardy fellows," he said, "and they'd settle down for the winter with two or three wives. And that goes back a hundred years. So after a time, there were lots of these creatures, neither white nor Indian. They started making their own babies and talking this talk that's half Cree, half Frenchie, and half whatever those Scotties talk. Once a year they make the trip to St. Paul to trade their hides and wheat. It's like the circus comin' to town."

"And their name?"

"Bois Brûlés? Means burnt wood—refers to their color."

"How will they make you rich?" I asked, fearing he planned to make slaves of them.

Flynn glanced about, as though the trees might steal his secret. "They will make me rich if they are real people, which I assert to you that they are."

"They seemed quite real to me," I said, not knowing how they could be otherwise.

Flynn put out his knobby hand and shook mine as though I had promised him my vote. "My friend," he said, "I'm glad to hear you say that, for if the Bois Brûlés are real people, as I say they are and you do too, then Minnesota is near the number of souls it needs to become a state. Now remember Indians don't count, but nothin's been decided on the Bois Brûlés—after all, they're part white. And since the sooner we become a state the better, folks have suddenly become open-minded on the question."

Flynn let it lie there, while I tried to solve the riddle. I couldn't.

"It's a matter of simple geometry," he said. "To count the Bois Brûlés, you have to draw the lines north to Pembina, and that makes a Minnesota with Kandiyohi smack in the middle. I'm very fond of these people."

Tom Flynn was unabashed. If the Brois Brûlés were judged real then his plan would succeed. And was there anything wrong with this? I couldn't see it if there were. I was sure that those with whom I'd just played music wished to be thought of as real. And right there, I began wishing for it too, thinking it might be good for me.

* * *

We reached Forest City late the following day. It wasn't a city; it was barely a town. But it did have a small inn, and that's where we stayed. At dinner that evening, Flynn and I shared a table with a young couple, Elijah and Loretta Woodcock. They had been married for a year but were only recently reunited, as Loretta had come west to join her husband in a cabin he had just finished.

Loretta Woodcock was plainly clothed but painfully beautiful. Her dark hair fell upon her shoulders in long curls, and I found myself stealing looks. Elijah Woodcock talked proudly about the land they were going to settle in a place called Green Lake. "There'll be a town there someday soon," he said, "and we'll own some nice pieces as our pay for sitting it this winter."

Mrs. Woodcock tried to look happy as her husband described the new land, but behind her stiff smile was fear. And why not? What sensible woman would not be afraid of such isolation—more so if she were to become with child. "I didn't think I'd be so well fed in the wilderness," she said, trying to be polite.

"Well, this is the end of the line," said Flynn. "It's all heathen land from here on. You know what they say: *No church west of St. Cloud. No God west of Forest City.*" Everyone made an effort to laugh, but the best Loretta Woodcock could do was to hide a grimace. I wanted to kick Flynn under the table. In the silence that followed, I thought about the land before us and about those who had lived there. And about how all of us at the table were searching for our dreams on land that once held theirs.

We set out the next morning on a route that went west, then south. The track was crude and our progress slow. Late the following day, we came upon a newly built cabin in a grove of box elder. "This is Noah White's place," said Flynn as we stopped before it. "We're nine miles further on."

The door to the cabin opened, and Mr. White came out to greet us. He was a solid fellow with large preacher hands and an odd roll to his gait, as though one leg were shorter than the other. He and Flynn laughed and slapped each other on the back. Flynn had brought Mr. White some supplies, and for dinner we had new potatoes and cooked pork, fresh out of a barrel. During the meal Mr. White took to teasing Flynn about his venture. "Why is any senator going to vote to come to this wilderness? They like their whiskey and their women."

Flynn laughed. "The great motivator," he said, pointing toward the ceiling as though the motivator was God, though we all knew that it wasn't.

"I suppose you'll be running for Senate yourself next year."

Flynn shook his head. "I'm going to do fine when the building starts," he said. "Just about everything that comes out here will come on our wagons. And don't give me that look, Noah. You're makin' the same bet, sitting here for some railroad." Mr. White smiled and didn't argue.

After the dinner I helped Mr. White wash the plates, while Flynn's men went out to sleep under the wagon. Flynn and I were to sleep inside, but before I could put myself under a blanket, Noah asked if I would play a game of checkers, seeing as how we would be neighbors soon. I agreed and we sat at the table as Cleo looked on. Noah won the first game, but I fixed him good the second, having learned a few tricks from the Johnson boys in St. Paul.

Next to us on a shelf was a book that I first thought was the Bible. On closer look, I saw it was a book of essays by Mr. Emerson, a man I had heard of but never read. When I was in school, Mr. Emerson's opinions were thought to be unsuited for young minds. I told this to Noah, and he offered to lend me the book.

"Won't you miss it?"

"I know it by heart," he answered. "Just promise that you'd walk across a frozen lake to return it."

"Without fail," I said. We stood and shook hands as though we had agreed to explore Manitoba together.

* * *

We left the cabin at first light and again headed south. The wind picked up, and leaves swirled about us like orange snow. Some hours later, we came out of the woods and stopped on the crest of a small hill.

"There," said Flynn, pointing forward. Up ahead on a rise of its own stood a cabin and behind it, through the trees, a large lake. As we approached, I could see two men stacking wood. Another man came out of the cabin when we arrived. Flynn looked at me. "Joseph, meet your partner."

"Well, I'll be," I said, looking at Owen Carter, whom I had not seen since he broke the mate's nose in Galena. Owen looked at me and smiled as though we had a secret.

"So you two know each other," said Flynn.

"Well, yes, we've met," I said, not sure what I should or shouldn't say.

Flynn seemed satisfied, and he motioned proudly toward the cabin. The logs were of good size and well chinked, just as he said they would be. The roof, however, wasn't done. Flynn saw my eye go there.

"You and Owen will finish it when we leave," he said. "And the door." I nodded, hoping that Owen had more skills with wood than I did.

The men then began to unload supplies: a small cask of nails, several others of wheat flour, lamp oil, corn meal, and sorghum blackstrap. There was a cask of pork and some sacks with dried beans, potatoes, and turnips. I went inside and found that the cabin had a plank floor and the promised iron stove. The two windows on the south side were covered by scraped deerskin.

Before dark, Tom Flynn and I walked up the knoll behind the cabin, stopping when we got to the top. "Guess where you are," he said.

"In Kandiyohi," I answered with new pride.

Flynn nodded. "Yes, but right now you're standing in the rotunda of the statehouse. It will overlook Lake Kasota behind and the capital square in front. Beyond that are the lots themselves—some two thousand already mapped."

I looked out upon this new city and saw not one thing made by man.

19

TOM FLYNN SNAPPED the reins. "See you in the spring," he called as the mules began to pull.

Owen gave a soldier's salute, and I raised my arm in farewell. "Next spring it is."

I thought we might watch Flynn's retreat, but only moments later Owen went behind the cabin and started riving shingles. I didn't want to look lazy, so I began to chop wood. Every minute or so, I would look out to see Flynn and company farther up the track. I wanted to chase after them.

In the afternoon, Owen climbed the roof and started pounding nails. I went inside and tried to clean a summer's cooking off the crusted pots. I had to use a hunting knife. Once the pots were respectable, I swept out the cabin, stoked the stove, and had a crock of beans warm when Owen came down at sunset. He gave an appreciative grunt, after which we ate in silence. Later, we sat in the lamp-light, I oiling my rifle, he carving a walking stick.

"I suppose," I said, "you didn't tell our employers about your mutiny on the river."

"No, I didn't," he said, unable to hide a grin.

"What happened in Galena?"

"Nothin'. Just told to stay out of trouble."

"You came to St. Paul?"

Owen gave a nod. "I worked on the wharf. Then I hooked up with Flynn. What about you?"

"I peeled potatoes at the big hotel."

Owen looked at my rifle. "You any good with that?"

I shrugged. "Been shooting since I was ten."

"Good. You can hunt then. I'll finish the roof."

We didn't talk much after that, and I didn't care. I was happy to be put in charge of something I could do. Beyond that, the hunting would give me opportunities to bathe and wash my clothes.

* * *

I rose early and was outside before the sun was up. Lake Kasota lay silent and gray, its far side hidden by the mist. With rifle strapped to my back, I walked along the shore, in places stepping over the birthroot that grew at wood's edge.

When the mist lifted, I got my first good look at the lake. It was larger than I had thought, stretching on to the east and disappearing behind a point of land. It would take hours to walk around, and if there were swamps along the edge, it could take longer still. I stayed on the near side, which was mainly dry and wooded land with small rises and few rocks. I saw no deer, but on my way back to the cabin, I shot a goose feeding in the pickerel grass.

Owen let out an approving yelp when he saw the bird, and later we sat by the stove and ate goose meat with grease-fried potatoes. Owen went at his plate like he hadn't eaten in a week. "How goes the roof?" I asked.

"Good," he said, wiping his chin on his sleeve. "But I want to get the planks for the door while we have the weather." He laid out his plan, and I said I would go with him in the morning. Then he went back to carving his stick. Didn't ask a thing about my hunting.

The next day we walked to a stand of oak whose leaves had faded but still clung to the branches. Owen picked a young, straight one, lined up the fall, and started in on it with the axe. The chips flew out in perfect order, and without a rest, the cut was made. Owen handed me the axe, and I circled the tree to begin my cut on the opposite side, a little below his. I was a good chopper but not near as strong as he, and when I was only partway in, Owen took back the axe. Soon I heard a loud crack, and the tree fell to the ground, right where he had aimed it.

"Now let's see what we can pry out of 'er," said Owen, taking off his shirt. He began the new cut about seven feet from the first. His shoulders and arms rippled as the axe came down. He was a strapping boy, the kind that had made my heart beat fast when I was a girl. I watched his every swing and felt like a thief. I wondered if later he might take off everything and dive into the lake to cool himself.

Once we had a free log, Owen set to work with a go-devil. In two hours we had three rough boards. We carried them between us, and before the sun was down, Owen had fashioned a door. He made hinges out of harness leather, and we tacked buffalo hide on the jams to keep out the wind.

That night I thought we might celebrate, uncork a conversation or two. But Owen just sat there and whittled his stick, so I decided to whittle mine by finding company with Mr. Emerson. I chose an essay on religion. He wasn't greatly in favor of it. He said we should investigate God's creation on our own, and his words brought to mind that sour apple Reverend Albright. In a wicked moment I wished I could have quoted Emerson during our walks and confirmed his worst suspicions.

* * *

I had been there a little more than a week, but something wasn't right. The silence we sat in was familiar, but Owen wouldn't look at me. I was somewhat acquainted with this as George Slater used to do the same—used to make me ask him to tell me about why he was bothered, instead of just saying it. Finally I had to speak.

"Owen, are you angry that I'm here?"

I thought he would say that he wasn't, but he didn't. Instead he gave me a hard look. "I don't like it when people aren't straight with me."

I felt my blood rush. "Straight with you?"

"You told me you were twenty-five. Probably said the same to Flynn. But you handle an axe like a girl. Probably can't shoot no better, neither. You're no more than twenty."

I wanted to curse, but I stayed even. "Yes. I'm not twenty-five. What's it to you?"

"What else you ain't tellin' me? Why are you in Minnesota?"

I was just about ready to tell him—ready to take my shirt off and let him figure that out. "I told you that true," I said. "I'm running away."

"From what?"

"Well, why you want to know? Want to claim the reward?"

I think that shamed him. "Joseph," he said, now looking at his feet, "I owe you for what you done for me at Galena, throwin' down my stuff an' all—"

"Listen," I said, interrupting, "you don't owe me. You're stronger than I am and can do things I can't. But I can shoot your eyeballs out at a hundred paces, and if you don't think so, we can see to that when the sun comes up. And if you don't want me here, just say so. I'll go back. You're acting like a bellyache. What haven't you told me?"

Owen's eyes avoided mine. "Nothin'," he said. "Nobody's got to go nowhere."

After that night we did better. We found things to talk about, though I was the one who told most of the stories. Owen liked the one about the poker game, and he couldn't get enough of my re-creations of the mate's bloody screams on the deck of the *War Eagle*.

During the day I mostly I hunted on the near side of Lake Kasota. I bagged a couple of rabbits and two more geese, but there wouldn't be any more of them, as they were leaving. I had yet to bring down a deer or even get a good shot at one. So one November morning, I went around the west end of the lake looking for better luck and was rewarded by finding fresh tracks. I was following them when I came upon a small clearing with charred remains. Something had been built there and then burnt. I kept following the deer, but never caught up. When I got back to the cabin, I told Owen about the burned place. He knew about it.

"There was a redskin huntin' lodge out there," he said. "Flynn's men burned it—said the Dakotas had no more rights."

"What if they come expecting it to be there?"

"That's what I said, but it was already burnt."

The two of us then talked about what we might do if there were trouble—how to better secure the door and signals we might give if danger came. Owen said he would make oak bars for the windows, so no one could come in on us while we were sleeping. For my part, I took a liking to a certain stray axe handle—a three-quarter hickory with a doe's foot. Owen laughed as I waved it about, fending off an imagined savage. I held no hatred for the Indians, but I didn't know what they thought about me. And we were very alone—the first of our race to live on this land. Beyond us, there was only the red man and his wilderness. We could travel a thousand miles and not come upon a road or a town or hear any word that we would understand.

* * *

The lake froze in early December, and a quiet fell over the land. Most of the birds had gone, and those that stayed weren't singing for mates. One evening I went out for wood and was stopped by the stillness. Above me the moon was bright, and around it shone a halo, as though announcing the coming of a king. The next morning, long feather clouds reached across the sky. In the afternoon they dissolved into a gray curtain behind which the sun was a dull, yellow spot. Snow began to fall before dark, and when I woke the next morning, it was boot deep and still coming down.

I decided to hunt. Along Basket Creek, I had luck in the snow—tracking game was easy. Taking note of the fresh wind, I put on every piece of clothing I had. An oilcloth draped my shoulders, and a stitched deerskin covered my head.

I walked the near end of the lake and then east along the far shore. I saw no deer. Finally, I crouched in a hollow to get out of the wind. It was snowing harder, and every creature of right mind had taken shelter. Well chilled and thinking to do the same, I turned and started back. Then I thought that I'd save a lot of time, an hour perhaps, by walking across the lake. The ice was strong, so that wasn't a worry, and even though I couldn't see the other side, I was certain I could to go straight enough to land near where I wanted.

I went out onto the frozen lake, not afraid of seeing no land but rather wishing for it. I wanted to float free in a white world. I got my wish soon enough—every feature lost to the snow. The wind came from this way and that, and the flakes danced around in the air. We never think of air as a thing like water, because we can see water and carry water. But now, with the snow giving it form, I could see the air. And I could see that it did not move as one but had swirls and eddies, dances and jigs. And if one thought, as some do, that the souls of those who have gone before still live in the ether around us, then surely I was seeing them as well. Many were out that day, dashing about and having a rather merry time. I supposed that they were all Indian souls, but they seemed to wish me no harm.

And seeing the air this way made me wonder about what other things might be around us—things we cannot see or feel. After all, if we were born without hearing, would we be able to imagine it? And did God even try to give us every sense at birth? Or were there ones He withheld, so we might later be surprised?

The wind swirled around me, and the flakes became tiny buttons that bounced off my sleeve. I thought of the warm stove. I kept going, knowing that I would come upon a familiar shore, but the lake's edge did not appear. I went farther. Nothing. I began to think I had turned somehow and was walking the length of the lake, away from the cabin, so I corrected for that. Still, I found no land. I remembered stories I had heard, stories about men who had gone out to the barn in a storm, their bodies found in the spring.

Finally, I came upon a shoreline, but none of it looked familiar. The snow had changed what little I could see, and for all I knew, I was, once more, on the far side of the lake. By this time my toes and fingers felt numb, but the choice was simple enough—I could go in one direction or the other. If I chose wrong, I would surely spend the night outside with no certainty of waking in the morning. Standing there shivering, I tried to imagine where I was—where the cabin might be. I shut my eyes as though some unknown sense would tell me, and indeed, I felt something glowing off to the right. The other way felt cold. I turned right and began walking through the woods, keeping the flat of the lake in sight. I saw nothing that I recognized, but then what would look familiar? I couldn't see but twenty steps, and with snow on everything, it all looked the same. My foot caught a branch and I fell.

Down in the snow, the wind left me alone. I felt tired and thought I might stay there and rest. Perhaps the storm would slacken, and I would be able to see more. I began to get drowsy, but when I nodded, my face pressed into the snow. I made myself get up.

The storm did not slacken, and nothing familiar appeared. Finally I stopped, but it didn't make sense to turn around. If I knew which direction to go, I still had the strength, but not knowing made me weak. I brushed the snow off a fallen tree and sat, not so much afraid as sad. I am telling this story, so we all know I survived, but at that moment my chances were fading with the daylight. I felt sorry for myself. No one fondly thinks about death, but we would all like, at the least, to have our passing noticed. But I knew that were I to die in that place, my death would cause no more ripples than that of a fly. Those back home wouldn't know. Who would tell them? I tried again to let the warmth of the cabin call to me, but I could feel nothing warm ahead and nothing warm behind. And no warm spot overhead beckoning my soul—none that I could feel.

Then I heard a sound. It might have been a limb breaking or, then again, a gunshot, muffled by the snow. The sound had not come from the direction I was heading, but I couldn't tell if it had come from behind me or from across the lake. I unwrapped my rifle and fired into the air. How far could it be heard? I waited. Then a dull report came in answer—definitely on my side of the lake. Heartened, I turned and trudged back through my tracks. After awhile, I fired my gun again. The reply came, louder now.

I stood close as Owen fed the stove—my fingers and toes still numb. "Thank you for coming out."

Owen nodded. "Got to look after my little brother." He then told me to get into bed. He'd make us something hot to eat.

I slept some, and when I woke, I heard the storm howling. Owen was at the stove mumbling, but I couldn't make out the words. Then I heard a sharp curse, and another. I thought that he had burned himself, but when I got up, I found him just banging things around.

"What's eating at you?"

Owen looked like he wanted to throw a shoe at me. "Well, maybe if you were older, you'd know."

"Oh, really?" I said, wondering what had happened to the little brother talk. "And what might I know if I were older?"

"Something about women."

"Is that all," I said, bothered and a little angry. "I was in love once, you know."

Owen's eyes grew wide. "How did you know it was real? How could you tell?"

"It's just something you know," I said, wishing I had not brought it up. I wanted the conversation back on him. "What's her name?"

"Allison Murphy," he said, his eyes not leaving the floor.

"From where?"

"St. Paul."

I was surprised, for I was expecting to hear Louisville, which is where he was from. "So what are you angry about?"

Owen let out a breath. "I want to marry her, but she don't want to marry me."

"Oh," I said, "I guess there's not a lot to be done then." That generous verdict echoed about the cabin, while I wondered what was to be said next. Something cheery about Mr. Emerson? The silence was broken by a gust of wind that shrieked like a banshee. Owen sat there churning butter on his insides. Then he looked up with animal eyes.

"She's a whore, Joseph. I bought her one night."

I held my face steady. "And from that one night, you asked her to marry you?"

"Well, it wasn't just one night."

"But was she the first woman you had been with?"

"Yes."

"Well, then."

"But there's no one else I want."

"How many times did you see her?"

"Four. On the last, I asked her to marry me. She patted me on the head and called me a *dear boy*. But I don't want to be no dear boy. I had to leave St. Paul. But now I can't stop thinking about her."

What could I say to my friend? A woman like Allison Murphy had traded all respectability to live beyond the reach of a husband—to live on her own and have money of her own and die, perhaps young, her own master. Having given so much to gain that freedom, why would she trade back to live in a sod house where the roof would drip dirt?

"What will you do?" I asked.

"I'll find some good land next spring," he said, his voice a mixture of doubt and hope. "I'll build a house, and when I've done that, I'll return to St. Paul. She'll marry me then."

I gave what I hoped was an encouraging nod. "Maybe she will."

We spoke no more of Allison Murphy, but I did hear her name again that night. I woke in the dark and heard Owen in great agitation, breathing hard and calling her name. I was aroused by these sounds. And by the thought of Owen's strong arms, and what he had in hand.

I wanted to go to him. I wanted to go to him and play the part of Allison Murphy. The sounds coming from him were more desperate and passionate than any I had heard from George Slater. And if I could have gone to Owen, been his lady of the night and then played the violin to cast a spell by which he would have forgotten all by morning, I would have done it.

20

OWEN PUSHED ON the door and stepped into snow that came to his knee. He muttered something and reached for the saw. A little later he returned with four saplings. Once they were warm, he bent them into bows and tied them back-to-back with soaked rawhide. Then the webbing. A day by the stove and they went stiff as iron.

It took some getting used to, but soon I was off hunting, fitted out with the trapper shoes Owen had made. I went away from the lake the first day but saw only one deer, and she a good ways off. The next day I couldn't find her at all. Owen stayed inside and brooded. And who could tell what he was thinking? Allison Murphy was probably at the heart of it, but I didn't care anymore. I was getting tired of his sullen moods and thought about paying a visit to Noah White. I had promised to cross a frozen tundra to return his book, and there just happened to be one right outside our door. I mentioned the idea to Owen and got a shrug in return.

I set out for Noah's on a still morning. The sky was a cold blue and sunlight leapt off every white thing. The snow made the land look smooth and easy, but traveling through it was slow and hard. My knees began to ache, and the sun had already sunk behind the trees when Noah's place came into view. I fired a shot and pushed on to the cabin. Noah opened the door as I got near.

"Oh, it's you," he said. "What's new in town?"

"Never mind that," I replied. "What's for dinner?"

Noah laughed and brought me inside, promising a meal of pork and beans. He seemed happy to see a human face, and I was happy to see his, though no one would think him a handsome man. He had the look of leftover parts—his ears didn't match, and his nose was a dumpling. And if you were a settler and his face a landscape, you might not homestead there because of its crooked places. But if you had a free afternoon and were looking for somewhere to explore, you might well choose it. And after a time or two, you might look forward to its glens and thickets and be sad if they were any other way. His dark eyes were alive, and it was fun to meet them when we talked.

Noah had been soaking beans, and that night he cooked them with the promised pork in a sauce of sorghum. After the meal, we sat before the fire and talked about the St. Paul and Northern, Noah's employer. The plan was to build a storehouse in the spring. Noah would run the depot for the men who would plot the track line.

"I can see you in a couple of years," I said. "A big watch in your hand, master of the station."

Noah laughed. "Better a watch than a hoe. What about you?"

"I want to raise horses," I said, curious as to what he'd say about it. "This looks like good land."

"It is," he agreed, "but you're a few years early. If I were looking to claim a piece, I'd go up to Manannah. Last I heard, folks there were getting along good."

"Manannah?" I asked, not sure if I were saying it right. "Where is it?"

"A couple of days north of here in good weather."

I thanked Noah for this advice, rolling the new word around in my head. *Manannah.* I wasn't sure if it were an Indian name or a Bible name, but I liked the sound of it.

"Well, are you a man of your word?" he asked. "Did you bring the book?"

"You saw it in my bag."

"What did you think?"

"I liked it most," I said, "when Mr. Emerson talked about nature."

"Ah, yes," said Noah, putting a hand to his breast. *"Nature never wears a mean appearance. Neither does the wisest man extort her secret."*

"Begging the author's pardon," I said, "I think I've seen nature wear a mean appearance. But did you come here for that? For nature?"

My friend shook his head. "No. I'm escaping my marriage or, rather, setting my wife free."

I was at a loss. "Where is she now?"

"Back in Illinois." Noah looked away as though traveling there in his mind. "She said she would follow me here, but we both knew she wouldn't. She married me but loved another man, and I didn't know that until she could barely stand the sight of me."

Noah looked down and fell through time. I sat there and wondered if all of Minnesota wasn't peopled by those who had lost at love.

* * *

The weather turned foul the day I got back to Lake Kasota. For the next week there was little that Owen or I could do outside. I felt trapped and brooded as much as he did. When things improved, I went out to hunt but came back with nothing. We decided to start in on the pork, and Owen took an axe to the barrelhead. There was a hiss, and the cabin filled with an awful smell. Owen dragged the barrel to the lake and put it under the ice. We then thought to open the second cask of flour. The first had been fine, but when we opened the second, it was covered in a black mold. And we had already lost our turnips and potatoes to a rot. It was early-January, and we had only a few lean weeks of food.

That night we ate beans, though with every spoonful, I felt anxious for eating what we might later need. Owen kept staring at the table. "One of us'll have to go to St. Cloud," he said. "Likely nothing in Forest City."

In the silence that followed, I considered the journey. What with the snow and all, towing a sled to St. Cloud and back could take a dozen days or more, assuming the weather held. I hadn't much the heart for it, the only attraction being the prospect of a hot bath.

"It's gotta be me," said Owen. "I can pull more. And you can hunt while I'm gone." I agreed, and we talked about what had to be done for his journey.

The next day Owen braced one of the sleds he had made for dragging wood and fashioned a harness by which to pull it. He warmed his boots by the stove and rubbed them with beeswax. For my part, I took two buffalo robes and sewed a sack for him to sleep in. Then I cooked our remaining bacon with a big pot of beans heavy with blackstrap, his food till he got to somewhere that had something else. Late that night I woke to hear him rustling about. He left without a word, as though he were going to fetch some water.

* * *

The days that followed were cold and dreary, the pewter sky sucking the very life from me. Then I fell sick. The fever lasted only a few days, but after that I couldn't find my strength. I stayed in bed. Cleo would come lick my face to ask if anything were wrong. I couldn't make myself hunt, though I grew hungrier by the day. I had become stingy with the food, not certain of Owen's return. I knew he would not abandon me, but what if he fell sick, as I had? He didn't have a bed or a stove—just two hides sewn together.

The nights seemed to go on and on, and even in the day, I had to light the lamp if I didn't want to stumble over things. The silence pressed in as though it were a noise. The wind could relieve it, and I welcomed that even when it brought the cold. There was too much time to turn things over in my mind. And once that began, it would go in circles. *How was it that I had come to be here? Did God have a plan for me? Was this punishment for my sins?* I began to imagine that hell was not the hot place so talked about, but rather a very cold one—like Minnesota. Why couldn't it be? Who did we know who could say for sure that it wasn't? Not Reverend Albright. Not Reverend Hale. And why were God's emissaries such dried-up strips of jerky? You'd think He'd have his pick.

* * *

The gray days were finally and blessedly followed by bright ones. The sunlight made me well. I went out with my rifle and headed away from the lake. I came across fresh tracks and followed them to a small meadow. There, on the far side were two does. They both ran when I fired, but one didn't get far. The unwounded deer came back to her sister. I shot at her, and she bounded off. I approached the fallen one. She was frightened and struggled. I took my axe handle to her head.

I set out after the other, following a trail of blood. Soon I saw her standing alone, looking unsteady. She saw me approach but merely watched with those big doe eyes, weak from her wound. I took her down with one shot.

There was plenty of day left, so I was able to bring the deer back to the cabin in two runs with the smaller sled that Owen had made for moving wood. I dressed them and buried the innards as deep as I could in the snow. Then I hung the deer side by side from a tree limb, high enough so that the wolves and bears couldn't get at them. I was quite pleased and wished that Owen could see the deer, as my hunting skills had come into question.

In the morning I walked out to check on my kill, but my heart near stopped, for not far away were three Indians staring at the hanging deer. They wore leggings and blankets, but how they stood the cold I couldn't say. I thought of the burned lodge.

I supposed the Indians to be Dakota Sioux whose land this was not long ago. They carried muskets and long knives, but did not act like they wished me harm, though who knew what they were thinking? As for me, I was thinking everything, most particularly that my gun was not loaded and by the door where it should have been. I wanted to run into the cabin, but didn't want to act like I had something to fear, or do anything that might make them think that I was alone. So I walked to where the deer hung and cut one rope. I pulled the carcass a step or two toward the Sioux then motioned for them to take it. I walked back to the cabin, expecting something terrible with each step. I went inside, and when I looked out again, my loaded rifle now at hand, the gift deer was gone and so were the Sioux.

I sat by the stove but couldn't stop shivering. Owen had been gone almost three weeks, and I didn't want to spend another night alone. I began to gather what I would need for the journey to Noah's. I quartered the remaining deer and put a piece on the sled. I made a nest there for Cleo.

Trudging in the snow to Noah's wasn't any easier the second time. Cleo and I got there late in the day, and again I announced my approach with the rifle. When we got close, Noah opened the door, and Cleo and I were both very pleased to enter his warm and tidy cabin. Ours had become cold and filthy. I unwrapped myself and then the frozen venison. Noah's face broke into a smile.

"So you got yourself a deer," he said, placing a fresh stick in his stove.

"Two," I replied. "But I've got only one now."

"Wolves?"

I shook my head. "No. Sioux. Three of them. I gave them a deer, and if it hadn't disappeared, I would have thought I'd dreamed them." I described for Noah my encounter and didn't pretend that I hadn't been frightened. I asked if he had seen anything of Owen.

"Yes. Several weeks ago. He told me of your troubles. I thought you'd come sooner." I reminded him that I was being paid to stay at my cabin.

We ate pork and beans again that night, as the deer was well-frozen. Noah wiped his plate clean with a piece of cornbread. "You were fortunate with the Sioux," he said, "what with their land stolen and their lodge burned."

I was surprised. "Don't they have new land along the Minnesota River?"

"What? Their feedlot? It's ten miles wide!" Noah stood and began to pace about like a schoolmaster. "Can you tell me, Joseph, why they were put there?" I shook my head. "Well, if we shipped them further west, say to Dakota Territory where there's lots of land, then some other white men would get their annuity."

"Can we not teach them to plant?" I asked. "The Mohawks where I grew up are good farmers."

"They may be," said Noah, "but not the Sioux. The brave could never bring himself to dig a potato patch. It's slave work. Women's work. They're finished. Remember those three you saw yesterday—you can tell your grandchildren."

Overnight it began to rain. In the morning the world was covered in ice. It remained cold and gray most of the day, and by turns we napped, talked, and played checkers. Cleo took a liking to Noah and made herself comfortable in his lap.

"I'm sure he's a lot better with you," said Noah, petting Cleo, "but I could barely get a sentence out of your partner."

"He will talk," I said, "if you wait a week or two."

Noah smiled. "He didn't say much, that's for sure. But he did say one thing. Said you're only twenty. Is that so?"

I forced a chuckle. "Some things are true for Owen," I said, "because he needs them to be true."

That hadn't really answered the question, but Noah didn't seem to care. "You know, Joseph, you remind me of a cousin of mine."

"Is that so?" I said, happy to be moving on.

"Yes. You're smart like she's smart."

She's smart? I grinned like he had told a funny story. "Well then, she must be real stupid, 'cause anyone sitting out here in the cold can't be smart. The smart ones are back in St. Paul. And that goes for you too, Mr. White."

Noah laughed and seemed satisfied. Cleo then stretched herself before settling back down into his lap. "Noah," I said, "in another month or so, I'll be done here. I don't know where I'll end up. Would you take Cleo?"

My friend looked surprised. "But, Joseph, she's yours."

"If I had a place of my own," I said, "I wouldn't part with her for the price of a horse. She likes it here. Please." He said yes and I felt sad.

I would have been content to stay at Noah's for the rest of the winter, but I owed Flynn a duty, and knew I should be at the cabin when Owen got back. He had spoken of trying a more direct route, so I couldn't be certain he would pass this way.

Late in the day the weather cleared, and after dark, the moon rose full. I told Noah that I would leave before dawn—moonlight on the snow had always been a fascination for me. Noah said he'd pack me some provisions. That night I slept with Cleo for the last time.

I woke in the dark not knowing the hour. When I poked my head outside, the moon was still high. I left quietly and started off across the frozen land, following the creek into a grove of box elder and cottonwood. The night was silent, and the clouds moved as phantom sailing ships. Each time the moon came out from behind one, the trees around me burned like lime as the silver light reflected off each branch and twig, covered still as they were with thick ice—a forest made of glass. A slight breeze would bring cracking noises, but a sudden one might break a tree into a thousand pieces as I looked on.

On a small rise I paused in the silence. I had seen the light of the moon on snow many times in New York but never in a landscape so untouched by human hands—no roads, fences, or chicken coops. I had not felt the loving presence of God in a long time, but now I gave thanks to Him for the beauty of this world. I felt blessed, chosen, and may I not be damned for saying this, but it seemed in that moment that God had brought me to that place so that He could look out over His creation and see it through my eyes.

For the next hour, the only sound I heard was that of the trapper shoes on the crusted snow and the sled rattling behind. When I stopped, it was so quiet I could hear my heart. Then out of the forest came a horrific noise that could only belong to a pack of wolves. A single wolf howling at the moon is one thing, and I had heard that many times where I grew up, but the sound that a pack of wolves makes is nothing like that. It's a chorus of shrieks that speak of torture and horrid death. My rifle was already on my shoulder, and I went to the sled and found the axe handle. I would have prayed for deliverance, but I didn't believe in it. If I were set upon, it would be my right to defend myself and the wolves' right to eat me. God would not shed a tear either way, or He would not have made the wolf.

I kept moving, holding to an even pace, trying not to spend my strength. Then I saw them—a pack of seven or eight coming down at me through the woods. I looked for a tree to go up, but the ones nearby weren't climbers. I chose a fat one to put at my back. My hand shook, and I hit it hard to get the tremor out.

Had they come at me fast, I couldn't have fought them. But since I wasn't running, and I knew not to do that, they advanced cautiously, baring teeth. I raised my rifle and fired at the closest. The report surprised them. The one I shot yelped and scrambled away a short distance. He fell, got up and then limped behind some rocks. Two of the others followed him, and then I heard an awful sound as though the two had set upon the wounded one. I reloaded and shot again, but I didn't hit anything, as the wolves were already moving away. And everything inside of me said to do the same. Now I went as fast as I could go. In a while the sun was up, and I heard no more of the wolves.

I saw my cabin in the distance and kept myself hidden. I watched for Indians but saw none. Finally, weariness and hunger drove me forward. About the cabin were no new tracks, and inside everything was as I had left it.

I built a fire in the stove, and when it was going strong, I sat in my chair and reached for my bag. As I opened it, a piece of paper fell out. I picked it up. There seemed to be some writing on it, but I couldn't make it out. I went over to the door and opened it partway, letting the daylight fall on the paper: *Dear Joseph. I know your secret. It's safe with me and Cleo, and if you ever need help, you can always call on us. Noah.*

I let out a groan. Noah knew. I paced back and forth trying to think of what it might mean. If he hadn't found a new way, Owen would stop at Noah's, and even though Noah had pledged that the secret was safe, how often do our intentions and actions follow a different course? That night my sleep was ragged.

The weather the next day was bright, but I stayed inside, too tired to hunt. Late in the day I heard a gunshot. I grabbed my rifle and opened the door. There, emerging from a grove of trees, was a man and a sled. I hurried out to meet Owen, thinking that he might be at his limit, but when I reached him, I saw that his eyes were full of life.

"Little Brother," he said with a grin, "we got some good eats."

I let out a happy yip and then insisted on the final pull. When we reached the cabin, I began to unpack. There was a shoulder of ham, a sack of potatoes, onions, dried beans in a sack, bacon, more bacon, flour, and jarred peaches.

"Where did you get all this?" I asked, amazed.

"St. Cloud," he answered, as if it were just down the road. "Weren't no provisions in Forest City."

"Must have cost a fortune," I said, shaking my head.

Owen laughed. "Didn't cost nothin'. When I got to St. Cloud, they sent a message downriver, and a letter came back saying to give us anything we wanted. Well, considering that they're sitting warm and getting ready to be rich, I wasn't shy." Owen began to unlace his boots. "And in case you were wonderin', I didn't go to St. Paul."

"Yeah, but you thought about it."

My friend looked up and smiled. "Yes, I did."

I wasted no time in cooking up the best meal I had seen in months, and I was glad to hear that Owen hadn't stopped at Noah's. He'd found a shorter way. That evening we sat and told our stories. Owen was asleep before I was done with mine.

* * *

What was left of the winter plodded on. In March, the cold lost its grip, and the snow melted back to the shaded places. Tufts of skunk cabbage poked up in the bogs, and the frogs began to peep at dusk. Then geese began to land on the lake. I was so happy to see them that I didn't shoot a one.

Our contract went to the end of the month, and as that time drew near, we began to wonder if we would see our employers. After a winter on this windswept hill, it didn't seem likely that it would be the capital of a great state, or even a lesser one. The end of the month came and went, and our spirits began to sink. We had each been paid a hundred dollars in the fall, but we had done what we said we would and wanted to be paid the hundred owed to us. We stayed on. A week went by. And another. I started shooting geese.

Then one sunny afternoon four men and a wagon appeared on the track. We waved like shipwrecked sailors. I was happy to see Tom Flynn and company, but I felt strangely annoyed as they moved into the house, easy as you please. Then Flynn unveiled a keg of beer, and all was made right. "To you brave gentlemen," he said, raising his cup to us.

"Can we drink to statehood?" I asked. "Is this still to be the capital?"

Flynn winced. "No, we're not a state. And as far as the new capital, we had a little trouble this winter. But now we're here, and you're gettin' paid."

"I'll drink to that," I said, and we raised our cups again.

Owen and I left the next day with handshakes all around. I had decided to go with him on his new route and bypass Noah White's cabin. Noah had been a friend, yet I felt resentful, as though he had meddled in my life. I didn't want to see his knowing looks. I didn't want to explain to him or perform for him.

Owen and I slept our last night together under the stars. The following morning we didn't bother with a fire as we prepared to go separate ways. He was heading to St. Cloud, while I was to follow a more westerly path that would bring me to the Crow River and then Manannah.

"Well, Little Brother," he said as we shook hands, "I hope you find your horses."

That was my dream, of course. Owen's was to marry his lady of the night. I had my doubts, but in the moment of parting, I couldn't discourage him. "And may a certain woman in St. Paul come to her senses."

Owen made a fist as though holding a coin he would never surrender.

21

THE SYCAMORES STOOD in the mist like rooted spirits. The path through them seemed enchanted, as though I might come out of the fog and find myself along Basket Creek. But the River Crow didn't turn into the Basket, and that was easy enough to see. There were no ledges or falls—it just meandered about like a lazy brown snake. I followed its course, and as the mist began to burn off, I came upon a sign rudely nailed to a tree: STARTS HERE, MEEKER COUNTY.

By noon, I could see the houses and barns of Manannah. People were all about, more than I would have thought to see—a celebration perhaps. Charred pork and sweet beans came to mind, but those hopes faded as I drew closer and heard shouting. I came upon a man loading a wagon, a woman with a crying child seated above. "What's going on?"

"The Sioux have risen!" he cried. "They're killing everyone!" The man climbed up and took the reins, but he could do nothing as the way was blocked by another wagon. He called on God to damn all.

A lanky fellow with a brimmed hat hurried over and gave no greeting. "You come in from the south?"

"Kandiyohi," I said, as though it were a town and not a cabin.

"You running from the savages?"

"None that I know about. What's happening?"

"Not sure," said the man. "A fellow came in from Henderson last night, scared to death. Said the Sioux were attacking the settlements."

I shook my head. "I haven't seen a thing."

The man said he was glad to hear that, though he didn't seem less worried. He put out his hand and introduced himself as Otis Whitmore. I told him my name. He asked what brought me to Manannah, and I said I'd come looking for work. Mr. Whitmore scratched his neck. "Well, our hired man left this morning, but we're not taking on help. Don't know anyone who would be. Half the town is leaving, and the rest of us are trying to figure out what to do."

A fine hello this was. I had gotten myself to Manannah, the town where Noah White said I should stake my claim, the town where people were "gettin' along good," last he heard. Now it seemed they were taking the place apart. And what should I do? Should I try to save my scalp and keep on going? To St. Cloud? To St. Paul? It wasn't a happy thought but then neither was being cleft by a hatchet. The best I could do was take a look at those who were fleeing and those who were staying. I did and decided to stay.

An hour later, the settlers who remained gathered under a hickory, maybe seventy or eighty in all. I stood back and watched as, by show of hands, the men elected a commander, a farmer named John Hillsboro, a former captain who had fought in Mexico. Hillsboro accepted the post wearing his blue army coat that no longer covered his belly. He didn't look impressive, but the townsfolk knew their man. His first words were an order. "Stop fortifying the farms," he said, eyes moving from man to man. "I want everyone here." Hillsboro then pointed to four houses that were to be the corners of a fort we would build.

I was part of the brigade that began work on the fort while others went out to their farms for supplies. Using fence rails, barrels, and whatever else, we made walls that might have kept out a stray mule. It looked like a barnyard after a windstorm. The next day we took it all apart as the trunks of young trees were brought in and stood upright. By the following afternoon, we had something that could pass for a stockade so long as you were coming at it from the west. It would take another day or two for the walls to meet on the other side.

Captain Hillsboro seemed pleased, and there was talk about how we could hold out in the fort for a week, if need be. By then the soldiers from

Fort Snelling would have arrived with cannon and bayonet—every hour surely brought them closer. We also waited for the return of a wagon that had been sent to St. Cloud to buy guns and powder. Some thought that it might come back with volunteers to help us. In the meantime, no one in Manannah worked for anyone. We all worked for each other, sharing the danger and the food.

Otis Whitmore introduced me to others, including his wife Mary and his brother James, a leaner version of himself. People were friendly, but no one was particularly curious about me. They had plenty to think about and were happy to see anyone who could lift a rifle. During the day, Otis and James would go out to the farm to check on things. Other men did the same. Hillsboro may have been the commander in the blue coat, but inside the fort it was Mary Whitmore who gave most of the orders. I stayed there and helped with what I could, most often standing guard, looking to the west for signs of attack and to the east for those of relief.

At night we sat about fires. People spoke of their former homes along the Allegheny and Shenandoah, now left behind with parents, sisters, or friends. Scraped clean of those attachments, like hides readied for a window, we sat in the dim light and awaited a common fate.

On the fourth afternoon, I was outside the fort standing guard with three others. Like grazing deer, we looked up at the same moment—a crack, a rifle shot. From the west, across the big meadow, a man with a rifle was running toward the town. He stopped, bent over, and then ran again, making hurried looks over his shoulder. Two men dashed out to meet him and as good as dragged him the last hundred yards. The wide-eyed young man was gasping for air. "Indians!"

"Did you see 'em?" Hillsboro asked.

"No. But Seth and Stuart sure did. Only an hour ago. They sent me back and went to warn the Brochners."

"We've got to go meet them," said one young man.

"Now, Wes," said Hillsboro, "every man is needed here."

The young man shook his head. "Seth's my brother, and I ain't gonna let him get kilt. He'd come for me."

The church bell began to ring, and the captain gave way. "Okay, but no more than five. And I want you to go no farther than Hollister Creek."

Wes looked about. "Who'll come with me?"

The feeling of danger surged through me like whiskey. I felt alive and closely bound to people I hardly knew. Faces spoke. Eyes told stories all by themselves. I raised my hand.

* * *

The five of us began at a slow run and soon got strung out in a line with me at the end. The track was rutted, and I was watching where each foot came down. I didn't want to twist an ankle, and I didn't want to be left behind, but that fear didn't last long. My time in Kandiyohi had made my legs hard. I could keep at it as well as any of them.

When we reached Hollister Creek, Wes held up his hand. "I'm going on," he said in a low voice. "You all stay here with Charlie; he's in charge." He looked about, daring anyone to mention the captain's order not to go farther. Then he looked at me. "Your name's Joseph, right?" I nodded. "Joseph, I want you to head up the creek and watch at the bend above. The rest of you set up here. If you hear me shoot, it's trouble."

Wes waded across the creek and started up the track. I crouched and crept upstream. At the bend, the bush willows grew thick on my side of the creek, good cover but no comfort, as every place was wet. There was nothing to do except nestle into the slop and watch for Indians. I tried to breathe quiet so I could hear the slightest noise, but that made things worse, for what forest does not have sounds? And you can make out of those whatever you wish, so in trying to hear Indians, I began to hear them, creeping closer but never appearing.

I couldn't say how long I was there, each minute was its own world. Then I heard a sudden noise, a splash. My hands gripped my rifle, and my eyes swept the far side. I could see every leaf that moved. No one. Then another splash, but this time I saw the stone that had caused it. I looked down the creek. Charlie waved for me to come.

When I reached him, Charlie put a finger to his mouth and motioned up the track where Wes had gone. By this time, whatever had been on the track was now in the bush. We took cover. I got behind a skinny birch which didn't hide a thing, but that's what was there, so I got behind it and pointed my rifle at the far shore. I heard the crunch of small branches. "Charlie," a voice called out. "It's us. Don't shoot."

"We're here," called Charlie. "Come across." Then out of the woods and into the creek came Wes and four other men, guns held high. When they got to our side, Wes said he didn't think they were being followed. No one had seen any Indians since the first sighting.

We returned to Manannah at a fast walk and in good spirits, entering the fort to the sound of cheers. Captain Hillsboro wanted a report. "How many were there?"

"I saw six or seven right out," said the young man named Seth. "But there were others in the woods behind. There might have been a dozen, maybe twenty. It looked like a hunting party."

"Hunting party?" said Hillsboro.

"Yeah," said Seth, "like we've seen before. If they had wanted us, we was easy pickin's."

"Well, you might be right," said Hillsboro. "Or perhaps they're just scouts. We'll have ten men awake at all times during the night."

That evening, the young men sat outside the fort and told stories of our afternoon sally. And much pleasure there was in the telling. "Hey, Charlie," said Wes, "for two bits, we'll tell Jenny Lindross that you shot yourself three Indians."

There were a few chuckles, but Charlie wasn't amused. "Keep at it, Wes, and you'll be eatin' dirt."

The girl that the boys teased Charlie about was serving food that night. She wore a smock of unbleached muslin, made grayer still by the smoke of the fire she tended. Her bonnet was simple, but from it escaped strands of fine brown hair that hung down in wisps about her face. As she spooned supper onto Charlie's plate, she gave him a look of relief—he had returned safe from the day's adventure. Charlie, aware that his friends might be watching, made a show of hardly noticing her.

Then it was my turn. Jenny ladled the stew onto my plate, and I looked up into a pair of light brown eyes, the color of the River Crow when struck by the sun. Jenny smiled, perhaps because I was new to town or perhaps because I was out with the boys at Hollister Creek. I couldn't tell, but Jenny smiled, and I felt a tremor.

That night I drew the early watch, and when it was my turn to bed down, I fell asleep within moments. But I did not leave the day's adventure behind, and this time, as I dreamt, the savages came across the creek. I was captured and forced to watch as Charlie, shrieking, was carved up before my eyes. Then I was stripped naked to meet the same fate, and when my nature was discovered, I was thrown over a log and abused in every horrid way. Then came the knives. I must have been crying out in my sleep, because when I woke, breathing hard, I could see others in the dim light, looking at me.

* * *

No more Indians were seen that week, but rumors arrived daily. This town or that had been wiped out. Soldiers were coming to help us. Soldiers weren't coming to help us. During the day men went out to their farms in threes and fours, well armed. Those who stayed in the fort shared the work, all except the McAllister brothers, who sat around and ate their grub. Willie and Jake had come to town hoping to buy horses cheap. They offered little, but more than would be gotten if the horses were run off by the Sioux. A few people did business with them, but no one sat and ate with them.

Captain Hillsboro went over to the brothers and asked for help in bracing the north wall.

"I ain't working for you, Cap'n," Willie said. "I ain't scairt of no Indians and don't care nothin' about your blue coat neither."

These were words that would have taken the skin off a man's back in the army or maybe got him tied to a post and shot. Hillsboro looked at Willie. Willie stared back. Jake kept his face in his plate, but I could see a flash in his eye.

Two older men sitting nearby rose to their feet. I did the same. The four of us would have been no match for the two of them, but the captain acted like he had the whole town at his back. "I think you best leave," he said.

Willie didn't budge, but his voice rose. "And if we don't?"

Hillsboro didn't try to match Willie's words but rather went the other way, to a whisper. "Just do it."

The moment teetered as though it were balanced on the edge of a table. Then Willie cooled. He and Jake finished eating and began to saddle up, making a show of being slow about it. They mounted and rode off at a walk, a string of four horses behind. One of the older men spat on the ground.

* * *

The next afternoon a wagon approached from the east. Everyone cheered as though it were a column of soldiers, but it was the Manannah men who had gone to St. Cloud. As they came to a stop, two repeating rifles were lifted high as proof of their success. They had four more in the wagon and a tiny cannon that could fire grape. They also had several St. Paul newspapers, and everyone wanted to know if the stories were true. One paper was held up, and there it was on the front page: SAVAGES ON THE FRONTIER! SETTLERS MURDERED!!!

"What about the soldiers?" someone called out.

"Ain't no soldiers comin'," said a man on the wagon. He endured a few curses and then defended himself. "I'm telling you there ain't no soldiers. They're just sitting around Fort Snelling." This news was greeted by angry shouts. What were the soldiers for if not to come help us?

That evening the newspapers were read aloud. The *St. Paul Times* told of an uprising in the south in which settlers, perhaps a hundred, had been butchered like livestock. The *Democrat* reported the massacre like it was news of a steamboat that had struck a log, tragic but not of great worry. J.P. Owen in the *Daily Minnesotian* went so far as to mock the story: "Immigrants may come on with safety. The purported Indian war is as great a humbug as excited mortals in Minnesota were ever known to invent."

"I'd like to bury an axe in his head," shouted one man. "See if he thinks that's humbug."

"They're all owned by the banks!" shouted another.

And so we gave voice to our opinions, but no one knew for certain what had happened. A massacre in the south, yes. But was the violence spreading? Could the newspapers be trusted? Would the soldiers come? Soon, it became clear that most of the men wanted to get back to their farms, soldiers or no soldiers. What good to be cautious only to starve? The best Captain Hillsboro could get was an agreement to maintain stores at the fort. I wasn't sure what it all meant for me. Then I remembered Otis Whitmore saying something about losing a hired man. I went over to where he was loading his wagon.

"Mr. Whitmore," I said, "would you be willing to take me on? I'm a good worker and don't eat much."

Otis looked me up and down, barely able to disguise his doubts. I certainly wouldn't be pulling any plow. "Let me talk to the others," he said.

Otis went over to James and Mary. They talked for a bit, casting quick glances in my direction. Then Otis nodded and walked back to me. "You can come on," he said. "Two dollars a week."

"I'll take it," I said, offering my hand. These were low wages, but I didn't care. I would have a roof over my head and food to eat. More important, I would get to know the land and people around Manannah.

After loading their wagons, most folks stayed put rather than go home in the dark. I played a few songs on the violin, but it was not a gay evening. We sat before the fire hoping the Indian scare was over—that petition no doubt contained in some prayers. I offered my own, for if it pleased God to let us live in peace, I would work that summer for the Whitmores. Then, if I found some well-watered land, I might stake a claim of my own.

22

THE WHITMORE HOUSE was a box made of bleached boards. The downstairs had a fireplace at one end and a nickel trim stove at the other. Upstairs were two bedrooms reached by steps that would have been a ladder had they been any steeper. I slept in the hired man's shed attached to the barn. It smelled like the animals, but I liked it well enough, it being off by itself.

Otis had planted potatoes the year before, but this year he was planting wheat—him and James working the double brace of oxen. I was given a spade to turn the plot for the roots and beans. I soon discovered that the loam on the Whitmore farm met every boast I had read in praise of Minnesota Territory. It ran black and deep and let go a ripe aroma that to a farmer might have been sweet but to me was rather sickly.

Otis was open and friendly. Wife Mary and brother James were not. James talked to me in an odd, suspicious tone that I pretended not to hear. Soon enough, it all got a little easier when I saw that James and Mary were no better to each other, like they had an argument going back to Indiana. For her part, Mary acted as though I were sitting in the chair that belonged to someone else. And maybe I was. As I would find out, Mary had given birth three times. A son had been stillborn in Evansville, and two daughters were buried out behind the barn, neither having lived a month. The lost children were remembered in the table blessing, every Sunday—their names spoken, followed by the words: *Thy will be done.*

* * *

By the last week in May, the roots were in the ground, and my corn and greens were up. And no Indians had come. The uprising had been real enough to those whose towns had been attacked, but that all stayed well south of us. Most of the Sioux, it turned out, had not risen. And almost all of those who had fled Manannah returned, wagon by wagon, a little sheepish, but we had all been chastened. Farmers carried rifles out to their fields.

One morning I was working in the garden when I noticed a grasshopper on a young plant. I plucked it off and then two more. I heard a shout and raised my head to see Otis running toward the house. "Locusts!"

We started three fires by the garden, but the insects were like driven snow. We used moldy hay, but the smoke bothered us more than it did them. They were on everything—the plants, our shirts, our faces, as though they would eat our flesh. The air smelled like something a dog had thrown up.

We fought with shovels and rakes and killed them by the hundreds to no avail. When the garden was beyond saving, we retreated to the house and stuffed rags under the door. Even so, they got in. One landed in Mary's hair. She tore at it, eyes wide with rage.

"I never wanted to come here!" she screamed at Otis.

"Mary, this isn't the time."

"Oh yes it *is* the time! You wouldn't hear me, Otis, you wouldn't listen to me. *We will leave it to God*, you said, and now our daughters lie buried in dirt that's covered in stinking death. May God be damned!"

Otis's hand hit Mary's face, and she fell back against the table. Her palm went to her cheek. "Go to hell!" she cried, and ran up the steep stairs. The trapdoor came down hard.

Otis gave James a desperate look, as though he had been the one struck. I saw no accusation in James's eyes and took care not to show any. I remembered very well the betrayal I felt when my husband bloodied my face. But Otis Whitmore wasn't drunk, and he wasn't George Slater. There were three dead children in this story and hurts I could only guess at. Faint sobbing came from above.

The next day the locusts were gone, but the smell lingered. Every green thing had been eaten, and all the people in Manannah had suffered the same. For all we knew, so had everyone in the territory.

That afternoon the town met to discuss what to do. As people gathered, there was speculation upon the meaning of the plague. Some believed it a curse called down by the Indians. Others saw God voicing His displeasure as He had done in the Old Testament. Whiskey traders and whores in St. Paul were offered as provocation. Or, perhaps, a sinner among us. Who could it be?

Captain Hillsboro took charge, and the Bible talk stopped. A company was formed to go to St. Cloud and return with more seed. In the meantime, any seed left got planted. On the Whitmore farm this meant potatoes, for they still had spud eyes from the year before.

The wagons returned from St. Cloud, and each day the farmers worked well into the dark. The new seed was hardly in the ground when Mary Whitmore came down with a fever. Soon she was delirious. Manannah had no doctor, so two neighbor women took turns bathing Mary and wrapping her in wet sheets. At dinner, Otis prayed. "Lord, Mary is a righteous woman. Forgive her anger. Spare her life." The words *Thy will be done* were not spoken. Otis had drawn his line.

With Mary ill, the cooking and washing fell to me while Otis and James worked the fields. My efforts were well received by Otis, and James too, although sometimes I saw a smile at the corner of his mouth as though I had been put in my place. I did try to act clumsy around the stove, but I didn't really care what James thought. It was work I could do, and so long as it didn't expose me, I wasn't ashamed.

The crisis passed, but Mary languished. Days went by, and she could barely get out of bed. One sunny morning Sarah Lindross and her daughter Jenny arrived. They had come to clean. I was happy for the help and for the company, Jenny's smile not forgotten.

"You keep a good house for a man," Sarah said as she looked things over. I nodded and wished I had been less thorough. The plan was to scrub every surface and boil every sheet and shirt. My part was to carry the water and keep the stove in wood. On one of these forays, I stopped to talk to Jenny, who was outside hanging clothes. A work bonnet held her hair, exposing a slender neck. I stole glances at it when I thought she wouldn't notice.

Jenny told me that she was sixteen, the oldest of four in a family come from Pittsburgh. I said I was also the oldest of four and from New York.

Her eyes grew wide. "You're from New York?" she said, as though the words conveyed a magic. "I should so like to see New York before I die."

"I'm not from the city of New York," I confessed. "I lived upstate. It's not so very different from here."

"But you have visited, surely."

"Of course."

"And is it grand?"

"Oh, yes! Very grand! Hotels and theaters on every street."

"And fine ladies and gentlemen in carriages?"

"That too."

I had never been to New York City, but saying so would have disappointed her and, I think, diminished myself in her eyes. I wished to do neither. And so I passed a pleasant afternoon, assumed by geography to be a young man of some breeding and rank.

* * *

In Manannah, the most elaborate of our simple pleasures was the Sunday afternoon picnic along the Crow. The children splashed in the river shallows, while everyone else stayed properly dry. Misguided propriety, but I wasn't going to do anything about it.

During the picnic, the young men and women, the unmarried ones, would gather a short distance from the others. There we would tease each other and tell our own stories. I listened mostly, but once in a while, I would tell a story of my winter in Kandiyohi. The one about the wolves gained me some notice.

But despite this acceptance, I remained an outsider when it came to the likes of Charlie, Seth, and Wes. I could skip a stone as good as any of them, shoot better than all of them, yet there was a certain bravado that I could not imitate, a bravado that had come to them at birth. Thus, at some point during these picnic afternoons, I would walk a short distance, sit by the Crow, and wander about inside my head.

Sometimes, Jenny Lindross would seek me out. We would sit there and talk, mostly when the others were off doing something loud. I don't think Charlie even noticed.

I did fancy Jenny Lindross—that is true. But I did not love her the way I had loved Lydia, and still did. Lydia was a wild creature whose fierce thoughts spilled out of her eyes. Jenny was gentle, at peace with that around her. So I did not and could not imagine myself running away with Jenny as I had imagined with Lydia. But I did think about her. One day someone would get to kiss that neck and look at the Jenny who moved beneath her frock. I should have put more distance between us, but I didn't want to. I liked when Jenny sat by me. And I marveled at how quickly a woman could be drawn to a man who wasn't one. I wondered whether a woman, any woman, wouldn't choose to marry a woman when the time came, if she could do so without penalty. The picnic certainly suggested it—the women sitting by themselves, the men in their corner.

One Sunday Jenny asked me to walk with her. We set off across the field in the late summer stillness, content to say nothing. We came to the stone fence and stopped in the shade.

"Joseph," she said as though some question had just come, "do you want a farm of your own?" I saw where this might be going, and I didn't know how to steer it.

"Yes," I said. "I was thinking of staking a claim this autumn. A little west of here."

Jenny paused and then lowered her voice. "Joseph, do you like me?"

"You know I do," I said. I didn't say more, and she knew I was keeping something from her.

"Joseph, you know what I want to know. Do you like me a lot?"

Suddenly, I saw the way.

"More than I should," I said, looking up.

"Why do you say it like that?"

I took a breath. "Because I have a sweetheart back east."

Jenny looked away. "Thank you for telling me."

"Jenny, I'm sorry. I should have—"

She cut me off with a wave of her hand. "What's her name?"

"Lydia."

"And you will send for her when you have a place of your own?"

"God willing," I said, knowing that God would never be willing.

Jenny gave a slow nod. "I'm sorry to hear this, Joseph, because I fancy you."

I wanted to draw her to me, but we weren't out of sight and it wouldn't have been right anyway. Instead, I met her brown eyes. "And I fancy you, my dear, beautiful Jenny. And if you must know, I shall be jealous of the man who will be your husband."

There was a silence. Then her face brightened. "And I shall be jealous of your wife." She leaned forward and brushed my cheek with a kiss.

* * *

A few weeks later I saw Jenny walking with Charlie and felt a pain in my chest. I told myself that this was as it should be. I had cut things off with Jenny as I should have with Lydia. I was to be alone, and there was nothing to be done. I wanted to be with Lydia, or even Jenny, but no matter how good a man I pretended to be, I could have neither. All I had won by my deceit was some imitation of freedom. Was it a fair trade? I couldn't say, but I knew one thing for certain—my condition was irreversible. Having risen, however imperfectly, to the rank of citizen, I could not go back to the indentured world of propriety and deference. Having spat freely into the fire, I could not now tend the fire and guard my expressions so as not to give offense. I was trapped. I could be no man's wife. I could be no woman's husband. That was my fate.

23

OVER THE SUMMER, I looked at land west of Manannah. I found some with wood and good water, but I didn't put in my stakes. No need—the rush of settlers had stopped. Trouble upstream.

It wasn't a complete surprise. Men had predicted a day of reckoning if the speculation continued, but those men had been mocked in the St. Paul newspapers as *spoilers* or *croakers*. Then the banks closed, and those same newspapers ran notices for sheriff's sales. Money disappeared. Recently wealthy men were said to be begging their breakfast on the streets of St. Paul. Otis told me I could stay on and work for no pay. I did and was happy to do it.

Just when things seemed darkest, a new entertainment appeared. It was a newspaper, the *St. Cloud Visitor*. And unlike those in St. Paul, its editor had a wry appreciation for the hardy people who worked the land. The Manannah farmers liked this. Soon enough, they forgave her for being a woman.

Jane Grey Swisshelm had left her husband to come west and start a newspaper. She was new to St. Cloud, so she called it the *Visitor*. Subscription for a year was two dollars, unless you couldn't pay that, in which case she would accept anything she could eat, wear, or burn in her stove—that's what she wrote. I sent the money, and the paper began to arrive.

Mrs. Swisshelm knew how to make folks laugh, and that was important, for sometimes that's all they'd be down to. She encouraged people to share food, play music, and dance. This ruffled the feathers of a certain

St. Cloud preacher, who one Sunday attacked the *Visitor* for encouraging wanton behavior. Mrs. Swisshelm was quick to reply:

> Reverend Inman takes the ground that dancing is inseparable from drunkenness and that when a woman is led onto the dance floor, she is disgraced. This is ridiculous, and the religious prejudice against dancing is without foundation. That dancing might be abused is no more an argument against it than gluttony is an argument against regular meals. I say, dance on!

And that, in essence, is what we did. It was the autumn of 1857, and people were making do with almost nothing. And while prices fell, what fell most was land, until you couldn't sell a piece for any price. Land for sale was everywhere. But you couldn't eat land or wear it like a coat, so why would you pay money for it?

Some farmers loaded wagons and headed east. *Go-backs* they were called, though it wasn't said unkindly. Indians could be fought, ruined crops could be replanted, but if the money to build the barn or purchase the seed couldn't be raised, what was to be done?

As people left, their homesteads came open to claim. One that I knew sat on the south bank of the Crow midway between Manannah and Forest City. It had been settled by a family named Howard, but now they were leaving. I went out to see if they planned to return. The answer was no.

The Howard farm could have been mine for no money the day after they left, but I wanted to be at peace with the spirits. We talked for a time, and I bought their place, or rather their improvements, for one hundred and fifty dollars. For that, they agreed to leave the small stove and the provisions laid up in the cellar. It still felt like stealing, but just like that, I had rights to one hundred and sixty acres with a small cabin, a garden, and a shed. All I had to do for title was live on it for three years.

That night I announced the news at dinner. Otis smiled, and James got up and shook my hand. "What are you going to grow out there?"

"Horses."

James shook his head. "You'd be better off with mules. If war comes—and by golly it will—you'll be a rich man if you've got a farm full of mules."

I laughed. What I couldn't say was that I wanted to raise horses because it had been my dream with Lydia and my promise to Helen.

Mary Whitmore displayed no reaction to my news. I thought it strange, even for her. At the very least, I thought she'd be glad to see me gone. But all became clear soon enough. As the conversation died back, she held up her hand. "I am going back to live with Margaret," she said, speaking of her sister in Evansville. "I am with child."

Mary looked hard at Otis, so I supposed he was hearing this for the first time. Otis kept still. He could have forbidden Mary to leave, but he had already lost three children, and two of those she held against him. Finally, he spoke.

"When will you come back?"

"When the baby and I are ready to live here, and this place is fit to have us. I want you to take me to St. Cloud, the day after tomorrow."

Otis threw down his fork and went out to the barn. All evening I could hear him hammering at the forge. Two days later, they left in the wagon. I wondered if Mary were truly with child.

* * *

A mist rose from the meadow, and the sun ate it for breakfast. Once the fields were dry, I hiked to a small rise and looked out at my land. The woods lay thick in the hollows, and the grass waved in the breeze. I could have rolled in it but didn't. There was wood to be brought in and roots to be dug.

I was at my new house but a day when I looked up to see a man on a horse coming toward me. He was coarse looking, and it took a moment to remember. It was Willie McAllister, the horse trader that Captain Hillsboro had come up against during the Indian scare.

"Why, pardon me," he said as he pulled up. "I was looking for Mr. Howard."

"The Howards are gone," I said, thinking he knew full well they'd left.

"So who are you?"

"I'm Joseph. I bought the place."

"Did you," he said, as though I were making up a story. "You new around here?" Willie didn't remember me.

"No," I said. "I worked at the Whitmore place this summer." I wanted Willie to know I had friends, and that seemed to be just what he needed to hear. He nodded, told me his name, and said he lived down the road. I was glad then that I had decided to come out. Had I waited till spring, not a hook or a door hinge would have been left, I was sure of that.

* * *

Several weeks later I went into Manannah for supplies. It was late November, but the cold hadn't settled in. There was mud everywhere, and the town looked neglected. The remains of the stockade were strewn about in careless piles.

I stayed the night with Otis and James. The house stank of wet wool, but I liked being there and having someone to talk to. And James was acting downright friendly. He asked me how I was getting on, and I talked about my growing pile of firewood, the leak in the roof, and Willie's visit.

"Stay clear of him," warned Otis.

"Oh, Willie don't bother nobody," said James. "Whatever horse thieving he does, he does it somewhere else."

I turned to James. "He steals horses?"

"He ain't even honest enough to do his own stealin'," said Otis. "I think he and Jake just go south and buy 'em real cheap from . . . well, I don't know who."

"I heard Jake's in jail in Dubuque," said James.

"I hadn't heard that," said Otis. "But just stay clear. That's what I'd do."

"Well, hold on now," said James. "Joseph wants to raise horses, and the cheapest ones just happen to be right down the road. People do buy from them, and I ain't seen no one go to jail yet." Otis shook his head but didn't argue.

That night I sat before the fire and read three weeks of the *St. Cloud Visitor*. Our editor, Mrs. Swisshelm, seemed to be in a running battle with the boss of Stearns County, one General Sylvanus P. Lowry. He was said to still own slaves back in Tennessee, and she wasn't about to let people forget it. Mrs. Swisshelm hated slavery, and there was hardly a week when she didn't write some protest. These were often firsthand accounts of cruelties she had witnessed in Kentucky, stories of young women stripped naked and whipped for doing no more than trying to defend their honor. Mrs. Swisshlem, I decided, was the bravest woman I had ever heard of. No cut hair or men's clothes for her.

* * *

That winter I slept like a bear. But I couldn't sleep all the time. I'd get to thinking, because there wasn't much else to do. I thought about my times in front of the fire with Noah White. I missed them now and began to regret that I had been so poorly mannered in the face of his sympathies. Noah had been my friend, yet I hadn't bothered to say a simple goodbye. And I knew him well enough to know that he had been hurt by this. He was living alone and not surrounded by friends. How could he have not felt the slight? But there was no seeing him now, or trying to make good on any of it. He was two to three days from me in the dry summer and more than twice that in the snow. And you couldn't tell from one day to the next what the sky was going to do.

I thought about Helen and wondered if this might be a place where she could come someday. It was so cold and dark, it didn't seem likely. But I had told her that I would have horses, and I would make good on that. The rest would be in the hands of God.

And then there was Lydia. Was she now engaged to a young man, or had I ruined her life? Did her thoughts still stray to me on occasion, or had she put me out of her mind? I had too much time to roll it all about, and a devil began to whisper in my ear. It told me to write to her. Of course, any letter I wrote would be denied her and taken by her mother. Then I remembered that she had a cousin in Minnesota—the letter might not fall under suspicion.

I thought of an apology for running away. I could say that I was not ready for marriage. That, at least, would confuse the matter if the letter were intercepted—I was certain that Lydia would read between the lines. I would simply say that I was raising horses in Minnesota. Perhaps I might hear back from her in a letter. That is what I thought about, at first. But then I began to imagine her actually coming to Minnesota. I imagined her sitting across the table, laughing and reading aloud from the *St. Cloud Visitor* as she had done with the *Honesdale Herald*.

These were, of course, the thoughts of a woman who was not right with herself or the world, but please judge me after you have sat alone in the dark for a whole winter. During the daylight hours, all four or five of them, I would vow not to write to Lydia, to leave her alone as I had promised myself I would. But then, in the dark, I would find myself composing the letter, trying to think of the words that might bring her to me. The sentences rolled about in my mind, over and over, till I realized that I would have to send the letter or go mad writing it every day in my head.

To help put my thoughts aside, I would sometimes play the violin, mostly canal shanties or drinking songs. I hadn't played "Laura's Waltz" in two years, afraid of being crushed by memories of Lydia. But one evening I decided to play that waltz. I *wanted* to remember. And something else—I wanted the violin to give me its magic. I had seen it work in Father's hand, and in my own. But never had I asked for all its power. What could it do?

I played the waltz once. Nothing changed. I played it again, slower. On the third time through, the room brightened, and suddenly I was able to see Lydia. She was in her yellow dress, looking out the window of the glass factory. I said her name, but she didn't move. Then I played the song again, thinking that perhaps if I just kept playing it, I would be able to step into that very room. And, indeed, as I played on, I saw her turn to me. She smiled. She could hear the notes now, and soon I would be able to go to her, put my arms around her, and kiss her . . .

I woke on the floor, the fire dead in the stove.

24

I WAS OUT in the woodlot before the snow was gone, cutting young trees for posts. My back took to the work, and my lungs liked the cool, early season air. I thought about horses and couldn't quite get out of my head what James had said about Willie—that people had bought cheap from him, and nothing bad had happened. His place was on the way to Forest City, just down the road a few miles. It wasn't much more than a tumbledown shack, but behind it was the darnedest collection of odd horses and Indian ponies. I saw a few that might be breeders and among them, a beautiful roan of sixteen hands that I wanted for myself.

A voice inside me said that I shouldn't buy a horse that might be stolen. But that voice wasn't very loud, and this may be a measure of how I had changed. Honesty wasn't dead on the frontier. It was just something you owed mostly to people you knew. Out here, men with advertised Christian virtue could forget the Lord's precepts when it came to those with dark skin, witness the very land we were on. And beyond that, people were taking liberties every which way with the homesteading law. I had been on the frontier long enough to know that if you busted and had no food or money, people wouldn't treat you any better if you'd never taken a short-cut—you'd just be out of luck.

Each week during the spring, I went into Manannah to pick up my *St. Cloud Visitor*. Mrs. Swisshelm's battle with General Lowry had gone on all winter, having moved beyond slavery to charges regarding public money—misspent or just plain missing.

Then one week, Mrs. Swisshelm's paper didn't come. What came instead was the *St. Paul Times* carrying the headline: "DISGRACEFUL OUTRAGE IN ST. CLOUD! PRESS DESTROYED!" The story said that the office of the *Visitor* had been entered in the night, the press demolished, and the type thrown into the river.

"So high-handed an outrage has never before disgraced our Territory!" said the *Times*. It then printed the contents of a note left by the intruders:

> Editor of the *Visitor*: The citizens of St. Cloud have determined to abate your nuisance. They have decided that your newspaper is fit only for the inmates of brothels. You will not repeat the offence in this town without paying a more serious penalty than you do now. The Committee of Vigilance.

I felt empty. Mrs. Swisshelm's experiment as a free woman had come to an end. She had gone out among them, and they had ruined her.

* * *

While setting posts in the near meadow I looked up to see a rider approach. It was Willie.

"Howdy, neighbor," he said when he got near. "I see you survived the winter."

"I did," I replied. "Now it's time to work."

Willie nodded then looked at the posts. "Heard you were building a fence—thought you might want some horses."

"I might," I said, trying not to sound too interested.

"Well, I have some nice ones. I'd give you a good deal."

"You'd have to," I said with a laugh, "because I don't hardly have any money."

Willie shrugged. "Who does nowadays? Truth is, it would help me to move 'em on. I'd take scrip for part of it."

A satisfied feeling came over me. I was happy to see Willie, because now I could explain to my better self that I hadn't gone looking for him. "Tell you what," I said, clapping the dirt off my britches. "When I get done here in a week or so, I'll come by."

Willie gave me a gap-toothed smile, while I looked back and imagined him and me standing side by side on a gallows in Missouri.

* * *

The next week brought the news that Minnesota had been declared the thirty-second state of the Union, the lines drawn all the way to Pembina, just as Tom Flynn had said. We were now genuine members of the best nation on earth, and a celebration was being planned for Forest City. That Sunday, five Indians with just bows and arrows could have walked away with all of Manannah.

At the celebration I ran into Otis and James. James was with his wife, Alice, recently arrived from Indiana. Otis was beaming. Mary had given birth to a boy named Isaiah. They would come out in the fall. I was happy for Otis and glad to hear that Mary had spoken true, though the thought of seeing her didn't warm me.

The other big news was that the *St. Cloud Visitor* would be publishing again. The story of Mrs. Swisshelm's troubles had been told all across the land, every newspaper feeling the duty to report the outrage. Money had been donated and a new press sent from Chicago. Mrs. Swisshelm was going to fight back.

Speeches were given that day, and the men who gave them had likely spent hours choosing the right things to say—wasted effort, because people were off laughing and drinking and didn't want to listen to pretty words. The men drank hard, and by late afternoon, their hoots and howls were a common sound. With that as a background, I played the violin and called a few dances, and people did dance. The finale was provided by some Manannah men who had brought the little cannon purchased during the Indian scare. They hovered and fussed and, with more trouble than I should have liked under hostile circumstances, made it belch fire and noise.

* * *

I finished the corral one morning in June and decided to take the afternoon and go over to Willie's place—maybe buy some horses. The day was warm, and I thought to first cool myself in the river.

The path to the Crow ran through a thicket, coming down to a bend in the river where the current had left an arm of sand. I took off my clothes and jumped in. Out where it was deep, I bobbed and floated. Then I went under and opened my eyes—above me the sun danced on the water. I went down deep and came up fast, breaking the surface like a fish chasing a fly.

Feeling refreshed, I swam over to where I had come in. My feet found the sand, and I rose from the water. I was reaching for my clothes when I sensed that I was not alone. I looked up to see someone standing on the high bank, not twenty steps away. The sun was behind him, and my eyes still stung with the water.

"Well, I'll be whipped." It was Willie. I could see him now, hands on his hips.

"Get off my land!" I shouted.

"Why, I don't see I have to go nowhere," he said. "You're the one who best git going."

"You leave me be, Willie, I swear."

He started toward me. "Ain't nobody gonna hear nothin'."

I waited till he was almost on me then ducked past him and ran up the bank. I was quicker than he was, but my bare foot hit a stone and my ankle turned. I got up, but by then, Willie was coming fast. He caught me as I reached the clearing, not far from the cabin. "I think you need some learnin' as to what's what," he said, turning me by the shoulder. Next thing, I was on the ground with a screaming pain in my jaw. Willie was on top of me, his filthy hands between my legs. He stank.

I tried to push him off, but he lifted his fist and brought it down. Everything went white with the pain. Then it went red, as blood poured from my nose. I lay there spitting blood and gasping while Willie tried to undo himself. His britches were stiff as leather, what with all the dirt and dried sweat—he needed both hands to get them down. Then I saw the knife hanging from his belt.

Willie fell on me again. I tried to bring my knee up, but that just made him crazy. "Goddamned sow!" he yelled, hitting me again. When my senses came back, Willie was inside me, grunting like a pig. I closed my eyes so as not to have to see him, but all the while I was reaching.

Willie jerked and the foul air went out of his lungs as the knife went deep into his leg—I stabbed him there because that's where I could, that's where my arm was. I pulled the knife out to strike again, but Willie reached for his leg and rolled to his side. I kicked free.

"Sonofabitch!" Willie screamed as he saw the blood flowing from his leg. He couldn't get up—I had driven the blade deep. He started pulling himself along the dirt, swearing and cursing. Wearing nothing but blood, I ran past him and grabbed the rifle hanging from his saddle. Willie kept swearing and taking the Lord's name in vain. My head hurt something bad, and I couldn't think with all those curse words flying around.

"You shut up," I shouted, showing him the bloody knife, "or I'll fix it so you never bother another woman."

That shut him up. But what sense did it make to tell him to be quiet when I was going to shoot him dead? It didn't make sense. Nothing did. Pain, fear, and anger all had their own ideas. And while one part of me was going to kill Willie, another part wanted him to go away. To disappear. And my wanting him to go wasn't even a thought. I just wanted him gone. I wanted the pain to stop. I wanted to wash myself. I needed to breathe.

For some moments I just stood there trying to catch my breath. With my one open eye, I watched as Willie crawled to the post his horse was tied to. I watched as he pulled himself up, hitched his pants, and yanked himself over the saddle, groaning with the pain. Willie then grabbed the horn with both hands, steadied himself, and threw a quick look. "See you in hell," he hissed.

That's what I needed to hear. I raised the gun to send him there. Even with one blurry eye, it was an easy shot. I aimed for his body, because I didn't want the chickens running around and pecking at his brains. And I'll give Willie this—he was outlaw enough to know that he'd get his when the time came, and he didn't seem to care when that was. My finger felt the cool, unfamiliar trigger. Pulling it required almost nothing, still I asked the Lord for strength, and that was a mistake. It was a mistake, because what

I heard in return was His commandment. I heard the commandment and didn't shoot.

Willie rode away slow, leaning forward, his arms wrapped around the horse's neck, because his legs couldn't hold. I threw down the rifle and ran into the cabin. I grabbed the vinegar and hurried back to the river where I washed myself inside and out. I couldn't get his smell off me.

25

CRIED THAT night, hoping it would bring sleep. But once the tears were done, I just tossed about till finally I got up and lit a candle. I walked over to the mirror, having stayed away from it in the day. Even in the dim light I could see that my face was purple and swollen, like that of some troll in a story to scare children. And there was a hard pain in my jaw that just wouldn't stop.

And what would happen next? Maybe Willie would be afraid for what he had done and wouldn't tell anyone. That wasn't likely, for one way or another, he was sure to tell. But perhaps when the truth about what had happened came to light, the folks in Meeker County would rise up in my defense, as they had when Mrs. Swisshelm was attacked. Willie would be run off or sent to jail, and I could continue on, known to be a woman but living as I wished. The comfort of that thought didn't last long. Willie would certainly seek revenge at a time of his choosing, and how could I defend against that?

The answer to that question flitted about the cabin like a moth. Then it landed on my shoulder and told me what I already knew—there was no way I could defend against Willie's revenge. And if I couldn't, it meant that I had to find Willie and kill him, before he found me and killed me. It was either that or run away, and I wasn't going to run. This land was mine—the only thing I had, and I wasn't going to leave it behind as I had left everything else. And if it meant killing someone who deserved to die, I would do it. After all, I had shown less mercy to poor creatures in the forest that hadn't done a thing to me.

I slowed my breathing so I could think. I felt cold inside. I would sneak over to Willie's place, lie in wait, and put a bullet through his head. I'd bury him somewhere—dirt here was easy to dig. And who'd miss him?

I took my rifle and some cornbread and walked east in the dark. When the sky began to lighten, I could see the outline of Willie's cabin. I crawled on my belly till I was in a place that gave me a clear shot. As morning broke, no smoke came from the chimney. Willie's mount was not there. He was not there.

I walked back, wondering why I hadn't killed Willie when I had the chance. I had every right. Of course, killing a man is not a natural thing, and God has told us not to do it. But that hadn't stopped me that very morning; why had it stopped me the day before? It was then that I realized how much of me had wanted Willie out of my sight. I wanted him gone. I wanted it all to have never happened, and that would have been near impossible if he were lying dead in the yard. And maybe God had spoken to me at that moment because I had the gun in my hand and He had to speak. And maybe He had let me walk over to Willie's place this morning because He knew Willie wasn't there.

That afternoon I bathed again in the river, my rifle nearby. I rubbed myself with mint leaves, but the memory of his smell didn't leave. Back at the cabin, I thought of hiding somewhere, till I healed. But where could I go? Then it came. I could go to Noah White. Hadn't he offered his friendship if ever I needed it? It seemed the perfect answer, but I hadn't slept at all the night before, and the journey over to Willie's had done me in. I was far too tired to think about leaving that day.

The next morning I forced myself to look again in the mirror. It was worse as the bruises had darkened. One eye was near shut, and I didn't want to be seen by anyone. I knew of a rough track that went south and ran into another that would take me to Noah's. It was a little longer, but if I went that way, I wouldn't have to go through Manannah. But I would be on the main road for a bit, so I decided to leave toward midday when fewer people would be on it.

With the morning to get ready, I found myself oddly tidying the cabin for my absence. I cooked some beans with molasses, which I put in a jar to carry with the remaining cornbread. I took ten dollars to bring with me and hid the rest of my money between the logs of the cabin. I packed a change of socks, hung my violin on the wall, and put out extra feed for the chickens. I was just finishing with this when I looked up to see a rider heading my way. I picked up my gun.

The rider came on slowly, a saddled horse in tow. I stood facing him, rifle cradled. The man pulled up a polite distance from me, a wiry fellow with a bushy mustache. I had seen him before but didn't know where. "Hello, friend," he said. "You're Joseph the fiddle player, are you not?"

"I am," I said. "And who might you be?"

"I'm Sheriff Jewett from Forest City. I seen you play at the celebration." He glanced at my rifle and then back to my face. "What happened to you?"

"I had some trouble," I said. "What brings you here?"

"Business," said the sheriff. "Probably the same trouble. Two days ago Willie McAllister rode into town more dead than alive. Lost a lot of blood. Claimed that you tried to murder him."

I wanted to yell every curse I knew, but I measured my words. "Sheriff, if I had tried to murder Willie, he'd be dead."

"But you did stab him?"

"I did. And I presume that in Meeker County it's the right of every man to defend himself. Did Willie say why I stabbed him?" I looked hard at the sheriff, but he was wearing his poker face.

"Willie said a lot of crazy things. He said that you tricked him, and then tried to kill him."

"Anything else?"

The sheriff paused. "Yes. He called you a she-devil."

That was it. My secret was gone. Part of me wanted to run, and another part of me wanted to lash out. But the sheriff knew his way around a situation, speaking slowly, evenly. "I would be obliged if you would tell me your side of things. You might begin—and I mean no disrespect—by tellin' me exactly how I ought to address you."

I cursed silently. "You should address me as Mrs. Slater." I hated to hear myself speak those words. After everything, I was, once again, the wife of George Slater.

The Sheriff nodded. "What happened?"

I took a breath. "Willie found me bathing in the river. He forced himself on me, but then I got hold of his knife and drove it into his leg." I paused for a moment, it all coming back. "I should have killed him, I truly should have. But then, of course, you might have some real business here."

"Still do," said the sheriff. "If what you say is true—and knowin' Willie, I could believe it—then you have nothin' to fear from the law. But I have a warrant for your arrest from the county attorney. I want you to give me your gun, and I don't want any trouble."

"Willie attacked me," I said, in disbelief.

By then the sheriff knew that I wasn't going to lift my gun against him. His tone became hard. "You can talk about that with the county attorney. And you can file a complaint against McAllister. But you're coming with me. Give me your gun. Now."

We rode slowly to Forest City, saying nothing the whole way. In town, people stared as we went by. The sheriff frowned. "I don't have no place for you," he said, "but I think Doc Blanchard might put you up. The county attorney will be back tonight. You'll see him tomorrow, and you can tell him what you told me."

The Blanchards' house was down a side road. When we got there, I stayed with the horses while the sheriff went to the door. He knocked and a gray-haired woman answered. The sheriff spoke to her and then motioned for me to come. He introduced her as Mrs. Blanchard and me as Mrs. Slater. She gasped when she saw my face.

Dr. Blanchard appeared. He was a short, balding man with spectacles. The sheriff told him that I was there to clear up a misunderstanding. That was silly, for from the looks of those in town, everyone had heard some version of Willie's story.

The doctor eyes ran over my wounds. "Please come into my office."

I stepped forward, but the sheriff blocked my path. His eyes narrowed under the brim of his hat. "You are not to leave here," he said. "Make a fool out of me, and you'll be sorry." I nodded, and he stepped aside.

The doctor led me into his office and looked closely at my head. "I want to put some salve on these cuts. Otherwise, there really isn't anything to be done. Are you injured . . . anywhere else?"

"It's all in the hands of God now," I said, wondering if some small part of Willie were growing inside me.

The doctor nodded in a way to show that he understood. "That was some bad business out there, Mrs. Slater. I'm very sorry for your trouble."

* * *

I slept a good part of the afternoon in the room the Blanchard's had offered me. At dinner I ate silently with the doctor and Mrs. Blanchard, glad they didn't seem to need conversation. After the meal, I said I'd wash the dishes. I was now Mrs. Slater, and that would be in keeping, though I was still in britches and had no thought of getting out of them. Mrs. Blanchard agreed, seeing I needed something to do. A little later, she came into the kitchen, a man close behind.

"This is A.C. Smith," she said. "He's the federal attorney at the land office."

Before me stood Abner Comstock Smith, though I only learned his full name later, for he was called "A.C." by everyone. He was lean and shaven and looked quite handsome in his canvas britches and calico shirt, open at the neck. I dried myself and through force of habit offered my hand. He took it, not quite sure whether to shake or not, so I helped out by shaking his. "I thought I might be of service to you," he said. "I hope I haven't intruded."

"No. I would be very grateful for any help."

Dr. Blanchard cleared his throat and nodded to his wife. "Me and the missus can go for a walk."

"Certainly not," I said. "Please stay and listen if you care to. I have no secrets now."

And so I told my story. I didn't mention Honesdale, just simply said that I had been abandoned by my husband and had left my daughter with my parents and set out to make my way in the world. When I tried to describe Willie's attack, my voice wavered. The event spilled forth in pieces, like the remains of a teacup on a stone floor. Mrs. Blanchard covered her mouth. Mr. Smith nodded slowly—I suppose to let me know that he was listening.

When I was done, Mr. Smith said he was sorry for what had happened and would speak to the county attorney in the morning. Since the warrant was for attempted murder, he didn't imagine there would be any trouble. He said he would help me if I wanted to file a complaint against Willie, but we could talk about that later. I thanked him and he left.

In low spirits, I went to my room. I just wanted to settle with the law, go back to my farm, and live there as a woman, if I could—if they would let me. But I wouldn't be just any kind of woman. Not now. I would be one with the every freedom of a man, starting with what I would wear. And close upon that thought, Mrs. Blanchard entered the room and offered an old night shirt of hers. I thanked her but said I had my own, meaning the rag that had once belonged to my grandfather. I wanted something familiar next to my skin.

* * *

I expected to see Mr. Smith early the next day, but the morning was near gone when he arrived, no smile on his face. "The county attorney," he said, "doesn't want to let you go just yet."

I could scarce believe it. "Am I to be put on trial for defending myself?"

"No," said Mr. Smith. "He's thinking about other charges."

"What charges?"

"I don't know. He seems to want to prosecute you for wearing pants and pretending to be a man—an offense against moral decency, whatever that is. Willie is to be left out of it."

"How convenient," I said, feeling myself flush.

"I'm sorry about all this," said Mr. Smith. "I won't lie. Richards is a difficult man. And worse, he's got ambitions."

"But the murder charge has been dropped?"

"Yes."

"Then why can't I go?"

Mr. Smith shook his head. "Richards wants you here. Now, he really doesn't have that say-so, and we could contest it, but it wouldn't do any good. And if you left town, people would be coming up with all kinds of ideas. By mid-afternoon, you'd be a bank robber, and by dinner something worse. We'll sit tight. Maybe when he thinks it through, the man will see reason. I'll find out tomorrow. In the meantime, I've sent for my friend U.S. Wylie in St. Cloud. He's a good lawyer and knows how to keep his mouth shut."

I was glad Mr. Smith's friend was a good lawyer and would keep his mouth shut, though I wasn't sure what part of this was still a secret. And why did we need another lawyer? The only bad thing I had done was go looking for Willie, to find him and kill him. But no one knew about that.

The next morning Mr. Smith returned and said that Mr. Richards had, indeed, filed charges against me—for wearing men's clothes and pretending to be a man. The trial was to take place in a week.

"Am I to be sent to jail?" I asked.

"They have to find you guilty first," said Mr. Smith. "And I don't think Judge Robson would send you to jail. And I don't think that's what our county attorney has in mind."

"What then?"

"I think he wants you run out of here. If you're found guilty, a criminal warrant can be filed at the land office. You'd be denied title to your land."

"They'd take my land? For wearing britches? That's not right!"

"No, it's not right," agreed Mr. Smith, "but if they get a guilty verdict and want to make an issue of it, they can. I'll do my best for you, Mrs. Slater."

It didn't make sense to protest anymore to Mr. Smith—he was on my side. "I am grateful for your help," I said, attempting to sound brave. I don't know how brave I really was, but I think life had already begun to put a crust on me. I wasn't standing there crying.

* * *

Two days before the trial, Mr. Ulysses Samuel Wylie walked into the Blanchard kitchen. I didn't know, at first, who he was, because I had imagined Mr. Smith's friend, the good lawyer who was coming to help me, as older—a man with large hands and a carved face. But that wasn't Mr. Wylie. He was a young man, with a sly grin, and a shock of orange hair. We were introduced and then Mr. Wylie turned to Mr. Smith, who was seated at the table. "Is there anything new?"

My attorney shrugged. "Just legal history, Useless."

I suppose that Mr. Smith called him that all the time, for Mr. Wylie seemed to take no notice. "What statute applies?"

"That, happily," said Mr. Smith, "is a problem for our county attorney. I don't think there is one."

I couldn't stay still. "Then why a trial?"

Mr. Smith took a breath. "Look. Out here the law is whatever Mr. Richards, Judge Robson, and the jury say it is. Mr. Richards, unfortunately, has already weighed in on the matter."

"And the judge?"

Mr. Smith cast a glance at Mr. Wylie—there was a story here. "I suppose for a complete picture," said Mr. Smith, looking back to me, "you should know that our judge, Charles Robson, is a man without humor. Add to that a courthouse that on Sunday is a church where Reverend Robson leads the prayers, and I'd say the slope is uphill. You may also be familiar with the recent news concerning Mrs. Swisshelm. Forward ladies are a topic of some disagreement these days. Where His Honor stands with all this, I can only guess, but I can tell you for sure that he dislikes me and Mr. Wylie."

This was more truth than I needed to hear. "Is there any reason for hope?" I asked, a little shaken.

Mr. Smith tried to steady me with a fatherly nod. "As long as we're able to stand up and say what we have to say, there is reason for hope. But we have to work with what we have. Now, for what it's worth, it would seem the law is on your side, or at least not against you. Also, I think Robson dislikes Richards as much as he dislikes me and Useless. He's got an opinion of himself, and I don't think he'd care to preside over a farce. So Richards may be on a short rope. We'll have to pick our moments."

"Speaking of our good friend, Reverend Robson," said Mr. Wylie, "what will Mrs. Slater be wearing at the trial?"

"I think what she's wearing now will be fine," said Mr. Smith.

"You might think that, but Robson won't. He sees her like that, there'll be hell to pay."

"Yes," agreed Mr. Smith. "Robson won't like it. But he doesn't like us anyway, so we're not losing much. We lose a lot more if we start acting like there's something wrong with Mrs. Slater's clothes."

"I won't wear a dress," I said. "If they want to parade me around in a dress, they can just send me to jail."

"Well," said Mr. Wylie, "I'm glad we're all agreed on that."

Just then Doc Blanchard entered the kitchen from the back door. He didn't look happy. "I was summoned by the judge," he said. "I've been ordered to make an examination of the defendant." He looked over to me. "I, of course, see people in their natural state all the time, but I have never been asked to examine someone's sex. If there's anything you wish to tell me, now would be a good time. We can forgo the examination."

"There's no issue of fact here," said Mr. Wylie. "We'll stipulate that Mrs. Slater is a woman."

The doctor shook his head. "I think they may still ask me to testify." He turned to me again. "You are a woman in every part of you?"

"Yes, I am a woman in every part of me," I said, annoyed, despite the doctor's obvious sympathies. "I have given birth and have the marks to prove it. And if you want to know what that's like, you could swallow a pumpkin whole and wait."

From her chair across the room, Mrs. Blanchard let out a hoot. Then everyone laughed, and we sat and had our tea.

26

I AWOKE TO the call of magpies and for a brief moment thought that I was back in Westerlo. Then I remembered—I was in Forest City, and it was trial day. They were going to shame me and take my land.

I rose to join Mrs. Blanchard in the kitchen. "Good morning, dear," she said, trying to be cheerful. The doctor came in, and his mood was more to my liking. His face was a rock upon which all pretending crashed and broke apart like water at the bottom of a falls. After a silent breakfast, he kissed his wife and forced a smile in my direction. I was to remain at the Blanchard house while they made the jury.

Mrs. Blanchard insisted that she clean the kitchen, while I got myself ready. There wasn't anything to get ready, so I just sat in the parlor and tried to read the *Daily Minnesotian*. But the print turned into a mosaic out of which jumped ugly faces. I had to put it down.

A while later a knock brought Mrs. Blanchard to the door. "I've come for Mrs. Slater." I got out of my chair, glad for things to be moving along, but when I saw Mr. Wylie, I took a step back. His orange hair had been smeared with pomade, and his hands were poking out from his Sunday clothes, which looked like they belonged to his big brother. Side by side, it might have been difficult to say which of us was on trial for pretending to be a man.

For the last several days, I had been worrying about our walk over to the courthouse. Might people gather to gawk? Might they follow us and say unpleasant things? As we left the Blanchard house, I kept my head down but soon realized I didn't need to. There wasn't a soul to be seen.

"Four farmers and two merchants," said Mr. Wylie as we made our way through the empty town. "A good jury, I think." He was trying to encourage me and doing a bad job of it. It didn't matter—I'd see for myself soon enough.

The town hall looked like a small barn, except that it had a door for people and a painted wooden cross hanging over it. We passed under and into the hall that seated perhaps a hundred and fifty, every seat taken. Why were they here? Didn't they have fields to tend or clothes to wash?

Heads turned as we came down the aisle. The swelling about my face had gone down some, but the purple bruises remained. I wondered whether those marks would bring sympathy or just be proof of my bad behavior. I didn't want to look at anyone—didn't want to see their delight in my troubles. But neither did I want to give them satisfaction by looking away, so I cast my eyes in their direction and erased their faces in my mind.

Mr. Smith rose and escorted me to the chair next to his. Off to the side were six men in a row and not one with a kind expression. Judge Robson came in wearing a black robe and a frown. He took his chair and brought down his hammer. "In the matter of the People versus Mrs. Lucy Ann Slater." He nodded to the county attorney.

In a freshly pressed shirt and hair slicked back, William Richards rose and addressed the court. "Your Honor, the people of Meeker County hereby charge Mrs. Lucy Ann Slater with wearing men's clothes to falsely impersonate a man, contrary to the laws of God, man and nature, practicing deceit and causing injury thereby to certain individual parties, to the moral fabric of the community, and against the peace and dignity of the State of Minnesota."

The judge turned. "What say you, Mr. Smith?"

My attorney stood and, of all things, seemed to suppress a yawn. His clothes were no different than those he wore every day; if anything, they were more rumpled. He paused and rubbed his nose as though thinking about his answer. "Your Honor, I ask for a dismissal on the grounds that no statute of the State of Minnesota or Meeker County has been violated. My client has broken no law and injured no person." Mr. Smith spoke simply and clearly. The motion seemed undeniable.

The judge shook his head. "It is quite clear, Mr. Smith, that a deceit has occurred. It will be the purpose of this trial to determine if any party has been injured or any law broken. Mr. Richards, continue."

My attorney raised his hand to show he wasn't done. "With the court's permission, I would also ask for dismissal on the grounds that my client has a right to a jury of her peers. Mrs. Slater is a woman. There are no women on this panel."

Judge Robson gave a look of warning. "Counselor, you see no women on this panel because, as you well know, in the State of Minnesota women do not serve on juries as a matter of law."

"That is my point, Your Honor. My client is entitled to a jury of her peers, and if one cannot be impaneled, the charges against her must be dropped."

"Mr. Smith," said the judge, taking on color. "I am aware of your political views. But I am not going to make new law here, and if you persist, I will have you removed and cited. Am I clear, Mr. Smith?"

My attorney lowered his eyes. "Yes, Your Honor."

I was a bit shaken by this. I glanced up at Mr. Smith, who, while keeping an outwardly repentant face, managed a small wink. I had no idea what it meant.

Mr. Richards rose. "I object to the defendant, dressed as she is in men's clothes. She mocks this court and these proceedings."

"Your Honor," answered Mr. Smith, "my client *is* properly attired. It is our assertion that by wearing these clothes, she has committed no offense. If the court requires her to change, it would prejudge the case."

Judge Robson thought for a moment. "I know of no precedent requiring a defendant to appear in certain clothing. Mr. Richards, begin."

The county prosecutor walked over to the jury and reminded them that it was they who would defend "the honor of our fair city." Then he called to mind that Minnesota had been a state for only a short while, so there had not been time to bring into law all that should guide our conduct—that we needed to consult common sense and precedent. He walked back to his table and picked up a dusty old book. "And what better precedent than the original laws of our land?"

"Oh, let me guess," said Mr. Smith, just loud enough for me and Mr. Wylie to hear.

Attorney Richards held up the book. He said it contained the laws of the Colony of New Haven. Then he opened to a chosen page and read aloud. *"Truth, whether through words or actions, is required of all men. Punishment will be given any person who wittingly maketh any lie, tending to the damage of any person, or with the intent to deceive the people with false news pernicious to the public weal."*

Richards looked at the rafters as though God Himself had authored those words. He held that pose for a moment and then looked back to the jury. "This is a simple law and a wise law. It identifies lies not just as spoken words but also as deceitful acts. It defines injury not only as damage to individuals but damage done to the public trust, the very well-being of the community. Think about that." Richards paused so they could.

"Now, let me read you another law of our forebears," he said, shaking his head, as though he were sad that it had come to this. "Some of you may find this harsh, but can we be lax when we defend the conduct we show our children? The law reads: *If any man lyeth with mankind as a man lyeth with a woman, both of them have committed abomination, they shall both surely be put to death. And if a woman change the natural use, into that which is against nature, she shall be liable to the same sentence."*

The courtroom was hushed. Richards closed the book with an unneeded slap. "I apologize to the womenfolk for having to sully the air around us with such language," he said, seeming not one bit sorry. "But here we see the intent of those who laid down the first laws of this land to keep the proper boundaries between men and women. Mrs. Slater has, most surely, crossed those boundaries."

"You dirty snake," said Mr. Wylie under his breath. I felt the same way and thought Mr. Smith would jump up and protest with passion. He didn't. He just got up and twisted a little to stretch his back. "Your Honor, may I inspect the volume from which our esteemed county attorney was reading?"

The judge nodded, and Mr. Smith picked up the book, turned some pages, and faced the jury. "I too should like to quote the code of 1650." He said the date slowly and clearly. Then he began to read. *"If any man have a stubborn rebellious son of sixteen years or upward, which will not obey the voice of his father or the voice of his mother; and that when they have chastened him will not hearken unto them, then shall his father and his mother lay hold on him, and bring him to the magistrates assembled in court, and testify unto them that their son is stubborn and rebellious and will not obey their voice and chastisement. Such a son will be put to death."*

Mr. Smith closed the book and let those words echo in the silence. "I shall not read further," he said, "but I know I could find similar punishments reserved for those who drink spirits and, if I remember correctly, kiss their children on the Sabbath." I glanced over and saw Mr. Richard's raise his eyes, as though Mr. Smith were making up stories. It didn't matter. The jury was watching Mr. Smith and he was looking hard at them. "Yes, the code of 1650 is a part of this nation's treasured history. But that code was *never* law in the *Territory* of Minnesota, and it is *not* law in the *State* of Minnesota, and I doubt whether any of you would like to make it so. After all, if everyone who told a lie were put in jail, we wouldn't have enough legislators left to pass another law to get them out."

There was laughter. Judge Robson pounded his hammer and glared at Mr. Smith. The judge seemed to be considering another rebuke, but, instead, he called a recess for the midday meal.

Mr. Smith let the courtroom clear before he walked me out the door and down the street toward the Blanchard house. "That was a bumpy beginning," I said.

My attorney knew that I meant the judge's order for him to say no more about women and the jury. "Well, yes," he answered, "but that's what we wanted."

"I don't remember wanting that."

Mr. Smith stopped and turned to me. "Mrs. Slater, what matters is how we finish. Now, as you know, Judge Robson has little sympathy for you or me, and he answers to the voters of this county. So it must appear that he has been hard on us all the way, otherwise, we can hope for no reason or kindness at the end. I'll let him bloody my nose another time if I can."

I looked at my attorney with new eyes. His common manner was something he wore like clothes, the wrinkles of which he had probably planned as well.

"I saw Noah White on the way out," I said, as we began walking again. "Is he to testify?"

"He's been called by Mr. Richards. So was Owen Carter."

I felt a sudden fear. "Where did they find him?"

"Somewhere south of St Cloud."

"Does he have a wife?"

My attorney shook his head. "I don't know."

* * *

By the start of the afternoon session, the heat had worked its way into every corner. A yellow dog in search of shade had wandered into the courtroom and fallen asleep in the back. And there weren't enough seats as people from the farther farms had come into town during the morning—come to town to see the show. The windows were opened to their fullest, so the folks outside could hear, and that worked well enough, I suppose, but no breeze came in return. People sat on the benches and fanned themselves.

Judge Robson came in, sat down, and told the county attorney to call his first witness. Mr. Richards called Dr. Blanchard. Mr. Smith stood up. "May I ask for what purpose this witness is called?"

A tiny smile made its way across Mr. Richard's face. "To determine for the record, the true sex of the defendant."

"But the county attorney asserts that my client is a female," said Mr. Smith. "*We* assert that my client is a female. There is no question of fact."

"I will permit the witness," said the judge. "I don't want any doubt about this. Now or later."

Dr. Blanchard got up and walked forward, not trying to hide his frown. He took the oath and Mr. Richards began. "Doctor, are you familiar with the defendant?"

"I am. She has resided in my house for the past week."

"Were you instructed by Judge Robson to make an examination?"

"I was."

"Can you tell the court the results?"

I did my best to look indifferent, but my clothes were coming off with a hundred people looking on. The doctor, who had made no examination, did his best to dampen the excitement. "I will simply say that by my observation the defendant, Mrs. Slater, is truly a woman."

"Could you be more specific?"

"No."

Mr. Richards let the doctor go. He then called out for Owen Carter. Owen had been seated in the back when we entered for the afternoon. He appeared very much the way he had in Kandiyohi, but he didn't look at me when he walked forward. He wasn't happy to be there, that was clear, and I had no idea of what Richards would ask him or what Owen might say.

Once the oath had been taken, Mr. Richards began. "Mr. Carter," he said, "you had occasion to spend time with the defendant. Would you tell us how that came about? When was it?"

"Two winters past," Owen said in a low voice. The judge asked him to speak louder. "Two winters past. We held a site in Kandiyohi for the new state capital. At least that is what we was told."

"Did you know that the defendant was a woman?"

"No," he said, looking down as a ripple of laughter crossed in the room.

"Did the defendant represent herself as a man?"

Owen thought for a moment. "Well, she let me think that she were."

Attorney Richards shook his head as though sorry to hear this. "And by this deception," he continued, "did she ever lead you to embarrass yourself?" I thought of Owen's cries in the dark as he pleasured himself with thoughts of Allison Murphy, but Owen just sat there, seeming confused by the question. "What I mean," said Richards, "is did you ever do things in front of her that you would not have done if you knew she was a woman? Things of a personal nature."

Owen's face was turning color. "I s'pose."

"I need an answer that is yes or no, Mr. Carter."

"Well, uh, yes, I guess. I weren't really paying much attention."

Attorney Richards nodded as if to say his worst suspicions had been confirmed. "And do you believe that you have suffered injury because of Mrs. Slater's deception? By way of these lies do you feel that something was stolen from you? A piece of your dignity, perhaps?"

I saw a flash in Owen's eyes. Maybe he didn't like how the county attorney was twisting things. Or maybe he just wanted to throttle me. I couldn't tell, but whatever it was, I could see the storm building as he sat there.

"Mr. Carter," said the judge. "Please answer the question."

Owen gave his head a slow shake like he was still sorting it out.

"Mr. Carter."

Owen cast a quick glance in my direction. Our eyes met for a brief moment and then Owen looked back at the county attorney. "No. Joseph never stole nothin' from me."

Mr. Richards decided to end it there, and as soon as he had taken his chair, Mr. Smith was standing in his place. "Mr. Carter," he said, "in the time you lived with her, did Mrs. Slater in every other way conduct herself honestly toward you?"

"Yes," he said, again looking down.

"Did she share in the work and the hardship?"

"She did."

"Was there a lot of hardship to be shared?"

"Well, it was cold that winter, and we ran low on food."

Mr. Smith nodded and walked away from Owen, as though thinking about his next question. He turned, no longer friendly in his manner. "Mr. Carter, you would have us believe that in all that time that you and Mrs. Slater were together, you did not observe that she was a woman?"

The suspicious tone of the question surprised me. Owen too. "I swore it on a Bible," he said, glancing at the judge as though for help.

Mr. Smith acted astonished. "How, Mr. Carter, is that possible?"

"Well, it were pretty dark most all of the time," Owen said with the slightest stammer, "and I weren't paying attention 'cause I had no reason to."

"In other words, Mr. Carter," said Mr. Smith, now looking at the jury, "you were giving her—though you didn't know she was a woman—you were giving Mr. Joseph Lobdell the normal courtesy of privacy that people give each other when they are in close quarters. Living where we do, we know it is not uncommon for people in small cabins to give each other privacy through inattention when no other means are at hand. This they do as a matter of course." Mr. Smith folded his arms. "Mr. Carter. Do you have any reason to think that Mrs. Slater didn't extend to you the courtesy of privacy that you extended to her?"

There was short silence before Owen spoke. "No. I would think that she did."

My attorney let that answer hang in the air. Then he said he was done. Owen got up, and as he stepped down from the chair, his eyes, again, came to me. But the moment didn't last long enough for me to even say a silent thank-you. He walked out of the hall.

Mr. Richards went back to his table and looked through his papers, while the room filled with the dull sound of people shifting about and saying this or that to the one next to them. It all became quiet again as Mr. Richards stepped forward. "The People call Mr. Elijah Noah White." I glanced about as did others. I saw Noah sitting off to one side. And he was looking about too, as if to see if someone else in the room would answer to that name. When no one did, he rose. He wasn't much to look at, standing there in his everyday overalls and walking forward with that odd gait of his and a wearing small grin as though he was somewhat amused by it all. I didn't think Richards knew what kind of fish he had on the line. The Bible was presented, and Noah declined.

"I will tell the truth," he said. "I don't need to swear it to God."

"Yes, you do," said Judge Robson. "You are in my court, and you will take your oath on the Bible or find yourself in the defendant's chair."

Noah gave a shrug and placed his hand on the Bible. By this time the flies had become a general bother. People used newspapers to drive them off, but they never went far. A large one took a liking to Mr. Richards. The county attorney first tried to act unconcerned. Then he waved his arm. The fly persisted. The prosecutor finally thought to walk back and forth. The fly moved on.

"I understand," he said to Noah, "that you spent time with the defendant two winters ago. Did she also lead you to believe that she was a man?"

"I believed she was," said Noah agreeably. "A better man than most I know."

I heard laughter, and Judge Robson turned to Noah. "You will confine yourself to answering the questions put to you."

Noah looked as though he wanted to answer back, but he didn't.

Richards started again. "Mr. White, were you injured in any way by Mrs. Slater's deception?"

Noah took a quick look around the room. "Well, I had to come here and testify," he said. "Lost four good-weather days. But that was your doing, so I guess my quarrel would be with you, sir."

Noah's poke at Richards brought more laughter. Judge Robson pounded his hammer. "I will not have you telling jokes in my courtroom! We all have better things to do!"

"The county attorney doesn't seem to," said Noah, showing no fear. "I'm happy to hear that there are no real criminals in Meeker County."

Judge Robson was about to explode. He was ready to put Noah in jail, and Noah was ready to go, that very fact maybe keeping Robson from doing it, uncertain as to who would appear more the fool. Mr. Richards said he had no more questions and went back to his table, looking like he wanted to hide under it. Mr. Smith, enjoying all the discomfort, was slow to take his place. He might have asked Noah something about my character as he had done with Owen, but he didn't. My attorney, it seemed, wished to make it plain that it was not *he* who had brought this witness to the room and it was not *he* who had brought this case to trial. He looked hard at the judge. "I have no questions."

Noah left the chair, and the judge watched his every step. A stray hiccup would have been enough to put him behind bars, but Noah took his seat and stayed quiet. I was now expecting to see Otis Whitmore, but neither he nor James was in the courtroom. Had they refused to come? Refused to be part of the lynching? Perhaps they had some unpleasant history of their own with the county attorney.

There was a recess, but I stayed where I was and examined the scratches on the table like they were some sort of map to get me out of there.

* * *

Mr. Smith stepped forward and called for Mrs. Lucy Ann Slater. I stood and walked to the witness chair. Every eye was on me—like crawling bugs. In that moment I was glad that I had not killed Willie. If this much trouble had come of a simple pair of pants, what could be made of a man with a bullet in his head?

The Bible was brought, and I swore to tell the truth. Mr. Smith approached.

"Mrs. Slater, did you ever tell anyone that you were a man?"

"I don't think I ever did. Not in words."

"But by your conduct and your dress, you did lead them to believe something you knew not to be true?"

"Yes."

"And so you did deceive people, even if you did not use words to do it. Is that so?"

"Yes, it is."

"Mrs. Slater, would you tell us why?"

I took a quick look at Mr. Smith for courage. "I had been abandoned by my husband and just wanted to live free here in Minnesota. On land of my own. And that would have been near impossible as a woman, so I pretended to be a man. I hoped that someday my daughter would join me."

"Thank you, Mrs. Slater." Mr. Smith seemed to think that was all I needed to say. He sat down.

Mr. Richards stood and slowly came toward me. I saw hate pour out of those small, gray eyes. I was expecting to tremble, but my eyes, fueled by a hatred of their own, did not turn from his. I was unmasked as a man, but defiant now as a woman.

Mr. Richards began his work. "Mrs. Slater," he said, "you took an oath to tell the truth in this courtroom, did you not?"

"Yes. You were here when I did it."

Richards glanced at Judge Robson to see if he would scold me. The judge fingered the hammer but said nothing. Richards pressed on.

"And that oath required you to tell the whole truth, did it not?"

"Yes."

Mr. Richards acted like a great curtain would now be pulled back. "So tell me, Mrs. Slater, when you deceived the good citizens of this county as to your true nature and let them conduct themselves unfairly in your presence, did you do this deception knowingly?"

I met his cold eyes. "I thought I made that clear already."

Attorney Richards then asked Judge Robson to instruct me to answer only the question asked and not to add opinions, and the judge did so. Richards then asked me the same question, and I said I did *knowingly* deceive people, at which point he walked back to his table as though he had won a big victory. Then he turned with an odd smile.

"Mrs. Slater, you have testified that you had hoped to live Minnesota in the company of your daughter, did you not?"

"I did."

"Well then, please tell us, Mrs. Slater, when your daughter arrived in Minnesota, were you to be her mother or her father?"

There was laughter. Mr. Smith jumped up.

"Your Honor!"

"Mr. Richards!" said the judge.

"Withdrawn," said the county attorney, not trying to conceal his smirk.

I felt the power of ridicule and stole a quick glance at the jurors. What did holding on to my land mean to them? Was there anything that Mr. Smith could say that would bring them to my side? They weren't there now.

27

JUDGE ROBSON STRUCK the table three times. The attorneys would now address the jury.

Richards rose and did his best to assure everyone that he was speaking, not just to the jury but to "all the honest, hardworking citizens in this land of steady habits." He said these words as though Mr. Smith would be speaking only to the dishonest, lazy ones. Richards went on about lines drawn in the sand and laws of God. He didn't mention any law of Minnesota that I had broken but instead offered his indignation as the true measure of my offense. He made it sound as though I carried some dreaded disease that would spread like pox among the children.

When it was his turn, Mr. Smith got up and walked in a slow circle. He spoke about "freedom" and "liberty." About how they need to get stood for every now and then. Mr. Smith then asked the jurors if they thought that they had the right, the liberty, to choose their own clothes. Or did they want the sheriff to do it for them? There was some laughter as he said these words, but the judge didn't move a muscle—he was letting him have his say. "We have come a long way since the days of the New Haven Colony," said Mr. Smith by way of summation. "Liberty is the gift we have brought to the world. Let us defend it."

Finished with the jury, Mr. Smith started back to our table. Then he stopped and turned to face Judge Robson. "Your Honor, I wish to petition the Court—"

The judge waved his hand for Mr. Smith to stop. "Counselor, you know—"

"What I know," said Mr. Smith, raising his voice in outright defiance, "what I know is that this trial is a minstrel show! It's an embarrassment! A travesty!" The judge tried to say something, but Mr. Smith wouldn't let him, as though Mr. Smith were the one wearing the black robe. I was surprised, for I had not seen this passion from my attorney before. And Mr. Smith was not speaking to the jury or anyone else in the room. It was down to just him and Robson, like they were going to finish it out on the street. "This woman," said Mr. Smith, pointing to me but still looking hard at the judge, "has cheated no one! Defrauded no one! And violated no law of this state! I know this and you know this. I move for a summary judgment."

The room was suddenly quiet. All eyes went to Judge Robson to see what he would do. And for all that had just happened the judge was strangely calm. "Are you done, Mr. Smith?"

"Yes," said my attorney, now speaking in a normal voice.

"You may sit down now."

Mr. Smith took his seat, and the judge turned to me. "Mrs. Slater," he said, his eyes meeting mine like a scolding schoolmaster, "I am offended by your conduct and think you should desist from it or leave the protection of our society. But juries decide matters of fact, and judges decide matters of law. And it seems there is no matter of fact at issue here. It is for me to act, and I cannot wash my hands of it, though I would like to."

The judge then raised his eyes and spoke to the whole room. "There have been in this trial references to the laws of God and man. Here, on Sundays, as you know, I pass on the Lord's Word as best I understand it to those who would listen. If Mrs. Slater has violated a law of God, then she will stand as a defendant without counsel, as we all will when we face that moment of truth. But in this venue, I interpret the laws of the State of Minnesota and those of Meeker County. And so I must dismiss the case against Mrs. Lucy Ann Slater, because no offense has been proven against her." He then brought down the hammer. "So be it."

A murmur of disapproval ran through the room. Mr. Smith stood and shook my hand. I wanted to throw my arms around him. Out on the street, we faced a gaggle of women who seemed angry at the outcome. I heard the words "harlot" and "Jezebel." With Dr. Blanchard and Mr. Wylie opening the path for us, Mr. Smith offered his arm.

The doctor's house felt warm and safe. Mrs. Blanchard was roasting a chicken, and Mr. Wylie and Mr. Smith were invited to dinner. Then Noah White appeared, all smiles. He gave a bow to Mrs. Blanchard and shook hands all around.

"We were very glad to have your sympathies," said Mr. Wylie.

Mr. Smith raised his eyes. "Yes. They almost cost us the case."

Noah laughed because he knew Mr. Smith didn't mean it. The he turned to me. Our eyes met and he took my hand. "Lucy Ann. Is it all right that I call you that? Or would you rather Joseph?"

I felt awkward. I was blushing. "We could try Lucy Ann," I said, "and see if anyone's at home."

"Well, Lucy Ann," said Noah with a grin, "I see that the Blanchard's have a checkerboard. Are you up to the challenge?"

"Yes," I said, "if I can be black."

* * *

At dinner, Dr. Blanchard asked me to say the blessing. I folded my hands and bowed my head. "Lord, thank You for the true souls You have put in my path. I have never known such generosity. Bless the meal before us and bless us to Thy purpose."

The food was passed, and then Mrs. Blanchard said that she and the doctor had been honored to have me as a guest in their home.

"I hope I haven't cost you any friends," I said.

The doctor laughed. "Oh, if I've ruffled any feathers, I'll be forgiven in a week."

"Yes," said Mr. Smith, "because it's you who stands between them and God, not Robson." There was laughter at this remark, and I did my best to appear merry, but underneath I was afraid. Mr. Smith seemed to sense it. "What will you do tomorrow?" he asked.

"I will go back to my farm," I said without much conviction. "I will tend to my garden and go to Manannah as little as possible. I just want to live in peace, if people will let me."

"You'll be surprised at how fast this will be water under the bridge," said the doctor. "The people around here are decent, despite what you saw today."

"And you needn't fear anything from Willie," said Mr. Smith. "We had a little conversation. He's gone and won't be back." I had already told my attorney, days ago, that I didn't want to file charges against Willie—I wanted the whole thing to be over. Now Mr. Smith had taken it upon himself to act on my behalf. I thanked him for his concern and his efforts. Then Noah asked if I would like him to come in the morning and walk with me on the road back home. I said yes.

*　*　*

We set out on the Manannah road, I still dressed as a man, but now known to be a woman. I liked it.

"How is my dear Cleopatra?" I asked.

"Oh, she rules the house," said Noah. "The hardest part in living with her is that when I'm deciding what to have for dinner, I end up thinking about what she might like."

I laughed. "Have they built the new capital?"

"Well, they built another cabin. But other than that, all that's there are thousands of stakes with colored ribbons. Looks like flowers in a meadow when you first see it."

Noah was in his own gleeful mood. He began to recount the trial, as though I hadn't been there. He remembered the county attorney as an amusing villain. I forced a laugh or two.

"You had us all fooled," he said.

"I didn't fool you."

"Well, you did for a while. Then Owen came by and insisted you were twenty. Something wasn't right. And as soon as I thought it, I knew it was true."

"So you just made up that girl cousin of yours?"

"No, you do remind me of my cousin. But you're right. I did mention her just to see what you'd say. You were light on your feet, but it didn't matter."

"But you didn't let on about it to Owen."

"Nah, I just wanted to help. To tell you the truth, I still feel that way." Noah stopped walking and turned to me. "Now, as you know, Lucy Ann, I am married. But if I wasn't, I would have you for a wife, if you would have me."

Noah searched my eyes, and I felt at once that his invitation was more than just suppose—his wife was never coming west. And neither was George Slater. And who was going to care anyway? Out here you could be a soiled dove one year, a farmer's wife the next and not have to sit in the back pew. I could live as Noah's wife. I could be Noah's wife. It was, in many ways, the perfect answer. I didn't want to be alone forever, and here was a man who loved me and who wanted to be with me, strange as I was. I was very fond of Noah and greatly enjoyed his company. And beyond that, I loved him. I did. I may not have known it until that very moment, but at that moment I did know it. I loved him. A woman might live five lifetimes and not meet an offer of such promise.

I trembled as the truth moved closer. I was unmasked as a man but still in disguise. I had traded Joseph for Mrs. Slater, but Mrs. Slater was further from the truth, because I didn't want to be with a man. I wanted to be with Lydia—or someone like her or someone like Jenny Lindross. So in that way, I was, as Lucy Ann, more the deceiver than I was before. And if I were to live as Noah's wife, I would have to play a deceiver's part every day for the rest of my life. I could not honestly lie down with him, so how could I marry him?

"Oh, Noah," I said, feeling my eyes water, "if I could be anyone's wife, I would be yours. But I can't. This may be hard to understand, but please try. I am more Joseph than I am the woman you might think you see. You were deceived once already. I could not do that to you again."

I watched as my words fell upon him like blows. I moved forward and gave him a clumsy kiss on the brow. "Noah, you have been the best friend I could ever have." This made me feel worse. I realized that nothing I could say would make him or me feel better. He had offered me his life—his very life—and words in return seemed like coins. I was breaking his heart. But better to break it once than to do it slowly over years.

Noah nodded as though he understood. He was considerate even in his pain. "If you would like," he offered, "I could stay with you until things settle down." It was a gallant, generous offer, and deep inside I wanted him to stay with me. But I said that I needed to be by myself. I think he suspected that I was lying, but he was in no position to insist. Just ahead of us on the road, a rough track branched off and went south, not the easiest path to Kandiyohi, but Noah decided to take it. He turned to me with a pained smile. "Good-bye, Joseph."

I should have gone to him and thrown my arms around him and held him as hard as I could, so he would know that I loved him, but I felt awkward and afraid. I stood where I was as he walked down the track. Even after he was out of sight, I fought the urge to run after him.

Walking west by myself, I tried to think of how things might be for me now in Minnesota. I should be happy. They had tried to take my land but failed. I still had my farm and what was left of my ambition. And why couldn't it work? If Mr. Smith was right, Willie was gone for good. Perhaps the people of Manannah and those of Forest City would come to accept me as a woman. Why not? Then I wondered if there were other women like me, women who wanted to be with women. There had to be. Maybe many. But how to find each other?

Perhaps my story—a woman put on trial for wearing men's clothes— would be retold in the newspapers, like the story of the attack upon Mrs. Swisshelm. Women who were like me might read it and take it for their beacon. They would find their way to my farm. We might become a family and, later, a community, like the Bois Brûlés. Then perhaps many would find their way to our village. And like the Bois Brûlés, we would work hard and act honestly toward all. And like the Bois Brûlés, we would wear bright colors, play music, and dance. These thoughts gave me some comfort as I walked alone toward my land and a new life.

When Willie's place came into view, my stomach turned. I thought about leaving the road and finding my way along the river. But I kept on, and there were no signs of life around the cabin and no horses. I felt a relief that came with a great tiredness. I thought of my bed.

My cabin lay in a hollow behind a grove of trees, so I could not see it until I gained the small hill to the east. When I reached the heights, I looked down and saw burnt logs and rafters still smoking.

As though in a dream, I walked closer. The shed was in ruins, and the chickens lay dead in the yard. I went to where the cabin had been and looked at the burned remains. There, along the back wall, was the charred neck of what had once been my violin.

PART III

Galilee

For seven years she roamed the mountains of Delaware, Sullivan and Ulster Counties. She lived in huts and hovels that she threw up with logs and bark, and appeared at the settlements only to dispose of skins or game to get ammunition and supplies.

—Frank P. Woodward, *Wayne Independent*, Oct. 19, 1928, describing Lucy Lobdell's whereabouts in the 1860s

28

A VOICE INSIDE my head begged me to turn back—had been begging all afternoon. But I hadn't listened to it, and now I stood before a white clapboard house. The elm tree in the back was larger than I remembered, but the crooked porch was much the same. I climbed the stairs and knocked on the side door. It opened to reveal a great turnip of a woman, none too pleased for being disturbed. "What do you want?"

I stood straight, as though that would hide my rags. "I would like to speak to the master of the house."

The woman grew larger still. "I am the master of this poorhouse," she said. "The men's beds are all taken, and we don't give handouts."

"I'm not looking for food," I said, hungry as a stray.

"Well, what then?"

"I'm asking after a girl who lives here."

"And who is that?"

I paused, barely able to manage the words. "Helen Slater."

The woman seemed briefly startled. Her eyes narrowed, and her voice dropped to a menacing whisper. "And what would your business with her be?"

The answer to that question was a box of stones that I had to lift and hand to her. "I am her mother."

The woman gave her head a quick shake, having supposed me to be a drunkard and a man. I thought she was going to tell me to go away, but she moved aside. "Come in."

The room smelled of soap and hot water, as two women were washing clothes in a tub off to the side. I was led past them, down a hall and into a parlor. The woman closed the door behind us and folded her arms. "I am Mrs. Florence McNee, resident housemaster. Who are you?"

"Lucy Ann Slater," I said, with a slight stumble. I hadn't called myself that in a long time. It didn't sound right. I tried again. "Mrs. Lucy Ann Slater."

"And you say Helen is your daughter?"

I nodded. "Does she still live here?"

The woman shook her head. "No. She's gone."

"Gone where?"

"To Pennsylvania. A farmer took her."

"A farmer?" I said, unsure. "And he will marry her?"

"No, dear," she said, seeming more kind. "He took her to live with his family. She will be his daughter. A good man, I think, or I wouldn't have let her go."

My feelings ran in all directions. I was glad that Helen was safe, pained to my soul that I wouldn't see her, and relieved that I wouldn't have to. Yes, I felt that as well. It had taken strength to set aside my fears and come in search of her, but those fears hadn't gone away. I looked back at Mrs. McNee. "When did she leave?"

The woman took a long breath. "Just a month ago."

Could this be? After years apart, had I missed my daughter by a matter of days? If true, there was only one way it could have come about. God had sent a Pennsylvania man to save my daughter from me. What other explanation?

The tears began. I hadn't cried for seven years, since the day I'd been attacked by Willie McAllister. But once that dam broke, the feelings that poured through were not just for the loss of Helen, but for everything—all my troubles at home, and those in Minnesota, and after that, the cold years alone in the woods. And then I must have fallen, for suddenly I was on the floor looking up at Mrs. McNee who was kneeling over me. Others were in the room. "Joan, heat water for a bath. Audrey, help me take her clothes."

"Shall I boil them?"

"Burn them."

A little later, I was in a warm tub. Mrs. McNee took a coarse cloth to me and then told me to lie with my head back. "There's no help for it," she said, taking a scissors and cutting my hair down to the scalp.

Once bathed and shorn, I was put into a nightshirt and led upstairs. I fell into a sleep that went on for a day. When I finally woke, I found myself in a real bed with ticking and sheets. I wasn't awake but a short time when Mrs. NcNee came into the room. She took the chair by the bed and patted my hand. I supposed she was there to say that it was time for me to leave, but she just sat there and looked out the window.

"I was married when I was sixteen," she said at last. "A year later I had a daughter, but I lost her when she was two. Scarlet fever. Everyone said it was God's will, but I could see no purpose to it. I cursed God and haven't been to church since. Then my husband died when his wagon turned over."

"I'm sorry, ma'am, about your little girl," I said, not knowing why she was telling me these things. "And about your husband."

Mrs. McNee gave a nod to accept my regrets, but she had more to say. "You should know that in Helen I found the daughter that had been taken from me. I did not want to let her go, but I believed she'd have a better life on Mr. Fortnam's farm. I miss her terribly. Then you arrive, and I don't know what to make of it."

I didn't know what to make of it either. Here was a woman who had seen Helen grow. Had given her love and been the mother I had not been. "I haven't seen Helen since she was small," I said.

I thought those words would condemn me in Mrs. McNee's eyes, but instead she smiled kindly. "Then let me tell you. Your daughter is as warm as the sun in the morning. Funny, brave, and kind."

Your daughter. Suddenly, I saw my little girl on the grass outside our house on Basket Creek, all of ten months, standing up and with shrieks of delight, taking her first steps. "Yes," I said, "she was like that, even as a little one."

There was a worried look behind Mrs. McNee's smile. "There's something you should know." I was afraid of it, but I met her eyes. "Helen thinks you're dead."

"And well she might," I whispered. What I would not explain was that I had been sick, sick for years, a fever of the mind. I had lived in huts in the woods, not much better than an animal. I didn't talk to anyone. I certainly didn't write letters. I didn't see or hear from my sisters, and that would have been near impossible, for how were they to know what state or county I was in, or even if I were still alive? It was all my doing, not theirs. I went into the woods, because it was that or be put in a cage. Later, when I was better, I did not want to be seen by anyone who had known me before. I was ashamed. I thought it best for all if I just stayed dead. But none of this I wanted to share with Mrs. McNee. She accepted my silence, stood, and ran the wrinkles out of her dress. "You can stay here, if you want."

I was weak and had no prospects. "Thank you," I said. "Yes. At least for a time."

"You know, of course, that everyone here works, from sunup to sunset—six days a week."

"I'll do anything," I said. "I'm good with an axe, and I can hunt."

Mrs. McNee looked amused. "Well, perhaps a wild boar for Christmas would be a treat. But first we must get you dressed. There's a room downstairs where we have some clothes. Why don't you go with Audrey and find a fresh dress to wear?"

"I don't want a dress." The words were out before I could grab them. But how to explain? "I'm sorry, ma'am. It's just I wouldn't know how to wear one. It's been ten years."

Mrs. McNee thought for a moment. "You can wear what clothes you like so long as you don't dishonor this house. Do you want to be called Lucy or Mrs. Slater?"

"Ma'am, if you don't mind, I'd liked to be called Joseph." And why did I have say that? It was the last straw, for sure—I'd be on the road within the hour.

The housemaster was not pleased and looked at me hard. "But you told me that your name was Lucy, Lucy Slater."

"It *was* Lucy," I said, almost pleading. "But it isn't now. Most people just call me Joe."

Mrs. McNee raised her eyes to the ceiling. "Lord knows I don't give people their names. Folks here can call you what they like or what you like—that's between you and them. And you can tell people about Helen or not. I haven't said a thing, and it won't come from me. I know a lot of things that I keep to myself. As for us, it's your conduct that's my concern. Live honestly here and we'll be fine."

* * *

The Delaware County Almshouse sat on the river flats across from the town of Delhi. It needed paint and leaned to the south, but the roof kept the rain out. The kitchen and eating hall were on the first floor, as was the large room off to the side where the men slept in bunks. The women and children stayed in the many small rooms upstairs. One of these, hardly more than a closet, was given to me.

After seven years alone in the woods, I had to learn again how to live with others. Mostly, I did what I was told and stayed out of people's way. I wore pants and a shirt, and when my hair grew back, I kept it short. I wasn't pretending to be a man. These were the clothes I wanted to wear, and no one seemed to mind. They called me Joe, for Joseph, or Jo, for Josephine, I don't know which because you can't tell how people are spelling things when they are speaking. I didn't mention Helen to anyone, and Mrs. McNee kept my secret. For the house register, I went by the name of Lobdell.

I worked that summer in the large garden out back. After hunting for so many years, I came to enjoy the dirt. It was alive and ripe. Caring for plants calmed me. Not so calming were the daily moans and howls from the building near the garden. It might have been a barn for chickens, it had that look, but it wasn't. It was a barn for the insane, and it never failed to throw a terror into me.

Mrs. McNee had strict orders to keep the inmates, as they were called, confined. But every now and then, when one seemed to have promise, the garden crew, with Mrs. McNee's consent, would ignore the order and bring the poor soul out to work. Sometimes the sunshine and companionship brought about a cure. It did good things for me. I had just spent seven years in the gray land between the dead and the living. Now I was back in the living world, but even so, it was a world without hopes or expectations.

And I didn't want any—they had only caused me trouble in the past. Now there was nothing for me beyond each day as it unfolded—one day and the next, trying to follow the Lord's commandments. People got used to having me around.

* * *

I had been at the almshouse for several months when one afternoon Mrs. McNee asked me to come to her office after dinner. I didn't like the sound of it. Once the table was cleared and the dining room swept, I went to her office where she was at her desk, making notes in a ledger. She asked me to sit and forced a smile in my direction. I wanted to run.

"I received a letter yesterday," she said. "It's from Helen."

I tried to calm myself. "Is she well?"

"Oh, she's fine," said Mrs. McNee, letter in hand. "If you'd like, I'll read it to you."

I nodded but was strangely afraid. I wanted to hear Helen's words but feared the failings they might call to mind. Mrs. McNee adjusted her spectacles.

"*Dear Mrs. McNee,*" she began, in a voice meant to enliven the words. "*I'm sorry I didn't write sooner, but the days have flown by. I was very sad when Mr. Fortnam took me away, but now I am content. Tyler Hill is a lovely place, and everyone has been more than kind . . .*"

Helen told about the Fortnam farm and her new brothers and sisters. She said that she worked long hours, but that she didn't mind, for everyone worked hard and she was treated well. She said that she missed Mrs. McNee very much and promised not to wait so long to write again. She signed it, *Love, your Helen.*

Suddenly, I felt bare. I had told myself when I left home many years ago that I was going to find work and a place for myself and my daughter. I failed. And somewhere along the way, I had begun to look for something else—freedom for myself. I had found it only in bits and pieces. But what good is freedom without love?

"She sounds happy," I said.

"Yes, I think so. But you worry, because people sometimes take a girl, and the child finds herself a servant." Mrs. McNee paused. "I will write back to her, Joe. Do you want me to say you are here?"

"Oh, please no!" I cried. "It's enough to know that she's well. If she thinks I'm dead, then perhaps that's for the best."

Mrs. McNee seemed startled by my outburst, but she didn't ask why it would be for the best. But then, of course, she might know. She, herself, had given up Helen, broken her own heart, and let Helen go so that she might have a real home. And now that she had one, was it for me to suddenly appear and curdle the milk? What did I have to offer, except my shame and destitution? Beyond that, I was sure that Helen would hate me less if she thought me dead, and in this, I was thinking more about me than her—about what I could bear. And I didn't want things to change for me. It might seem that I had fallen as far as a person could—that I had nothing to lose—but that wasn't so. I had been to a place far below. I had been cold, hungry, and lonely enough for ten lives, and I never wanted to go back. At the almshouse I had a bed to sleep in, food to eat, and people to talk to. Things I hadn't had for years. And if you haven't had those things, you don't think of them as nothing.

* * *

When the weather turned and the ground became hard, those of us who worked in the garden were offered to the townsfolk as house helpers. The fee for our labor, paid to the county, was small, so many people took this service. But suspicious eyes fell on any new arrival who might be a thief as well as poor. I thought this peculiar, for in my experience, poor people were no less honest than others. Often, I found them more so. Still, because I was new and a little strange, I was given work two days a week cleaning the courthouse and the sheriff's office, where my good conduct was thought assured.

Sheriff Evans was at his desk the day I first came.

"And what can I do for you?" he said, leaning back in his chair.

"I'm Joe Lobdell, sir," I said, in military fashion. "I'm a resident of the County House and here to work."

The sheriff shrugged as if to say it was all right with him, whatever the county wished to send. My hair was still short, and I was wearing trousers, but he knew, of course, who I was and that I was a woman—my story had made the rounds. I think he was a little amused, but whatever he was thinking, he didn't make my time difficult. He went about his tasks, and I went about mine. Had it been my choice, I would have remained at the almshouse and done any kind of work, just to be with people I knew and not have to think of things to say to people I didn't.

Curtis Evans was a close-shaved man with a tarnished pistol on his hip. He lived just outside of town with a wife and two daughters. I learned this from Mrs. McNee, for the sheriff and I didn't talk much. That changed one afternoon when Evans saw me stop to admire the rack of rifles chained to the wall. "You know what you're looking at?" he asked. I nodded. "You know how to shoot?" I nodded again. "Well, I'll be damned."

"Most likely," I said. That answer made him laugh. The sheriff then took out a key and unlocked the guns, pulling down a breach-loading carbine he was fond of. I saw his surprise when I held it with ease.

"I used to hunt," I said. "Along the Delaware. And in Minnesota."

The sheriff gave a disbelieving look. "You were in Minnesota? When?"

"Before it was a state."

I handed the rifle back, and he leaned it against the wall. "I had thought to go myself," he said. "How was it?"

"Cold in the winter, but I liked it fine."

Evans smiled. Maybe he didn't believe me. For my part, I hadn't spoken of Minnesota in years.

"Did you see Indians?" he asked.

"Not many. Most of them had been penned up."

"Lucky you weren't there for the uprising."

"Oh, I was. It just wasn't as big as people first thought."

"No," said the sheriff. "I mean the one three years ago. Hundreds of settlers were killed—entire towns wiped out."

Entire towns? I remembered the fear I had seen the day I walked into Manannah.

"Do you remember what towns?" I asked. "Would the names Manannah or Forest City sound familiar?"

The sheriff shook his head. "No. I just read that they got burned. Then they sent in the soldiers and rounded up all the redskins. Had a big hangin' day. They won't be bothering anyone now."

Hanging day? I felt a rush of sadness for the settlers and the Sioux. And then the questions: What about the people who had offered me their kindness—the Whitmores, the Blanchards, Noah White, and Jenny Lindross? What had become of them?

29

WHEN SPRING CAME, I contrived to continue my work in town. By then, Sheriff Evans and I got along pretty good. I liked when people stopped in and passed the news or played checkers with the sheriff. Sometimes, when he wasn't there, they'd ask questions of me. When would the sheriff be back? Had the mail come in from Oneonta? Laugh if you care to, but each of these was evidence that I was, indeed, a living person. And to have it be a true test, I waited to be spoken to. I don't know what they said about me when I wasn't there, though I did hear that some people teased the sheriff by referring to me as the deputy. But in my presence, nobody went out of their way to be mean about my clothes or short hair, an unexpected acceptance that I wanted to keep.

When the men played checkers, I would usually find a way to watch from a polite distance. I liked the game and hadn't forgotten the tricks I had learned in Minnesota. I would see things that others didn't and often had to hold my tongue. But one slow day I didn't hold my tongue but instead challenged the sheriff to a game. I had overstepped my bounds—I was not his equal. But there was no one around, and the sheriff agreed to play. I beat him that first time, and from then on, it wasn't hard to get a game out of him. He was eager to get back at me, and he did, often enough. One afternoon he caught me daydreaming and jumped me twice.

"What were you starin' at?" he asked, taking my pieces.

"The cells in the back," I said with a yawn.

"They're the same ones that were there last week."

"I thought they might be," I said, taking the bait, "but are they the ones where they kept the Calico Indians?"

The sheriff dropped one of the checkers and looked at me like I might be a ghost. "What would you know about that?"

I paused, because I knew a lot of it. The struggle between the farmers and the fancy-name landlords—Van-this and Von-somethingelse—had gone on for most of my girlhood. "Back then," I said, "we lived a little east of here—out near Schoharie. Men were called to help the farmers. My father went out. Were you here then?"

"Oh, I was," said Evans with a smile that meant more than he was saying.

"You were on the other side?"

"It weren't no *other side*," he said. "It was the law."

It all came rushing back. My father going out in the night. My uncle Tom getting arrested and losing his land. Land on which he'd built a barn. "The farms should belong to the people who clear the land," I said, repeating what I had heard many times when I was a girl.

The sheriff shook his head. "The land belongs to the person who holds the deed!"

"Deed?" I said, unable to let it be. "A deed that came from some duke or earl? We had a war to end all that if I remember my lessons."

I wasn't saying anything new. Neither was he. This was an old argument—we both knew how it went. So I was surprised when I saw Evans getting worked up. "They had no damn right to break the law!" he shouted. His knee hit the checkerboard and the pieces went flying.

I wasn't going to say anything back to that. I just ducked down and tried to pick up the checkers, but the sheriff told me to get out.

I didn't tell Mrs. McNee about my argument with Sheriff Evans. I was afraid. There I was, once again, making a mess of things. And what would happen now? After all, if I were not good enough to work at the jail, would I be allowed to stay at the almshouse? Perhaps the sheriff would make up some story that had nothing to do with the farmers' uprising. He could say almost anything. But I couldn't bring myself to tell Mrs. McNee—even for her to know my side of things. Like every child in trouble, I hoped it would go away on its own. I wasn't due at the jail for another four days, and I was certain by then I would hear not to come. When that didn't happen, I expected the sheriff wanted to tell me himself. But he wasn't at the office when I arrived, so I started cleaning in the back. Evans came in soon enough, didn't say a word and went about looking through the mail.

So that was how it was going to be—back to us hardly talking. I regretted it, but I was relieved and kept on with the work, making my way into the front with the broom. A little later the sheriff put down his reading. "Listen," he said, "I was an up-renter because my Pa was an up-renter, and that was the way it was. It mostly depended on if you owned your land and who your friends were."

"I think it was hard on everybody," I said, looking for common ground. "Whoever was on the other side, well, I guess it was natural to think the worst of them. Did you hate the Calicos?"

"Oh, I hated them all right," he said, showing a little color.

"Why? They were just farmers."

"Not after dark, they weren't. One night they caught me on the Bovina road. Tied me up and told me they were gonna to hang me. I was eighteen. Near pissed my pants."

"And?"

"They had their fun and let me go. Then three of them got arrested for tarring the land agent and were locked up, right back there, just as you said. Their friends decided to get 'em back and put out the call. They had three hundred men on horseback right outside of Delhi, blowing those horns all night and promising to burn the town and turn it into a cabbage patch. You remember that?"

"No," I said, a little put off. "I was just a girl on a farm. All I remember is the coming and going—Mother pleading with Father, begging him not to go out."

Evans glanced over his shoulder, as though to make sure no one else was in the room. "You ever see those costumes?"

I smiled to myself. "I found my father's in the attic," I said, having spoken of that to no one.

The sheriff's eyes grew wide. "Did he have the mask?"

I looked at Evans. For a wicked moment I wondered if my father had been one of those who had caught him and scared him near to death. "You pissed your pants, didn't you?"

"Well," he said, not denying it, "you find yourself alone at night surrounded by men in painted sheepskin and see how well you hold your water. People were frightened out of their wits. Some of the old folks thought it was the real Indians come back. Matrons hid toasting forks about the house, determined to defend their honor. We sent riders to Albany, but for all we knew, they'd been caught and hanged from some tree."

I picked up the broom. "I see Delhi is still here."

"Yeah, well, we had guns too, and more to eat than they did—them riding around like that. But then Sheriff Steele got shot over at the Earle farm. Caught a bullet in the gut—took two days for him to die. Then all hell broke loose. Soldiers came and over two hundred men got arrested. If you so much as gave a glass of water to a farmer who wasn't payin' his rent, you were guilty of Steele's murder—that's how Judge Parker saw it."

"I know," I said. "My Uncle Tom was one of them. He was in church that morning, thirty miles from the Earle farm. Spent twelve months in jail just waiting for a trial."

"But not your father?"

"He wasn't arrested."

That much was true, but my father might have been, having been accused by people whom he had thought of as friends. This I learned from my mother later on. Most of the bad things had happened west of us, but something inside father got broke back then. Neighbor testifying against neighbor. Who would be arrested next? Some men were waiting to hang. Finally, Father sold our farm and moved us all to a new place along the Delaware. At the time, I saw it all as a big adventure and not a flight from ugly memories.

"Are people here still angry?" I asked.

"You bet they are," said the sheriff. "And you'd best know where they stand on that one before you scratch the scab."

I stopped my sweeping. "So I've learned."

* * *

By my second winter in Delhi, my duties expanded, and I was sent to work two days a week for Mrs. Elizabeth Caldwell, a widow who lived in a large house west of the square. By then, I was a common sight in town. A spinster in pants.

I had learned from Mrs. McNee that Mrs. Caldwell had a sister in New York, a daughter in Buffalo, and a husband in the grave in Tennessee. But Mrs. Caldwell didn't share a word of this with me. She gave instructions and, after that, nothing that could be thought of as conversation.

She walked with her hands clasped, back straight, as she moved about the house without a sound. From what I could see, she might have been born into this world with a gray head of hair and a hooped petticoat. Her face, stern and still beautiful, seemed like a doorway to a dark room. The house shared her mood. Upstairs were three bedrooms and a staircase to an attic that Mrs. Caldwell visited on occasion. I was never given any duties there. On the first floor was a dining room with an oak table that seated six. There Mrs. Caldwell would take her tea and look out over the empty places to a window and a meadow beyond.

While dusting in Mrs. Caldwell's library one afternoon, I paused by the fireplace and looked at the books. One caught my eye, and without thinking, I took it down. I opened it and began to read, just to remember the feeling, having not read a book in ten years. The words tumbled off the page as though they were musical notes that formed not a sentence but a song.

"What are you doing?"

I turned and saw Mrs. Caldwell by the door, standing there like the queen of Prussia. Almost weekly, Mrs. McNee had told us never to touch a personal possession of our employers. Now I had one in my hand.

"I know I shouldn't have taken it down," I stammered. "I just did."

Mrs. Caldwell was not moved. "What book is it?"

"One by Mr. Dickens," I said, taking a quick glance to be sure. "*The Pickwick Papers.*"

Hearing this, her face softened. "Joseph, have you read any books by Mr. Dickens?"

"Yes. When I was young. I read this very book, but I couldn't tell you much about it now."

"And were you Joseph then?"

"No. I was Lucy then."

"Why did you change your name?"

I looked at the floor. This was a story too long to tell, but neither could I lie. "I gave up my name when I gave up my daughter. Anyone who gives up her daughter cannot be a woman, surely not a mother." I stopped, certain that I had said too much. Mrs. Caldwell wanted to know more.

"Where is your daughter now?"

"In Pennsylvania. But until two years ago, she lived here in Delhi. At the almshouse."

Why had I told her that? I hadn't told anyone, and now Mrs. Caldwell knew and was more curious than before.

"What's her name?"

It was my fault. I had brought her to the secret, and now I couldn't put another name on my daughter. "Helen. Helen Slater."

The woman seemed to lose her balance. "Helen Slater is your daughter?"

"Only by birth, I'm ashamed to say. Did you know her?"

"Helen? Yes. She worked in this house."

Now the floor seemed to move under me. Had Mrs. Caldwell also been a mother to my little girl? Was I in some strange station of hell? I gathered my courage. "Did she work here long?"

"Not long enough. Someone stole her from me." Mrs. Caldwell appeared distressed. "Joseph, I must tell you that she said her mother was dead."

"And well she might say that. In any case, God has told me that He wants me to have no more to do with her."

Mrs. Caldwell gave a disbelieving look. "How did He tell you that?"

"By taking her from here a month before I came. I am to leave her alone. He is watching her now."

Mrs. Caldwell nodded as though to say she understood. I couldn't tell what she was really thinking.

The following week Mrs. Caldwell again found me dusting in the library—this time, no book in hand. I waited to hear her instructions, but there weren't any. Instead she asked if I had read anyone besides Mr. Dickens.

"Yes, ma'am," I replied, trying to remember things from a long time ago. "I've read William Thackeray and Mr. Hawthorne and some of Mr. Emerson."

"You read, then, *The Scarlet Letter*?"

"I did."

"And what do you suppose Mr. Hawthorne was trying to say?"

I think this was Mrs. Caldwell's test to see if we were talking about the same Mr. Hawthorne. I hesitated but a moment, for I remembered the book. "I think he was saying that there are things we know about and things we don't."

"Indeed," she said with an approving nod. "Joseph, would you like to borrow a book now and then?"

Had Mrs. Caldwell offered me a gold coin, I could not have felt more excitement.

I said I would, and Mrs. Caldwell went over to the bookshelves and started running her finger over the books, looking for something. "Here," she said, pulling out a book and handing it to me. "You might like this." On the cover in gold letters was the title, *Adam Bede*, and the author, George Eliot.

"I don't think I've read anything by Mr. Eliot," I said.

Mrs. Caldwell let out a sound that I had not heard from her before, something like a chuckle. "Well, I'm sure you will like it. More so when you know that Mr. Eliot is really a woman." She paused to measure my surprise. "And I have a few other books by women who first wrote as men. You might like this."

She took down a book titled *Jane Eyre*. I hadn't heard of it, but Mrs. Caldwell said it was now very famous and that the author, Miss Brontë, had first published it under a man's name. She handed me the book, and I brought it back to the almshouse where I read it in my room at night. I took delight in Miss Eyre's adventures and more delight in the news that women were now writing books of their own, and that they had begun by disguising themselves as men. When I finished *Jane Eyre,* there was another book to replace it, and thus my world began to grow.

But the books that I borrowed changed little between me and Mrs. Caldwell. It was not like years earlier when I would talk about books with Burton in the dining room of the Hotel Wayne. They didn't lead to conversations. Mrs. Caldwell might ask me a question about the book I was returning. I would reply, and she would nod her head and say, "Yes." That I had read it seemed enough for her. And in this way and others like it, Mrs. Caldwell remained to me more a spirit than a body of flesh. On some days, she seemed only half there, part woman, part shade, come back to this world to watch over needy souls like myself, as though it were she, and not Captain Caldwell, who had fallen at Shiloh.

30

A S THE SEASONS passed, I rose in the ranks of the poorhouse.
Unlike many who lived there, I knew my grammar and could write
in a clear hand. I became a *senior resident* and was given the duties of cor-
respondence. For this, I got two dollars a month and my own little table in
Mrs. McNee's office. I also wrote letters for Sheriff Evans. He said things
sounded better when I wrote them.

Every four months or so, a letter from Helen would arrive. Mrs. McNee
would take it to her room and read it to me the following day. Helen's
letters told of the difficulties on the Fortnam farm—the washouts and the
droughts, the coughs and the fevers, the bossy sister and the nosey aunt.
From our distance, Mrs. McNee and I watched Helen grow up. Then one
day she wrote that she had met a young man named David Stone. She said
she saw his soul the moment she laid eyes on him. I felt uneasy. I hoped
that she would bide her time and not, like her mother, rush into something.
Of course, I couldn't write to tell her this, because I was too ashamed to
bring myself back from the dead.

* * *

I was working on the ledger one chilly autumn day when I heard my name
called. I came onto the porch and saw Mrs. McNee and a man I didn't
know standing by a wagon.

"Joe, there's a woman here. Help this man carry her inside."

In the wagon, a woman lay as though dead. The man took her shoulders and I her feet—she weighed almost nothing. We carried the poor creature upstairs, down the hall, and onto the spare bed in my room, Mrs. McNee close behind.

"Where's she from?" asked the housemaster.

"Don't know," said the man. "I found her at the rail station, on her knees shiverin'. My house ain't fit for a mule, so I brought her here."

Mrs. McNee thanked the man, calling him a Samaritan. She told Audrey to take him downstairs and give him a meal. We undressed our visitor and found her hot. Mrs. McNee passed over her with a wet cloth, and I dried her with a towel.

The woman lay there for two days. At times, when she stirred, I sat her up and got her to drink. The fever continued. On the third morning, I brought her tea with sugar, thinking I would wake her, but her eyes were open when I came into the room. "Who are you?" she asked in a thin voice.

"I'm Joseph," I said, setting down the tray. "What's your name?"

"Marie. Where am I?"

"You're safe, Marie. At the almshouse. In Delhi."

"Oh," she said, though I'm not sure she understood. I got her to take the tea, and in the afternoon, I brought her soup. I tried to feed her, but she wanted to do it herself. When I handed her the spoon, she used it to point.

"That bed," she said. "Who sleeps there?"

"I do," I said, thinking that would assure her.

Marie gave me a funny look. "Joseph, are you a man?"

I laughed. I hadn't thought of how it might be to wake in a strange place and see someone who looked like me. "No, I'm not."

"Are you a woman?"

"Yes."

"Then why do you wear those clothes?"

"Because I like to."

Marie nodded, but I could see that my strange appearance was more than she cared to think about. And when I asked where she was from, she shook her head to say she didn't want to speak of it.

Two days later Marie was still in bed but better. She was thin as a goat, but her eyes were bright. She was sitting up and eating porridge when Mrs. McNee came into the room, house register in hand.

"We need to make this official," she said to Marie. "What's your name, dear?"

Marie turned and gave me a frightened look, but I didn't know how to help. She turned back to Mrs. McNee but hesitated. "Marie Louise . . . *Martin*," she said finally, her voice suggesting that the last name was not her real one.

Mrs. McNee ignored the confession and wrote in her book. "Where are you from?"

"Jersey City."

"What was your business on the railroad?"

"I can't tell you."

"Nonsense," said Mrs. McNee. "Of course you can."

Marie pulled the blanket to her chin. "I am disgraced."

Mrs. McNee gave a tired smile. "My dear, in this house, we are all disgraced. That is our specialty. But we must contact your family."

"No!" she cried. "I'd rather die."

Mrs. McNee paused then patted Marie's hands as if to say there was nothing to fear. For the present, no more questions.

I had been at the almshouse for four years and had a room alone, except when the other bed was needed. Marie was left with me, and I was to care for her. In a few weeks, her face filled out, and the color came back to her cheeks. She was pretty, and much younger than I had first thought. Nineteen, she said. She was well-spoken, but careful not to talk about her past. Her few possessions were kept in a double-handled cloth bag that she kept under her bed. Of worldly goods I had less than she did. My one visible possession was on the table—the book I was reading, which, of course, wasn't mine. Marie asked about it, and I said that I had borrowed the book from a woman I worked for in town. She picked it up and brightened when she saw it was *Villette* by Miss Brontë. "I love Charlotte Brontë," she said. "I wanted to be Jane Eyre when I was fifteen. Didn't you?"

I smiled and told Marie that I hadn't read *Jane Eyre* when I was fifteen, but rather just two years ago, but, yes, I did like the book. And that, I think, was the beginning of our friendship. Her question showed that she thought of me as a girl in my younger days, despite my present appearance. I liked this, for many people couldn't seem to see me that way, as though I must have been a very strange creature back then just because I was one now. Beyond that, having a book in common gave Marie and me the feeling that we shared certain secrets. But not all secrets—her past was still not to be spoken of, and neither was mine. We were, of course, bumping into these walls all the time.

One night as we were preparing for bed, Marie was so forward as to ask if I had ever done something very bad. "I mean," she said, "something so bad that it could never be undone. Something that hurt the ones you love."

Such a thing to ask. And of me, in particular, for what hadn't I done to hurt those I love? On another day, I might have found a way to avoid the question, but just then it seemed easier to answer. "Yes," I said. "If you must know, I have."

Marie arranged herself on the bed. "I'm strangely comforted."

I gave a short laugh. "Well, I'm glad my sins can do good for someone."

"Perhaps even more if I knew what it was that you did. Does anyone here know?"

"No, Marie, they don't," I said, annoyed that she was ignoring our rules. "And what about you? You would know my greatest sin and not even tell me your real name?"

That did it. She buttoned up. Seeing how things were, I picked up my book and began to read. A minute later Marie asked the name of the book. I let out a breath. It had been on the table for the past two days, so I knew full well that she knew, but I told her it was *Silas Marner*, by George Eliot whose real name was Mary-something. I think she knew all about George Eliot, but she was playing the child, so she just nodded, and I went back to the book. A minute later she spoke again, now asking if I would read to her. I paused as though considering, but I already knew that I didn't want to—my reading was my world. But I couldn't think of a good way to say this. Finally, I gave up and turned back to page one.

Despite my misgivings, I liked the reading almost right away, and from then on, we didn't miss a night. Soon we took turns, I one night, Marie the next. To keep our voices low we pushed our beds together. And I didn't mind revisiting the first part of *Marner*. Despite the dreary landscape, the book now took on the qualities of adventure, as though Marie and I were out on the moor together with the evils of the world hiding in the weeds.

Once done with *Marner*, we decided to go back to *Jane Eyre* to have the fun of reading it together. But the book didn't capture either of us the way it had before. Rochester, who, in the first reading, had come galloping in on a huge stallion, appeared the second time almost a bumbler—never able to say what he needed to say and always sighing, *Jane, Jane.* I began to imitate his moaning and soon it became our private joke. And the foolery didn't stop with just Rochester. We made fun of Jane too, though we both still loved her.

Sharing stories at night reminded me of when I was a girl in Westerlo where we would begin our peas and beans in boxes set inside the window. There they could grow safe from the cold, and when it was time, we would take them out and put them in the ground. Reading books with Marie was a little like that. It was safe. We could laugh at the vanities of others. We could speak with certainty about what this one should have done, or how foolish he had been. We could judge harshly and be mean to no one.

One night as we were getting into bed, Marie broke our rule about questions and asked if I belonged to a church. I looked away from her as I tried to sort it all out. I hadn't prayed to God since I had been out in Minnesota. And as far as I could tell, God had forsaken me and I Him, and who had acted badly first I couldn't say. And that was no short story, so I gave a short answer in its place. "Not anymore."

"But you did?"

I put my pillow up to the wall and leaned against it. "I was a Methodist, Marie. But I was cast out of that church. Twice, in fact."

"Whatever for?"

"Once for daring to speak at a meeting. The other because my minister feared I was something of a God-in-nature philosopher."

"Were you?"

"I didn't think of it that way, but maybe I was. And now you."

Marie stood and pulled the curtain over the window and then sat again on the bed. "Our family belonged to the Church of New Jerusalem."

I shook my head. "Never heard of it."

"It was founded upon the teachings of Emanuel Swedenborg. He lived in Sweden, two hundred years ago."

"So you haven't met him?"

"What do you think, Joseph? Did you ever meet Jesus?" I had to laugh, but Marie was not in a joking mood. She wanted to tell me about this Swedenborg. She called him "extraordinary," which right away made me not like him. According to Marie, the man had studied medicine, philosophy, minerals, and other things I can't remember. She said he engraved maps, constructed musical instruments, and designed a machine to fly through the air—and another that would go under the sea to attack boats from below.

"And he is your spiritual leader?" I asked. "This man who designed machines of war?"

Marie ignored me. "Swedenborg had a dream where an angel of God told him to bring the truth to the people. He was a changed man. He had conversations with spirits. The queen of Sweden summoned him and asked him to speak to her dead brother, the prince of Denmark, I think. He came back with a message, and she near fainted away, for it contained a secret that only she and her brother had known."

"We have people who do similar things here," I said, trying to act more respectful. "The Poughkeepsie Seer comes to mind, though many thought it was just parlor tricks. But what did Mr. Swedenborg preach that you find so remarkable?"

"Many things," said Marie. "He denounced the churches for being rich when so many people were poor. He said the kingdom of heaven is open to any and all and not just those who have read the Bible or been blessed by a priest."

"Did they nail him to a cross? That's what they do to people like that."

Marie smiled. "I think I see, Joseph, why you were thrown out of church. But you're right. When he was eighty and could barely walk, he was put on trial and branded a heretic. My church began after his death."

"And is it still your church?"

Marie shook her head. "No. I abandoned it and everyone I cared for, for what I thought was love and freedom. I have only one thing left."

Marie reached down for her bag while I thought about what she had said—abandoned all for love and freedom. A moment later she handed me a small book: *The Teachings of Emanuel Swedenborg*. On the inside was the inscription: *To our dearest Marie Louise, with love, Mother and Father. December 25, Year of Our Lord, 1863*.

I opened it and read, letting fate decide the passage:

> Priests ought not to claim to themselves any power over the souls of men, because they do not know what the interiors of a man are. Still less they ought to claim the power of opening and shutting Heaven, since that power belongs to the Lord Himself.

I closed the book and looked up. "My, my," I said. "Who do we have here?"

Marie smiled. She thought I was speaking about Mr. Swedenborg, but I was wondering about her.

31

WE HAD TOLD each other something of our former lives. I was a cast-off Methodist, and Marie was a follower of a man named Swedenborg. Not our darkest secrets, but even so, we didn't revisit them. We went back to where we had been, reading to each other but not speaking about the past. She wasn't ready, and as for me, I had built a safe place at the almshouse, and much of it had to do with not telling. I wasn't afraid of being judged. I wanted to forget.

But now, the quiet me who had lived secure was being confronted by another me, a me who wanted things—things I could only dimly remember, like laughter. Marie had poked holes in the walls I had built, and light was finding its way in, enough so that I suspected I would tell about myself if she asked. And soon enough she did ask, though it was more like barter. I would tell her; she would tell me. After months of not speaking about anything prior to the almshouse, Marie was now excited by the idea. Before I had a chance to say anything, she had the candle in front of my face, demanding that I swear before the flame that I would forever guard her secrets. She then brought the candle to herself and made the same vow in reverse.

The next day Marie was as cheerful as toast with jam. I felt like cold soup. And why was I to be the first one to tell? How had that been decided? My dark mood followed me into the office where none of the columns in the ledger would agree.

But when evening came, I did my best to rise to the occasion. I helped Marie smuggle tea and sweet bread to our room. With these as our blood-and-flesh communion, we again boldly took our oaths before the candle. I thought Marie would blow it out—I had imagined a dark room—but instead she set it on the table, still lit. She then made a nest for herself in the corner where the walls met. I did the same at the end of the bed, feeling awkward.

"One more thing," I said. "Swear that you are not St. Peter and this is not my final interview."

Marie smiled. "No, Joseph, it's just me. Now stop trying to wiggle away."

"How should I begin?"

"Tell me your earliest memory."

I thought for a moment. "I remember being behind our house when I was very little. There were people about. It was a picnic, I think. And there was rope around my waist that was tied to a tree."

Marie laughed. "Like a dog?"

"Yes. Apparently I liked to wander."

I told Marie about our farm in Westerlo. About my sisters and brother. About how Father taught me to ride a horse and play the violin. How he took me out behind the barn and taught me to shoot a rifle. I bragged about being a good student, but Marie wanted to know about the boys. I told her about William Smith who took to walking with me after school. About how Father saw us and forbade it.

"Soon, we were hiding notes for each other," I said, enjoying the memory. "Innocent notes, but they seemed daring to us."

"And your father found them."

"No. You should let me tell the story. My sister Sarah did. I wanted to strangle her but couldn't, because she would tell. So she teased me until I lost interest in Mr. Smith."

I told Marie about Henry St. John. About how he had fallen sick and died. I think the story affected her more than me in the retelling, the years gone by having erased the pain. After Henry, of course, came George Washington Slater.

"He was a handsome, wild boy," I said, feeling yet a little pride in his good looks. "And disturbed, a quality that I somehow found attractive. I was drawn to him but still mourned my Henry, so I couldn't really give my heart to George. Father didn't like him, and I was unsure myself, so when Father said I should go away to school, I agreed."

I then told about my years at the academy in Coxsackie, where I had lived with my aunt. And about how Father had moved the family to Basket Creek, where I had joined them. And how, a year later, George Slater had knocked on our door.

Marie liked this part. "You must have been excited to see him."

"I was," I confessed. "Imagine, his coming all that way. So when George asked me to marry, I said yes." I stopped as it came rushing back.

"It did not go well with him?"

"You could say," I said, not able to meet her eye. "After our wedding, there wasn't a single day that we were both happy at the end of it."

I described George's suspicions and wild accusations. How I had to run back to my father's house and how George had left. I told her about the birth of Helen, adding quickly that she was grown now and living in Pennsylvania, hoping to head off questions and not giving pause for any. I told of my hunting along Basket Creek, housekeeping for Raspy Winthrop, and his crude offer of marriage. And that was as much as I could do for the night. I didn't want to talk further about any of it, particularly about Helen.

The next day the floors in the almshouse had an odd slope—not the feeling I had hoped for. Digging up the past was a bad idea. I was done with it and would tell Marie after dinner. But when we got to our room, I saw her expectant face and lost my resolve. I went on with my story, telling her about my decision to change my clothes and run away as a man—perhaps not a complete surprise, considering my appearance. But the dancing school *was* a surprise. Marie had many questions, and she couldn't stop asking about Lydia. It took me all night to get through Honesdale, and it would have gone longer if I hadn't put an end to it.

The following night Marie was with me every step through Minnesota—the winter in Kandiyohi, the attack by Willie McAllister, the trial, Noah's proposal, and finding my cabin in ruins. "Oh, Joseph!" she cried, scarcely able to believe it. "They burned your house! Where did you go?"

"Back to Forest City."

"But wasn't that where they had the trial?"

"Yes, but that's where I ended up. I think most people were decent to me, or maybe they weren't. I couldn't really tell. I was sick. But it wasn't the normal kind of sick. I just couldn't make sense of anything. People looked strange—I would shout at them. They didn't know what to do with me. Finally, they raised some money and sent me east."

"Back to New York?"

"Yes. Father met the train. A letter from Dr. Blanchard said I was to arrive and not well. Father took me home, but I had no fever, so in a day or two everyone thought I'd gotten better. And, of course, they had questions. Dr. Blanchard had told them about the trial."

"But you were found innocent!"

"Not in their eyes. I think Mother blamed me for what Willie did. And I was too sick to say anything that made much sense. Someone might be in the room, but it felt as though they were shouting down a well. They turned on me. My brother John was harsh, and so was Sarah, who was getting ready for her wedding. I was spoiling everything."

"And Helen?"

"She wasn't happy to see me either. I was just this strange person who made everyone upset. She was seven then and didn't look like the child I had left behind. God knows how much I had changed in her eyes. When there was shouting, she would run to Mary. It became impossible. I had to leave, though I was still not well. I took my rifle and went into the woods to join Gelerama, an old Lenape woman I knew who had a stone hut at the head of the valley."

"You went to live with an Indian woman?"

"Yes, but she wasn't there. Her things were, but she wasn't. I think the wolves had gotten to her. Her place became mine."

Marie sat there wide-eyed, the blankets bunched around her as if she were in the hut on a cold night, bears outside the door, which there had been on any number of occasions. I told about hunting for deer and bringing the meat to trade at the store at Long Eddy. Marie asked about Helen.

"I would see her maybe once a month. Mother started having her spells again. And it all seemed to have something to do with me, as though I were the bad seed that had sprung not out of but into her. By this time, the very sight of me set her off."

"Were you afraid?"

"I was for Helen. Mother started calling her *Lucy*—my name. One day I came home and heard her yelling at Helen, calling her Lucy, and swearing that she would drive the devil away. I ran into the kitchen and saw a knife in Mother's hand. Helen was huddled in the corner, crying. I grabbed her and got her out of there. She was not sure about me, but she was more frightened of Mother. She stayed in my stone cabin for five days in the cold. I knew it couldn't go on, but there was nobody I could bring her to."

"Not your sisters?"

"Mary was married and gone by then, and Sarah, who was close by, was trying to have a child of her own. Besides, we had both said too many horrible things. There was no one. So I took Helen's hand, and we walked three days to this very house. I told her that I loved her and hoped I would come back for her. She grabbed me and begged me not to leave, promised she would live with me wherever I wanted, that she didn't care how cold it got. But I told her again she must stay. She became still, and sat down, her face unmoving, broken by betrayal. That's the last memory I have of my child."

Marie sat in silence. "Oh Lord," she said finally. "You brought her here. You brought her here yourself. And then left her."

"Yes."

"Why didn't you stay?"

"I couldn't."

"Why couldn't you?"

"I was not well, Marie," I said, trying to tell the truth but feeling the shame. "I was only a half-step away from the insane in the backhouse. Closer than that. I would have been locked up with them, and Helen could have listened to her mother howl at night and visited me as I sat in my filth. Better to go off and be eaten by wolves."

"Perhaps you just *thought* you couldn't be with people."

"No, Marie. Nothing was right. Everyone wished me harm."

"So you left your daughter here and went back to your cabin?"

I shook my head. "No. I didn't go back. I didn't want to be me anymore. I moved a couple of counties north and built myself a new hut deep in the woods."

"How long did you live there?"

"Five years. Something like that. I lost track."

Marie looked startled. "You lived by yourself in the woods for five years?"

"I told you, Marie. I wasn't right."

"But you seem fine to me, Joseph. Truly. More in your right mind than most people I know."

"Well, I did get better, but by that time, I really didn't know how to do anything but live in the woods. Then one day I thought I'd go to Delhi and find some sort of work. I would wash floors, sweep the streets, anything, so I could see Helen now and then." I paused while I remembered the day I arrived.

"And when you saw her?"

I took a breath. "I never did. God sent a Pennsylvania farmer ahead of me—a month before I came. He took Helen out of this house, to be his daughter. And so I have replaced her here where you have found me."

It was done. I had spent three nights taking Marie from Westerlo to Delhi. I didn't feel unburdened, and I didn't feel closer to Marie. I wanted to run away and thought I might when the morning came. I blew out the candle and lay down. Marie stayed where she was—frozen by the cold disposal of my daughter.

A little later, I felt her hand stroke my head.

32

MARIE DID NOT begin her story the next night. She was tired and wanted to do the telling when she wasn't. I didn't care.

Three days later we both felt better. We again smuggled tea up to our room. This time I sat in the corner and she on the end of the bed, arranging herself one way, then another. "Oh," she said. "Now you must help me. Where should I start?"

"Your name, I think, would be a good place."

"Oh, well, yes. My name is Marie Louise *Perry*."

"And where are you from?"

"Abington, Massachusetts, though mostly we thought of ourselves as from Boston. Now, of course, in Boston there are Perrys who are very wealthy, but we, I'm sad to say, are only second cousins."

"So you are not rich. I was so hoping you were."

Marie smiled. "No. I'm sorry to disappoint you, but we weren't poor. Father had a store. We had a house just south of town with a garden and a carriage barn."

After having been so shy about it, Marie spoke easily about growing up in Abington. She told me that she and her sister had attended the girls' academy and worked in their father's store after school. She was happy, she said, until she turned sixteen. Suddenly, Sunday afternoons were no longer for friends or walks in the woods. She was to stay at home and receive callers.

"I hated it. Boys—you couldn't call them men—who mostly fidgeted and tried to think of things to say, and I, of course, would have to sit there, wanting to scream, and agree that, yes, it was a very lovely day. Then one afternoon, out of the blue, John Ferguson asked me to marry him. I said right out that I didn't love him."

I laughed. "You said it like that? Did he take offense?"

"He didn't. I think he was relieved, having been put up to it by someone who said he must now find a wife. So Mr. Ferguson stopped coming, but Willard Hoskins started coming more. One Sunday, he showed up on our doorstep, smelling of witch hazel and patting his pink neck with a handkerchief. I wanted to run."

"Did you try to discourage him?"

"I couldn't. He just told me in a rush that he wanted my *hand in marriage*. Said it would be *advantageous*. That his *impressions of me* were of the *purest* kind. Oh, Joseph, you should have seen him, hair greased and parted down the middle. And that stupid handkerchief! Finally, I got a word in and said no. He then asked if he might leave with some *glimmer of hope*. I said I thought it best if he didn't."

"So you are not here because you were forced to marry him?"

"No, but if I had married him, this is exactly where I would be. But it wasn't just him. I had two more of that sort. By this time Mother was worried, and not just her. One evening my aunt Augusta came to dinner. In our first moment alone, she took my hand. *I've brought you a little something*, she whispered. *From Boston!* She handed me a small box. What do you think was in it?"

"A potion?"

"No. A pair of lady-plumpers." The silence that followed conveyed my ignorance. "My goodness, Joseph, you *have* been out in the woods for a while. Lady-plumpers are ceramic pieces that you put in your mouth to push out your cheeks so that men might find you attractive. Aunt Augusta was almost in rapture. *This will be our little secret,* she said. *They are the fashion!*

"I thanked my aunt, though I was mortified and wished that she and everyone else would take no interest in my affairs. I hurried to my room, but when I got there, what do you think I did with the plumpers?"

"You hid them under the bed."

"No. I placed those melted down tea cups in my mouth. I stood before the mirror and wondered if I looked better with my cheeks puffed like a squirrel. And, of course, it was almost impossible to speak. My aunt said that one merely needed to practice, starting with simple things such as *How very interesting* and *Do you really think so?*" Marie garbled these phrases, and I couldn't help but laugh. We paused for tea.

I was enjoying myself. I liked Marie's story, despite her discomfort at having to drive suitors away with a broom like they were young bears snuffling around on the back porch. But when she began again, there was a different look on her face. She spoke of a young man named James Wilson. He had been hired by her father to work in the store.

"He was handsome and mannered," she said as though it were all a long time ago, "said to be on leave from university, awaiting an inheritance. Soon, he was moved from dry goods to clothing because he was good with people about clothes and had a keen eye. Two of them. They were gray and unafraid, and when they were on me, I knew it, even when my back was turned. Had he made his advances early on, I would have rejected him out of instinct. But he had patience. And his silent looks did more to my heart than any words could have."

"He did not approach you?"

"No. He kept his distance. I would be the one to find some reason for us to speak. *Did the red cloth need to be reordered?* This went on for some time, but once he was sure of my attraction, it changed. He would find me alone, in the stockroom or upstairs with the fabrics. His attentions were at first tender, but soon his lips were hard upon me, and his hands followed closely behind. He was insistent, and after all the pretending by the others about their pure intentions . . . well, I liked it."

"Weren't you afraid?"

"That too." Waves of feeling crossed Marie's face and crashed into those going the other way—anger, sadness, and perhaps still a longing for the passion. She gave a sorry laugh. "I was in a state of sin for the liberties I had permitted him, so, as you might imagine, I spent some time wondering about what God thought of it all. I prayed and asked forgiveness. I vowed that James would not touch me again, but as soon as he came near, I went weak. His hands were on me, and I let them do what they wanted. Then he took my hands, and I learned what he wanted. By then, I was given over to it, eager to touch him and please him. Only lack of opportunity kept me from even greater sin."

I felt a strange disapproval. "What did you think would come of it?"

"James did the thinking. He proposed that we run away. He said that Father would not consent to our marriage, though it was not clear as to why. I believe now he was stealing from us, and that was the real reason he wanted to be gone. In any case, may God forgive me, I helped him steal more."

I wasn't sure that I had heard her right. I was about to ask, but I saw Marie start to tremble. Then out of her mouth came sobs, words, and sudden gulps for air as though she had forgotten how to breathe. "I have sinned . . . and when the time comes . . . I will stand before God . . . ask His forgiveness . . . but how could I ever again stand . . . before my father . . . having stolen from him?"

Marie wept. I wanted to offer sympathy but couldn't bring myself to do it. I would never have stolen from my father. She tried to explain.

"I had money coming to me upon my marriage, so I thought at the time that what I did was—that's not true. I knew it was wrong. Horribly wrong. I stole money from the safe. James, of course, had told me about his inheritance. I cared little for his money, but the story, I suppose, kept me from asking questions. We would pay everyone back when the money came through—a thin thought by which I betrayed my father."

Marie was in distress, and I suggested that perhaps she had gone as far as she needed to for the night. But she said that if she stopped, she wouldn't be able to start again. So she kept going and told how she and James had taken one of her father's carriages into Boston and then traveled by train to New York. She told how a ferry had brought them to Jersey City where they were married by someone who James said was a judge and how quickly thereafter James Wilson became someone she didn't know. In this, of course, I was not only her sister but her twin. And now I did feel sympathy.

"I think his greatest pleasure was in ripping me from my home and my church," she said. "Think of it—more powerful than God. But once he could have me anytime, it wasn't half the fun. Love really didn't exist for him. He just knew its language, like the way he sold cloth to ladies."

Marie said that they rented a shabby room above a bar run by a woman named Olga and her daughter Ulena, a heavy-set girl who cursed and belched like a man. For all his supposed manners, James took a liking to them, and Marie said that she heard his voice coming from the landlady's room across the hall on several occasions.

"What was he doing there?'

"Discussing business, he said. Wouldn't say what."

"And the inheritance?"

"Oh, yes, that. When I brought it up, James said that there was more delay and that he had to look for work. His search must have taken place in the bars around Jersey City, judging from his condition when he returned. God knows where else he'd been, but his interest in me lessened even more. All the while, our money, our stolen money, was draining away."

The candlelight didn't soften the devastation on Marie's face. "You poor child," I said, giving voice to the years between us. "Did you want to go home?"

"Go home?" she said in disbelief. "How could I go home? What trust hadn't I broken? What sin hadn't I committed? Too many letters to be sewn on one breast—I should look like someone's discarded sampler."

Marie shook her head as though she couldn't believe her own story. "I took to walking the streets while James was off doing I didn't know what. Saint Mary's was two blocks away, so I spent part of each day there, pretending to pray, just to have somewhere to go. One afternoon I came back and found James and Ulena on the floor behind the stairs. At least I presume it was Ulena, for all I could see was a fat rump sticking up in the air, an image I shall not soon forget."

A silence followed. I could hear someone moving below, but the rest of the house was quiet. Marie looked away.

"She was slovenly, Joseph. She was fat and slovenly, yet he preferred her to me. She could excite him with her barnyard manners, and I could not."

"Surely, you left him then."

Marie shook her head. "No. He left me. That night—with Ulena, our money, and a good portion of the week's receipts, if the landlady's fury the next morning was any measure. She said that she was going to the police and would have me arrested for robbery. I had to leave."

"But you were done with him."

"Not quite."

"What do you mean?"

"Oh, Joseph, you'll have a good laugh over this. Really, you will." Marie paused to gain courage. "I chased after them."

"Chased them?"

"Yes, as though she had stolen my shawl. Olga said they had been seen at the train station. So with the little money left in my purse, I bought a ticket, thinking I would find them in some town where the train went, for whatever good that would have done. I hadn't eaten in days. I wasn't well. I boarded the north-bound train and then I don't know what. I woke up in this room."

33

WITH OUR SECRETS told, our friendship grew. My work in town kept us apart during the day, but at night, Marie and I would talk or share a book to all hours—our consumption of tallow approaching scandalous. And we would always begin by reading a passage from the Bible or one from Swedenborg. It was Marie's idea, and I came to like it. It reminded me of the times when Mother would read from the Bible as we sat before the fire, John in her lap and Mary in the crib. Soldiers and shepherds came to life, and after a time, there were psalms and parables that I knew by heart. Some of these I recited when it was my turn, though most often, Marie did the Bible reading. It was ointment to her wounds—if God could forgive her, all was not lost. She was younger than I and felt her shame more deeply.

After the evening devotion, our reading went in every direction. There were stories about love found and love lost, all of them taking place in English settings. And stories of inheritance from long-forgotten uncles finding its way to some unsuspecting but goodhearted soul, as though something of the sort was out there for all of us. We liked these stories, but Marie and I were overtaken when we read *Woman in the Nineteenth Century*, a book that Mrs. Caldwell had finally thought us ready to read. It was by Margaret Fuller, a well-known New England thinker. I had never heard of her, but Marie had, being from that place where those philosophers seemed to grow on trees.

Mrs. Fuller was an advocate for women. She chastised those who "make the lot of the sex such that mothers are sad when daughters are born." She spoke of the great lack of fairness between what is offered to a young man and a young woman. Most of these thoughts were not new to me, just said better than I could ever have said them. But Mrs. Fuller wrote other things that *were* new to me—about the nature of the sexes:

> Male and female represent the two sides of the great dualism. But, in fact, they are perpetually passing into one another. Fluid hardens to solid, solid rushes to fluid. There is no wholly masculine man, no purely feminine woman.

I had never before heard or read such a thought, though I had been wrestling with this question for many years, always wondering whether I was one thing or another. But here was someone who seemed to say that I could be a woman and still have part of me that felt like a man. And that it was all quite natural. Had she still been living, I would have written to her.

* * *

One Sunday in April, Marie asked if I would take her to church. I put on a clean shirt, and we walked over the bridge to Delhi. We had our pick, but we chose the Baptist church because of the forsythia by its door. We waited till most had gone inside and then entered and sat at the back. There was nothing in the sermon worthy to repeat, but we both liked the singing. On our way home I bought Marie an ice cream with my senior resident wages.

Once over the bridge and away from town, we went for a walk in the meadow along the river, stopping under an apple tree dripping with blossoms. I made fun of the morning's preacher, who reminded me in no small way of Reverend Albright.

Marie laughed. "I think, Joseph, we should start a new religion. The ones we have are so dreary."

"If I can be the bishop," I said.

"No bishops or priests in this religion."

"Oh?"

"And there'll be no churches."

"A religion without churches?"

"Yes. Three or four times a year, we'll gather in a field like this and have a picnic. Then we'll form a circle, and those who want to speak about God, or anything else, can."

"All right, I'll do that. What else?"

Marie thought for a moment. "Well, God is to be referred to as *She*."

"Just to be contrary?"

"Not at all. God gave birth to the world, so I think it's evident. And in this religion, we're going to take care of certain things on our own—like God isn't going to have to worry about whether we covet our neighbor's wife."

"That would be all right?"

"No, it wouldn't be all right; it just wouldn't be God's job to worry about it. Joseph, do you really think He keeps track of our every selfish thought? Never mind does He have the time—why would He want to? I rather think that at the end, He picks us up and pings our hearts the way we do with an apple to see if it's crisp. If He hears a good ring, He's satisfied."

I smiled. "You're saying *He,* again, my dear."

As we walked back through the field, Marie took my hand, letting it go when our house came into view. We had spent the entire day together—gone to town, sung hymns, eaten ice cream, and invented a religion. After dinner we sat on the porch swing, drifting in thought as the tree frogs gave a concert, the kind of moment you wish you could keep in a bottle. Marie was entranced. "Joseph, do you think that where we go when we die, there will be sounds as beautiful as this?"

That night, in our room, Marie sat beside me on the bed. "Joseph, I want to know something."

"Of course. What it is it?"

Marie looked at the floor. "What about Lydia did you love the most?"

Lydia? I was surprised, for Lydia was far from my mind. I thought for a moment, trying to answer her truly. "I think, Marie, what I loved about Lydia was that she didn't imitate anyone."

I didn't know what Marie was looking for, but that wasn't it. She just nodded and lay down where she was. Three breaths later she propped herself up. "Joseph, do you think you could ever love me the way you loved Lydia?"

"No," I said without thinking it through. "I loved Lydia the way I loved her. I love you the way I love you. Only with you, it's better because I'm not hiding anything."

"Then you do love me?"

There it was. And why hadn't I seen it before? "Oh, my dear Marie. Yes, of course, I love you. I do."

"In the same way?"

I hesitated, not sure.

"Oh, Joseph. How direct must I be? You would be the man, so be one." She reached down and pulled her nightshirt over her head. I saw her nakedness and her fear. I took her hand and looked into her eyes. Then I let myself look at her small, uncovered breasts. My lips wanted to go there, and my face wanted to press into her white belly. I wanted to feel it on my cheeks and eyebrows.

"Joseph, please kiss me."

"In a moment," I said. I sat up and took off my shirt. I then blew out the candle and lay beside her. She was breathing in short, uneven gulps. I gathered her to me, and we began to breathe together—slower, longer. We kissed and then some more, until our bodies were pressing hard against each other.

Nothing in my marriage bed had even suggested the exquisite pleasure that I found with Marie. It rolled over us again and again, and when one of us would start to drift off, the other would begin, and we would come back to each other, till the window began to show light.

When I returned from town the next day, I saw Marie in the kitchen. She looked a little worn around the eyes, but otherwise present enough for someone who hadn't slept the night before. The only odd thing was that she wouldn't look at me. What was this about? Was she feeling uneasy? Was I now another mistake she'd made? At dinner, she sat away from me, and with some worry I stole glances and studied her face. She felt me do it and gave the slightest wave, as if shooing a fly. Then she bit her lip to keep from smiling.

That night I thought we would talk about what had passed between us, but when I got into bed, Marie reached for me. We kissed and gave ourselves to the moment, muffling our sighs. We had found a new world.

34

LIFE HAD BEGUN anew. I felt hopeful, and with it, afraid. I had been safe in the almshouse for years, my land of no dreams. But now there was love, and with it danger. The first, of course, was having that love discovered. Marie and I had to be careful with our affections, both inside our room and out. Each day we wove a small, gentle web of deceit, and I knew that every time I had done that in the past, I and someone I loved were the ones who got caught in it.

But that spring no one seemed to pay Marie and me any particular attention. The conversation was mostly about Dr. Herman Fromwitz. Herr Fromwitz, as he liked to be called, was an inspector from Albany who started visiting the almshouse every two weeks or so. He strutted like a rooster and smelled like raw bacon.

The doctor's visits were at first inconvenient. Then they were bothersome. Everyone tried their best to keep the place running at a merry clip while he was about, but Fromwitz found fault with everything, and none of it made sense. If you were cooking the meal, you should be making the beds—if you were feeding the goats, you should be mopping the floor.

When I asked Mrs. McNee about these visits, she said they had to do with the wretched people out back. "The state is going to build them a hospital," she said, raising her eyes in mock prayer. "It's been talked about for years. In the meantime, instead of sending money so that we might properly care for them, they send us Dr. Fromwitz—an alienist, I'm told."

Mrs. McNee said that an alienist was a person who treated afflictions of the mind, but I never saw Fromwitz spend any time in the backhouse.

And his training must have been in more than just the mind, because Herr Fromwitz played the part of house doctor on almost every visit. His patients were always women. He had an uncanny eye for seeing illness before the woman herself was aware of the malady. One day I overheard him tell Audrey that she looked pale. Mrs. McNee was standing nearby. "There's nothing wrong with her," she snapped.

Fromwitz gave the housemaster a cold look. "I am the doctor here. And you would do well to concern yourself with the proper management of this house. I will be making my report."

Mrs. McNee glared at him but dared say no more. If the doctor reported that she was the cause of poor conditions, then the County Board would dismiss her, because that was easier to do than to fix anything. She had no way to fight back.

One day Herr Fromwitz came into the house while Mrs. NcNee, Audrey, and Marie were scrubbing the floor. His hat was hardly off when he demanded to see the roster of residents.

"It's the same as it was last week," said Mrs. McNee, still on her knees.

"Oh, no," said Fromwitz. "It can't be the same, it's a new week." The doctor lifted his chin and patted his chest. "That's what's wrong with this house—no one does what they're supposed to. This will be in my report, Mrs. McNee."

I watched this exchange from the kitchen doorway. It took all my restraint to keep from picking up the mop water and dumping it on his head. I was on the edge of saying something, but before I could, Fromwitz walked over to Marie, who was now standing. He placed his hand on her cheek. "You don't look well, my dear. Do you feel all right?"

Marie pulled away. "I feel fine."

"No, you're flushed. Come into the office. I'll have a look at you."

Fromwitz tried to take hold of her hand, but Marie wouldn't give it. He reached for her again. By this time I was across the room. Herr Doctor didn't see me till I grabbed his shirt and pulled it tight to his fat neck. He stood on his toes to breathe, his eyes mad with fear. "If you touch her," I said in a growl, "I'll make you a gelding and feed the leftovers to the dogs, though I doubt it would be much." Then I brought my free hand hard to his soft belly. Fromwitz near fainted when he felt the knife go in. There wasn't any knife.

I released him, and the man, or whatever you would call it, fell over himself trying to get away. When he got across the room, he turned. "You're going to be very, very sorry," he said, trying to assert himself. I stepped forward as though to go at him, and he jumped behind Mrs. McNee. Then he grabbed his hat and ran out of the house.

As soon as the door slammed, I knew I had done bad. My impulse to protect Marie had brought heavens-knows-what upon us. And Mrs. McNee was in the most danger. "I'm sorry," I said to her. "I couldn't help it."

The housemaster was pale but composed. "It's all right, Joe. I won't be here much longer, anyway. If it's not this, it will be something else."

"Did you see how that rodent ran out of here?" said Audrey. We all laughed and that made things a little better for right then.

* * *

Two weeks went by, and Dr. Fromwitz did not come back. A hope kindled that perhaps we'd seen the last of him. Then he returned. He wasn't as brash now. He just walked around nodding, as though to let us know that he was seeing everything, and we weren't going to pull any wool over his eyes. Then one afternoon Sarah knocked on my door and said that Mrs. McNee wanted to see me. I went downstairs. The housemaster was in the parlor, and behind her was Fromwitz.

Mrs. McNee's face was ashen and her voice unsteady. "As master of this house, it is my duty to inform you that you are no longer a senior resident. You are to remain here as . . . pauper insane."

My face felt hot. "What does that mean?"

"It means," said Fromwitz, "that the state is building you a new home where you and your kind can live without bothering anyone. You're a ward of the state, and I can have you put in jail. I can have you put in the pens out back or, if Mrs. McNee will promise that you will not run away, you can stay here. But you can't work in town, and you can't leave this house, and if you do, I will have you hunted like a mad dog, and Mrs. McNee will pay the consequence."

Fromwitz put on his hat and walked out. I stood without moving. So did Mrs. McNee. "There was nothing I could do," she said finally. "But you stay or go as you see fit. I'll not stand in your way."

I glanced at Marie, who had come in and seen most of it. "I'm not going anywhere."

The order from Dr. Fromwitz took me from town and put me back in the garden where I weeded and planned revenge. I imagined a Calico Indian meeting him on the road at night. I remembered my father's costume and thought I could fashion a decent imitation from the used clothes in the storeroom. Perhaps Marie would join me. It wouldn't take much to scare Fromwitz. I thought of displaying knives and nooses while Herr Doctor quaked. And then leaving him on the road, without a thing to wear. I imagined him, pig naked, knocking on doors. And people telling him to go away.

I didn't quite find the moment to share this plan with Marie. She was talking about us running off together, but I said no. I said that the trouble with Fromwitz would all blow over like a summer storm. After all, we had more friends than he did. Fromwitz might be able to order me into the backhouse, but he couldn't keep me there. And as long as Marie and I could still be together, we were safer where we were. So we stayed, and nothing bad happened. Fromwitz came, and I managed to keep out of his way. He seemed just as willing to keep out of mine. I began to think that things would, indeed, blow over. Then one afternoon I came into to the house to find Marie crying.

"What's happened?"

"I don't know," she said. "I was in the kitchen and Sarah came and said that there was someone at the door asking for me. I went into the front room, and there was a man I had never seen before, a man with a waxed mustache and a derby hat. He asked if I were Marie Louise Martin, and I said yes, but I couldn't think of who would know me by that name. The man looked at me and then said there was some mistake—that I wasn't the Miss Martin he was looking for."

"Well, perhaps, that's it. Some sort of mistake."

"But it wasn't, Joseph, because I saw his eyes."

I didn't like the sound of this, but I told Marie that we should stay still for the moment. Wait for things to sort out. Marie agreed, and we didn't go to Mrs. McNee about the man, but Sarah must have told her.

A week later, Mrs. McNee called me into her office. She had an official-looking paper in hand. She didn't try to smile.

"I have a letter from a detective agency in New York," she said. "I'll read what it says."

> In your house there is a woman going by the name of Marie Louise Martin. We believe she is a woman named Marie Louise Perry who we are searching for on behalf of her family. We have sent a man, and her description matches that of the missing woman. As stewards of the law, you are required to tell us if this woman is really Marie Louise Martin. Or is she Marie Louise Perry?

It was done. Mrs. McNee was required to tell the truth, and I could not lie to her.

"Well, they've found her," I said.

"And I must write to tell them. You know that, Joe."

I nodded and said that I would go tell Marie. I found her in our room, and when she heard the news, she began to cry. "Oh, Joseph. I can't go home. I'd rather throw myself in the river."

I stayed by the door. "Perhaps," I said, "going home is for the best."

"I won't do it," she said calmly so I would understand. "I won't. Joseph, we can take to the road. You can be my husband; I shall be your wife. We will go from farm to farm and offer ourselves for work. We'll find some-place where we can live in peace and speak to people about the goodness of God."

"But we would be paupers," I said. "I've lived that way, Marie, but you never have. You should go home."

"No!" Marie caught herself and lowered her voice. "No, Joseph, I wouldn't survive a week. I'm not afraid of poverty. I'm not afraid of death.

Whatever happens to me, I just want it to be mine. Of all people, you must understand that."

I had stayed in Delhi under the threat of being locked away, because I believed us safer in the almshouse than out on the road. And I would have continued to stay were it possible. But it wasn't. Marie and I would either leave together, or she would be brought home against her will and I locked up when the time came.

"Then I pledge myself to you, Marie," I said, wondering what would become of us. "I love you and will never abandon you."

"I pledge myself to you, Joseph," she answered. "You will always have my heart."

We sealed these vows with an embrace and then calmly talked about what had to be done. I sat with Marie as she wrote a letter home:

> Dear Mother and Father,
>
> You have found me. I have been living in the almshouse in Delhi. I am, as you may guess, no longer the wife of James Wilson. He was not the man I thought. It cost me everything to learn that. Please know that even though I betrayed you, I never stopped loving you. But I can't come home. And so I do not expect to see you again in this life, but know that I pray that we will see each other in the one to come. Please follow me no more.
>
> Your loving daughter,
> Marie Louise

The letter went out the next day, along with Mrs. McNee's reply to the agency in New York. That week, I mended socks while Marie looked through the storage room for anything that might be useful on the road. She went up to Mrs. Caldwell's house to secretly say our good-bye. I stayed at the almshouse, not wanting to do anything that might ruin our plan. I didn't visit Sheriff Evans, and we said nothing to Mrs. McNee, though I'm sure she knew.

35

WE CREPT OUT of the almshouse and down the Hamlin road, a bag over my shoulder and one over Marie's. We walked while the moon was up and all the next day. We nodded small greetings to those we passed and feared the sound of anyone coming from behind. I knew Sheriff Evans wouldn't let Fromwitz order him around, but I didn't know how big a crime this was—my leaving Delhi—and who else might be set on my trail.

On the third afternoon, the Hancock bridge came into view, our passage to Pennsylvania and safety. I found myself trying to walk quiet—might we yet see armed men, or hear them coming at a gallop? But no guard was on the bridge, and the only horse to be heard was pulling a wagon.

I looked out at the Delaware and remembered another bridge that had taken me over that river, one that had carried canal boats—an enchanted bridge. Once across it, fishes and loaves had appeared, complete with raucous nights in a tavern, dinners with accomplished men, and the love of a beautiful woman. But that was miles downstream and sixteen years of water.

Marie felt none of my haunting. She let go of my arm and skipped across the bridge as if she were ten. I didn't join her. Parts of me still felt like a woman, but no part felt like a girl. When I caught up on the other side, Marie had a mischievous look on her face. "I've been waiting to show you this," she said, reaching into her bag. Her hand reappeared, and in it was a roll of paper money.

"Where did that come from?" I asked, fearing the answer.

"Our dear Elizabeth Caldwell. One hundred dollars!"

"That woman is not of this earth."

"Oh yes she is," said Marie, laughing. "And she told me to tell you that if you break my heart, you'll have to answer to her."

"You told her?" I said, feeling alarm. "I mean, not just about our leaving, but about us?"

Marie met my eyes. "She sends her love."

* * *

In Pennsylvania, we didn't have to stay out of sight or look over our shoulders. We could smile and say hello to strangers who would smile and say hello to us. And for the first time in many years, I was again posing as a man. It was easy. I looked the part now—the hard living in the woods had seen to that. And Marie was on my arm. People would look at her pretty face and not think a thing about me.

We followed the river downstream and later slept beside it. The next day, we traveled inland on a narrow road. It was late afternoon when we walked into the village of Galilee. The second house we passed had a fence with small white roses. At the gate there was a sign: *Dr. Arlyn Powell, Justice of the Peace.* I stopped walking and took Marie's hand. "Marie Louise Perry, will you marry me?"

Her eyes grew wide. "Oh, yes, dear Joseph, yes! But do you think it's wise?"

"That's not a quality I'm known for," I said, making her laugh. We had talked about living as man and wife and had even made vows, but neither of us had imagined a ceremony, until now. I put my hands on her shoulders and looked into her eyes. "I want to be married and not pretending."

I opened the gate and we walked up the path her arm in mine. The door was answered by a plump woman in an apron. I gave a slight bow. "Is the judge in?"

"He is. What may I say is your business?"

"We would like to be married."

The woman's face lit up. "Oh my, well, yes. He is here. Come in. When were you thinking of?"

"Today, if it can be done."

"Today, yes, well. Let me call my husband, and he can tell you. Please take a seat."

Marie and I sat on a cushioned bench in the small parlor. A few minutes later Judge Powell entered the room. He looked just like Mrs. Powell—they might have been a matched set of rag dolls at a church fair. The judge wore a vest and spectacles, and I could not tell right away if he would be stern or accommodating.

"So you'd like to get married," he said, as though the thought were both question and answer. "Want to do it today. Well, I see no reason why not. Just give me a little time to finish what I'm doing and prepare the papers. It will be five dollars—three of that goes to the county."

"Will you stay for dinner?" asked Mrs. Powell who had just joined us. "I've a chicken in the oven, and we'd love to have you join us."

I looked at Marie and she smiled our acceptance. The world seemed perfectly happy to have us wed. Mrs. Powell went back to the kitchen, while Marie and I sat there, holding hands and whispering like school children.

A little later, a neighbor, a Mrs. O'Connor, appeared with her young daughter. Mrs. Powell, who now seemed to be running things, told me to go join the judge in the garden. She and Mrs. O'Connor would attend to Marie. I found Judge Powell standing by a budding hawthorn. I stood quietly beside him and watched a humming bird make its rounds.

A few minutes later, little Karen O'Connor came down the path carrying a daylily. Some distance behind walked Mrs. Powell and Mrs. O'Connor. Then Marie, holding a bouquet of iris and columbine. Purple verbena had been woven into her hair, and she floated down the path like a seed of milkweed.

With Marie at my side, Judge Powell asked if I would love and honor her until the day I died. I said I would. Marie was then asked if she would love, honor, and obey me until the day she died. She said she would. I was then told that I could kiss the bride and that was the first time our lips met as married folk, and the first time we had kissed with anyone looking on. We didn't have to hide.

When the ceremony was done, Marie and I went for a stroll. We walked a short distance till we found a spot under an old maple where we sat and listened as the birds made their evening calls. Marie's hair, which had been pinned up for the ceremony, had begun to pull loose. Strands fell down the sides of her face, while her eyes danced like sunlight off a lake.

"Joseph," she said, "I've been given a new life."

"I feel the same," I said. And yet as I spoke those words, I also felt a strong upwelling of sadness. It didn't push the happiness aside, but it was there all the same. And I didn't want to hide a thing from Marie, so I told her. "I feel like crying for some reason. Isn't that odd?"

"I don't think so," answered my wife. "I could too. And I don't believe they'd be tears of joy, as some would say. I think that when you feel happiness like we do now, you go deep into the well where all that has happened is stored. And you cannot draw water of any particular kind, for it has all mixed."

"Surely so," I said, looking into Marie's beautiful face and wishing not to think of the dark things lurking in my well.

When we returned to the house, Mrs. Powell asked if we had a place to stay that night. We said no, and she showed us a room with a posted bed that looked out at the garden. "We keep this room for our son and his wife when they come to visit," she said. "You will stay here tonight." Marie looked at me with big eyes and then gave Mrs. Powell a hug that almost knocked the dear woman over.

At dinner, Judge Powell said grace. He asked God to protect us and provide for us. It seemed to me that He had already begun. On the table were greens, sweet potatoes, and warm chicken. "Where will you be going?" asked Mrs. Powell as the food was passed. "Do you have work?"

"No," I said, "but we're hoping to find some."

"Well, I don't know of anyone looking for help, but there are many farms to our west. I'm sure you'll find something."

"We also want to spread the good news of the Lord," said Marie. I felt uneasy hearing these words. I knew that Marie was earnest in her desire to serve God, but I was not confident on how it would be received.

"Oh," said, Mrs. Powell, "do you belong to a church?"

"No," said Marie, "we believe that many paths lead to God. We follow the teachings of Jesus and those of Emanuel Swedenborg."

Mrs. Powell turned to her husband. "Arlyn, have you heard of a Mr. Swedenborg?"

"Yes," said the judge. "They had a church in Harrisburg when I was boy."

Mrs. Powell seemed delighted and gave her benediction. "Well, I don't know this Mr. Swedenborg, but if you follow the teachings of Jesus, you will never be lost to each other."

That night, Marie and I slept in the Powells' beautiful bed with its feather mattress. Our kisses did not last long, for we were tired from the walking. In the morning, I woke to see sunlight streaming through the curtain and my wife sleeping beside me. Marie opened her eyes and smiled to see me there.

After a breakfast of bread and jam, we said our good-byes and started up the road.

The land was indeed enchanted—the day before had proved it. We had been given flowers, good food, and a soft bed, all in exchange for declaring our love. I thought we might go from town to town and marry in each one.

* * *

We traveled west and every day found shelter, often doing chores for something to eat. But it wasn't until we crossed into the next county that we found steady work. The farm, nestled in a narrow valley, belonged to the Spencers, an older couple whose children had left. I chopped wood for them, cleaned the chicken coop, and helped bring in the hay. Marie worked inside. Mr. Spencer, lean and weathered as a fencepost, was pleasant and glad for the help. Mrs. Spencer was his opposite. Just moving about the house brought on her heavy breathing. Her flushed face seemed locked into a frown.

Marie and I slept in the barn loft. We were warm and comfortable but could light no lamp for fear of the hay. Our end of the barn was close to the house, so we often heard pieces of conversation and became privy to Mrs. Spencer's every dissatisfaction. We kept our secrets by talking softly to each other in what we called our barn voices.

On Sundays, Marie and I would walk about the meadows and the glens. We found a waterfall and built a campsite near it. I made a shelter using a piece of canvas borrowed from the barn. We slept there on the warm nights.

Beneath the falls, the water had carved a pool in the rock. We sometimes bathed there, though even in July the water was cold. One Sunday I rose early and started a fire beside the pool. I fed the fire all morning, and by noon, when the ashes fell away, eight large rocks glowed like embers. I pushed them with a sturdy stick, and one by one they went in, each letting out a loud hiss. A little later, Marie and I slipped into water that was silky and warm. We lingered and talked the early afternoon away, kissing and floating entwined. Finally, quite pickled, we left the water to seek the sun.

Marie lay naked in the meadow, and I sat and gazed at her. Her fine brown hair seemed to play with the freckles on her back. She was thin at the waist with a plump little bottom that I loved to look at. After a time, she rose and pushed me down and began to run her eyes over me. Then her loving touch.

If anyone should tell you that a woman cannot find satisfaction with another woman, I can be your witness to say it isn't so. We both found our pleasure that afternoon—several times. And in being outside and not covered by a ceiling or a blanket, our love seemed almost like a sacrament. And if God had wanted to show His disapproval, He could have sent the rain or a stroke of lightning, but instead He sent dragonflies and sparrows.

36

DURING THE WINTER, Marie and I slept in the small room behind the Spencers' kitchen. Mrs. Spencer was in bed much of the time with a variety of complaints. We did what we could to be helpful, but she became increasingly disagreeable. In the spring, Mr. Spencer, with apologies, asked us to leave.

After three days on the road, we came upon a farm belonging to a widow named Emma Winslow. The corn fields were abandoned, but there was still work to be done around the house and in the garden. We were given a bedroom on the second floor.

Emma Winslow liked to tell stories, and sometimes I thought that was the reason we'd been taken on. Over dinner, she would talk about the boyish things Mr. Winslow had done during his courtship or about their children and the trouble they got into when they were little. Marie and I wove a sparse tale, saying that we had owned a small farm but had lost it by misfortune. We really didn't have to say more, because, soon enough, Mrs. Winslow would be telling us about a cat that chased a bear or a daughter who snuck pie to the chickens on Christmas.

On Sundays, I'd hitch the mare to the carriage and off we'd go to the Baptist Church. After service, we might take Mrs. Winslow visiting, and on those occasions we wouldn't get back until it was almost dark. On one such evening, I attended to the mare and then joined Marie and Mrs. Winslow on the porch. Fireflies by the dozens were around the yard. I sat next to Marie, while Mrs. Winslow moved gently in her rocker.

"Pastor Caulfield spoke to me after service," she said. "He asked if you might want to join the church."

Marie gave me a quick look, no question in her mind. "Please thank the pastor for us," she said. "We would like to continue to attend, but we don't wish to join. We have our own faith."

"What is that?"

Marie sat up in her chair. "Well, we believe that God is all around us and within us and that we find Him most easily when we look for ourselves."

"My goodness," said Mrs. Winslow, "you sound like those New England philosophers we hear about from time to time."

"Well, yes," said Marie, "but we are followers of Jesus, nonetheless."

Mrs. Winslow thought for a moment and then spoke of the picnic that we'd been preparing for. The gathering at her farm was an annual event, begun when she and her husband had small children.

"We always have a devotion," she said, "and it's never led by a minister, always by one of us. Perhaps you, Marie, or you, Joseph, would lead us this year? You can say what you just said to me—that was beautiful. Just speak your heart. Only a minute or so.

My knees felt weak at the thought, even seated as I was. Marie, however, loved the idea, and she wanted *me* to do the speaking. Before I could say a thing it was decided. Later, when we were alone, I told Marie that she should have talked to me first.

"Talked to you?" she said, not trying to hide her annoyance. "Isn't this just what we imagined? People gathering in a field and speaking plainly to each other?"

"I don't know these people, Marie. What should I say?"

"I think you should tell them about that time on the prairie when you were alone in the snow, about feeling that God was seeing the world through your eyes."

"And be stoned as a heretic?"

"Well, find something else then. Is standing up for the Lord really such a chore?"

I was a coward, and my wife had shamed me. I agreed to do it, but I promised myself that the names of Emerson or Swedenborg would not pass my lips. I would speak of Jesus. That week I read the Gospels, though

I was not much in the spirit to start. But then certain passages came to life, ones that Marie had read to me in the almshouse. And one in particular, about what Jesus had said to His disciples just days before the Romans drove spikes into His hands. I put it to memory but still hoped for rain.

* * *

The picnic day dawned fair, and wagons began to arrive around noon. We had a hog roasting on a spit, and people brought fresh bread, bowls of greens, and pans with berry pie. Women sat on blankets and talked like schoolgirls while the children ran wild and the men stood in knots and complained about the price of feed.

As the sun moved lower in the sky, Mrs. Winslow came up to the field and stood on a large, flat rock near the center of the meadow. Her neighbors gathered on the ground that sloped away, as they had done for years. "As you know," she said, "Joseph and Marie have worked here since early May. I have asked Joseph, on short notice, if he would bring us the afternoon devotion." She looked at me and nodded.

I stepped onto the rock, feeling unsteady. I clasped my hands and squeezed as though that might keep my voice even. "Marie and I have been blessed," I said, "to have found our way to Mrs. Winslow's door and to your beautiful valley."

I looked over to Marie and she gave a reassuring smile. "In the Scripture we read that the disciples came to Jesus, afraid, for the end was near. But Jesus told them not to fear because His Father would watch over them for they had taken care of His Son when He was cold and hungry. But the disciples could not remember these things. *When, Lord,* they asked, *did we see you hungry and give you food? Where was it that we saw you a stranger and took you in?* And Our Lord said to them, *If you have done it unto the least of my brethren, you have done it unto me.*

The stillness was broken only by the sounds of children down below. I looked about to see open faces. My words came easier. "Now there are some who say that we should look for God in Nature, others say church. Both are surely good, for has He not said that He is everywhere? And if this is true, might we also look for Him inside those around us, and inside ourselves? And I believe *that* is what Jesus was saying—that He is *within* each of us. *If you have done it unto the least of my brethren, you have done it unto me.*" I paused for a moment then gave a slight nod. "Marie and I thank you for your kindness."

Amidst the murmur of *amens*, I went over to Marie and she embraced me. People came up to us and offered simple words of appreciation.

* * *

A little later in the summer, Mrs. Winslow had a bout of indigestion. We didn't give it much thought, but her complaints kept on. As the winter approached, she had trouble holding down food. The doctor came and gave her laudanum. Things improved for a time, but then the tonic only made her tired.

Mrs. Winslow grew weaker as the winter dragged on. In the last week of March, her daughter Julia arrived from Wilkes Barre. Her mother had written about us, but Julia seemed to have heard every kind word as evidence that we had tricked the old woman and taken advantage of her. We were surprised, for in Mrs. Winslow's stories, Julia had been a mischievous but endearing little girl. Now she seemed made of spite, and by her looks, you might have thought we had something to do with the illness.

Julia had been there only a week when at dinner she started telling us about her visit to town. "I heard that on Sunday Reverend Caulfield denounced devil worshippers said to be in our midst. They give little sermons trying to lure good Christians from their churches. Perhaps you know who he is talking about?"

I gave Julia a cold look. "I know that your mother asked me to give a short devotion in the meadow last summer. I did so, and everyone was kind."

"They were being gracious to Mother. I want you and Marie to go."

I glanced at Marie and saw her flush. "We'll go, of course," I said. "We'll say good-bye to your mother."

"No, she is too ill. Don't disturb her. I won't permit it."

Marie and I found work at a farm ten miles away. A few weeks later we heard that Emma Winslow had died. We went to her burial, but Julia made a big show of not speaking to us. Reverend Caulfield's crusade against devil worshipers had taken hold. People turned their backs to us—even those who were at the picnic and who had come to us with earnest handshakes and smiles.

Marie and I went south to get away from the rumors, but our evil reputation seemed to precede us. We found work now and then, but it never lasted long, and usually, we were paid in poor food. What money we had ran out, along with our luck. In the town of Preston, they put us in jail and told us to leave in the morning.

We were weak and hungry. Had there been a way to give up, someone to surrender to, I would have done it. Had there been a way to put Marie on a train back to Boston, I would have done that too, with or without her consent. But as it was, we walked on, as beggars.

In Stroudsburg, we were left alone for a few days, but we could find no real work. The sheriff, an unpleasant man named Briscoe, said he was going to arrest us if we didn't leave. I began to shout at him. People stopped and watched.

I might have done better to speak differently to the man, but I had laid up a lot of anger from the things that had been done to us, and it all spilled out. Marie and I got put in the Stroudsburg lockup.

37

THE BUNKS IN the Stroudsburg jail were rough planks. The food was oatmeal, and we were glad to have it. The judge would return in a few days and let us go upon our promise to leave town. That's what we were told.

On our second day as his guests, Deputy Hastings took pity and passed me his *Stroudsburg Sentinel*. I had been pacing back and forth, and would have happily read the train schedule. But I never got to the trains, because on the first page, set in large type, were the words OUTRAGE IN DAMASCUS! The story told of a dastardly attack on a young woman who had been beaten, raped, and then thrown off a bridge into the Delaware River. She'd been found the next morning, barely alive. Then my heart made a fist—the woman was identified as the adopted daughter of David Fortnam of Tyler Hill, Miss Helen Slater. This had to be a dream. I shook my head and looked again. No, I was awake and the newspaper was real.

"Marie!"

She came to the small window between our cells, and I handed her the paper. A moment later she cried out. "Oh, Joseph! That poor girl! Helen. What are we to do?"

"I know what I'm going to do," I said. "I'm going to get out of here and hunt those villains like dogs." I ran my tin cup on the bars to get the deputy's attention. He wasn't amused.

"Those bastards raped my daughter!" I yelled.

The deputy gave a disbelieving look. "You saying that girl's your daughter? She ain't nobody's daughter. Paper says she's an orphan."

"No, she's mine! Let me out of here!"

In a clearer mind, I would have been less insistent, for we were to be set free in a day or two. But now I wanted out on a claim about a story in the newspaper, and they weren't going to be "taken for fools." That's what the sheriff said.

Days passed. Then a week. The time had now gone when we should have been released. I was furious but could do nothing. My daughter's attackers were getting away.

On the ninth day, Sheriff Briscoe walked back to my cell. "You're going now," he said as he unlocked the door. Then he clapped a set of irons on me. "You're going to New York, that is. It seems you have some friends there."

"What?"

"We have the warrant. And, yes, you were telling the truth about the girl, except it seems there's some other question." The sheriff curled his lip. "I think we ought to make an inspection. See what's what. Wouldn't want to arrest the wrong person. So if you've got a willie, let's see it. Take them britches off."

"I'm not taking off nothin'," I said, pulling away.

"Maybe you need a little help," the sheriff said, stepping toward me.

I raised my shackles, but he just laughed. "Whatever happens, it's just you trying to escape custody, so I don't care how much of a brawl you make. I'm gonna see what I want to see."

I thought of my daughter at the hands of men who would rape and murder without a thought. I considered the sheriff one of them, and I was prepared to make him pay a price—I didn't care what happened to me. Then Marie's voice came from the next cell. "Sheriff?" she asked calmly. "Do you have a wife and children? Do you go to church? Do you care what people say about you?"

I think the sheriff had forgotten Marie was there. He quickly sobered and decided to get rid of us both. He opened Marie's cell and told her that she was free.

"I'll go where my husband goes," she said.

"Your husband?" he said. "You call whatever that is your husband?"

I was led outside to a wagon and loaded onto the back where there was a little hay, one blanket, and a hasp to which I was fastened. The deputy snapped the reins, and I began the slow journey from Stroudsburg to Delhi—in irons, like I had killed someone.

Marie walked behind, crying. A mile out of town, the deputy stopped the wagon. "Get on," he said. Marie thanked him and climbed up beside me. Three days in the back of that wagon was agony. Marie did what she could for me, but the trip was hardly any better for her.

* * *

Late on the third day, we pulled into the yard of the Delaware County almshouse. A man I didn't know came out, a pistol strapped to his leg. He was with Jennings, a resident I knew. Deputy Hastings got down and went over to the men. A moment later he turned to me. "Mrs. Slater, this is Herm Cranston, housemaster. You are in his custody."

"Where's Mrs. McNee?"

"I don't usually talk to crazy people," said Cranston, "but the old hag is gone. And you and your kind are one of the reasons. Deputy, if I could call upon you for one last service? Would you help Jennings escort Mrs. Slater to her cell in the backhouse?"

"I'm not going there!" I shouted, suddenly realizing that they were going to lock me up with the insane.

"Yes, you are," said Cranston, "and that's where you're gonna stay."

Marie tried to say something, but Cranston shouted her down. "Watch yourself, missy," he warned. "Step on this property, and I'll have you arrested."

Marie glared at him. Cranston gave a small smile. "Take the inmate up." Deputy Hastings took me by the arm, and Jennings led the way. I didn't fight. It wouldn't have done any good, and I didn't want to give this Cranston character a show. We went upstairs, Jennings opened a door, and in a moment, I was alone.

The pen was eight feet square with a bunk, a corn shuck tick, and a slop bucket. The place stank. There was no window, just a diamond-shaped hole in the door and a narrow opening at the bottom. A little later, a bowl of gruel slid through it.

"Who's there?" I said.

"It's me, Jennings," came the answer in a hushed voice. I ran to the hole and peered at him. "I'm sorry for your trouble, Joe," he said. "I'm not even 'sposed to say nothin' to ya, and iffen I know Cranston, he's countin' the seconds."

"What happened to Mrs. McNee?"

"She's gone. You did right, Joe, to leave. Things are bad now. No one works in town anymore. The garden's gone to hell. Cranston thinks he can get things to grow by pointing his gun."

"Where's Marie?"

"She went to town, but Cranston's expecting somethin'. And he says he'll shoot anyone trying to get you outta here, including Miss Marie. I gotta go."

"God bless you, Jennings."

I felt afraid for Marie, for I knew she would come. In another day, I was more afraid for myself. I was inside a ship that had sunk at sea.

On my third night, I woke to a faint tap on the door. "Joseph?"

I was up in an instant. "I'm here, Marie," I whispered. "How did you get in? You're in danger."

"Never mind that. Listen. I met with Mrs. Caldwell. I think she's going to help. And I talked to the sheriff, or at least I tried to. He wasn't happy to see me and said right out that he didn't want to know anything. He said he hoped you wouldn't break the law."

A dog out back began to bark—the neighbor's bitch.

"Marie, Cranston will shoot you if he catches you here."

"Then listen. Be ready. I don't know when."

* * *

Days went by. Nothing happened, and no encouraging message found its way to me. I began to despair. I could not imagine anyone lasting more than a week or two in this hell before his humanity was extinguished for all time. Why was this allowed? It would be more kind to shoot the insane. Truly.

I tried to think of things to do to keep myself from coming undone. I made a crude clock by marking the travels of a sliver of light that came from the outside through a crack. I tried to think of ways to open that crack so that the light might be a fraction larger. I found a nail that I could grip. It wasn't loose, but the wood around it was old and dry. I tapped it a little each day with my shoe, and then slipped the lip of my tin plate under the head to see if it would come out. A few days of trying, and I had the nail, about the size of my little finger.

I used the nail to widen the crack in the board, but I took care not to work it too hard—I had plans for it. If I were to remain penned up, I was certain that Cranston, at some time, would come to admire his work. And when he did, I would act broken, and I probably would be broken by then, except that I would have saved just a small piece of myself for the occasion. I'd wait for him to relax or turn his back, and then I'd spring up and bury the nail in his neck.

A day or two later, a fever came on. I lay in the darkness, sweating and aching. Now where was the broth, the soft word, or the hand to the brow? I thought about my mother. I strained to remember when I was young and she loved me and took care of me. Why had she changed?

The sickness stayed for a week. When it left, I tried to keep track of the days, but couldn't. At times, I cried for the lack of anything else. No messages and no Marie. Had she been arrested? I had no way to find out, for the man who brought my food was someone I didn't know, and he wouldn't say a thing. I stopped hoping for rescue, because the daily dimming of that hope was more than I could bear. I began to think of other uses for my nail—a particular vein in my arm called to me.

"Joseph, we're here." I had heard Marie's voice before—been woken by her voice on several occasions only to discover that the voice was just a wish inside my head. Marie spoke again, so I answered into the dark. What came in return was something that made me think I wasn't dreaming. It was a man's voice I didn't recognize. "Joe," he said in a whisper, "we're going to pry the hasp. You ready?" I said I was, and then I heard some tapping and a few grunts. Then louder tapping and low cursing.

"Joe," said the man, "it's stronger than we thought. I've got a bar, and I'm ready to do it, but it's gonna make a lot of noise. You and Miss Perry will be on your own. Understand?"

"Do it," I said, not lowering my voice.

There were three hard bangs and the sound of groaning wood. The inmates in the backhouse began to howl, along with all the dogs on the west end of Delhi. Three more bangs, and the door flew open.

"God bless you, gentlemen," said Marie. All I ever saw of my rescuers was a pair of shadows fleeing down the hall.

Marie found my hand and pulled me behind her, down the stairs and out into the yard. Several rooms in the house were already lit. Cranston's voice could be heard above all. "Herbert, Jennings! Get the clubs!" Then he was on the porch. "What's going on out there? Don't play any tricks. I've got a gun!"

Marie and I ran behind the chicken coop, which gave us cover till we got around to the side of the house where Marie had hidden her bag. From there we couldn't see Cranston, but from his shouts it seemed that he hadn't moved off the porch. Then a shot was fired. It couldn't have been fired at us, but we ducked anyway and crouched low as we hurried across the front yard, moving toward the road and freedom.

Suddenly, a man came out of the dark. He was coming around the house from the other side and nearly ran into us, a stick or a club in his hand. A terrified moment later we recognized the man as Jennings, and it took about the same time for him to see it was us.

Cranston's voice came from out back. "Jennings, anything out there?"

I knew that Paul Jennings wished us no harm, but I also knew him to be obedient. I didn't dare speak, nor could I plead with my eyes because of the dark. I stopped breathing.

"Can't see nothin'," he shouted.

38

WE WENT FROM town to town, but Pennsylvania was not the friendly place it had been during our crossing two years before. Our clothes were ragged and worn, and that's all people seemed to see. Some were just plain mean, as though we had insulted them by our misfortune. And people tried to take advantage of us, thinking I wouldn't notice, but I noticed all right. I saw most everything and wasn't taken in by their smiles and promises. Once they knew that I was on to them, they wanted us gone, and that meant we had to look for another place. I was tired a lot, and there was a squeezing pain in my head, something that had begun in the back-house. I tried to hide this from Marie, for our troubles were hard on her, but sometimes I couldn't. Often the pain would stay all day and into the next.

We tried to find out what had become of Helen, but we were care-ful not to ask too many questions, remembering what had happened in Stroudsburg. Every now and then we would hear some version of it, and almost every story had Helen back at the Fortnam farm. Some said that she had been driven mad—others were just as certain that she had recovered. Everyone agreed, however, that her attackers had been arrested, and then, without so much as a trial, let go.

I wanted to avenge this crime, but as it was, I couldn't even feed my wife. And beyond that, I could feel myself slipping back into that dark place—the one I knew well from my years alone. Voices echoed strangely now, and heads began to look large. I could hear people talking about us, though they might be miles away. I trusted no one and saw twisted faces behind every smile. I didn't know where it would go or what would become of me, though I had seen what had happened to my mother. Marie begged me to be better with people and trust them more. I did make myself act better, though I couldn't trust them no matter how hard I tried.

* * *

That winter we found work at a farm in Monroe County. We received no money, but Marie kept telling me not to say a thing. So I held my tongue, even though I knew what they were up to. But all my minding my manners did no good, for one day the farmer announced that he had heard about us and didn't want us around anymore.

We walked a long way, and just as I thought we would die of neglect, we found work. It was on a farm that belonged to an older, childless couple north of Waymart. The Matlows were strict and stingy, but Marie told me to behave myself, and I did. Weeks went by, and nothing bad happened. We had Saturday afternoons and Sundays to ourselves, and on these days, we explored the upper meadows and ridgelines and found a shallow cave in a rock outcropping. Remembering our camp at the Spencer farm, we made the cave our new camp and stayed there on warm nights.

We did all that the Matlows required and got paid with thin soup. So as not to spoil something else for us, I spoke as little as possible. But they kept asking questions—questions about us. Marie could always answer these questions in a way that seemed to satisfy them, but sometimes Marie wouldn't be there. And I couldn't keep track of everything she had said, and even when I could, it never came out sounding right when I said it. And every time I told them something about us, which usually wasn't true, they'd go ahead and ask another question.

Then one morning Mr. Matlow said that he was going to the village and would be back in the afternoon. I didn't like the look on his face. A few hours later I was out back tending the hogs when a carriage pulled up. Out jumped a man with a pistol strapped to his leg—that devil Cranston! I had been betrayed. All their questions so that they could get some reward.

Cranston came toward me in an easy manner, thinking perhaps I didn't recognize him. I wasn't going to let him slap irons on me, like that fiend

Briscoe, so I waited, and when he got close, I hit him hard in the knee with the bucket. That put him down.

"You didn't fool me," I shouted, "and you're not going to catch me neither." I ran down the road and then up into the forest. I went to the cave, thinking that Marie would know to find me there.

The next day Marie did come. She looked like she hadn't slept the night before, and she was crying. I was certain that Cranston had done something mean to her, but she was angry at me. "Joseph," she demanded, "why did you do that to Mrs. Matlow's brother?"

"He was no brother," I said, thinking that they had lied to her. "It was Cranston. You know, from Delhi."

"Oh, Joseph," she said with a sob, "it wasn't. I saw him. I guess you could say he looked a little like that man, but not that much."

I wasn't sure if Marie had seen the same man. Maybe they had played a trick on her. I said that I would die before getting locked up in the backhouse again, but Marie didn't seem to care about that. She said I was lucky that the man wasn't badly hurt, or the sheriff's men would be at the cave instead of her. She said she would keep working for the Matlows, but I had to promise never to go there. She would bring blankets and food. She said I needed to calm down and forget about the backhouse.

* * *

I stayed at the cave, and Marie came by every couple of days. I didn't mind being by myself—I had done it for years. Sometimes I'd snare a rabbit, and I'd have that rabbit roasting when Marie came on Sunday. When the berries started coming, I went out and picked—picked enough so that Marie was able to trade for them. And as long as I stayed in the woods, I was all right. But as soon as I went near any settlement, I wasn't. All things made by man seemed ugly, the same way things had looked when I spent my years alone in the woods.

With so much time to myself, I thought about everything. I thought about this earth, and about God, though I no longer thought about preaching the Good Word—I was cured of that. I didn't pray much, but when I did, it was to ask God to bring His judgment in time for me to see it. Let it come. Let His judgment rain down from the sky. I thought it was overdue, for if we humans had been sent here to do the Lord's work, then surely by now He must be disappointed.

That thought was not new to me. It came to me first when I was living in the woods some ten years before. The war had started, and they had built a small factory in the next valley. It was to tan hides in the acid made from tree bark. They called the new town Acidalia, as though it were a flower.

One day I went over to see. The hillsides were stripped and covered with skinned logs. The bark with its acid had value, the soft wood underneath not so much. It wasn't worth the effort to haul the logs to Long Eddy. So there they lay and would lie till they rotted, which made it seem like murder. Down below were piles of scraped cow hides, and nearby, in open-sided barns, large cauldrons of boiling acids were tended by half-naked Irishmen, no better than savages. The smell was something awful, and if they had been stirring sinners into this soup instead of cowhides, it would have been the perfect picture of hell. And all of it so that men could make boots that other men could put on, so they could march to great fields where they would line up and shoot each other, fall down dead and rot like the naked logs.

So the Lord's certain disappointment was not a new thought, but while I sat by our cave one afternoon and waited for Marie's next visit, the thought that should have followed this revelation finally came. It occurred to me that we humans were not here on this earth to do the Lord's work but to do the Devil's work. If we did the Lord's work, then everything we made wouldn't look so ugly, and we wouldn't hurt each other in so many ways. What we call the Lord's work are minor efforts to undo some awful thing done before. No matter how righteous our thoughts, it's all a costume for the Devil to walk about in—all a disguise.

Why hadn't I seen this before? I didn't know, but it didn't matter—I was seeing it now. The Devil had fooled everyone, but in the end, he hadn't fooled me. I had discovered him and not God inside myself, and now I knew how I could still serve my Lord and turn the tables on the Devil. I would take myself to the quarry and throw myself off the ledge. If each one of us did that, we could put an end to all the defilement. And at the very least, I would set Marie free, for it was now clear that I was the weight chained to her leg.

The quarry was not far, just up a hill above the Waymart road. I walked to the rutted track that led to it and began to ascend the incline, feeling calm. But then it occurred to me that perhaps the Devil *wanted* me to throw myself off the cliff. Maybe he did, because he knew that I knew the truth. He wanted me gone, so I wouldn't tell anyone.

I turned around and in a few minutes regained the road to Waymart. I would go to town and warn people—tell them what I knew. I headed for M'Ginty's tavern where there were sure to be people, even in the day. I wanted to tell as many as I could, as soon as I could. I knew that the Devil would try to stop me.

There were only a few people on the street in Waymart, but when I entered M'Ginty's, sure enough, men were there. I tried to tell them. I tried several times, but no one would listen. I began to shout. "The Devil is within us!" People began to yell back at me. I didn't know what they were saying. Then I was being grabbed and pushed. I pushed back, and a man fell over a chair and into a table. Someone hit me and I hit him back. I tried to tell them again. "The Devil is within us!" There was more pushing and yelling. Something struck me from behind.

39

I AWOKE WITH a sharp pain in my head. A row of steel bars stood an arms-length away.

"Good morning," said a voice.

"Who's there?"

I saw something red move. It turned into the shirt of a man in a chair. "I'm Deputy Simpson. You feeling better?"

"I'm not sure. My head hurts."

"Well, you'd do well not to drink so much."

I didn't want to argue. "Where am I?"

"In the Waymart lockup. You caused quite a ruckus at M'Ginty's. If you'd just been drunk, I could let you go, but things got broke. In a few days, you'll go to Honesdale. See Judge Tompkins."

Honesdale? "No!" I said as clear as I could. "I don't want to go to there."

"Oh, I wouldn't worry," said the deputy. "Tompkins ain't hung nobody for a few months now."

I laughed. Moments later, I realized that I hadn't laughed at anything in a long time. I hadn't laughed since before I'd been locked up in Delhi. My head hurt something bad, that was true, but the squeezing feeling was gone. Deputy Simpson just seemed ordinary.

In the afternoon, Marie arrived, and behind her veil of concern I could see a slow boil. This was the final straw. She asked if I were all right, and I said that I was except for my head.

"You're head's been hurting for a good while," she said, without sympathy.

"Well, that part doesn't hurt now. To tell the truth, Marie, I feel better."

Marie looked down at the floor.

"Marie, please listen," I said, taking her hands through the bars. "I think I'm better." I wanted to show her that the darkness had lifted, so I let go of her hands and danced a little jig and sang. *"I'm Captain Jinks of the Horse Marines, I feed my horse on rice and beans, and often live beyond my means . . . ."*

If anyone else had heard me, they'd have thought I was crazy for sure, but Marie saw this silliness as part of my old self and smiled. "I'll tell you who's full of beans," she said. Then a sad look crossed her face. "The deputy says that you are to go to Honesdale."

"I can't go there, Marie."

My wife heard the fear—she knew my story and knew that if I went to Honesdale, my old self might never come back. She didn't have to think about it. "I'll go tomorrow," she said, "and see if I can talk to the judge."

* * *

Marie was gone for four days. On the morning of the fifth, I saw her enter the sheriff's office and hand Deputy Simpson a letter. The deputy led her back to the cell.

"You're to be let go," she said with a tired smile. "It's done."

"What did you do?"

"I wrote a letter. To the judge. I said I was your wife and we were Christian people, and if you were released, I'd see to your conduct. It took two days to get to see him, but he agreed."

This was happy news, but I felt a rush of sadness as I began to think about what might come next. "I've ruined everything," I said, wanting to free her.

Marie didn't agree. "We have another chance, Joseph."

"I've wasted them all," I said. "We've nowhere to go."

Marie shook her head. "You're wrong." She then said that she had been

to see the pastor of a local church. He knew of someone who would take us in and give us work, at least for a time.

We left Waymart and took the road east, our new home four or five miles outside of town. Along the way, we stopped by a stream. Marie took a knife to a small loaf of bread and then brought out a piece of cheese she had been keeping as a surprise. She put a thick piece of it on the bread and held it out to me. Her hand shook. Then her lip began to quiver. "I have something to tell you, Joseph."

I knew that she was about to announce that the house and work we were walking toward were for me only, and that she was going to return to her family. I looked at her bravely and vowed not to try to change her mind.

"Yesterday, as I left the courthouse," she said, "I was approached by a woman. She asked if I was your wife." Marie paused as though to gain courage while I looked for somewhere to hide. "When I told her that I was, she said that her name was Lydia Montrose, but that you had known her as Lydia Watson."

I stood there mute, unable to breathe.

"She asked if I knew who she was. I told her that I did and that you had always spoken well of her. I felt afraid, but her eyes were kind. She said that she wished to meet with you and asked if I would consent. I told her that I had no reason to prevent it. She said that she would be at the Rolling Marble, the inn at the crossroads in Walton, one week from today at noon. She wants you to be there."

Meet with Lydia? I couldn't think of it. I didn't want to. "Look at me, Marie," I said. "I'm like a savage brought in from the mountains."

"Then we shall have to do something about that." Marie put the rest of the bread into her bag. "We have a week. You can make your decision as the days go by, but in the meantime, I will set about to get you ready. I think you should go." And there was Marie, ready to help me meet a woman I had known, under a lie, twenty years before. My dear wife was kind and resolute. No comments with sharp edges.

She opened a sack she had been carrying. Inside there was a plaid shirt, canvas britches, and a pair of boots—used clothes that she had been given at the church in Waymart. The shirt was clean and bright and the britches were a little worn, but in better condition than my own. We went to the

stream and Marie scrubbed me down with soap and a rough cloth. Then she sat me on a rock and cut my hair.

* * *

I reached the Rolling Marble sometime after the noon hour. Once inside, I was approached by a man who asked if I were Joseph Lobdell. We went down a short hallway, and he gestured toward a door. I passed through and into a large room with a polished oak floor. A woman was standing by a window, her back to me.

"Joseph?"

"Yes, Lydia."

She turned, and I walked to her, stopping on the near side of the window, its width between us. We stood facing each other. There was an attempt at a smile, but she did not offer her hand. She was more round than when I had known her, but a very handsome woman, as Marie had told me she was. Her eyes shone like wet stones, but her smile looked weary.

On the road I had practiced my apology. Now the time had come, but the words got sticky. "I . . . have thought of this moment for many years . . . or rather what I mean is that I prayed that someday I . . . might . . ." I took a breath and started again. "I never wished to deceive or…"

Lydia cut me short with a laugh. "Oh, that. It was only a small inconvenience on my part. How was it for you?"

"I never wished to deceive you, Lydia," I said, pushing forward. "I lied to you, because I loved you."

The woman before me was not moved by these words. "Could we not say that about every lie we tell? And why didn't I see it?"

"You never thought it?"

Lydia shook her head. "No. But as soon as I heard, I knew it must be true. I was in pieces. I felt as though everyone was talking about me, and for a while, they were."

"How did they find out?"

"Father ran into a man who knew you. I heard them planning some awful thing."

"Thank you for warning me," I said, as though it had all happened days ago. I was not entirely sure if I were in an actual room or having a dream. But Lydia seemed very real and strangely at ease with it all.

"You know, Joseph, I might have gone with you—I so wanted to get away. But I have found happiness in a place I hadn't expected. In any case, not in Minnesota."

"I went there, Lydia," I said, interrupting her. "I went to Minnesota."

Her eyes grew with surprise. "Did you really?"

"Yes. I claimed our land. It was beautiful. I would be there still, but they found me out. I was ruined and sent home. Then my family drove me off."

I told Lydia about living in the woods, the almshouse in Delhi, and meeting Marie. I didn't say a thing about Helen. It would have taken a good while to tell about her, and I was ashamed.

"And you love Marie?" Lydia asked, inviting me to speak of her.

"Yes," I said. "I love her and owe her my life. She had money and a family in Boston, but she chose to go with me."

"She probably proposed to you as well," said Lydia, a slight smile in her eyes.

"She did," I said. "Or rather, she is the one that said we should go off together." I paused for a moment. "But then, unlike you, she knew the truth." Suddenly, the past came rushing in. I bit my lip. "I'm so sorry, Lydia . . . I was going to—"

"It's all right, Joseph," she said. "That was a long time ago. And maybe for the best. Sure settled things with David Horton. Remember him?"

"Of course," I said. "Every girl remembers David. What happened?"

Lydia smiled. "He married Dorothy. And I was *not* the maid of honor."

"But you found someone else?"

"Oh, yes," she said, as though the thought amused her. "Well, if you remember, I was quite certain about what I did and didn't want. So the joke on me is that my three children inhabit my heart in such a way that I could not imagine a world without them. Howard, my husband, is a good man. He is married to his commerce, but I have come to see that there are illnesses far worse. He lost his first wife, so he carries a sadness inside that I cannot touch, and in an odd way, that makes us equals. He is not threatened by my moods or opinions."

"I never knew you to have any," I said, trying to keep the smile off my face. For a blessed moment, we were back in the glass factory, laughing and making fun of everyday things.

Lydia seemed to lose herself in thought. Then she spoke. "I have begun attending meetings, Joseph. Meetings to extend the vote to women. Last year, I went to Saratoga Springs. Alex, my oldest daughter, came with me. And I organized a meeting here in Honesdale this past summer. Mrs. Stanton spoke. I spend my days raising my children and working for the vote. And you, Joseph, you've been in trouble?"

I didn't know how much she had heard. "Yes," I said. "Mostly of my own making. I have spells when I am not myself."

"We all do."

"Not like these. I do bad things and say bad things and, most of the time, I don't remember. My mother had a similar affliction. Marie usually gets me out of trouble, but I'm afraid I'm drowning and will pull her down."

"Then don't," Lydia ordered. "Marie has given you her life. You must protect her."

There was a silence. Then a pained look crossed Lydia's face. "Joseph, I am grateful that we have been able to see each other, but this will be the last time me meet."

"I will do whatever you say, Lydia."

She nodded. "Good. Then one week from today I want you to come back here, to this room. Someone will be here and give you a letter from the bank. With it, you and Marie can purchase a small house with a garden where you can care for each other. I will do this with the consent of my husband, but to everyone else, this must remain a secret."

I was amazed. How had I deserved this? "I can think of nothing," I said, "that would bring more joy to Marie than for us to have a place to live. But there is no way I can return the kindness."

"Not to me, perhaps." Lydia's brow tightened as though thoughts were fighting inside her head.

Then it came. "I have seen Helen."

I had no words.

"She lives near Galilee," said Lydia, trying to explain. "On occasion, she comes into town. It was when she had her great trouble, that I discovered who she was, a shock to be sure. I thought I would never see you again, but then your daughter was in our midst and in need. I befriended her and looked out for her in the way an older woman can. She has no idea who I was to you. In my moments with her, Joseph, I found some peace about us, strange to say, and in this small way, you and I have shared a child. She is a beautiful woman and by all appearances happy now. I don't know how much you know of her troubles."

"I read about the attack," I said. "How is she now? I heard of a young man named Stone. Are they still to marry?"

Lydia took a breath as though not knowing where to begin.

"No, she didn't marry Mr. Stone, but she will have to tell you about that herself. What I can say is that six months ago she married a young man named James Crawson. I was at the wedding. And the last time she was in town she brought other news. She is with child. You should go to her."

I was flooded with shame. "And present myself how? All I have ever given her is abandonment."

Lydia gave a look of reproach. "Helen has known more than her share of sorrows, but she still manages to see the good in things. She has found the courage to face the world. You should find the courage to face her." Lydia picked up her gloves.

"Thank you, Lydia," I said, bowing slightly. "I know Marie would thank you as well."

"Take care of her, Joseph. You are blessed to have her. Good-bye."

I remained where I was and watched Lydia walk across the room. Soon, I heard a carriage door and then the sound of horses.

The Apparent Widow

Lucy, Helen, and Marie After 1876

GIVEN THE ERA, Lucy's* temperament, and her declining state of mind, the chances were small that she and Marie Perry would live out their days unmolested. According to the *New York Times*:

> In 1876 they were living in a cave in the Moosic Mountains, near Waymart, Penn. Lucy Ann continued her use of male garments. She was arrested one day while preaching in the above village, and lodged in the Wayne County Jail. She was kept there several weeks. Her companion finally prepared a petition to the court for the release of her "husband" from jail on account of "his" failing health. This document was a remarkable one, and is still in the records of the Wayne County Court. It was couched in language which was a model of clear and correct English, and was powerful in its argument. It was written with a pen made from a split stick, the ink being the juice of poke-berries. Lucy Ann Lobdell was released from jail.

The *Times*, in a separate article, reported that after Lucy's release, she and Marie Perry encountered "a lady who was particularly charitable to the couple." The story alleged that the unnamed benefactress "was years ago engaged to be married to Lucy Ann, the latter having spent some months near Bethany dressed as a man." The *Times* also reported that Lucy Ann and Marie, after having lived much of their time together in barn lofts, caves, and shanties, and with some apparent help from the former

---

* Note: In this section and the one that follows, I refer to Lucy as Lucy and not Joseph, and I use female pronouns. I do this for simplicity. It conveys no attitude or judgment toward Lucy's (or Joseph's) personal journey, which I honor. And just which of the modern labels of sexual orientation or gender should be applied to the historic Lucy is something I will leave for others.

betrothed, "went to Damascus, Penn, and in 1877 purchased a farm, which they occupied and worked together."

Whether it was a farm, as the *Times* said, or a house with a garden, or just a piece of land upon which Lucy and Marie built a cabin, the idyll was not to last. In two years, Lucy Lobdell was again in trouble and in custody. According to Robert E. Pike in his 1959 article in *New York Folklore Quarterly,* "the result of the court proceedings was that the 'husband' was returned to Delaware County, New York, and once more became an inmate of the poorhouse at Delhi, and when the pauper insane of New York were removed by law from county to state asylums, she was sent to [Willard Asylum for the Insane], Seneca County, New York, where she died in 1889." Pike's account, while substantially correct, was in conflict with that of the *New York Times,* which claimed in its lengthy obituary that Lucy Lobdell died ten years earlier, in 1879, "after a brief illness." The *New York Sun* published its obituary in 1885, claiming that "the Female Hunter of Long Eddy" had died in June of that year. As records show, none of these dates is correct, but Pike was right in asserting that Lucy had been placed in an asylum in Seneca County, New York.

Willard Asylum, it should be noted, was due south of Seneca Falls. Thus, in 1880, Lucy Lobdell found herself behind bars just a few miles from the Wesleyan chapel where the first American women's rights convention had been held in 1848 under the direction of Elizabeth Cady Stanton and Lucretia Mott. While an inmate at Willard, Lucy became the subject of two articles of presumed scholarship, both printed in the periodical *Alienist and Neurologist*. The first, by Doctor P.M. Wise, was published in January 1883 and titled "Case of Sexual Perversion." The second, somewhat derivative, was by James G. Kiernan, published in April 1891, and titled "Psychological Aspects of Sexual Appetite."

According to Dr. Wise, "Lucy Ann Slater, alias, Rev. Joseph Lobdell, was admitted to the Willard Asylum, October 12th, 1880; age 56 [actually, 51], widow, without occupation and a declared vagrant . . . She was dressed in male attire throughout and declared herself to be a man, giving her name as Joseph Lobdell, a Methodist minister; and said she was married and had a wife living. She appeared in good physical health . . .

and gave responsive answers to questions . . . Her sexual inclination was perverted."

In reviewing Lucy's history to explain her condition, Wise asserts, "She was peculiar in girlhood, in that she preferred masculine sports and labor; had an aversion to attentions from young men and sought the society of her own sex." From what is known of Lucy's girlhood, this characterization seems to be an error or an invention. Nevertheless, Dr. Wise proceeds to take the enlightened position of the day that persons such as Lucy should not be subject to criminal punishment. "It would be more charitable and just," he concludes, "if society would protect them from ridicule and aspersion they must always suffer . . . by recognizing them as the victims of a distressing mono-delusional form of insanity. It is reasonable to consider true sexual perversion as always a pathological condition and a peculiar manifestation of insanity."

In his article, Dr. Wise tells of Lucy's relationship with a "young woman of good education." Wise doesn't name the woman, who was surely Marie Louise Perry, but says that the two of them, "strange as it may seem," formed an attachment of mutual affection, which he called "Lesbian love." It is unlikely that Wise coined the term, but *Swade's Lesbian Tribal Chant History* claims that the Wise reference is "the first time Lesbian is used to denote woman loving woman as opposed to an inhabitant of the Isle of Lesbos." Jonathan Katz in *Gay American History* characterizes Wise's article as "one of the earliest American reports of Lesbianism."

The doctor's log at Willard Asylum records that Lucy's mental state deteriorated while she was there. Entries like "dementia increasing" and "perversion of sexual inclination continues" are typical. They go on until 1890. The final entry says: "Continues in good bodily health. Has improved somewhat and says she has gotten over her old ideas." Improved or not, records show that a year later she arrived at the state psychiatric hospital in Binghamton, New York, where she stayed until she died in 1912, at the age of eighty-three, after thirty-two years as an inmate in state mental institutions.

* * *

After having been abandoned by her father and surrendered by her mother, Lucy's daughter Helen spent a major portion of her youth in the almshouse in Delhi, New York. Then she found a home. According to Professor Robert Pike, "a rich but childless farmer named David Fortman [Fortnam], of Tyler Hill, Pa., happened to be in Delhi and with a friend he visited the almshouse. Lucy's little daughter was then 8 years old [more likely 12], a bright and pretty child. Fortman took her home with him to live with his family, and he and his wife became so fond of her that they legally adopted her."

Again, Pike's account is accurate in substance but not detail. Fortnam was not childless. Helen's true status in the household may be indicated by the 1870 Wayne County census, which lists David Fortnam and his wife Emiline living in Tyler Hill with their children Thomas, 21; Lavina, 10; and Iona, 8; and Helen Slater, "domestic servant." "Adoption" of children out of the almshouse as a source of unpaid labor was a common practice of the day and not considered demeaning. Helen's indentured employment brought her out of the institution and into society and thus, as a trade, was fair for its time. Beyond that, it also appears that Fortnam tried to look after Helen like a father and protect her, though in this he was not successful. Also employed on the Fortnam farm was a man named Thomas Kent, who saw Helen as an easy mark. Helen already had a romantic attachment to a young man named David Stone. She found Kent crude and rejected his advances. According to the *New York Times,* Mr. Fortnam then found it necessary to discharge Kent "for certain base proposals made to the girl . . . [Kent] then commenced circulating injurious reports against Miss Slater."

Shortly thereafter, on the evening of July 16, 1871, Helen Slater was set upon by four men, beaten, raped, and then thrown off the Cochecton Bridge into the Delaware River where, presumably, she was supposed to die. But Helen washed up on a sand bar and was discovered the next day near death, but alive. The *Wayne Citizen* called the attack "the most atrocious piece of villainy ever perpetrated in Wayne County." More specific words denoting rape were not acceptable in print, so the preferred term for the crime was "outrage," although some accounts solved the problem by using the words "roughly treated." For a time, Helen's condition was critical. It was said that she had been forced to inhale chloroform, which, along with the beating and time in the cold river, rendered her unable to identify her attackers.

"Suspicion fell upon those who had been circulating reports to her discredit . . ." said the *Herald,* "[Kent] hastily crossed to the New York side of the river." The *Wayne Citizen* picks up the chase: "On Saturday evening, circumstances justifying the measure, two young men named Thomas Kent and John Geers were arrested in Cochecton, on the charge of abducting the girl, outraging her, and attempting to murder her subsequently . . . more arrests will probably be made." Two others were arrested, but as Helen was slow in her recovery, they had to be released for lack of evidence. They disappeared. "Kent, the fiendish abductor," reported the *New York Times,* "managed to escape the justice he deserved."

In time, Helen regained her senses and her health. She then resumed the affectionate relationship she had with David Stone, and the two let it be known that they wished to marry. Helen's foster father, David Fortnam, gave his approval, but David Stone's widowed mother would not. Helen Slater was in for yet another, almost unbelievable, cruelty of fate.

According to the 1877 account of A.C. Smith, "Stone's affection was undiminished. He still pressed his claim for her hand. At length, when their marriage seemed certain, Mrs. Stone revealed a state of affairs which fully accounted for her opposition. She told her son that she was not a widow, and that [George] Slater was his father as well as the father of [Helen]." The *New York Times* also reported this story saying, "She in time recovered her mental and bodily health only to learn that the young man she was to marry was her half-brother, being the illegitimate son of her father, [George] Slater, according to the testimony of people who professed to know."

After abandonment, servitude, rape, attempted murder, and shocking disappointment, one might wonder what the world looked like to Helen Slater. What is known is that after a few seasons had passed, Helen met a young man named James Crawson, and they were married. A year or so later, they moved to Sayville, Long Island, where she gave birth to two sons, James and Bruce.

When James was only two, he was, for reasons now unknown, sent up to Basket Creek to live with Helen's aunt Sarah, who lived at the head of the valley. In her later years, Helen returned to Basket Creek and lived by herself but within easy distance of James and his wife Minnie. James and Minnie had three children: Myrtle Mae, Mildred, and Vincent. These children had children and, to this day, descendents of Lucy Ann Lobdell live along Basket Creek.

* * *

When Lucy Lobdell was arrested for the final time, Marie Louise Perry followed her to Delhi as she had done before. This time there was no daring escape. According to Robert Pike, "The Delaware County authorities refused to provide further for Marie Louise Perry ... To get rid of her they told her Joe was dead." This was probably the impetus that led to the obituary in the *New York Times* that bore the dateline "Delhi, N.Y." Marie may have known or suspected that her husband was still alive, but she participated in the fiction that he was not. William B. Guinnip had contact with Perry during this time, and forty years later, in 1924, his recollections were published in the *Wayne Independent*:

> Nothing more was heard from them for some time; then Maria Perry
> appeared saying that her husband, Joe, was dead. Maria picked berries
> to sell, and slept during the summer wherever night overtook her. The
> people of the locality were kind to her and she did not find it hard to
> find someone to take her in when winter came. Her baggage she kept
> for a long time at the home of Rueben Comfort, and she stayed for as
> long as a week at a time at our house.

Guinnip's account is in accord with another notice that appeared in the *Honesdale Herald* in 1882:

> The Female Hunter's wife was in town today, selling wintergreen ber-
> ries. In all the fact or fiction that has come before us, we have found
> nothing more strange than the strange companionship or relationship, as
> they claim, of these two women. Both educated, the wife exceptionally

so, asking odds of no one, living by themselves, one in male attire and the other in her proper dress, seeking with earnestness a living in the few avenues left open to them, always consistent, always true to each other in trials and adversity, their strange conduct may well excite more than a passing interest. Old age is creeping upon them, yet they resist its ravages as stoutly and as successfully as the most favored. Always gentle, always quiet, defrauding no one, striving in humble yet honest ways to care for and protect themselves so they may be left alone to work out their own "problem of life."

This article was written by Thomas J. Ham, editor of the *Herald,* and it is clear from its content that Ham was not aware that Lucy Lobdell was no longer free or was, according to the *New York Times*, already dead. Several weeks later, however, Ham received a letter from the subject of his story.

"I do not write this for insertion in your paper," wrote Marie Louise Perry. "I do not seek fame, but as you kindly state, far prefer to work out unmolested my own *problem of life*."

Acknowledging that the letter was not intended for publication, Ham published it anyway, saying that Perry "so well expresses her views on matters of public interest, we take the liberty of putting it in print."

In her letter Perry offered her appreciation for the "kind sympathy" evident in Ham's notice, but she went on to voice her own thoughts:

> I am sorry you did not dwell longer upon "the avenues to employment" not being more "open" to persons of my sex. If, instead of styling me "The Female Hunter's Wife," you had said his *apparent widow*, I think the expression would have been more correct. I do not know why the companionship of two women should be termed "strange." Men are often seen in close companionship, and, Mr. Ham, my sex are not inferior to yours.

Perry went on to describe a woman's tenuous position in society:

> The abuse and injustice which she often has to endure, and which has such a crushing influence upon her existence, seems to be a wrong on the part of the administrators of the law and the voters who create

them. If woman has no voice in the making of the laws of our country, she should as recompense, be granted sufficient other privileges to pre-serve her equality of rights. How this is to be done is the information which many of the stern sex seem to need. Will you find it convenient to inform them? You will thus oblige a friend and sister.

Marie Louise,
the Apparent Widow.

Shortly after this letter was published, and perhaps because of it, Marie Louise Perry decided to leave Wayne County. According to William Guin-nip, "One day she said she was going back to Boston, and started off, intending to walk the whole distance."

Hardships Willed to Be Forgotten

Author's Afterword

I HAD LIVED along Basket Creek for twenty years and had never heard of Lucy Lobdell. Then one morning Jack Niflot asked if I would meet him for lunch at the East Ridge store in Hankins.

When I got to the store, Jack was seated in the back, a leather case on the chair beside him. He was a square, chunky fellow, then about sixty-five, a councilman for the town of Fremont, a trustee of the village church, and the founder of the Basket Historical Society. For years Jack had worked for the *Sullivan County Democrat,* and he had the practiced eyes of someone who has witnessed a variety of human folly played out on a small stage. His most recent project had been a book published by Praeger the year before, a collection of letters written by six brothers in the Union Army to their sister on Basket Creek. *Dear Sister* had barely come out when Jack was struck down by a heart ailment. He had just emerged from his convalescence.

Once I was seated, Jack leaned back and asked if I knew who Lucy Lobdell was. I shook my head and asked if I *should* know. He gave a sly smile and said that I might have heard of her, since my old farmhouse was said, a century ago, to have been haunted by her ghost. Having assured my attention, Jack went on to say that Lucy had lived along Basket Creek before the Civil War, and that he'd spent years collecting anything on her that he could find, making a pest of himself at libraries and historical societies and sifting through boxes of letters in the attics of Basket Creek old-timers. He had planned to write a book about her, but no longer felt up to it. As he told me this, he reached into his leather case, picked through papers, and pulled out a copy of something from the *New York Times*—an obituary dated October 7, 1879.

"DEATH OF A MODERN DIANA" was the headline. Next in smaller

capitals: "THE FEMALE HUNTER OF LONG EDDY . . . DRESSED IN MAN'S CLOTHING SHE WINS A GIRL'S LOVE."

The story was long and complex, more like a feature article than an obituary. When I was done reading, I looked up at Jack. He said that most of what was in the piece was accurate, but some of it wasn't. The biggest mistake, he said, was that Lucy wasn't dead when the obituary was published—wouldn't be for years.

Basket Creek passes through fields and over rock ledges as it runs down a narrow valley to the Delaware River. The first white people to settle along the Basket were John and Mary Gould and their eight children, who in 1842 took possession of nine hundred acres at the head of the valley. When the Civil War came, six of the seven boys volunteered. More than one hundred years later, their letters home would be gathered into a book.

Also arriving in that first decade were James and Sarah Lobdell, who came with their son John and their daughters Mary, Sarah, and Lucy Ann. They settled midway up the Basket at a place where the valley briefly leveled to provide land for grazing and then dropped off to create an ideal spot for a sawmill.

A few years after the Lobdells, Patrick and Ellen O'Meara moved to the Basket from County Tipperary, having escaped the natural and human cruelties of the potato famine. The O'Mearas settled on a hundred acres overlooking the east branch of the creek and right away set about harvesting hemlock bark and maple sap while they cleared the fields and built a barn. As their farm prospered, a larger house was built around the first to accommodate a growing family—four sons and three daughters. In time, the boys left for New York City to become policemen. Mary, Elizabeth, and Ellie stayed on at the farm.

Ellie O'Meara never married and lived until the late 1950s. She had earned something of a strong-minded reputation when she was young, but even as an old woman, Ellie was dauntless. "I have tapped the big maple," she wrote to a friend when she was eighty-four. "Only one spike, but it will keep me busy when it comes time to boiling." As the last link to the first settlers, Ellie embraced her duty as local historian by, as she described, "taking notes of passing things and hardships willed to be forgotten." She assisted Leslie LaValley in the preparation of *The Basket Letters*, a book about the region's early days. She was particularly involved in the chapter on the Lobdells and their notorious daughter, for whom she had a special fondness.

My wife, Jean, and I purchased the O'Meara homestead in 1980. At that time, the house was showing its age—objects rolled freely on sloping floors, copper plumbing was strapped to the walls, and, upstairs, the roof of Patrick O'Meara's original dwelling, chimney and all, protruded awkwardly through the attic floor. Much of each weekend was spent sweating pipes and patching roof leaks.

When our children came, the old house was once again filled with activity. There were the sounds of babies crying, dogs barking, and people laughing at the kitchen table. The echoes of these moments joined those of the first settlers and then radiated their warmth back into the rooms, creating the feeling that life, however out of plumb, was good.

The O'Meara farm is seven miles over the hill from Fremont Center, a tiny town with a sometimes-open gas station and one church. The Fremont church had been Methodist, but during the 1990s, declining membership had led the Methodist Conference to the difficult decision to close the doors. The remaining parishioners wished to continue, and what followed were negotiations and lawsuits.

The pastor of the Fremont church was (and still is) the Reverend James O'Rourke. Born Catholic, a long-distance truck driver by profession, Pastor Jim had come to the ministry late in life. From the pulpit he preached on the power of love, and his week was spent living his words, often shouldering the cares of others. This he did for a remuneration generously described as *gas money*—less than one might think, for often the highlight of each Sunday was when the good pastor, in his early seventies, silver-haired, handsome, but a little overweight, roared up to the church astride his 800cc Kawasaki Vulcan.

It was during this time that I began to count myself among those who wished to save the old church—it might have been the twin to the Baptist church into which I was born. On my way to service in those days, I would pick up Thelma Herbert, a church elder who lived between our house and town. In doing this I was completing a circle that had begun many years ago, for as a girl after the First World War, Thelma would set off on foot for church in Fremont to be picked up most Sundays by Ellie O'Meara, driving a wagon and team of horses on her way to Saint Mary's in Obernberg.

Thelma was a connection not only back to Ellie but back to a time when the Fremont church was robust with children, choirs, potlucks, and picnics. No more. Thelma still sat in the second pew, but the voices behind her had dwindled. Those of us who remained would bravely fight our way through each hymn and, after the service, retire to the annex, where we would drink instant coffee and eat the dry cake left over from the weekly senior's card social. During this snack, gossip was exchanged and, for a time, the Methodist Conference spoken about in somewhat un-Christian terms. It was here one morning that Jack Niflot asked if I would have lunch with him.

I think a nonfiction book about Lucy's life is what Jack had in mind when he handed his research to me. His previous efforts and my own were in this realm. The problem was, although the outlines of Lucy's story could be confirmed by newspaper articles, letters, and other recollections, the core, the very essence of what would be interesting, wasn't there. Thus, any purely factual book that I could imagine was destined to be hollow.

In 1982, an historian from Minnesota, Mindy Desens, wrote to Jack, looking for information about Lucy. She was working the story from the western end, where Lucy had become known as the "Wild Woman of Manannah." Desens confessed to Jack that the project had become an obsession. "I had a dream the other night." she wrote. "I had Lucy by the shoulders and I was shaking her, begging her to write a memoir so we could know about her life after 1855." Desen's frustration was similar to my own following my meeting with Jack, and not long after, I concluded that Lucy's memoir, the one that she had promised to write, would have to be found. Then I too began to have dreams.

I am usually polite with people who believe in channeling. I don't. That said, I must relate that this book was written with the aid of numerous four-in-the-morning sessions with Lucy. It is quite normal, of course, for authors to wrestle with language in the dark late at night. In this case, since the entire story is told in Lucy's words, it was always her voice that rattled around my head, giving the sensation, at least, that my imagination had been captured by her spirit and not the other way around.

I was well into the project before I discovered what Jack had meant when he told me that my house was said to have been haunted by Lucy's ghost. I ran across it in one of the *Basket Letters*. As the story went, when Ellie O'Meara was a girl and acting a little frisky and tomboyish, the neighbors would say, "Sure, if it isn't the Female Hunter come back to live with us." So sometime in the 1880s, Ellie O'Meara was said by her neighbors, in a light-hearted way, to be the reincarnation of Lucy Ann Lobdell. Not the kind of haunting one would make a movie about, but then, more than one hundred years later and up late at night in the attic of the same house, I had plenty of time to wonder just what the official definition of haunting should be.

After I had begun work on this book, a difficult time occurred for my family. Our house, the O'Meara homestead, burned to the ground while we were on vacation. Every physical object that connected my wife Jean and me to our past was wiped out in an hour, along with a beloved four-legged friend. The cause of the fire is unknown to us, but the circumstances surrounding it—too complex and bitter to recreate here—were such that arson would have to be a strong possibility.

But an odd thing happened beforehand. As we were departing for North Carolina I heard a warning voice in my head. I stopped the car in the driveway, went inside the house and gathered all of Jack's research and all my work on this book, threw it into a box, and carried it over to the garage, where along with my garden tools it survived the blaze. I have wished many times that I had paid more attention to that voice.

For several years after the fire, I was not able to work on the book, as a great deal of energy went to re-creating a secure situation for three children and to building a new house where the old one had been. During this time, I did not have conversations with Lucy, and I wondered if, after such an absence, she would come back. Do spirits perish in fire?

One Sunday, while we were still living in a rented house in Pennsylvania, I felt the impulse to drive over to New York and attend church in Fremont, some forty minutes away. I arrived late—not uncommon for me, even when I lived nearby. When I came through the door, I saw several people standing by the great table at head of the church. Reverend O'Rourke was with them, and seeing me come in, he asked if I would come forward and serve as a witness. I walked to the altar and stood beside him. The couple holding the baby I had not seen in church before, but I knew who they were. It was a beautiful morning in May, and I was, quite by accident, participating in the christening of the great-great-great-great grandson of Lucy Ann Lobdell, a moment of some meaning for me.

One year later, our family returned to our land along Basket Creek, where I was able to resume work on Lucy's memoir. This is her story as I have heard it. It has been a long journey and a great privilege.

Lucy Ann Lobdell in braids, beads, and feathers, circa 1853.
Photo courtesy of Crawson family of Basket Creek.

"IN THOSE DAYS, Lucy wore her dark hair in two long braids and must have resembled an Indian, tanned from exposure to sun and wind as she roamed over the forested hills and dark valleys as yet untouched by the pioneer's axe. She was an expert shot and often spent days away from her house, following old hunters' paths made originally by the Indians, finding shelter at night under some over-hanging ledge. Deer, bear, and panthers were plentiful then, and wolf signs were not unusual."

—Ellie O'Meara, from *The Basket Letters*

Acknowledgments

THIS MEMOIR IS fiction—an amalgam of real and imagined events and real and imagined characters. In most cases, where the events of Lucy's life are reliably known, the plot and personage of the memoir conform. Where gaps occurred, I invented. Where accounts conflicted, I made a choice. The attempt was not to produce a literal history of Lucy Ann Lobdell, but rather to explore, within the framework of her story, a more shaded, uncertain, and interior landscape, terrain that could not be traveled without first being conjured. I am indebted to those who kept the historical record from which I drew—a line going back over one hundred years. Thank you Jack Niflot, Ellie O'Meara, Thomas J. Ham, Leslie LaValley, A. C. Smith, Robert Pike, William Guinnip, Frank Woodward, Gloria McCullough, Mindy Desens, Susan Crawson Shields, Bambi Lobdell, and others— people who valued Lucy's story and passed it forward.

During the years of this book's gestation, I benefited greatly from friends who offered insight. Many were accomplished writers, some were skilled editors, others just friends whose opinions I valued. Thank you Franca Bator, Anneke Campbell, Emily Ennis, Kate Gallagher, Karen Gormandy, Andrea Henley Heyn, Debra Howard, Liz Huntington, Martha Kaplan, David King, Margot Livesey, Karen Macbride, Bernard McElhone, Laura Moran, David Surface, Roy Tedoff, Elizabeth Tuck, and Amy Lear White.

Thank you Michael Collier and all the fine folks at Breadloaf Writer's Conference, and Anne Greene and all the good people at the Wesleyan Writer's Conference. Thank you friends at the Hudson Valley Writer's Center. Finally, I would like to thank my wife, Jean Macbride, for her patient and steadfast support during the many times I was away in the nineteenth century.